Forged by Shadows

SHADOWED SOULS SERIES
BOOK ONE

MADDISON COLE

Dedication

To the Brightest Star in the sky.

To the Reason I began writing.

To the Woman who beat so many odds.

Thank you for hanging on long enough for me to make you proud.

Please check the Trigger Warnings below before diving in. If you're a dark romance lover, you can skip through. You belong here.

- Death of a parent
- 1:1 Bullying
- Stalking
- Blackmail
- Gaslighting
- Invasion of Privacy
- Dub-Con
- Voyeurism
- Exhibitionism
- Implied incest
- Spanking
- Eyes Open/Eyes on Me sex
- Possessive behaviour
- Mention of body dysmorphia
- Suicidal thoughts
- Mentions of childhood abuse
- Mentions of neglect, poverty
- Therapy sessions
- Depression
- Drug/alcohol use
- Flashbacks/Nightmares of sexual trauma

And if you're still here...enjoy, you dirty bitch.

AVERY

PROLOGUE

Breathe. Don't forget to breathe. Stop wringing the hem of your dress. Sit up straighter. Face forward. Don't appear irritated by whoever dared to laugh at the back of the room. Ignore the flash of cameras. Remember who you were raised to be.

Despite my inner chastising, each inhale coincides with a stabbing pain in my chest. If I wasn't surrounded by people watching my every move, I'd give into those urges rising within. To scream, lash out and smash a whole bunch of shit. Not the appropriate response in front of the press and celebrities streaming into the room at their leisure.

I steal a glance at the back of the room. Anger flares within me, a brief, hot flame that quickly extinguishes, leaving only the cold emptiness behind. They have no idea what this day means, what I've lost.

The service is twenty-three minutes late so far, and apparently I'm the only one counting.

From my seat in the front row, I watch those shuffling forward to pay their respects to the open casket. I listen to their wishes for eternal peace, and nod politely when they offer rehearsed condolences. The question in their furrowed brows bounces off the practiced mask I keep firmly in place.

What's going to happen to you now? Where are the rest of your family?

Sighing, I stare longingly at the huge portrait at the front of the room. Usually, the conservatory is my favorite place to be. Filled with light and the scent of freshly cut grass drifting in from the rolling gardens. But not today. Today, the plush cream sofa, hanging plants and rows of bookcases have been removed. Instead, chairs dressed with teal bows divide the guests into two clear categories either side of the walkway. Those who knew my mom personally, and those who wish they had.

A hushed silence settles behind me, the low click of the rear doors being closed exploding within my head. I quickly glance to the wall of glass before me, dampening the impulse to vault over my mom's casket, use my body to smash through and run until I collapse. The press, who have permission to be here, would have a field day. My lips part, precious air slipping inside.

Don't freak out. Don't make a scene.

I close my eyes for a moment, feeling the weight of the grief pressing down on me. It's a suffocating, relentless force, threatening to pull me under. How am I supposed to keep going without her? She was my anchor, my guide through every storm. Now, I'm adrift, drowning even, and no one nearby is coming to save me.

My gaze returns to the portrait, and I imagine her smiling down at me, offering the comfort I so desperately crave. I want to feel her arms around me, hear her voice telling me it's going to be okay. But that's not possible any more.

There's a brief disturbance before the doors click shut again, snapping me back to the present. I take another deep breath, forcing myself to remain composed. This is what she would have wanted – for me to be strong, to face this with dignity. I can do this. I have to do this. For her.

A body crashes into the seat next to mine, arms locking around my numb torso. I flinch at the sting jolting through my hands, only now realizing my nails were embedded into my palms.

"Shit, Avery. I'm so, so sorry I'm late." My best friend, Meg, whispers as my adoptive father walks down the central aisle. "The security outside is unreal." Using my shoulder to sweep her brunette hair aside, Meg's head nestles in the crook of my neck. Meg's presence is a balm, settling over me like a weighted blanket.

Fuck. I hadn't even considered that she might have been stuck at the gates, no doubt with many others trying to get into the funeral of the year, as if it is a red carpet event. To be fair, I haven't considered anything in the past few weeks I've spent laying in bed.

Tears gather in my eyes, the finality of what's about to happen making me dizzy. I watch the tired, well-dressed man take his place beside his wife's body without really taking notice. Her portrait stares at him, a humble smile on her perfectly painted face. Jade colored eyes glimmer from within the canvas, an incredible accuracy to their unique brightness. She is stunning. *Was* stunning.

With love in his wrinkled features, Nixon begins to speak with more composure than I could have managed.

"Thank you all for coming. Today, we gather to remember a remarkable woman whose radiant spirit illuminated the lives of all fortunate enough to know her. My beloved Catherine. Her infectious laughter has echoed through every room in this house, and her love, compassion and understanding is what made it a home for our two beautiful children."

Nixon smiles towards me kindly, ignoring the obvious which everyone else has noticed. The empty seat and unclaimed flower buttonhole at my side. "I hope you will join me in celebrating her life and giving her the send-off she deserves."

Nixon continues to deliver a flawless eulogy which drifts between heartfelt and poetic, enthralling those watching within the room and down the camera lens. To the rest of the world, she was a coveted model, an award-winning actress. A charity fundraiser who invested her time and money into saving countless lives - including mine.

I was just a poor, abused girl in the right place at the right time. No one usually adopts an eleven year old, but typically that same coveted model, award-winning actress and charity fundraiser wouldn't have driven in a shady neighborhood and happened to spot said-eleven year old abused girl digging in the trash for food. From the moment she found me, there hasn't been a day that Cathy Hughes hasn't seen me well fed, cared for and loved.

She was the woman who saved me from the depraved life I was born into. The woman who showed me love and warmth. Who would snuggle under a duvet and read with me whenever she wasn't away working. I bite my bottom lip hard. I still can't believe she's gone.

The rest of the ceremony passes in a blur of camera flashes and repetitive eulogies from actors who barely knew her. By the time the service comes to an end, the only thing distracting me from my itchy eyes is the growling in my stomach. I can't remember the last time I ate, as if surviving today was all I could focus on and I didn't spare a thought for what happens now.

Nixon rises from the seat he took beside me, holding out his hand. His peppered dark hair has been styled back from his handsome yet weary face, an impeccably crisp navy suit clinging to his frame that seems at odds with the stubble lining his jaw. Blue eyes settle on me, a look of adoration passing through his features.

"You did good, sweetheart." My chest swells, preceding the dam breaking and all of my withheld emotion flooding free. *I need to get out of here.* Inhaling my first full breath since I heard of that fatal car crash, I rise to my feet. Nixon and I approach the casket, taking turns to place one last kiss onto her forehead. Long eyelashes fan her rosy painted cheeks, her chocolate brown hair pooling around her favorite chiffon dress.

"Thank you for showing me how to love," I whisper. Nixon catches the tear that leaks from my eye with the back of his hand before it can land, pulling me into his side for a hug. His strong heartbeat and gentle scent of cigar allow me to briefly hide from the imposing stares and cameras.

Bright flashes assault us as we push our way, arm in arm, through the crowd waiting to offer their support. Meg steps into my other side, creating a wall which sees us to the rear conservatory doors. The crowd falls behind, hands patting our backs and stroking my long, blonde hair. More cameras flash, more false sympathy. Shrugging them off, I blink several times to banish the sparks from my vision. All of a sudden, I'm peering up into the most intense emerald green eyes. His presence hits me with the weight of a dumpster truck. I recoil on instinct before the anger breaks through.

"Wyatt." Nixon nods to his son in greeting, not seeming at all pissed Wyatt missed the majority of his own mother's funeral. I reckon Nixon expected nothing less. Wyatt's attention stays focused on me, a scowl forcing his sharp jaw to appear deadly. Dark curls fall into his face; the scruffy skater boy look at odds with the suit and tie sitting lazily on his muscled frame. Leaving the top few buttons of his white shirt undone, the edges of black ink lingers just beneath. I purse my lips.

I refuse to let him intimidate me today.

As soon as the doors are opened at his back, I barge onwards. My shoulder connects with his ribs, hurting at least one of us, and I drag Meg with me. A shudder rolls through my spine, a headache quickly seeping in. I desperately shove aside the awareness of his body, firm and unmovable. The smell of his expensive cologne, the way his green eyes drag over me like prey. Fuck, I really try, and fail miserably.

The cameras follow, constantly flashing, waiting for the moment I snap and give them a real headline. That's the only thought which keeps me from flipping out. Entering the kitchen, I hunt for privacy as the caterers usher everyone else away until they're ready. Meg and I slip behind the door, slumping against wallpaper flaked with real gold.

"Psst," our cook, Nancy, ducks her head around the corner. "We'll direct the guests into the ballroom. Grab what you need and escape while you still can." I manage a small smile at Nancy's wink, her hair neatly contained in its black net. The staff here are like extended family, since I rarely leave the mansion. There's been no need. My tutors come Monday to Friday, Meg is here more than she's home on the weekends and the dance studio is my safe haven. Meg doesn't waste a second, grabbing a bottle of champagne from an ice bucket and an entire tray of canapés before we rush upstairs to my bedroom.

Slamming the door shut with her back, Meg hands me the bottle so she can fan herself. "How does Wyatt get hotter every time he comes home?" My mouth drops open and I stumble while kicking off my heels. Dropping heavily on the bed, Meg dives next to me a moment later, her smile too mischievous.

"That's seriously not the first thing you're going to say after I just said goodbye to my mom," I scoff, turning my attention to the bottle's cork. I probably shouldn't drink before the burial, due to take place in the gardens in an hour, but I don't know if I have the energy to leave this room again. I've already put myself through a whole morning of being ogled at. I'm the Rapunzel in this tower, hidden away from view, often left to her own devices. My grief is private, as my life used to be.

"Oh, please," Meg nudges my arm. "You were totally thinking it too." My best friend, ladies and gentlemen, and her uncanny ability to hide any real hint of emotion. I suppose it comes with the territory being a therapist's daughter. My therapist.

Jumping up, Meg locates a black baseball cap, turns it backwards and uses it to pin up her hair. Despite wearing a dress, she gives her best Wyatt impression, and I wish I could say it's the first time I've seen it.

"Yo, Aves. I'm just too manly to admit my feelings, but at least I'm hot," she mutters huskily. There's an excessive amount of jaw stroking and hip jerking. "You know I hate being around you but I'm such a douche, I can't keep my eyes off you." Grabbing a handful of her imaginary ballsack, Meg snarls her top lip and snakes her head from side to side. An uncanny resemblance, truly.

A laugh is forced past my lips. A stab of guilt quickly accompanies it. I shouldn't enjoy any part of today – not even the distractions Meg is trying to provide and especially not at Wyatt's expense. I turn my attention back to popping the champagne with a dramatic flow of bubbles, which Meg rushes to catch in her mouth. I call her a few choice words, taking a swig from the bottle myself. Sinking against my headboard, we sigh in unison.

"He won't stay," I comment into the quiet which settles. My foot is tapping. "He never does." Describing mine and Wyatt's relationship as love/hate is putting it mildly. As long as I'm around, he refuses to spend a single night in his own home, preferring to hide in his fancy boarding school. And in the summers, if all other options fail, he stays in the pool house. Anything to avoid seeing me.

"It's not your fault, Aves. None of it," Meg returns to her own voice, picking at the tray of canapés. "I'm going to miss Cathy too." I lean into her, nodding absentmindedly. I hear her words, I understand their truth, but it doesn't matter. If I wasn't around, Catherine would have spent more time staring at her son's face in real life, rather than through the photographs lining her dresser. I prefer the photos personally; they are the only way I know what Wyatt's smile looks like.

"Hey, remember the time we spent all day trying to make that fort in the living room?" Meg perks up. I smile distantly.

"No matter how hard we tried, it just kept falling down."

"Your mom had barely put down her travel bags when she called for the staff to help us. Within an hour, we had the most epic fort around the TV. It had multiple rooms and snack compartments. We refused to come out, sleeping in there for three days until Nixon started complaining that the manor looked like a squatter's spot." I snort a laugh, drinking more champagne.

"She stayed in there with us, watching old movies, stargazing at the projector. Mom may not have always been here, but when she was, her attention was solely on us." Meg's arm slides around my shoulder, hugging me into her.

"Her attention was solely on you, Aves."

True to my word, I don't resurface for the rest of the day. Meg and I eventually shed our black, tight-fitting dresses and replace them with sweatpants and hoodies. The afternoon is lost to snacking and binging a new romcom series. I barely take any of it in, but the background noise helps to block out the burial happening beyond my balcony. Mom would understand. I've never been one for living in the spotlight. I will grieve on my own terms, in my own time. At some point, I dozed off, only to be woken by Meg sneaking back into bed with a tub of ice cream and two spoons.

Orange tones begin to bleed into the sky through the windows. Car engines signal the departure of guests until the noise on the floor below has decreased significantly. With every muffled goodbye, my heart eases slightly knowing this difficult day is nearly over. I'm practically a puddle of relief when my door abruptly flies open loudly, the intrusion of muscle making me screech.

"Dad's office. Now." Wyatt's deep voice commands our attention, despite speaking fairly quietly. The death glare in his green eyes leaves no room for negotiation, so I jump down from my high bed and gesture for him to lead the way. Three steps out of the door, I stumble and crash into Wyatt's back. He steps aside, watching me fall ass over tit onto the floor.

"You're fucking wasted," he growls in the base of his throat. "Today of all days." Striding away, Wyatt's dress shoes click on the marble staircase until he's out of sight. Meg slides her arms beneath mine, helping me to stand. Her wobbly smile and unfocused eyes aren't any better than mine, as I spy the several wine bottles littering my bedroom floor. Fuck, I didn't even notice her sneaking them in, or that I was drinking all day on effectively an empty stomach.

"You've got this," Meg tries to bolster me. It doesn't help much when I have to hug the railing down the stairs and slide one fluffy sock in front of the other to reach Nixon's office. The door is open, two figures shrouded in the fireplace's glow waiting for me.

"Come on in, sweetheart," Nixon coaxes. I manage to reach the high back armchair and settle myself down, keeping my gaze on the man across the mahogany desk. "Ironic, isn't it?" He chuckles to himself. "The one thing Cathy wanted, and it's finally happened when she's no longer here to see it." There's no need to ask what *it* is. Wyatt and I haven't willingly been in the same room in years.

Holding a glass of gin in his hand, Nixon seems to have given up on his appearance for today. I'm sure he'd rather a whiskey, but he refuses to stock it. His hair is disheveled, the plum-colored tie hanging uselessly under open buttons to reveal his graying chest hair. Not even the sharp jawline and high cheekbones he and Wyatt share can stop him from appearing defeated in the fire's flickering.

I dare to steal a glance at Wyatt, but he keeps his face forward. A tick beats in his clenched jaw, waiting for Nixon to continue.

"We could have been a proper family. A complete one," he babbles on. I look away, tears blurring in my eyes. If Nixon cracks now, there's no hope for me. Mom was taken from us so suddenly, so viciously. The morticians are miracle workers for the way she appeared today, not a single scratch visible of the car wreckage she was pulled from, killed on impact.

Nixon chuckles to himself again, but his pale eyes look blank and glazed. Throwing the rest of his gin back, Wyatt's scowl deepens in my peripheral vision while I fiddle uncomfortably with the hem of my hoodie.

"Things change, today." Nixon seems to sober slightly, staring intently at Wyatt as if I'm not in the room. "I must return to my business in New York tomorrow evening. It is imperative that Avery is cared for." I chew on the inside of my cheek. I've been left alone many times before, under the supervision of my tutors and the house staff. Keren has upped my therapy sessions to twice a week for the time being, and I have a ballet exam fast approaching. Plenty to keep my mind busy. Nixon thinks carefully over his next words and delivers them with brutal confidence.

"This year's semester is only a few weeks in. I've spoken to Dean O'Sullivan, and Avery starts at Waversea College on Monday morning. I've set her up with a dorm, and you, Wyatt, will look out for her."

The silence which follows is filled with tension; a physical pressure I can feel pushing onto my chest. Wyatt's lack of reaction scares me more than if he'd flipped the table, his eyes turning murderous. More than that, the sinking ball of dread in my stomach explodes, my thoughts racing around my delayed and sloshy brain.

I...I can't leave. I rarely ever leave the mansion. It's my home, a safety barrier between me and the outside world. And Nixon intends to drop me into a school, in Wyatt's dorm building and expect him not to kill me in my sleep? I'm hyperventilating before Wyatt's even blinked.

"Please Nixon," I breathe, layering on the sweet and innocent appeal he usually caves for. "That's really not necessary. I'm happy here on my own. Even if I wasn't about to turn twenty-one, I have everything I need to look after myself. Let me stay," I flutter my lashes for good measure. Nixon's blue eyes soften. *Hook, line and sinker.* Nixon may be ruthless with everyone else, his son included, but he has always been softer with me. Reaching over, he takes my hand over the desk, stroking the back with his thumb. Wyatt growls once again.

"Seems I'm not needed, as usual. I'll see myself out. Thanks for the party." Wyatt rises from his chair and walks towards the door too damn casually. As if the entire world owes him a favor. Immediately, Nixon drops my hand, his posture strengthening. The emotions so recently swimming in his eyes disappear.

"Don't take another step!" I flinch at the sudden roar, twisting my face away. It's involuntary, but seems to irritate Wyatt further as he tuts. My nostrils flare in irritation. If he'd let me handle this situation delicately, if he'd just kept his mouth shut, Nixon wouldn't now be using his closed fists on the desk to push himself upright. Struggling to calm his voice, Nixon's eyes shoot daggers at Wyatt, still braced by the door.

"You will clear your schedule to show Avery around campus. You will make sure she settles into her new room. You will ensure no one bothers or distracts her from her studies. And so help me, if you want to continue living with my financial support, you will be a suitable guardian to your sister."

"She's not my fucking sister!" Wyatt shouts back and suddenly I'm transported back ten years in my mind. To a long summer in a new house with a spoiled little shit glaring at me. Even back then, his perfectly styled ash brown hair and taste for expensive clothing enhanced the brat he was, thinking he deserved whatever he wanted without ever having to work for it.

It was explained to me that Wyatt had no prior knowledge of my arrival. The Hughes' weren't in the market to adopt until a small, filthy child stumbled into the road in front of their car. I understood, and I was just so thankful to know where my next meal was coming from. So, for years, I tried to find common ground with Wyatt. I gave him the space and patience I hoped he deserved. But he preferred boarding schools to his own home, and soon enough he stopped coming back during the holidays too. Wyatt made himself a ghost, only his memory left within these walls. And I stopped giving a fuck.

Blinking back to the present, I balk to find Nixon has moved. A harsh crack reverberates from behind, silhouettes bouncing around the exposed wooden panels of the room. I spin in my seat, gripping the arm rest. Wherever Nixon hit Wyatt, it's not apparent. The two are locked in a stare-off, but it's Wyatt who bravely closes the gap to bump his father's chest.

"You can give her our last name, give her half of the inheritance, parade her around like your perfect angel. But she is not, nor will she ever be, my sister."

And there's the truth.

Fury bleeds through Nixon's features, the strain of the day becoming even more evident. He grabs Wyatt's collar in both fists. Standing nose to nose, Nixon's tone lowers to a threatening level I've never heard before.

"Avery has been more a part of this family for the past ten years than you have. I buried my *fucking* wife today. It's all of our responsibility to see Avery is safe, and time for you to step up. Don't push me, Wyatt." He shoves his son backwards.

Refuse, I beg inside my head. *Keep refusing until Nixon lets me stay.*

With a lasting death glare at me, Wyatt leaves, making sure to slam the door harshly. Foreboding settles over me. On top of everything I've lost today, the lifestyle I love has just been snatched away and Wyatt is supposed to be the one *keeping me safe*. Something tells me, my big brother will do everything in his power to ensure the exact opposite becomes my new reality.

AVERY

CHAPTER ONE

Meg's sickly pink BMW rumbles to a stop before a gigantic building of brick and light. Every window is illuminated against the fall of evening, figures moving within cramped dorms. My stomach churns as Meg switches off the engine, a pair of fluffy dice swinging from the rear-view mirror. We remain there, locked in place until various sources of music and chatter mingle with the balmy air leaking through our open windows.

"It could be fun," Meg offers for the hundredth time. I can't spare her a look of bravery, my mind reeling. There is nothing fun about the bad omen before me. Forced social interaction, the onslaught of noise, being forced to share my space with a complete stranger. And somewhere within those walls is a fake brother who hates my guts. This is my new hell.

"You would fit in here much easier than I ever could," I sigh. I wish Meg was coming with me, but her athletic scholarship is at a state school miles away. Lacrosse is her speciality, becoming the first junior captain, whilst juggling the swim team, business studies and debate club. It's no wonder she hides at the Hughes mansion on weekends, needing to escape it all. Everything Meg has in this life, she's had to work for. But at least she has teams of friends and an incredible amount of group chats to fall back on. Without my tutors, dance coach, therapist...I have no one.

I take a deep breath, hoping my fear is masked from a bunch of basketball guys who wander past. Their jerseys are black with yellow trims, baggy around thickly-corded muscles coated in sweat. One looks back, throwing a wink at me before he empties his water bottle over his dark, messy hair and shakes it out. I sink back in my seat, flinching as Meg rests a hand on my arm.

"You'll be fine," she promises, leaning across the console to press a kiss to my cheek. I know I'm keeping her from the long drive she has to make back, but Meg refused to let one of the chauffeurs bring me. She stayed all weekend, advising me on what to pack while I looked longingly out of the window after Nixon left for New York. I'm used to waving him goodbye, but this time I'm not going to be there when he returns.

Nodding, I pretend to find my resolve as I exit the car and grab my bags from the trunk. One medium-sized case for my clothes, a smaller one for my make-up, toiletries and shoes, and a backpack with my laptop, notepads-essentially everything I'll use for class. *Class.* I shudder to myself. Leaning through the driver side window, Meg returns my hug with equal vigor and pulls away to smooth the two tendrils of long hair out of my face. Her pale blue eyes appear gray, swimming with unshed tears.

"You've never needed Wyatt before. Don't give him that power over you now." Meg whispers in my ear. I know she's right, but her words almost cause me to break. Waving goodbye from the curb, I hold the tears back. The night air grows heavy, my feet barely cooperating as I make my way to the building entrance and duck inside. Voices echo through the halls, doors slamming shut, laughter ringing out. I keep my head down, tackling the staircases with quiet resolve. Something I can attribute to my ballet; upholding stamina in the shittiest of situations.

Reaching the fourth floor, I enter a network of cramped hallways, tracking the numbers on closed doors for the one I've been allocated. Nixon forwarded on all of the emails from the Dean, including my dorm room, directions, a campus map and my class schedule. Music blasts from the doors left wide open, and I peer into each one, wondering if Wyatt will be on this floor too. I hope not. Sweat starts to bead on my forehead, my arms burning from my suitcases as I start to gather some attention. Wolf whistles follow me down the hall, throngs of college students stopping to assess me as fresh meat while shouting to be heard over one another.

I spot my dorm up ahead, the last one on the end. A group of girls huddle in the doorway, their brows raised when they see my approach. In a flurry, they rush past me, their giggles filling the air. My stomach cramps tightly but I refuse to let it show. Straightening my spine, I step into the room I'll be spending my foreseeable future in.

The room is small, two twin-sized beds against opposite walls. Separating them is an elongated desk for both of the occupants. On one side of the desk, beside a pot of brightly coloured highlighters and post-it notes, a strongly-scented candle flickers.

"What is that?" I inhale deeply. "Gingerbread? Maple syrup?"

"Cinnamon apple," a fiery redhead replies without looking up from her phone. She's lying on the bed closest to the window, scrolling endlessly and tapping her foot to a song in her head. I inhale again, deciding it's a pleasant smell despite originally being overwhelming.

Entering the room, I ditch my cases by the foot of the empty bed and sink onto the mattress. It's not as giving as what I'm used to, but the stiffness in my limbs will take what it can get. Eventually, my roommate glances up, her eyes studying me for a moment before she speaks.

"You must be Avery," she comments. She doesn't smile or grimace, as if she doesn't know what to make of me quite yet. I nod, pulling my hair free of its ponytail before a tension headache sets in. "Welcome to Waversea, I guess. Everyone is super excited for your arrival."

"They are?" I balk. There goes my careful constructed plan of laying low. The redhead hums, sitting upright.

"Oh yeah. You've been the hot topic all weekend. I gave up closing the door, bored of the insistent knocking and questions I couldn't answer. Now you're here, you can answer them yourself."

"What...what kind of questions?" My shoulders sag inward, a feeble attempt to protect myself. This is what I was afraid of. A strange unknown place, surrounded by people eager to know every shred of my business. The tabloids are the worst for it, but at least they weren't in my personal space everyday. I could block them out, locked away in my tower like Rapunzel. The redhead shrugs.

"Many of them are about your brother. What he likes, how he smells up close. If you've ever walked in on him in the shower, if his dick is really as big as they say. Things like that." My jaw drops, flames heating my cheeks. She laughs, waving my embarrassment off. "Don't worry about those bitches. They're desperate for Wyatt's attention in any capacity, whether it comes from befriending or bullying you. There's a target on your back, Avery Hughes. You should probably get a full night's sleep before the war starts tomorrow." The redhead laughs and starts to roll over. I straighten all of a sudden, my nostrils flaring. I may be timid, unused to college dynamics, but I don't take kindly to threats.

"And are you one of the bitches I should be on the lookout for?" My voice is steady. Her smile deepens. Her laughter grows louder, as if I've missed the joke.

"Your brother holds no interest to me. I'm gayer than a leprechaun scissoring a unicorn upon that magical rainbow in the sky." I blink several times, not sure how to respond. Maybe I do still need to look out for my roommate, but not in the way I thought. I can hear Meg in my head, tutting at me. She's gay, not a serial rapist. I hope.

"I'm McKayla, by the way," she fills the silence. "Just Kay is fine. I'm done for tonight, I've got track practice at dawn. Lock the door before you turn in." This time, Kay does roll over, pulling the covers up to her vibrant red hair. My eyes flicker to the doorway, noting the shuffle of steps and whispers nearing. I move in a flash, shutting and locking the door before my shadow has a chance to grace the grubby hallway carpet.

My hands are shaking as I silently unpack my clothes into the dresser and change out the bed sheets for a fresh set. Tomorrow will be a full-on day indeed, but not one I will be tackling without the right mindset. Starting with banishing the rumors I have no doubt Wyatt helped to create.

When Kay said she was leaving early, she wasn't kidding. I glance across the enclosed space, finding her bed empty and neatly made. Daring a glance at my phone, it's just past half five. I groan, pulling the covers over my head to block out warm rays of sunrise leaking through paper thin curtains.

After years of watching Wyatt sneer in the face of being ridiculously spoiled, I've tried my best to not follow suit. I don't ask for much beyond my means, working each Christmas in soup kitchens and asking for birthday gifts to be donated rather than receive them myself. But to a certain degree, it's impossible not to miss the blackout curtains, plush duvet and deep memory foam mattress I've become accustomed to.

Thinking ahead, I start to mentally play out the day, pre-empting and preparing. The cafeteria food won't be what I'm used to, the on-campus supermarket probably stocking brands I've never heard of. Then there's the thought of communal showers, which I'm dreading. It'll be an adjustment, but I haven't always lived this life. I once ate whatever crumbs were left behind and washed with the last drop of hand soap I could conjure from an almost empty pot.

I slip into a half-dazed state where the two versions of my life bleed together and somewhere along the way, I fail to remember which girl I am. The timid one sporting bruises, or the untouchable heiress who locks herself away. When I stir once more, it's with a dull headache starting to throb behind my eyes. Pulling the covers back on a sigh, the light is temporarily shrouded by a large silhouette looming over me.

"Ahh!" I scream, throwing a fist wildly. It connects, but doesn't pack half the punch my self-defense teacher taught me. A deep chuckle rumbles through the room.

"Oh, you're going to be fun," the figure muses and steps back. Watching me for a moment longer, while I clutch the cover to my heaving chest, he wanders towards the doorway.

"Who the hell are you?!" I find my voice. When he twists the latch from inside, my eyes widen. "And how the fuck did you get in here?!"

"Tsk, tsk, Peach. Do you kiss Nixon with that dirty mouth?" he chuckles again. I'm stunned, desperately trying to take in the stranger's features. Floppy brown hair flicks in all directions, as if it's been styled to look like he's just rolled out of bed. There's nothing to note about his clothing; sweatpants covering his lean legs and a pair of Air Jordan's on his feet. From the short sleeves of his t-shirt to his knuckles, he's coated in ink. A colorful mismatch of images that don't merge together, but rather tell individual stories. Secrets ready to be cracked open, but not by me. Definitely not by me.

I don't know this man, and I'm certain he doesn't know me. Upon opening the door to leave, another body suddenly appears and crowds him back inside. This is turning into an early morning circus and I'm the only spectator.

"Fuck's sake, Garrett," the man growls. His hair is trimmed short, causing the sharpness of his jawline and cheekbones to appear razor-cut in the artificial light streaming from the hallway. Slapping Garrett on the back of his head, he also turns to assess me too closely. I fight against the urge to shrink back under his all-seeing gaze. "Wyatt told us to watch her from a distance," he grumbles, his words not meant for me. Garrett is stroking his head, a wide smirk on his face.

"Give me a break, Axel. I wasn't going to wake her with my cock in her mouth." He rolls his eyes while I hide a whimper and shift further beneath the covers. "I just wanted a closer look. Besides, someone needs to give her an official tour."

"And you thought you were the best man for the job?" Axel scoffs. "I just watched you scale the drain pipes and climb through her bedroom window." I inhale sharply, eyes darting to the window in question. Note to self - replace all of the locks pronto.

Axel doesn't take his eyes off me, standing shoulder to shoulder with Garrett at the foot of my bed. The pair seem to draw all of the air out of the room, making it hard to breathe, let alone scream at them to get lost. All of my training, every scenario of my past I've replayed in my head, pinpointing where I could have fought back or been stronger. Gone. I'm still just as easy to trap, and that drives more of a knife through my chest than the two sizing me up in my pajamas.

"Dammit, Garrett. You never do as you're told," Axel sighs, clearly the sterner one. Then he snaps an order intended for me. "Get yourself sorted. We leave in ten minutes."

"Erm," my mind trips over itself. "Thanks but...no thanks. I have a map, I'm sure I'll be just fine." They give me matching condescending smirks, but I hold my ground. It's my first day, the first chance to make a good impression. I'm sure as shit not going to be caught trailing the men who have been ordered to 'watch me from a distance'. Garrett breaks his stare first, placing a hand on his friend's arm and giving me a pleasing eye flutter.

"See, she's so cute and naive," he pouts. "I reckon we could keep her, just for a little while." My brows furrow but Axel sighs again, stretching out his neck.

"Ten minutes." The pair retreat, leaving me alone with my heart pounding in my chest. I stare around the room, hunting for a means to escape. How close are drain pipes beyond the window?

"I don't hear any movement in there, Peach," Garrett calls back. "I can always come and give you a hand if needed." There's a swift 'oomph' where I imagine Axel has hit him again, but I don't wait around to see if he'll deliver on that promise. He's already climbed through my window once this morning.

AVERY

Whatever picture I'd created in my mind of Waversea College, I'm left reeling at the reality. It's much bigger and busier than I'd expected. Students cram into a canteen for breakfast, eagerly hunting for a free seat. Their desperation is exasperated by the multiple cafe's we've passed, which are also packed from window to wall, many resigning to stand in small groups and nurse their coffees. Curious eyes catch mine whenever my kidnappers aren't looking. Whether Garrett actually notices any of the people darting out of his path remains to be seen.

"Over there is the art block," he throws his hand lazily to a parallel building through the hallway windows. I'm distracted once again by his colorful tattoos. They're an array of illustrations, none matching but all slotted together in a makeshift sleeve. Cartoon characters, flowers, skulls, even some popular logos.

"And connected to that, the music rooms. Generally, if I'm in the mood for a decent blowjob from someone who knows how to tongue a flute, while another paints my chest with a 'We Love Garrett' masterpiece, that's where I go." Axel groans, shaking his head but doesn't hit his friend again. I try not to choke on the pastry I was handed at the beginning of the tour and ordered to eat on the go.

"Someone," I mutter around a mouthful. The pair don't hear me over the rush of those responding to a distant bell. That's what he said - not a woman, not a female, but someone. Suddenly, I slow to assess how

Axel's bicep brushes Garrett's repeatedly. Purposefully. Whenever they're forced apart by a railing or similar, they automatically draw back towards one another. We move from one block to the next, the names of lecture halls becoming a blur. Breaching the main courtyard, I stop at the top of the steps.

The buildings here are different, older. Creating a rectangle around a central fountain, four gothic structures stretch wide and high, more windows than I can comprehend catching the morning light. Directly opposite, a huge window of stained glass sits directly between a huge arched doorway and the brass bell in a clocktower. The courtyard, complete with stone benches and carefully curated flowers, is so out of place. I have to look back into the corridor behind, checking I haven't stepped into some other dimension. The hallway is quieter now, everyone in class. On that thought...

"So, yeah. Thanks for the tour and breakfast, I guess, but I'm going to get to class." I reach into my bag to find my timetable. A weird, high pitched whine causes me to stop.

"Noooo, you can't leave now!" Garrett frowns over his shoulder. "We're about to get to the best bit." The pair of them turn fully, standing shoulder to shoulder. Their gray tracksuits hide none of the muscle lingering underneath, their hands pushed into pockets. Their eyes are on opposite ends of the color scale, shining hazel and deathly darkened. Garrett smirks while Axel watches me with caution. An angel and a demon, tempting me to stray from what I should be doing. From where I should be.

"Seriously, I'm good. I have to go." Gripping my bag's strap like an anchor, I rush back into the building, hoping the door closed before they saw me stumble. What the hell was I thinking - complicity going along with their tour? Now I'm late and lost, only knowing of the best alcoves to be fucked against a wall without anyone nearby realising.

I waste so much time trying to center myself with the map. Up to now, I've only ever been homeschooled in a singular room. My longest commute was from the study to the ballroom-turned-dance studio. When I make it to English Lit, the door is ajar. I raise my hand to knock, but the talking inside has already gone silent. Dozens of students spot me through the glass, their assessment already beginning.

On an exhale, I push the door open and nod to the professor. Mrs.

Patrick, as the plaque on the door states, signals for me to take the lone seat in the back row without any embarrassing introductions. I'm thankful for that at least, knowing whispers and stares can't be passed behind my back. My blonde hair falls forward, creating a curtain around me as I fumble through my bag with shaky hands. My breathing is hitched, becoming stuck in my chest. I block out those who peer back when my highlighters slip and scatter across the floor.

I still, staring at the wood on the desk. It's smaller than the dining table I'm used to. A simple square, not big enough to fit both my textbook and notepad on, never mind my water bottle and pencil case. Isn't that what college students have at all times? I can't risk to look around and see, my cheeks on fire and nails embedded into my thighs. This was a mistake. I shouldn't be here.

A hand appears before me. Tanned, long fingers unfurl their grip from my highlighters, revealing a small square of paper. 'Hi.' The two letters stare up at me beside a smiley face. I can't help but respond with a tilt of my own lips. Tucking my hair aside, I twist to reply and nearly choke on a gasp. That tanned skin melts away from the crystal clear blue eyes glimmering at me. His face is as flawless as the cut of his jaw, the outline of his adam's apple. Fuck, he's gorgeous.

Clamping my mouth shut, not trusting myself not to squeak and interrupt Mrs. Patrick's lesson for a third time, I lean over the scrap of paper. 'Hey,' I write back, and slide it onto his desk. He chuckles quietly while I focus on clamping my thighs together. Right, no - focus. That's what I'm supposed to be doing. Although everytime I look up at the whiteboard, I'm instantly reminded I'm in a room full of people and my head begins to swim. Instead, I use the curtain of my hair to block everything out, only listening to the stern voice relay the pros of allegory and taking notes.

When the bell goes, I jump a few inches out of my skin. Hands instantly grab my arms, giving a reassuring squeeze until I'm settled back in my seat. Those blue eyes seek out mine, silently soothing me as the rest of the class pack up and promptly leave.

"It's okay, you're doing just fine." His whisper has more reassuring weight than he could possibly know. I melt, my chest finally unfurling. I visibly sag, my breath rushing out in one.

"You think? I'm certain everyone can tell I don't belong here."

"Really? Maybe my radar is off." My smile is genuine, mirroring his. Everything about this guy is warm and soothing. "Attending Waversea means you're either disgustingly rich or incredibly smart."

"Which category do you fall into?" I ask. His blue eyes and blond afro contrast with his tanned skin, such an exotic mix that I can't stop staring at. *Fuck, I'm staring.* Slowly standing, his hands linger until I'm steady. That smile doesn't leave his handsome face as he drops another note on my desk and strides away. I can't help but watch the snug fit of his jeans, the easy swagger of his stride. Is this what college really is? Impending panic attacks and raging hormones?

"Miss Hughes," my name is snapped once we're alone. I collect my books and join Mrs. Patrick at the front of the room. "Class starts promptly at nine. I'll ignore it this time, but two lates in one week will be reported to the Dean." I nod, biting my lip.

"I'm sorry, I got..." *Distracted? Kidnapped?* "Lost." The middle aged woman with cropped, light hair and a cane regards me for a moment. She nods as if to dismiss me, but her voice carries as I reach the door.

"You won't be given any free passes in my class, Miss Hughes. Regardless of your family ties." My mouth drops open, my palm on the threshold. Despite the flames I feel taking root in my cheeks, my back straightens.

"I wouldn't dream of relying on such a thing," I state, my nostrils flaring. Perhaps I appear hostile, but Mrs. Patrick seems to be at ease with my stance. It's best we clear up now that I will work for my degree and have no intentions of skating by on reputation. No doubt that's what Wyatt is doing, wherever he is. Entering the hallway, I realize it's awfully quiet again and rush to my next lesson. The one I've been most looking forward to. Performing arts. The only problem is, that block is all the way across campus.

By the time I drop onto my bed that evening, forgetting the mattress has no bounce, I'm calculating ways to change my identity and start a new life in a new state.

"Good first day?" Kay asks from her bed. She doesn't bother to put her phone aside and actually look at the defeat in my features.

"I was late to every class, subjected to multiple warnings from my professors, whispered about by most, stared at by everyone, almost had four panic attacks and ate my lunch in the toilet. What do you think?"

Grabbing my covers, I roll myself towards the wall and give into the emotion clawing at my throat. I control it for the most part. The tears fall silently, the spasming of my chest subsides with exhaustion. I miss Meg, I miss my home. Still fully clothed, I relent to the darkness slipping in while clutched in my hand is that crumpled note I've kept with me since English Lit.

'I'm Dax.'

CHAPTER THREE

"Miss Hughes," Mrs. Patrick regards me with surprise as she enters her classroom. She glances at her watch to confirm that I am, in fact, early. I've been here for almost an hour, since it's where I opted to eat breakfast. Waking at the crack of dawn with Kay wasn't easy, but I'm determined today will be a better day. That, and I didn't want to risk waiting around for another morning break in by Garrett. I'd showered, dressed and given myself an entire pep talk before the sun had come up. I've been through worse than this; I'm just not used to being so visible.

The room begins to fill as I'm turning to a fresh, clean page in my notebook. I write the date in scrawly cursive, dotting the i's with hearts and underlining with a pink highlighter as a body settles in beside me. I can't withhold my small smile as I tug at the hem of my denim skirt. Turning to my neighbor, I'm horrified by the large perm and garishly bright lipstick smiling at me like a deranged poodle.

"You're Avery, right?" the girl chews on a wad of gum. The desk on my other side scrapes as it's dragged closer.

"Wow, are you naturally blonde? Your hair is so smooth," another female comments while stroking my straight locks. I flinch away from her. Through the students nearby, I scan for Dax. He enters the room, raising a brow at my new friends and grins, settling in the front row. I register too late all of the desks nearby have been etched closer, caging me in.

"You smell nice, what are you wearing?" A girl with french braids bends back and actually sniffs me.

"Um, I...don't we have to keep the same seats?" I ask quietly. Their combined laughter has me shrinking in my seat.

"Oh, she's so cute. This isn't elementary school," the Poodle gently smacks my arm. My chest feels tight. I focus on the back of Dax's head, willing him to turn around. Then I can plead with my eyes for him to save me from the five girls all twisted in their seats, openly ogling at me. In the shitshow that was yesterday, Dax was the only part I didn't entirely detest. I always have radiated towards those who seem steady, dependable.

"If we're ready, I'd like to begin," Mrs. Patrick says in our direction. The girls turn back and nod, while the one who keeps touching me brushes her knuckles over my face.

"I need your skin regime pronto," she whispers and I push her off, weirded out by her need to groom me like a chimpanzee. It's only when I'm writing down the topic of today's lecture that I realize this is a double lesson. It's going to be a long morning.

By lunchtime, I'm desperate to crawl back to my room and hide. Instead, my stomach is forcing me to seek out food. The cafes are packed once again, but the canteen is a no go. Even through the doorway, every college movie cliché comes to life before my very eyes. Taking the long route past Garrett's ideal closet for something he referred to as 'Downward Dog for Dick', I manage to find a kiosk shrouded in the smell of coffee. I wait patiently, despite those who push into the line, to buy a meal-deal and large latte before hunting for some solace. It comes in the form of a quiet courtyard which was missed off my tour.

The gardens have been well kept, colored flowers trailing a pattern of stone pathways. At the end of each, wooden structures and benches are encased in waterfalls of wisteria. Lilac, purples and pale blues. The air is fresher here somehow, calmer and quieter. I can't believe my luck that one of the benches is free and I rush to claim it for myself. Setting my backpack by my feet, I lay out my coffee, sandwich, cookie and bottle of water on the wooden slats.

"You like order, don't you?" a smooth voice sounds. I look up to see Dax hesitantly nearing. Relief floods me. A friendly face, that calm presence. I quickly shove my lunch into my side, gesturing for him to join me.

"It's not like OCD or anything," I blurt out and then reign myself back in. "I'm used to having a bit more personal space. That's all."

"Ahh," he smiles and lowers onto the bench. "Are you staying in the dorms? The communal showers must be fun."

"No one seems to use them at four a.m." I smile around my coffee. Sipping, I almost moan at the warm liquid running down my throat, at the quietness in this part of campus. "Peace at last," I sigh. Dax watches me intently. His blue eyes are so bright, akin to my own. Looking away, I scramble for something to say, but he beats me to it.

"What's your major?"

"Dance - ballet specifically. I'm taking English Lit for extra credit."

"Wow. You don't like having a social life either?" Dax muses. I half smile, half shrug, eating my sandwich. Nixon's choices had been a surprise to me too. He knows I live to dance, but I have to settle for the two lessons a week I can get. The fact I wasn't placed in something akin to business and finance puts me at ease. Nothing to indicate I'll be a part of the family business, sat in an office next to Wyatt for the rest of my life. No, thank you. After I've graduated, I'll return to the manor and remain there. Set up a home business, work via my computer. This whole ordeal will be chalked up to experience.

"What about you?" I shift the conversation back to Dax.

"Same about English Lit. I'm majoring in biomedical engineering."

"Wow, that's-" the bell goes in the distance. Damn, already? Dax stands in one smooth motion, collecting up my now-empty coffee cup and sandwich packaging. He shoots me a wink and a mix between a wave and a salute. I sit there a few more moments, enjoying this feeling of...I'm not even sure what. But it's not panic and it's not misery, so I'll take it.

"There you are!" Good feeling's gone. The loud exclamation cuts through the serenity that the courtyard tries so hard to maintain. A mess of floppy brown hair bounds over, strong arms scooping me right off the bench. I struggle against Garrett, arguing and pointing towards my backpack. Axel appears to collect it and follows us into a side alley. "Time to finish our tour," Garrett swats my ass. I fall deathly still.

"Touch my ass again and I'll-"

"Oh Peach, please don't finish that sentence. We're near the Handjob Hideout and Wyatt would kill me." My eyes fly over Garrett's shoulder to a wooden bench shrouded by a curtain of wisteria, and then to Axel, who merely shrugs.

"Disobedience is his biggest turn on." I immediately stop wriggling but release an exasperated sigh.

"At least let me walk. This is degrading." With a chuckle, Garrett lets me slide down his body. It takes everything to ignore the hard planes of his chest, his abs and the arms which set me upright without any strain. Both he and Axel wear t-shirts and gray sweatpants, not that I'm looking south of their waistbands.

Snatching my backpack, I wait for my head to stop spinning under the guise of letting the pair leave the alley first. They lead me on what I can only believe is a wild goose chase, and it takes forever. We cover miles of campus on foot, until an uncomfortable layer of perspiration coats my skin. I tug at my button down blouse, the pretty one with a small daisy print. At least I had the good sense to wear my sneakers. These fuckers are getting on my last nerve, despite giving me a reason to miss Classical Studies. I release a shaky exhale, which Axel presumes is for exhaustion. He stops so suddenly, I almost crash into him as he kneels.

"Come on Princess, your carriage awaits," he pats his back. I scowl at the name and stomp past him, the truth locked behind my sealed lips. They think I'm pampered, not knowing I was starved and beaten for most of my childhood. They think a walk across campus would tire me, unknowing my ballet classes last for entire days sometimes. Dancing helps me to forget.

'*The best bit*', as Garrett previously described it, is a domed building at the end of a long driveway. The parking lot is surprisingly busy for the time of morning, a constant to and fro of men mainly. Gym bags slung over shoulders, tight vests stretched over firm chests. Beyond the building, a dense forest spans the landscape, hinting at the edge of campus. Garrett flies past in a fit of excitement, skipping down the sidewalk, his floppy dark curls flying around wildly.

"Ta da!" Garrett throws his arms up at a flag hanging high on a silver pole. I take my eyes off the white dome and tilt my head. When the wind blows just right, the flag unfolds to reveal an image of the man bouncing on his heels underneath. Smiling broadly, frozen in time with his biceps flexed around a basketball jersey. Garrett's name is printed in bold.

Following suit, a series of flags sway further down the sidewalk, each with a different team player featured. Axel is actually smiling in his, the gentle wind giving the illusion of dimples. Beyond him, a tanned man I can't quite make out from this angle, then another with shoulder-length and wavy hair like a surfer. There's no mistaking who's at the very end - Wyatt. He is not smiling, one eyebrow cocked and his arms crossed over his chest. Typical.

BEEP. BEEP. A blaring horn makes me flinch. An SUV swerves half onto the sidewalk right in front of us. Like the glossy paint job, the windows are an opaque shade of black. The window lowers revealing the intense blue eyes I was so recently having lunch with. Dax looks over me with confusion.

"What the fuck are you doing here?" he asks of me, but I don't get the chance to answer. Axel brushes past, opening the rear door and mumbling it wasn't his idea. Garrett is still bouncing around like an excitable puppy.

"I'm doing as I was told," he grins. "Meet Avery, the kid sister." Dax's frown turns to a look of horror. He swallows, choosing to stare at a spot over my shoulder. I suppose that means we aren't friends any more.

"Wyatt said, *in no way, shape or form,* are we to interact with her." My cheeks heat now that the conversation seems to be happening over my head.

"Exactly!" Garrett throws his arm over my shoulder. I shove him off. "And Wyatt knows I always do the opposite as I'm told, so by telling me to stay away - he was actually inferring I should get as close as humanly possible."

This time when his arm lands heavily on my shoulder, his large hand gives my left tit a squeeze. I hold my stance, relying on years of self defense classes to keep me calm. Another voice starts arguing from the driver's seat while my hand gently sinks into my bag. My fingers lock around my pepper spray, bringing it to my side. Every movement is tracked by Dax, his icy blue stare sizing me up but he says nothing.

I exhale slowly. When my chest has fully deflated, taking Garrett's hand with it, I turn into his body. The spray is unleashed on his eyes as my knee is unleashed on his groin, slamming home hard enough to burst his balls if I'm able to catch them just right. He screams beside my ear, then drops like a sack of shit on the ground. My heart thunders as Dax catches my eye, a word soundlessly leaving his mouth.

Run.

DAX

I watch the scene unfold with an odd sense of detachment. *Avery fucking Hughes.* She's not supposed to be here. She definitely shouldn't be with Garrett and Axel, heading to the gym. Directly into the lion's den where Wyatt will be waiting. What the fuck were they thinking?

"I think I'm in love," Garrett croaks against the ground. Avery stumbles a few steps back, a world's worth of unanswered questions passing her features. Finally turning to run, as instructed, Garrett's hand wraps around her ankle, jerking her to the ground. She hits the concrete hard, but that doesn't impact her tenacity. Kicking, scratching, shrieking. Had it been anyone half as obstinate as Garrett, she might have stood a chance. As it stands, he's army-crawled up her body and is gyrating his crotch into her face, yelling 'kiss it better'. I can't fully comprehend the ridiculousness of it all, when Wyatt's face lights up on the dash display. At my side, Huxley groans and accepts the call.

"Hey man," he attempts to sound relaxed, despite running a hand down his face.

"Hey, I had to circle back. Left my damn phone at the house. I'm just coming up Belfield Drive now. Be there in-" Huxley is out of the driver's seat before Wyatt finishes his sentence and I rush to disconnect the call. Wyatt isn't at the gym, he's barely a road away. I doubt any thought is considered as Axel also abandons the cab, helping to wrangle a struggling Avery into the trunk. Her language is colorful, her skirt hitching up to the waist. Screaming she's going to kill us all, the trunk slams closed and an eerie silence falls over the SUV. No banging, no juddering. I peer back to ask if she's okay when the orange Nissan turning the corner catches my eye. The boys jump back in their seats as Wyatt pulls to a stop by the driver's side window.

"What are you guys doing here...on the side of the road...not in the gym?" Wyatt asks slowly, his brow raised. Huxley flexes his hands on the wheel.

"Just a flat," he bites the inside of his cheek. "It's all sorted now." Wyatt looks over the SUV disbelievingly, keeping his gaze narrowed.

"Okay then. Let's not waste any more of practise sitting out here." Wyatt smoothly drives ahead, finding two parking spaces side by side. The tension in the SUV is crippling as we follow at a snail's pace.

"She's so quiet," Garrett whispers, a pained groan in his voice. "Why is she so quiet?" I catch him in the rearview mirror, rubbing at his reddened and sore eyes.

"How the hell are we going to lie our way out of that?" I jerk my thumb at the invalid. Reversing into a space, Huxley declines to answer either of us. One by one, my best friends slide out of the car, stepping into Wyatt's side. His back is rigidly straight, his foot is tapping the ground. He's pissed.

"You coming?" he scowls at me when I hesitate half out of the door.

"Uh, yeah. I just need to grab my bag. You guys go on ahead." I attempt a cool smile. I can sense Wyatt's irritated groan rather than hear it, and he refuses to move. Slinking around the back, I open the trunk, locking eyes with Avery. Her arms are crossed, her scowl an exact replica of Nixon's and Wyatt's. Reaching over her, I grab my duffle bag from within the junk Huxley left in here, hovering over her face.

"I'm going to leave the trunk popped open. You need to get out of here. The gym is Wyatt's domain. If he catches you anywhere nearby-"

"No, thank you." Avery states matter-of-factly, crystal clarity in her blue eyes. I trip over my words.

"No...you don't want to be let out of the trunk?"

"No, thank you," Avery repeats. "I want to lie right here and stew in my hatred for Wyatt and his stupid friends and all the stupid shit in my life that he is responsible for." My mouth opens and closes a few times.

"That's the most passive-aggressive thing-"

"Dax! Come on!" Wyatt storms towards me. Avery laughs bitterly.

"Daddy's calling," she muses just as Wyatt slams the trunk closed without looking down. I know he doesn't hear it under the skid of his sneakers, but Avery's small, mocking laugh follows us. I sigh, shoving my hands into my jean pockets while Wyatt's hand clamps around my nape. He urges me into the gym where I ignore the receptionist and head for the staircase.

On the level below, I empty the contents of my locker out onto the wooden bench in the middle of the room. My jersey, shorts, sneakers and hand towel. As I change, my back turned away from the rest of the team, Wyatt takes my day clothes, anally slapping the wrinkles out and folding them until they fit perfectly back into my locker.

"Head in the game," he nudges my shoulder. In Wyatt's language, it's practically a hug. "We can't let those fuckers from Radley get too comfortable on top." He leaves me for a moment of solace, but I don't let myself linger. Tying my laces, I'm running out on the court for the last few drills. Huxley throws the ball hard into my chest, his hands raised for me to reciprocate.

"Well? Did you get rid of it?" he leans in, his chocolate eyes boring into me. I give a quick shake of my head, throwing the ball back. We sidestep and duck under the next pair throwing their ball over head and repeat. We keep going until there's a comfortable warmth burning through our calves, then Wyatt barks out formations to try. It's not as easy as usual, given that Garrett is sitting in the stands with Axel applying a cold compress to his face.

At least the whole team is present today, including the subs who normally spend each game on the bench. I suppose it's helpful for them to get some practice in while Garrett isn't showboating across the court. We work the newbies hard, repeating the same moves until they can get their feet moving quick enough.

Waversea has a reputation for a winning basketball team, most going on to play professionally. Playing ball is just a release for me, a way to stay close to those I've come to call family. Us five shared a room at boarding school and it was no mistake we all got into the same university. I'm sure it had much to do with Wyatt pulling strings. We're his family; any one of us being left behind wasn't an option.

"Completely pathetic," Wyatt scowls at the end of our allocated time on the court. The netball girls have already begun to filter in, posing on the bleachers in an attempt to get our attention. A few offer to take care of Garrett's weeping eyes, the promise of nurse's outfits being mentioned. Axel shoos them away, guiding Garrett into the locker room like a blind man.

The subs of the team have the good sense to grab their stuff and leave. They'd be the first to feel his wrath. Wyatt kicks the metal gate blocking off the supply closet. I feel the jarring sound down my bones, opting to shower beside Huxley rather than engage.

"He's not handling her presence here very well," Huxley groans quietly. I face the tile, lathering up and washing off.

"Has he even seen her yet?" I ask. Huxley shuts off the faucet, chewing his inner cheek.

"No. And we need to keep it that way."

"For both of their sakes. There's only so many injuries I can keep up with." Axel mutters, handing us both a towel. Due to his goal of being a sports physiotherapist, he's the one attending to all of the sprained ankles and cramps on the court, and repercussions of the fights between the team behind closed doors. Wyatt's a ball buster - it doesn't always rub off well with the subs.

"You'd better keep a tighter leash on Garrett then," I sigh. He tries to object as we re-enter the main section of the room. Wyatt is lifting Garrett's chin, peering at him with clinical awareness.

"An oil spray, huh? I don't know what kind of car oil can burn this way. I'll have a doctor at the house for when we get back." Wyatt withdraws his hand before he notices the way Garrett is leaning into his touch, seeking a trace of affection from the one man who refuses to indulge him. Axel takes that mantle most of the time, and when he's unavailable, I draw the line at some light spooning.

Wyatt turns to the rest of us, grabbing his bag. He doesn't bother changing since he'll be heading to the gym and for a swim any moment now. "If he can't play the Fresher's Rally next weekend, we'll have to decide which sub to train up in his place."

"Yes boss." Huxley grumbles, dragging his pants on. Wyatt's eyes close briefly, a long exhale escaping him.

"Look guys," he runs his hands through his dark hair. "I just need something to focus on. I know I'm not the easiest to live with right now.

I'll...work on it." I nod, Axel pats his back while Garrett wraps his arms around Wyatt's waist.

"It's okay, Riot." Garrett nuzzles his hip. I crack a smile at the childhood nickname, noting the tension that eases from Wyatt's shoulders. He pries Garrett off with a soft chuckle.

"You're lucky you're cute." Wyatt leaves, shaking his head at himself while Garrett lights up with reddened heart eyes. I'm pretty sure Wyatt just made his entire year. Huxley shoves my clothes into my chest, reminding me there's a captive in the trunk we should release. I groan, explaining that she wanted to be left there. She's got her phone, a cookie and water from lunch. She might have decided to take a nap for all I know.

The four of us head out, spotting Wyatt setting up beside the running machine, headphones on and head bopping. He loves exercise at the best of times, but it's common knowledge Wyatt works out his stress through physical exhaustion. It's usually around each holiday when he's been forced to return home or every Wednesday after his mom would call. I wonder what he'll do on those afternoons now.

Exiting the gym, Huxley stops dead. I slam into his back, quickly followed by Garrett and Axel in mine. "The fuck," I grumble, extracting myself from the Dax sandwich I unknowingly entered into, then I see it. Huxley's SUV, exactly where we left it, its windscreen, lights and windows smashed in. The glossy white paint has been scratched and dented in numerous places. A crow bar I'd barely registered in the trunk has been artfully placed on the dash.

"No, no, no, no," Huxley babbles, suddenly rushing forward and almost being run over. I wave an apology to the oncoming car, the rest of us close behind. "The tires. The leather," Huxley whimpers from behind his hand. I stare inside at the torn material, then to the back where Avery seems to have kicked the seats out. I have to hand it to her, this goes way above passive aggressive. Peering through his sore eyes, Garrett bursts out laughing.

"Oh please, please, please let me be the one to punish her!"

"Punish who?" Wyatt's voice says from behind, his steps slowing. We all turn in unison, side stepping as if we could block his view of the damage. "These were dropped in my bag," he produces the SUV's keys and throws them at Huxley. "What...the fuck happened here?"

"I... There..." I swallow hard. "I'm sure there have been reports of rabid raccoons on campus." Huxley over-nods in agreement.

"Oh yeah, nasty buggers those things!" We both murmur words like, 'horrid', 'disgusting', but Wyatt tilts his head.

"Raccoon's carved a giant 'F U' into the hood of your car?" His dark eyes settle on Huxley. I feel the moment he's about to crack, but it's Garrett who breaks first. Damn Wyatt and his teasing compliments.

"It was Avery! She followed and attacked me! Pepper sprayed me right on the sidewalk, I was defenseless. She must have stalked the SUV all the way here. You're right Riot, she's batshit crazy!" My mouth drops open and I shoot Garrett a wide-eyed look. Wyatt barely reacts, minus the vein in his temple which throbs when he's exceedingly mad. Coolly walking over to his Nissan, his dark eyes appear black.

"I'll handle this," is all he says, dropping into the driver's seat and speeding away. Both Axel and I slap the back of Garrett's head.

"What the fuck?! What were you thinking?" I half-shout, drawing a small crowd of spectators now. Garrett has no right to look sheepish, but he does and shrugs anyway.

"Better her than us, right?" I've known Garrett for years, I know his mind and ways. Yet I can't believe he's feigning innocence in this. I grind my teeth together, taking off on foot.

"Wait, Dax," Axel calls. "Where are you going?"

"I'm going to find her before Wyatt does!" Breaking out into a full run, turbulent emotions crash within my chest. Why did it have to be her, from my English Lit class? Why couldn't she just be a simple, nice girl? One that could have possibly been mine. Heavy pounding falls into step with mine, and I look in surprise to see Huxley at my side. "Dude, what about your car?"

"That's Garrett's mess to fix. When it comes to keeping Wyatt out of jail, I'm with you." Dread drags me down, the very real possibility of what we might find setting in. Surely Wyatt wouldn't really hurt her in all the ways he's described. Surely it was all talk...

AVERY

CHAPTER FIVE

I have to hand it to Garrett. The gym might actually be the best part of campus, given how good the coffee is. My vantage point from the second floor cafe is ideal for a spot of people watching over the parking lot, hidden behind the sheen of glass. The warm mug in my hands covers my smile at the view. Garrett blindly feels out the car's door handle. Axel has taken the driver's seat, putting the SUV into a crawl. I can imagine the grinding of alloys on tarmac as the car appears to limp down the driveway. Idiots.

No doubt Wyatt zoomed off in search of me, as if I'd be waiting somewhere obvious like a sitting duck. Instead, I'm two pain au chocolats deep and had a lovely afternoon admiring my handiwork. Bidding Ross, the barista, goodbye, I shoulder my backpack. The rest of the cafes' visitors have opted to sit on the far side, watching out over an outside arena. I spot a vibrant red-head gliding around the track, gracefully jumping over the hurdles.

"Kay," I smile. Making my way through the gym, inhaling the chlorine from the swimming pool, I make my way outside. It's turned out to be a glorious day, my mood lifting with the bright sun and clear skies overhead. Kay is in her element, her eyes squarely focused on her horizon. I sit in the bleachers, watching her outrun and then overlap all others. Slowing at a gentle jog, the spell is broken and she spots me.

"Look who's found herself in my neck of the woods," Kay pulls out her Airpods. "You seem much happier than last night, and this morning," she grins. I almost blush, reminded of how I complained at the early wake up as if it were her fault and not an active decision I made for myself.

"I'm caffeinated," I answer. Kay makes an 'ahh' sound in understanding. Dropping down beside me, I offer her my water and she happily accepts.

"So, what's brought you here?"

"You wouldn't believe me if I told you," I chuckle. Kay gives a 'try me' look so I relay the past few hours, not sparing any details. Not about Garrett's dick being thrust into my face, my stubborn-off with Dax or the excess of cocks I scratched into the side and back of the SUV.

"Holy shit!" Kay doubles with laughter, unable to catch her breath. "Where the hell did you learn to escape from a car like that?!" I smirk along with her, keeping the answer locked within.

There are certain scenarios I experienced as a child which haunted me night after night. So when I was assigned a self defense trainer, I had very specific requests. The hope was, if I felt well-equipped enough, I could chase away the nightmares. Today was an added bonus I couldn't have set up better myself.

"I was wondering if you had dinner plans," I change the subject once Kay has settled, looking out over the track.

"My, my. Are you asking me out on a date, Avery?" she holds a hand to her chest. I roll my eyes.

"You wish," I snort. Something about Kay's demeanor, the light-hearted edge to her tone, is easy to vibe with. It's like a whole different person when she's not engrossed in her phone and ignoring the rest of the world. "There's so much I still need to be caught up on. I was hoping the offer of good food and wine might encourage you to indulge me."

"Okay well first off, people our age don't talk like bored, middle-aged wives. If you want to get me drunk and spill the hot gossip, all you had to do was say so. I've got some pink gin beneath my bed, you hardly taste the alcohol until you can't see straight," Kay begins to stand. I jump up to stop her.

"Um, I would probably avoid going back to the dorm for a little while. Is there anywhere else we can go?" Kay looks over my blouse and denim skirt, then her own polo shirt and leggings.

"Yeah, I know somewhere. I hope you're prepared for this crash course on how things run around here. It's a lot to take in." Leading me through an archway to exit the arena, Kay's lingering smirk doesn't rattle me as I'm sure is intended. It's day two at Waversea and I've had a morning break-in, been kidnapped twice and lied to multiple times by faces I don't know whether to lick or punch. A crash course is exactly what I need.

Kay climbs the steps, guiding me into a quiet whitewash house on a relatively quiet street. Not what I expected on the rich side of campus, from the frat and sorority houses lined in two neat rows. I suppose it is only Tuesday; the parties will be reserved for weekends.

Stepping into a circular entrance lobby, the low hum of chatter soon becomes apparent. Women cross the landing atop wide stairs, most smiling down sweetly. Either side of me, two matching living areas suggest this building was originally two houses, the central wall knocked through to make one, giant home. The decor is classic, cream with ascents of soft, pebble gray. Huge sofas face flat screen TV's mounted up high, twin fireplaces are set in stone feature walls. Feminine touches arise in pastel pink pillows, fluffy blankets, scented candles and bouquets on low coffee tables.

Kay leads me into a dining room, the hint of a kitchen through wide archways beyond. None of the girls studying at the long table flinch or perk up at the sound of my name, as Kay makes introductions. *Finally*, I smile to myself. *A hint of normality*.

"Mind if we join you for dinner tonight?" Kay rubs small circles over a brunette's shoulders. They share a secretive look. "My new roomie here has some questions she needs answers to."

"More the merrier," the brunette directs my way. Mandy, I believe her name is. Kay strokes Mandy's hair and announces she's going for a shower. Before exiting the room, she pulls out a chair and pats the back, indicating I sit down. I do just that, tucking my backpack beneath my legs and cross my fingers. Everyone seems so intent on their work, I don't want to disturb them. Pulling out my phone, I shoot a quick message to Nixon to let him know I'm doing well and settling in nicely. All lies, but I don't want him to worry. The three dots of his reply appear and then quickly vanish. He must be busy at work.

"How are you finding Waversea?" A voice floats to me from a beautiful young woman with incredible blue hair. The light shade matches her eyes, her full red lips turned into a kind smile.

"Oh, it's been interesting," I huff beneath my breath, tucking my phone away. Her expression is strangely understanding. "Sorry, it'll take me a while to remember everyone's names."

"Sophia," she reaches across another girl with long braids to shake my hand. "Yeah, it's quite the adjustment." When Braids gives up trying to finish writing her sentence, she drops her pen and turns to face me.

"Lizzy," she nods as a way of greeting. "Obviously you're on much more of a backfoot than us. An announcement went out on the student forum that another Hughes would be starting here. It doesn't take a genius to spot you, all wide-eyed and innocent." My eyes do indeed widen, a blush coating my cheeks. Mandy leans on her hand.

"I'm sure we're not the only ones who have been curious about you. Have you met them yet?"

"I presume you mean Wyatt's thugs. And yeah, I've had the unfortunate pleasure." A series of laughs sound around the table, from those participating in the conversation and not.

"They're not thugs," Lizzy twists further and knocks my knees. "They call themselves the Shadowed Souls." I snort but she gives me a somber look. "It's from their childhood days. Five young boys who had their individual struggles but found a family in each other." I wrinkle my nose but dare not say anything further. A contemplative silence has fallen over the room, so I shift my questions elsewhere.

"So how do I get them to leave me alone?" The small laughter is back, pens scratching on paper. Lizzy hums to herself, double underlining key words in her notes.

"As long as you avoid Garrett's attention, you'll be fine." Her eyes glance my way when I remain quiet, a slow blush on my cheeks. "Oh no, what did you do?"

"I mean...well, technically he started it. But I suppose I..."

"She pepper sprayed him and kneed him in the balls," Kay strides back into the room, freshly showered. Her red hair is dripping on a pair of flannel pajamas. She must crash here often. The general consensus around the table is utter shock before the hysterics kick in. Kay had a similar reaction in the arena. Hounding laughter echoes around the room, more than a few mutters about me having a death wish filtering around. I swallow hard, trying to calm my erratic heart.

Thankfully, as more girls enter, the task of dinner shifts the attention. Many hands work in unison, practiced roles becoming apparent. Those who aren't cooking either wash up as they go or clear the table, setting places. It's more sophisticated than the pizza boxes I was expecting. Wine glasses are placed by Lizzy, Chloe flittering just behind to fill them.

"What's the special occasion?" someone I haven't met before asks. She's on cutlery duty. Mandy snickers from across the island.

"It's Avery's funeral. Take a good look guys. She might not be around tomorrow." Meanwhile, I sit there like a melon, not wanting to get in the way. A round of chimes and vibrations go off in unison, apparently on everyone's phone except mine. It goes ignored as bowls of spaghetti bolognese are dished out, the space filled with idle talk. I half listen into two conversations, eating and sipping the wine. I need a refill before I've finished my bowl, battling with my own nerves to relax. This is fine. More than fine; it's pleasant. The first glimpse of hope I've had since arriving at Waversea.

"I'm dreading Harcombe's assignment being set on Friday," Kay is groaning. "He purposely handpicks what you're worst at and spends the rest of the semester watching you squirm. It's borderline sadistic." Mandy pouts in sympathy, reaching up to brush sauce from the corner of Kay's mouth. The flirtatious looks between them seem private so I twist and enter into Lizzy's lengthy rant on gender equalities between the tutors. Spoiler alert, there's five more men than women apparently.

I hug my glass, happy to be forgotten. Invisible in plain sight. The more they talk, the more I drink. The more I drink, the more I relax. This is fine. Eventually, my bowl is swept away and replaced with a small plate hosting a slice of lemon cheesecake.

"It's vegan," says the blonde who puts it down. "Just in case you were wondering." I inhale the intense lemon scent wafting my way.

"And homemade?" I hazard a guess. She makes a cute gesture, somewhere between a nod and a scrunch of her nose before moving on. Over dessert, a few questions come my way. I manage to dodge them all with simple answers. Yes, it was lovely growing up with the Hughes'. No, I didn't get a horse for every birthday. I murmur a thank you when condolences are offered, just glad there were no questions regarding Wyatt's showering habits. A few rise, taking the crockery into the kitchen. I'd love to see the chore chart, I muse to myself as I quickly follow.

"Here, let me," I move towards the stacks of bowls and plates mounting up. A girl with heavy bangs bats me away.

"It's okay, we've got it. But you can recycle the wine bottles if you like? There's a green trash can out back." She juts her chin towards the side door as her hands are submerged in soapy water. I smile, gathering the empty bottles into a large cardboard box. Yes, that I can do. The door is opened for me and I make an attempt at some sort of curtesy as I pass. It's getting dark out, the last glows of a golden sunset disappearing over Waversea's campus.

I leave the porch in search for the trash cans, spotting them in a corner where the garage and fence meet. The fences on either side are tall, giving the illusion of privacy. Dropping the box on the ground, I open the can lid just as a hand clamps over my mouth.

"There you are," a deep voice mutters into my ear, dragging me back into the shadows. I scream into the large palm, struggling to no avail. A hard body pins me in place, a rumbling chuckle reverberating through my back. Twisting my head to the side, the hand shifts to cup my jaw. I squint at the six foot silhouette, a shiver running through me. Just as I'm wondering if Wyatt has actually found me, a tongue is drawn along my cheek, lingering at the corner of my mouth. "Mmmm. You taste like lemon. And here I thought you were all peaches."

Garrett. I should have known. I exhale, my posture no longer as rigid.

"Oh, it's just you." I don't know if Garrett sees my eye roll, but his chuckle suggests he does. The hand on my jaw lowers, wrapping around my throat.

"I wouldn't relax. You really don't know me yet." I'm spun again, and pushed through a side door. The garage is colder than the main house, flecks of street lamps slipping through the roller door on the other side of the space. I glimpse shelving units, a covered car, glints of clutter before I'm shoved horizontal across a table. The wood is uneven and smells like some kind of paint or varnish. Garrett's hands are too large, too quick for my current state, locking my wrists behind my back with something akin to a cable tie. The chill on my thighs is an abrupt reminder that I'm still only wearing a denim mini skirt.

"A punishment is owed, Peach. Since you seem to like my balls so much, I'll put them in your court. What would you rather be subjected to - Wyatt's hazing or my idea of dirty discipline?" His weight settles over my ass, the rounded point of his elbow leaning in the center of my back. I'm gasping, struggling to breathe as my mind spins. Usually, any situation that puts me at a disadvantage has panic clawing its way up my throat. So why not now? Because I've had mostly a bottle of wine to myself and I think Garrett is all talk, that's why.

I don't give him any type of reaction, especially not the one he's hoping for. I won't scream, I refuse to beg. Pushing off me, his hips keep me pinned in place. Fingers touch my thighs, feather light and tracing patterns.

"Tell me you want my punishment." His own voice is thick. I clench my teeth together, remaining stubborn to a fault. Those fingers round my muscles and squeeze, digging in firmly. "Say this is what you want," he grinds against me. I feel a quiver low in my belly, the haze taking over.

"I'm drunk," I murmur, sinking my teeth into my bottom lip when he rolls his groin against me again. The hands holding me in place roam further up to the edge of my panties.

"Tell me which you choose." It's a plea hidden inside a threat. I shudder properly this time, subconsciously wanting to shift his fingers to dip inside the fabric separating us.

"I...I've been drinking," I whimper in a small voice. Garrett growls, suddenly shifting to grab my hair and wrench my head back.

"You're barely tipsy. It's your last chance before I decide for you." From this position, my back is bowed, my ass pushing against him harder. Garrett, the man I assaulted merely hours ago. He wants retribution, but he wants me just as much. In this scenario, he can have both and I'm seconds from giving it to him. The taunting, the teasing were as good as foreplay. "Your silence is damning," Garrett answers for the both of us.

Tearing my panties down to my knees, the cold air is a shock against my wetness. The wine in my system helps to quash any shyness, my cheek pressed against the wood to ground me. For the longest moment, Garrett doesn't touch me. I'm aching for his devilish nature to take charge, to make me forget who I am and why I'm here for a short while. Then all at once, a tongue runs up the center of me. I grind my hips into the table, my mouth open on a silent groan. It comes again, long, lazy licks from clit to ass. I tilt up to anticipate him, widening my stance.

"Feels good, doesn't it Peach?" Garrett breathes beside my face. I startle but he preempts me. Shoving my head back down against the table, his mischievous eyes consume mine as another lick consumes my pussy. The hot mouth closes around my clit, sucking sharply.

"Who is that?!" I cry out, a bolt of electricity pulling my limbs taut.

"Who do you want it to be?" Garrett retorts, his smile widening. A moan passes my lips, heat skating through my core. I buck now, finally listening to the small voice I'm sure is supposed to be my conscience. I should have taken Wyatt's hazing. At least then I'd have known exactly what I'm getting and from who. Unless....no, no way. "No need to say it out loud, Peach. Keep your fantasies locked inside where no one can find them."

I squeeze my eyes closed, unable to withhold my following whimper. A deep, unspoken fantasy presents itself, unraveling within my mind. The mouth on me knows exactly what I like, switching between sharp sucks and languid licks. My ass is spread, a mixture of cool air and heated breath skating over me. I don't know if I'm shivering or shuddering, until that devilish tongue pushes inside of me. I shift, tugging on the ties at my wrists. I need to move, but even if I were able, I don't know what I'd do. Push him away or pull him closer.

"I...please..." I hear myself saying without realizing the plea had left my mouth. Garrett cocks his head, shifting his hand so that he's gently stroking my hair.

"What do you need, Peach?"

"More," I arch my back when the tongue enters me again. He fucks me with it, lapping up any taste I permit him. Garrett chuckles, watching me with fascination.

"You heard her. More," he orders. Two fingers replace the tongue, slamming home in one, hard thrust. I jerk upright on a gasp, which Garrett uses to his advantage. His mouth closes over mine, his tongue skating over mine. I surrender to his kiss, a hot and bruising fight of our lips. Garrett swallows my cries when those fingers twist, withdraw and repeat. Every time, stars burst behind my closed eyes, my body too rigid. Something has to give, like a wave on the precipice of pulling me underwater. It needs to break. I need it to break.

Garrett throws my throat high, stealing kisses from my parted lips. His other hand works its way across my chest, into my blouse and pushes my bra aside. I can't deny how my nipple pebbles or how I lean into his palm. He chuckles darkly against my cheek, dragging kisses across my jaw.

"Not going to pepper spray me this time?" The smile against my ear is almost enough to snap me back to reality. Almost. This is Garrett's big idea - to have me not only willing but begging for his touch. I'm too far gone to be denied now.

The mouth closing around my clit once more works in time with taunting, twisting fingers. Garrett teases my nipple, pinching tighter. The noises leaving me aren't ones I've allowed before. Even with previous partners, I've been careful. No one gets to see me surrender. Using his grip on my throat, Garrett raises my head higher and gives himself full access. As soon as he draws me into his mouth, the wave within crests its peak.

Simultaneous pulls on my nipple and my clit, synchronized clenches of hands on my throat and inner thigh. I rock back, bearing down on the one providing my pleasure. He works me into a frenzy as I clench around him, screaming as much as Garrett's hold on my throat will permit. Those fingers pick up their pace, chasing my pleasure. Drawing it out for an eternity. I slump against the desk, panting, shaking. I can't draw a full breath, unable to form my next coherent thought.

"How was that a punishment?" I ask hoarsely. The ties at my wrist are cut free.

"You'll see," Garrett muses, lowering my arms gently. I figured he'd be out the door but he remains, massaging my shoulders out. Beneath his fingers, the true strength of an ache becomes apparent, the lack of blood flow starting to circulate back to my hands. His accomplice lifts my panties back up my legs, pulling my skirt down to cover my dignity. It's a little late for that. I could lash out, twist and demand to know who it is, but I don't. Whatever just happened, the strange role play situation I found myself in, I don't want to break the illusion. Deciding I'm ready, Garrett lifts me upright, straightens my blouse and places a tiny kiss on the end of my nose.

"Once I find something I like, I don't let go. Your orgasm effectively just signed your life away. I'll see you in the morning, Peach." He smacks my ass on the way out and for once, I don't retaliate. I'm too busy trying to keep myself steady against the table to move for now. My body is sated, yet hungry for more. Long, long after the garage side door has clicked shut, I exit into a silent street. My legs are wobbly as I half-sprint back to my dorm, rushing to check the window is firmly locked. Only then, in the solace of my own space, do I drop onto my bed and stare at the ceiling. What the fuck just happened?

AVERY

CHAPTER SIX

I wake with a start. It's bright. It's late. An arm is draped heavily over my waist, a body spooning my back.

"I swear on my life Garrett, if you-" My hiss is cut off by a grumble, a head of flame red hair popping up over my shoulder.

"Wha- what happened?" Kay rubs her dark eyes, glancing at her smart watch. "Shit!" Flinching away from me, I watch my roommate collapse off the bed and rush to grab her clothes and toiletry bag. "This is why we don't get shitfaced on weekdays! I've missed cross country. Where the hell is my bra?" Kay stops dead in the center of the room, nothing left to the imagination in her vest and panties. "Wait...did we..." I watch her gesture between the two of us and peer back to her own, perfectly made bed. I gasp.

"Oh God, no! No, no, no," I shake my head. The ache between my legs has stemmed from a very different source. Kay's shoulders relax but she snorts.

"Okay, good. No need to deny quite so much. It's not like you could handle-"

"Don't you have to be somewhere?" I blurt out, blushing furiously. Kay remembers herself, hurrying to grab her gym bag and flee the room, rushing to the showers. I groan, dragging the covers over my head. If there ever was a day to lie here and hide from the world, this is it. For the first time, I question why I'm still going along with Nixon's decision to move me here. Prior to last night, the prospect of living a life my mom hadn't carefully manufactured had its minor appeal. Akin to a social experiment. Well color me socially satisfied, because Garrett forced me to toe a line last night that I wasn't prepared for.

Who do you want it to be? His question has rung through my half-sleepy state all night and when I finally managed to find sleep, green eyes awaited me there. I can't be having these thoughts, thinking of him this way. I just wish my mind would get the memo and stop bringing the fantasy back to life every time I shift and feel the blissful ache between my legs. Yep, a day in bed sounds perfect.

BANG. BANG. BANG.

"Fuck my fucking life," I grumble, throwing the cover aside. Wrapping the cover around my nearly-naked self, I trip over the backpack at the end of my bed. Kay must have brought it back for me when I passed out last night. I momentarily pause to check my phone is in the front pocket. It is, but the black screen of death is all I get.

The banging on the door continues until I fling it open. The air is sucked from my lungs. Wyatt fills the doorway, crowding me back a few steps. Hatred rolls off him in waves, his intense green eyes glowering. They scan my face, my bare shoulders and the sheet clenched to my chest. I watch the pure disgust wash over his features before I snap back into myself.

"What the hell do you want?" I scowl back just as hard. Closing the door behind himself, Wyatt presses his back against it, refusing to come any further into my space. My heart hammers in my chest. Is this about last night; does he know what Garrett did? Was he actually there?

"What the hell happened to you?" He is momentarily distracted by the red welts circling my wrists. I roll my eyes. Well that answers that.

"Is there a reason you're in my room?" I crane my neck to meet his eyes. Wyatt shakes his head, remembering himself.

"I'm only going to give you one warning," he says darkly. His chest rises and falls heavily in a navy t-shirt, his dark jeans and black hightop sneakers left in a wide stance. Every muscle is rigid, causing veins to line his arms all the way down to clenched fists. The fantasy I've been replaying all night dies a sudden death. Wyatt would never touch me in any way other than to cause pain, and now I'm glaring at him, I wouldn't want him to. It's easy to create delusions about a figment of my imagination, but Wyatt is nothing more than the spoiled asshole who hates me. Holding himself flush against the wall, he inhales deeply to steady his disdain.

"Stay the fuck away from my friends. They don't know what a leech you are." My mouth drops open.

"A leech?!" I struggle to maintain my cool façade. A fresh lash of anger races through me. I've been an idiot, letting myself forget just how callous Wyatt can be. Convincing myself that now we're older, he might just be able to redeem himself. "You're unbelievable," I shake my head and turn away. I can't have this argument without clothes on. Tugging a hoodie over my head, I hold the cover in place until it's pulled down to my silky pajama shorts. That will have to do.

"Do you have any idea what it was like every christmas, birthday, thanksgiving?!" I spin around and throw my hands out. Wyatt's gaze lingers on my bare legs, his top lip hitched in disgust. "There was always a place set for you at the table, presents under the tree. Every holiday brought a lingering sadness that you weren't there. Mom would have done anything to have you come home."

"False," Wyatt snorts and looks away. "She wouldn't get rid of you. And she wasn't your mom." I'd heard similar before, but a sudden thud of hurt hits me center in the chest. Ten years. I was adopted ten years ago. I haven't spent a single night away from the Hughes Manor prior to this week, but it'll never be enough in Wyatt's eyes. I'll never be one of them.

"She was more mine than yours," I sigh, releasing my anger. The only person it will affect is me. "You weren't there, Wyatt. You sent her tulips each mother's day, but lilies were her favorite. You ignored all of the tickets she sent for galas or basketball games. She only wanted to spend time with you."

"Then she'd have worked harder. She'd have come here, or at least met me halfway. I was a child!" Wyatt slams his fist on the door. I just manage to conceal my flinch. "Why was it always up to me to make the journey? Why did it always have to be on your terms, at your home?" My mouth parts, the sliver of a young boy with a chip on his shoulder slipping through. He doesn't even see the manor as his home any more.

"Wyatt, it was always-"

"I refuse to spend one night wherever you are." And there it is. The walls slam shut behind his green eyes, the asshole is back. Leaning back on my desk, I feel myself deflate. We're forever going to run in the circles of the same argument, neither of us escaping the endless cycle.

"Then I feel sorry for you. The next time you think about all of the time wasted, remember it's all because of your own stubbornness." Lowering my gaze to the space between us, silence settles over the messy room. Kay's usually neat bed is crumpled in her haste to grab what she needed from the overhead shelves. She knocked over a pencil pot along the way. I toy with one of those pencils now, rolling it beneath my foot. The quiet is unnerving, but I have nothing else to say. Finally, Wyatt shifts and opens the door.

"Stay the fuck away from all of us. They're my real family. You can't have them too." He flashes me a dare with those vibrant green eyes and I suddenly find my voice.

"Please extend the same courtesy their way. I wasn't the one crawling into Garrett's bed on my first day." Wyatt's gaze darkens. He nods and exits the room, taking all of my gusto with him. At the click of the door, I shrink into a ball on my mattress. That's the longest I've been in Wyatt's presence, and the closest he's permitted us to get. In my head, I've built him into more than a man. A monster of nightmares. A looming reminder that I'll never be a Hughes in the ways it matters.

After several steadying breaths, I build up the bricks around my heart and put my phone on charge. As soon as the screen lights up, I'm invested in searching for an outlet. Wyatt's had my fear for ten years; I refuse to give him another day. I'm a student of Waversea now and I intend to live like one.

AVERY

"And one, two, three, four," Miss Nightingale calls across the studio. In a long line of pink tutus, girls hold the barre and move between positions. Pointed toes, extended arms, confident postures. I'm a few from the end, feeling the stretch from the top of my head to the arch in my feet.

"Turn out your toes, ladies. Remember, ballet is a conversation between body and soul." Her voice reverberates throughout the mirrored room. I watch my own reflection as it obediently moves in tandem with my body. My muscles scream in protest, but it's a familiar pain, one that comes with discipline and determination. One I've learnt to depend on.

"Five, six, seven," Miss Nightingale walks the length of her students as the music swells in the background. We twirl, a continuous wave of pink tulle like petals caught in a gusty wind. The world blurs into a mixture of wood and mirrors, my own reflection rushing back at me as I spin back around. My breath is shallow but steady, maintaining rhythm with the counting in my head. My fellow dancers are echos of each other —synchronized, poised and focused. A bead of sweat trickles down my forehead, threatening to sting my eyes but I blink it away quickly.

"Eight," Miss Nightingale commands, her tone unyielding. My feet obey before my mind can process the order. Plie, releve, sous-sus. The routine courses through my veins as naturally as my own blood. The burn in my calves is igniting slowly but surely now, rising like a crescendo to meet the burning determination nesting in my chest. The mirrors reflect dozens of identical faces, each etched with the same grimace of pain and intense concentration; faces striving to master an art that demands perfection from imperfect creatures. Miss Nightingale's voice rises above the symphony of exertion.

"Nine! Ten!" She concludes with a dramatic flourish of her hands, sending waves of relief coursing through our synchronized bodies. But mine isn't buzzing with relief; it's victory. The victory of surviving my first week at Waversea.

As we all lower our arms, groans ripple through those collapsing along the edge of the mirror. I find my bag and lower cross-legged, not making any effort to talk to anyone. Whether it's my reputation for being a skilled dancer or a Hughes which has circulated, no one showed me any kindness when I entered the studio. Rather, there were hushed whispers and side glances. I don't care either way; I'm just happy to have a place to dance.

Taking a long drink, I glance at my phone. Meg is on her way back home for the weekend, sending all of the crying emojis that she's not heading to the manor with her pjs and face masks instead. Only a week ago, we were toasting my mom's life in my bed. A single week and I barely recognise the girl with sunken eyes in the mirror. Socialising doesn't suit me, I quickly decide.

At least Garrett's fascination appears to have passed. I haven't so much as seen a basketball player since Wyatt left my dorm room, and I've skipped all of my English Lit classes to avoid Dax. The emails from Mrs. Patrick are becoming rather caps-lock shouty, but I can't bring myself to face him yet. Not because of Wyatt's warning. In fact, due to said warning, I almost skipped in and shoved my tits in Dax's face that very day. Instead, I decided it's not worth wasting any more time thinking about.

Shooting back a message that Meg is welcome to come and take my place here, another notification appears at the top of the screen. The recipient is unknown. Various other cell phones ring out at the same time, causing Miss Nightingale to bark at us all to silence our devices. I hide mine underneath the lip of my bag, opening the student message center.

A round of excited chatter leaks through the girls who have been invited, while those who aren't pout. I can't deny the weird, satisfying sensation I feel from being invited myself. What was I just thinking about hating to be social? Whatever it was, apparently the part of me hoping for acceptance speaks louder. My thumb hits the RSVP button before I overthink the outcomes, then send a screenshot to Meg. She'll be so proud I'm embracing university life. Quickly noting the address is on the same street as Kay's sorority friends, Miss Nightingale snaps her fingers.

"Up you get! Time to go again!" She commands sharply. We reset, taking our positions once more and clinging to the barre for support. The tension is palpable, the room now evenly split by giddiness and envy. Miss Nightingale instructs the pianist to play. "One, two."

I keep my focus steady, feeling my muscles tense and flex with each movement. Right foot forward, left hand stretched out-the motions are second nature. My movements are fluid. Graceful arches, poised extensions. Around me, the room is filled with exasperated sighs as some girls struggle to keep up.

But there's no room for sympathy in ballet. Five minutes under Miss Nightingale's watch and I can already tell she's going to be my favorite. Her face is pinched, her graying bun perfect. In a black leotard and longer skirt, her slender body is flawless despite being around fifty. Beneath her rule, every pirouette will have to be perfect; every leap must reach the heavens. It's grueling, exhausting, and I can't wait.

"Miss Hughes," she calls over at the end of class. I change my shoes, releasing my hair to flow across my shoulders. "Walk with me," she commands, not bothering to wait for a response. My heart finds a rapid rhythm as I rush to gather my things and follow her down the long corridor. It's dim, save for the flickering lights that sporadically illuminate our path. Her sharp heels click against the polished marble flooring, ringing through the empty hallway as we weave past the vacant studios. A gust of cold air toys with my hair as we venture deeper into the building, forcing me to pull my chunky-knit cardigan tighter around my shoulders.

"Your pirouettes are impeccable," Miss Nightingale begins after a prolonged silence. Her voice is crisp and clear, much like her persona. "But your grand jeté needs work." I nod, her critique not altogether unexpected. In the past few weeks, or since before mom's death if I'm being honest, I've let myself slip.

We stop suddenly at a large wooden door. Miss Nightingale rummages through her purse for keys, before pushing it open. Stepping into a room, I brush my fingers over rails filled with costumes of every kind imaginable; ornate tutus covered in sequins, tulle skirts draped over mannequins, feathers strewn about on tables. The scent of old fabric and lingering perfume consumes me. She selects one hanging from a rack - an enchanting piece in a shade of soft rose with silver accents. Holding it against my body, she looks at me with an unreadable expression.

"Have you considered dancing as a career? You could be something special, if you keep practicing." I blink a few times, glancing across the dressing room. I see what this is now. An intervention. My personal dance teacher has given me the same speech multiple times over the years.

"I do love ballet, but no," I push the hanger away. Miss Nightingale's lips purse, the lines around her mouth becoming visible.

"What are you scared of?" Her sharp eyes narrow. Maybe my problems seem trivial to someone who has seen more of the world but I stand by my decision.

"Ballet is like therapy to me. If I do it professionally, it will become laborious. And in the dark times I need the release, I won't be able to lose myself to the music in the same way. It's all I really have that's all mine and no one else can take away." I lower my gaze to the floor, hearing the years of tutors telling me which direction my life should go in echo within my ears. Everyone believes they know what's best for me. "I know you won't understand," I sigh.

"I do, in fact. I also now understand why you're such a natural. You have the drive, the passion." I look up at this, sharing a brief smile with Miss Nightingale I doubt others ever see. She walks towards a row of glittery blazers, picking an invisible piece of lint off the shoulder of one. "Should you change your mind, there's a showcase at the end of the semester with agents coming to watch. The starring role could easily be yours, should you want it."

"Thank you." Setting the dress back on the rack, I spare another moment to stroke the stiff tulle skirt. Perhaps one day I could be this girl, dancing in eight shows a week, attending glamorous parties. I haven't expanded my mind that far before, preferring the safety of the walls I know. There's dangers lurking in the real world, unfathomable pain and horrors I won't survive a second time. But maybe, just maybe, the exhilaration of endless possibilities is enough to outweigh the bad.

It's late in the evening when I leave the studio. The sun has cast long shadows across lively streets, bathing everything in a golden glow. The haunting melody of the piano still rings in my ears. Theodore, as he introduced himself after he stayed late to play for me, smoothly rolled from one classical piece into the next. My every muscle aches from exertion, yet there's a spring in my step as I reach my dorm building.

"Oh hey," Kay looks over her shoulder as I enter. She's holding two mini dresses on hangers and using the window's reflection to hold each one over herself in turn. "Have you seen the posters around? There's a fresher's Sports Rally tomorrow afternoon, and a party afterwards. I'd ask you to come but it's invitation only."

"You mean, this invitation?" I wave my phone. Spinning in a flash, Kay's smile grows, her excitement palpable.

"Nice! None of my friends are going so I was worried I'd be alone. This worked out brilliantly!" Suddenly, she's fawning over me. A small voice in the back of my head tries to break through but I shove it aside. Convenience or not, there's a fluttering in my sternum. I'll be heading out on a Saturday night with my roommate, aiming to get wasted and laugh myself stupid. In the spirit of deciding what kind of girl I want to be, this is a good start.

While Kay finishes picking her outfit, I grab a towel. If my social meter needs to be fully charged for tomorrow, a shower, fluffy pajamas and an early night is in order.

"I have dance in the morning, but we can meet back here and get ready for the rally together? I'll bring lunch." My teeth sink into my bottom lip as those flutters intensify. These are the times I miss Meg the most. She wouldn't have needed the bribe of lunch, she'd have been here regardless. Kay looks over, seeming unsure until a smile breaks across her face.

"Sounds great."

CHAPTER EIGHT

The rally is busier, louder and far more coordinated than I expected. Starting in the open stadium, I'm happy to let myself become lost amongst the masses. Officially kicked off by the school band, brass instruments blare out a tune which soon becomes familiar. Our fight song. I'm in awe of their smart uniforms, of how they're in sync and of their team spirit. It feels...good. I can feel myself buying into it. Cheerleaders take to the grassy floor next, flipping and twirling with an athletic grace.

From a middle spot in the benches, Kay squeezes between a group of girls with yellow ribbons braided into their hair and face paint around their eyes. I wave shyly and settle down, tucking my skirt beneath my butt. A couple of guys slap high fives over my head. The scent of sweat and popcorn mingles in the air. Vibrations from the music and cheers beat within my chest.

I should hate it. I've spent the last ten years hiding away, and before that...well, I'm not going that far back right now. Maybe I'm losing my damn mind or maybe I'm channeling my inner-Meg, but I think I could get into this team spirit thing. Promote the planning committee, I'm hooked.

A multitude of visiting schools take part. The best of the best in soccer and American football. Each game brings with it a newfound sense of excitement from those filling every seat, with Waversea taking all of the winning trophies. I clap when I should, cheer when others do. A cute guy buys all the girls hot dogs and before long, I don't find it as difficult to blend in as usual. But then the crowds are herded like sheep by the cheerleaders towards the gymnasium.

My heart thumps faster just walking through the doors. I clutch my bag strap tighter, weaving through the students decked out in yellow and black, their school spirit on full display. The bleachers are packed, a sea of bouncing bodies and waving arms, a kaleidoscope of the opposing school's colors - red and white. Kay grabs my wrist, dragging me to a seat in the front row. Huge overhead screens display the words 'Waversea vs Radley', before spanning the audience in full HD. Kay squeals when the camera passes us, distracting me just as the basketball players bound out onto the court.

My spine straightens. Their jerseys, black with yellow trims and lettering, gleam under the harsh lights. Well-defined muscles flex. The distinctly-feminine roar all around the gymnasium is deafening.

Huxley is the biggest of the bunch, broad and cocky. His shoulder-length blond hair has been pulled back into a top knot. Axel and Dax nudge shoulders, their leaner frames a contrast of tanned and pale. And then there's Garrett; arms covered in those brightly colored tattoos. I need to explore them more closely sometime.

Garrett's dark eyes land on me and the smile drops from my face. Jogging over, Garrett drops onto one knee, takes my hand and kisses the back of it. I blush furiously, seeing my own face appear on the overhead screen. There's a mixture of whoops, boos and gasps all around. I set my jaw, tearing my hand from his grip. He must have known I wanted to blend in, to disappear in the crowd and not be put it in the spotlight. Yet he singled me out just so. Leaning back in my seat, I place my sneaker on his shoulder and push him away. Garrett tumbles onto his back, a belly-filled laugh tumbling from him. The camera catches it all.

"Looks like we have some feisty fans in the audience today!" the tannoy calls. I fold my arms, shrinking into my seat. Despite my death stare, Garrett blows me a kiss and heads back to his team. That's when my eyes land on Wyatt. He's leaning against the basket pole, clasping his wrist in front of him. His jersey is the same as everyone else's, but he somehow makes it seem more imposing. The black nylon blends into his dark hair, pushed back from his face. Even from across the court, I can

make out the sharp line of his jaw, the bump of his Adam's apple, the black ink tipping just above his neckline. His lethal, green gaze is solely on me. Then he blinks, and forgets I insist.

Starting their warm-up drills, the Waversea Warriors are passing the ball in quick, practiced motions, their sneakers squeaking against the polished wood floor. Each time a ball swooshes through the net, the crowd erupts, a collective roar of approval that makes me grin despite myself. Fuck Wyatt, and fuck Garrett. I'm a part of this school too now, I'm going to enjoy this. That's my last thought as a box of popcorn is put in my hands by Kay.

Of course, the Waversea boys win. From the first bounce of the ball, Wyatt's team owned the court, their movements sharp and swift. I don't know anything about basketball, and relied heavily on those nearby telling me who was in the lead, but I do have a keen appreciation of sweaty, muscled men. Not usually ones who showboat so often, but after a while, I saw the appeal. The crowd's enthusiasm was contagious - integral really in spurring them on. The chants, the cheers, the synchronized clapping. I found myself clapping along after a while, all earlier reservations melting away.

The winning players are announced one by one to receive their medals, each player stepping into the center of the court to thunderous applause. They look so confident, so in their element. They're at home here, under the bright lights with everyone watching. Cameras snap pictures, their smiles practiced and seamless. A proper bunch of showboaters.

This isn't just about the game. It's about belonging, about being part of something bigger than themselves. And no doubt, about getting girls. There's a whole row of them jumping around in teeny cheerleader uniforms, bouncing their boobs for attention. Kay and I don't hang around to see those same cheerleaders rush forward, or the lingering touches on biceps or fluttering eyelashes. I don't need to see what comes next. I have a party to get ready for, and maybe tonight, I'll be the one giving the demands when it comes to my pleasure.

Pounding bass from the house can be heard from streets away, drawing in the selected attendees like the pied piper. Strobe lights penetrate the night's sky, creating a spectacle for those who weren't invited but have come to linger outside anyway. Kay's arm is linked in mine as we push our way through, a half-empty bottle of wine in her other hand. She started early, whilst scrunching her red hair with mousse, giving it a kinky effect around her large hoop earrings. Her see-through red lace top, with a black bra underneath, blends into a deep burgundy skirt. Some may say it's too much red, but not Kay.

The security on the door is a little overkill, six-foot-something of bulk wearing sunglasses and an earpiece. He checks our phones and admits us into the chaos within. I imagine when not filled with drunk, horny students, the house is an amazing place to live.

"Why's it called Thorn Manor?" I ask, peering at the words carved into the white stone above the doorway. Kay mumbles into my shoulder.

"There used to be three brothers who lived here whose last name was Thorn. The rumors about them are *wild*, but they've got nothing on the new occupants." Her eyes glimmer with mischief.

"So, who's house is it now?" Kay's laughter rings out over the din of music as she nearly trips over her own feet. I use my grip on her elbow, steadying her against me. She grins up at me through wine-stained lips and hiccups. On second thought, I can't pinpoint when she started drinking.

The security guard permits us entry with a grunt, echoed by Kay's squeal, and we step into the huge lobby. Rivaling the size of the sorority house, whoever decorated this one has finer taste. A range of shades from white to black, laying heavily in the dark grays, cut clean shapes across the walls and floors. The overhead chandelier is dimmed, making it almost impossible to recognize anyone in the various adjoining rooms. We step into a whirlwind of pulsating music, laughter and the occasional shriek. The smell of alcohol and weed is heavy in the air.

Moving together, Kay and I remain side by side, arm in arm. Past the throng of bodies on the dance floor, through the mass of people in the kitchen hoarding punch bowls. A few wolf whistles ring out while we fill plastic cups, and I realize belatedly they're for me. Reaching across the island littered in bottles, my high-waisted shorts rise even higher over fishnet tights. The black heels help my legs look incredibly long.

I turn and raise my cup in thanks, Kay being quick to drag me away. Compared to hers, my top is simple; white and long sleeved, dipping low in the cleavage. I thought she'd lead me into the rave taking place, but instead, Kay rounds the stairs. As we ascend, I note the rich wood paneling on the walls contrasting with the modern art. The room we enter is quieter, filled with plush couches and scattered groups of people lounging about. Another chandelier hangs from the ceiling casting a soft glow onto our faces.

A woman in a smart dress shirt detaches from a group when she sees us. Her tie is the same blue shade as her mohawk, both swaying as she makes her way over, eyes fixed on Kay. My presence is completely ignored and instantly forgotten by Kay. Charming.

While the pair chat each other up with hazy enthusiasm, I glance around the room again. The air is different here - cleaner, less chaotic but still carrying that undercurrent of wild unpredictability that comes along with house parties like this one. I feel a tap on my shoulder and turn around to find a slightly intoxicated cheerleader.

"Hey, you're not Sophia," the cheerleader slurs, squinting up at me through her heavily mascaraed lashes. She stumbles slightly and I reach out to steady her, careful to keep my plastic cup from spilling.

"No, I'm not," I reply with a chuckle. "I'm Avery."

"Oh." Her face falls slightly before brightening again. "Well, that's okay too!" She exclaims, throwing a friendly arm around my shoulders and leading us back to the group she'd detached herself from. I'm thrust into their girly giggles and matching uniforms. Black with yellow trim; the Waversea colors. The cheerleader who brought me over introduces me as Audrey, her words slurred and eyes heavy. I go along with it, giving a small wave.

Despite being cheerleaders, I'm surprised by the easy way they accept me into their bubbling conversation. I have to let go of the clichés, I berate myself while drinking my punch. Even still, I find comfort in their physique, their posture, the way they laugh and glance around as though they're always watching for an audience. A slice of predictability is needed sometimes. They're in the midst of 'Would you rather be chased by a snail your whole life or a lion for half an hour a week?' when the door slams open. On instinct, I shrink into their group.

The original cheerleader who approached me squeals, standing on her tiptoes to get the newcomers attention. He's tall and built with a shaved head and an easy smile on his face. Dimples pop in his cheeks, ones I've only seen on his gym-side flag. His dark eyes meet mine through the crowd, recognition flashing across his features.

"Ahh, fuck," I watch his lips move and smile drop. More figures move in behind him and I don't need to look to know exactly who they are.

"I hope they choose me," one of the cheerleaders beside me gushes. I down my drink and grab her arm, yanking her down a few inches to my level.

"Choose you for what?" I hiss. She looks at me like I'm stupid.

"What we're all in here waiting for," she bobs her eyebrows. My face scrunches up as I look for Kay. She wouldn't have come to this room with the intent on catching the basketball team's attention. The cheerleaders, maybe. But alas, she's disappeared.

Tugging my phone out of my cleavage, I look down for a split second when the girls around me part and the air changes. Axel hastily turns me towards the back wall as music starts to play. Not the thumping, fist pumping kind like downstairs, but the type you'd receive a lap dance to. Pulling me against his body, his solid chest leans against my back.

"Just go with it," he mutters in my ear and sways slightly. We're turning ever-so-slowly, step by step, to the bitter disgust of the cheerleaders watching on. The room rotates at the will of the firm arms caging me. The door comes into view and after checking over his shoulder, Axel releases me. "Get out of here." I don't need to be told twice.

Rushing for the hallway, my hair is suddenly caught. I'm being yanked backwards, screaming and gripping the hand twisted in my blonde locks. Coming face to face with Wyatt's furious green eyes, they slide over my shoulder.

"Tsk, tsk, Axel." His gaze briefly wanders to his friend. I can't bring myself to worry about Axel right now. Out of his usual casual wear, Wyatt's body seems bigger in a black shirt. The buttons have been left open down his chest, revealing swirling dark ink and the hint of defined muscle. He smells incredible, expensive. I jerk away, trying to rip my hair free from his fingers. With no such luck, Wyatt bundles me down the hallway and into an empty room.

I double take as I'm released, then pushed along to sit. I know in theory Wyatt is a Hughes, but the replica office to his father's is the first time I've seen evidence of it. The desk is wide and mahogany, home to an antique lamp and cigar box. My eyes linger briefly on the decorative engravings before moving on. Persian rug, black shades, lit fireplace; it's all here. Using the armchair's high-back to their advantage, I can only look forward as the shadows close in. Wyatt takes front and center.

"What are you doing here?" He pops his knuckles on the desk behind him. Crossing one fishnet-clad leg over the other, I do want I do best. Act nonchalant and get under Wyatt's skin.

"I mean...I was planning on getting shitfaced and dancing until dawn, if that's quite alright with you?" Wyatt's jaw tightens, a flutter beating in the low fiery glow.

"I thought I told you to stay away from us." His voice is so thick, I have to suppress a responding shudder. Sighing, I pull my phone back out of my cleavage and slowly turn the message high for all to see.

"Well, someone decided to invite me." Wyatt snatches it from my hand to peer closer. A long pause follows. I don't try to understand the conversation happening between their eyes. Garrett and Axel take a guarded step closer to the chair arms, while Dax and Huxley hang back. Finally Wyatt draws himself back up to full height, slowly rolling his shirt sleeves up to the elbow. I'm sure he believes he's being threatening.

"Apparently there's no easy way to get this message through your skull, so let me be painfully clear. You are not welcome in my house, near my friends, at the gym." Wyatt lets his voice turn to a drawl, talking as if I'm stupid. What a surefire way to get my back up. "If you see me around campus, get out of the general vicinity. Do you understand what I'm saying?" He drops forward, juddering the chair as he grips the arms. His green eyes fill my vision, the darker flecks within them more prominent than usual. My nostrils flare as I huff through my nose.

"Last time I checked, I'm a fully fledged student here," I prod my finger in Wyatt's chest. "Just. Like. You." There are murmurs behind, hushed warnings to quit while I'm ahead. From where I'm sitting, shrouded in Wyatt's shadow, I'm firmly on the backfoot regardless. I might as well have a reason for his hatred, other than merely existing. Indecision crosses Wyatt's face. I reckon he's either going to headbutt or bite me, but instead, he pushes himself away.

"You're nothing like me," he chuckles darkly and rounds the desk. I don't see the cue but a bag is promptly shoved over my head. It's thick, making it hard to breathe. Hands grip my wrists when I try to shove it off, my entire body being manhandled. I'm carried out of the chair and dumped upright. Someone is still holding the bag around my head so I use my freed hands to lash out. Wood meets my fingers, snapping my nails on impact. I feel out the flat planks surrounding me as Wyatt's laughter freezes my movements.

"I want you to remember, I tried to warn you multiple times. You're just so fucking stubborn." There's a distant slam, like a ream of paper hitting the desk. "I have friends in the administration offices who kindly let me borrow your therapy transcripts before they were passed along to the counsellors. There's so much to work with in here," he muses. I feel around more slowly now. Three walls, empty slots where shelves once were, metal hinges for a door. If I had to hazard a guess, I'm in a closet, pinned in place by fear and the hand lightly clasped around my throat. My head is shaking but no sound comes through my lips.

"Fear of dark, enclosed spaces. The smell of whiskey causes flashbacks," Wyatt makes a noise in his throat. Blood rushes in my ears as the hand holding me slips away. That's it, hazing over. I will my heart to settle and for legs to move. Before they get the chance, a sudden shattering just above my head makes me scream. I duck, covering my head despite the bag protecting me from a downpour of glass. Whiskey explodes around me and when I finally manage to run, I slam into the now closed door. A lock clicks.

"No, no, Wyatt!" I scream, dragging the bag off my head. It makes no difference. The closet is pitch black, only wide enough for me to stand upright inside. I pound my fists, screaming at the top of my lungs. Someone in another room might hear. Grabbing for my phone, I remember Wyatt has it, the bastard. I fall still and quiet, pressing my ear to the wood. I convince myself they've left until a low sigh sounds through the door.

"Hopefully this conveys the message once and for all." Wyatt's voice is as clipped as his footsteps, echoed by the others leaving the room. My heart threatens to burst out of my chest.

"Guys, wait! Garrett, Dax, please don't leave me here!" I've resorted to pleading. My breathing kicks up to a worrying pace, an impending panic attack about to hit. The whiskey makes me gag. My memories awaken as if they've been lying in wait, hovering on the edge of my consciousness for this exact moment.

"No!" I scream again, but my voice echoes back, a mocking reminder of the times I've been trapped before. This isn't like the trunk, where I had the light of my phone, the boys on the other side of the divider and managed to maintain the upper hand. This is complete and utter blackness, an abyss forcing me back into a past I'd been doing my damnedest to forget. The effect of it was like a punch in the gut, and my knees buckle. There's nowhere to go, my legs crushing against the wall.

It isn't long before the panic attack hits hard; a crushing weight on my chest as if the walls really were closing in on me. My breaths come in ragged gasps, beating against my ears with painful loudness in the tiny space. The darkness swirling around me is a living thing, pressing in tighter as each second passes.

Focus on what you can touch, Keren's voice rings in my mind. Out of all of our therapy sessions, this is the one feat we could never manage. Even with the help of hypnotism, I can't break my reaction to tight spaces. It's not like claustrophobia; it's a deep seated terror that I'll be left and forgotten. That'll I'll die trembling and alone. Like my mom, I vaguely realize as the tears begin to fall.

With trembling hands, I feel along the walls for some sort of handle or latch. Tracing the coolness of the wood under my fingertips, stroking the rough grain against my skin. But there is nothing. Wyatt has created the ideal prison for me.

"I'm gonna kill him," I seethe, clenching my fists. That, I can focus on. My undeniable, all-consuming hatred for Wyatt. Finding a position crammed against the wall, crunching glass beneath my heels, I do something I have never managed before. I welcome the memories of my past, but in place of a fragile young girl, I picture Wyatt. Topless, scared, screaming Wyatt. Let his body be beaten, let his tears drip onto the hardwood floor. Let him suffer and starve.

My breathing slows, my fists relaxing. The panic swirling stalls, settling like a heavy ball of lead. It's not gone, but it's somehow less. A strange, creeping smile grows upon my face and a flicker of hope ignites in my chest like a small flame. Perhaps I should thank Wyatt for making me face my demons. Now I can bring a whole world of pain he isn't expecting. Maybe then he'll learn to leave me the fuck alone.

CHAPTER NINE

"I'm so sick of this shit," Wyatt groans, throwing a dart. It swoops high, bouncing off the backboard and missing the target. His shoulders sag with the weight of his sigh. I lift my hand to pat his back, but I don't follow through. I can't bring myself to comfort him right now. Instead, I step up for my turn. Acting casual is the best way forward, despite the crippling ache in my chest.

Similar feelings are rippling behind me. On a low sofa across the abandoned games room, Dax is incredibly quiet, nursing his drink and tapping his thumb on his knee. By the pool table, Garrett and Axel have turned into each other, taking comfort in stolen touches and muttered reassurances. The only one of us who doesn't care that there's a girl locked in the closet upstairs seems to be Wyatt.

His next dart sails aimlessly past the target and clatters against the wall behind it. The sound resonates through the silence in the room. Taking a shot of vodka straight, Wyatt sways on his feet, accidently bumping me aside. Garrett and Axel exchange a glance, but they don't dare say anything. We're all used to Wyatt's dark, withdrawn moods, but getting himself unstably drunk is new. Every aspect of Wyatt's life, of his personality, is about control. Strict, meticulous control.

I straighten my shoulders and take my turn at the dartboard, my mind hardly focused on the game. I nail a bullseye without trying to. The metallic thunk of the dart hitting home rings out, a harsh interruption to the tense quiet. For a moment, we're all staring at the dartboard, as if that lone dart has all the answers we're too afraid to speak. Finally, Dax drains his drink and shatters the silence.

"We can't just ignore her," He says gruffly, his tone laced with frustration and worry. His icy blue eyes are hard when they meet mine, but there's fear there too. Fear for the girl upstairs, fear for us, fear of what will happen if we don't calm Wyatt down soon.

Wyatt doesn't look at any of us, let alone respond, as he retrieves his darts from various corners of the room. His shoulders are rigid with tension and I have a gut feeling that anything we say won't sit well with him. Garrett's hand finds Axel's in silent solidarity as they brace themselves.

"Wyatt," I sigh, taking one for the team. This time, I do grab him by the shoulders, stilling his movements. "Maybe you should find someone to take your mind off...things?" I offer. My smile is weak, and he sees straight through it.

"Don't do that."

"Do what?"

He scoffs, shrugging me off and downing someone else's shot.

"Don't send me off for someone else to deal with." His green eyes are blurred but his scowl is in full force. My gut plummets to be on the receiving end of it for a change. Turning to face the three on the sofa, Wyatt accidentally stumbles into the table. Drinks topple and spill onto his plush carpet.

"I've been there for each one of you. I spent months cuddling Axel at night while Garrett was in the hospital. I memorized the entire medical physics textbook so I could push Dax through his entrance exams. And you of all people, Huxley, understand how it feels to be completely isolated while everyone else is watching."

"I know, I know. You're right," I attempt a different tactic. Ganging up on him isn't going to get us anywhere. I break through something as his façade cracks. The fragile boy he keeps hidden deep, *deep* inside, makes a brief and rare appearance.

"It's my turn to be supported. You may not feel what I feel, but I expected you all to step up. I told you what her being nearby does to me. I can't...There's just..." Any trace of weakness is quickly shut down. Grabbing a bottle by the neck, Wyatt launches it across the room in a similar fashion to the one he shattered over Avery. "You know what, fuck the lot of you. I'll let someone else deal with my anger." I hang my head as he storms away. God help whichever cheerleader volunteers.

"And the girl?" Garrett asks tentatively. He's taken a protective step in front of Axel, as if such a question might cause another bottle to be thrown.

"Do what you want," Wyatt throws up his middle finger as he exits, taking the tension with him. We stand for a while, stewing in regret. I'd known Avery's presence on campus would affect him, but I should have been more active in making sure their paths didn't cross. Speaking of which, who fucking invited her?

"Dudes. We're shit friends," Dax groans, leaning his elbows on his knees. He's toying with a cigarette in his fingers.

"We're not shit friends," I roll my eyes. "I'll stand with Wyatt against the whole freaking world, but I'm not in the market of using someone's fears against them." My eyes drift to the hazel ones determined on staring at the floor. Out of the five of us, Axel had the hardest time reading Avery's transcripts. She's a survivor, that's for sure, making far more progress in opening up about her past than he ever has. Now it's being used as a weapon against her.

I throw the rest of the darts in my hand, all three hitting the board without trying. Then I finish my drink, wiping my mouth with the back of my hand.

"Right. I'll go get her," I announce. I don't trust Dax not to get ahead of himself, sporting his puppy dog eyes, and the torment twins won't be any good to anyone for the rest of the weekend now. Garrett smiles, hiding everything behind that simple gesture.

"I'll be on Axel-watch. This is the epitome of a triggering situation."

"I'm literally right here," Axel finally steps out of Garrett's shadow but leans on him anyway. Their fingers intertwine and they start to walk on by. I step into Axel's way, chasing the misery in his eyes.

"Come here," I open my arms and draw him in for a hug. His head lingers on my shoulder and if anyone were to happen upon us now, they'd get the wrong impression. The Shadowed Souls formed from a bunch of needy kids who wanted to feel included, but over the years, it became so much more than that. We separated, we suffered. Now back together, we're inseparable and some of us are still healing.

For Axel, he relies on physical love in whatever form it comes in. I release him, letting the pair leave and give Dax a stiff warning to stay in his seat.

Taking the stairs two at a time, I enter the study. What strikes me first is the quiet. Just like with the trunk, she's so quiet and I spend a few moments assessing if she's managed to break out of the closet door. I'm sure if she had, the room would be as wrecked as the SUV in the garage. The keys are still on the desk beside her phone and a brown folder brandishing her name. Nothing is out of place. Deeply exhaling, I collect the keys and unlock the door, slowly turning the handle. Pulling it open, I wince at the mess I might find inside, when a blonde tornado launches herself at me.

"Holy fuck!" Glass shard in hand, I narrowly avoid losing my eye, gripping Avery's arms and holding her back. Her blue eyes are feral, and despite my steel grip, she continues to jerk and buck against me. "Hey, hey! I'm not going to hurt you! I came to let you out." Avery pauses, sizing me up like her next meal.

"Did you stand aside while he locked me in?" she asks and gives me a whole three seconds to hesitate on an answer. Gritting her teeth, she jumps for me again. Her wrists are so small in my hands, easy for her to twist and break free. Her clenched fist punches me in the jaw before the glass is pressed against my throat. I back up, hitting the wall and holding my hands where she can see them.

"Whoa! Let's just take a breath, try to-"

"If you tell me to calm down, it'll be the last thing you do." Avery's hand on the shard is unwavering. Her whole body, in fact, is completely steady. I'm careful not to swallow, or shudder against the knee she has pressing into my balls.

"I'm not going to hurt you," I say tentatively. A drop of scarlet red rolls down Avery's arm. "You're bleeding. Let me help." Against my better judgment, I cup Avery's hand and gently pull it away from my throat. I pluck the thick shard from the whiskey bottle from her grip. She permits it, now that she's distracted by the open cut on her palm.

Keeping my hold loose, I manage to guide her through the hallway. A few people jump out of our way, the whispers already starting to circulate as I pull Avery into my bedroom. We head straight for the bathroom where I grab a first aid kit from the bottom drawer. When I turn back, Avery is sitting on the countertop, her hand under the faucet. I watch her in silence, thankful the wound isn't too deep.

"Would you really have cut me?" I need to know for future reference. I won't be the first to aid her next time if it's going to cost me. Avery gives me a half-shrug which is just as terrifying. She didn't even know. It takes a while for the bleeding to slow, after which I pat her palm dry and apply a dressing. Then, I wrap a bandage around her hand. All the while, my thumbs stroke the lingering bruising around her wrists at any chance they get. Does she have any idea how beautiful she was, restrained and wanting? How good she tasted? I push away the thought.

"I want to go home," Avery sighs, leaning back against my mirror. I look away from her raised chest, her slightly parted legs. Garrett isn't here to persuade me that the best kind of payback is oral.

"I'll walk you back to your dorm," I reply hastily. Getting her out of Wyatt's vicinity is what's best for both of them. Avery shakes her head, staring vacantly across the room.

"Not the dorm. I want to go *home*." She bangs her head back against the mirror. "I miss Meg. I miss my mom and Nixon. I hate it here. I hate always being late. I hate having nowhere private to just be myself. Everyone is always watching. And every time I try to do what normal students do, Wyatt and his asshole friends are there to throw me into a spin."

I can't comment, being one of those asshole friends myself.

"I just...I can't keep..." Avery struggles to find the words, tears threatening to fall. I act on instinct. Pushing my way between her knees, I do what I'm best at. I wrap my arms around her back and force her into my chest.

"I get it," I try to reassure her. Avery laughs bitterly, refusing to hug me back. "No really. I've spent long enough around broken people to understand. You need something solid to hold onto."

She waits a beat, then tentatively winds her arms around me. The man she almost put in the hospital ten minutes ago, but I have a feeling nothing is straightforward when it comes to Avery. She hasn't lived in the real world. She doesn't have any point of reference for social situations, and has somehow found herself at the heart of the most fucked-up friendship group around. At least while she's hugging me, I know she isn't plotting my death. Avery's breath hitches, her head becoming heavy against my chest.

"I can't depend on you." I agree with her small voice, but I refuse to let her go just now. The music and laughter from the party simmers on the level below. Wyatt will have found someone to distract him by now. Axel has Garrett, Dax has his terrible smoking habit. What or who does Avery have?

When I can't handle my own train of thought any longer, knowing I've always been a soppy drunk, I release her. Bracing myself on either side of her legs on the counter, my head lowers.

"Okay, let's make a truce. Anytime any of us annoys you from now on, I'll let you beat me up. I volunteer as tribute and all that. You can restrain me if you like, but I need you to promise me one thing." Bringing my face up, her perfume mixed with the stench of whiskey hits me.

"What?" Avery's eyes return to mine, suspicious and curious.

"Lead with your left hand. We can't let anything come between you and your multicolored highlighters." A smirk hitches the corner of my mouth in an attempt to dissipate the thick atmosphere. Avery's brow rises.

"Dax?" she guesses.

"He may have mentioned it." I leave out that he didn't know who she was at the time. It was nice to see him giddy for a change, talking of a cute girl in his class. Then it all came crashing down.

Slowly sitting upright, Avery enters my personal space. Her eyes are all encompassing; the palest blue flecked with light green. Her lips are full, slightly parted. In a stolen moment that has no business happening, my gaze roams over her body. I'm used to girls toting around this house in bikinis and heels, nothing left to the imagination. But not Avery. Her long sleeved white top hugs her curves, the black shorts sitting high on her waist. Even though they needn't be, her legs are covered with fishnet stockings. She's like a present, ready to be unwrapped.

"I'm going to move away now," I breathe, ignoring how I feel the words bounce off her lips. My hands grip the sides of the counter as Avery slowly nods.

"Okay."

"Just gonna...back away and leave," I repeat. Maybe if I say the words enough, my body will follow through.

"Wyatt will kill you if you don't," Avery also tries to convince me.

"He'd bury me six feet under." My eyes dip to the junction of her thighs. I know how tight she is, how beautifully she glistens. I swallow thickly, on the verge of panting. "Why is forbidden fruit so tempting?"

"Because it's forbidden," Avery whispers with a smirk that is almost my undoing. At the point where I decide I'm not going to deny myself a second longer, the loud shrill in my pocket saves us both. Dragging the device out, I hand Avery her phone and shove myself away for good. She makes a disappointed noise in her throat and I'm right back again.

"What's wrong?"

"My roommate," Avery sighs and turns the screen to face me. I'm affronted by a photo of a blue tie hanging on a door handle, accompanied by the words *DON'T COME HOME*. We share a quick glance, a question in our tipsy gazes.

"Hit the shower. I'll make you up a bed on my floor. But don't get any ideas. If I took this any further, Wyatt would have my balls."

"And we wouldn't want that," Avery smiles at last and slides off the counter. I pause at the sarcasm in her tone. I think Avery would be exceedingly happy if my testicles were hung in the study as a decorative ornament. The shower is switched on behind me and I feel like I should receive a medal of honor for making it all the way into my bedroom without looking back. Just as I lose my nerve though, my cock straining in my pants, I turn to see the door being slammed shut in my face. I guess I'll just jerk off into her pillow instead.

AVERY

CHAPTER TEN

A pinging sounds beneath my face, jerking me upright. I fumble with my phone to silence it before anyone else hears.

"*Shit, shit, shush!*" I whisper as if the device can hear me. Managing to find the snooze, I slump back onto the fluffy blanket. My head is spinning, an empty bottle of gin knocking my knees as I draw them into my body. Settling back into a hungover, miserable state, the sudden realization of what my alarm was for physically slams into me. Fuck, I'm going to be late.

I scramble to gather my phone, bag, and heels, stopping in the middle of the darkened room. A deep inhale and rumbling exhale comes from the four poster bed, Huxley's outline strewn across the covers. There isn't an ounce of fat on him, every limb honed with defined muscle. His blond hair is scruffy against the pillows. I glance from my fishnet stockings and crumpled shirt to the dead-like figure on the bed. On second thoughts, I can't attend my appointment like this.

There's a solid wood dresser, each drawer presenting neatly folded stacks of clothes. I 'borrow' a white t-shirt, pair of gray sweatpants and patterned boxers, before heading into the bathroom. Huxley doesn't stir once. After quickly washing, scrubbing my face and finding a pack of new toothbrushes in the vanity, I dress in his clothes. The sweatpants have a drawstring, the t-shirt I twist at the side to reveal my navel. It'll have to do. Across the far side, I'm provided an escape into another bedroom. Thankfully, this one is empty. I raid the wardrobe for shoes, finding a pair of sneakers which are only a few sizes too big. That's what laces are for I guess.

Cracking the door, voices travel from downstairs. All male. Wyatt is shouting, Garrett is laughing, and Axel is trying to mediate.

"What the fuck were you thinking?" Wyatt barks, evidently slamming something soon after. I creep out into the hallway, careful to stay against the far wall. "I told you to keep the fuck away from her."

"Ohhh," Garrett exaggerates. "I thought you said 'keep fucking her'." His laughter is infectious. I find myself smirking, despite no doubt being the subject of their conversation. Just knowing there's someone else in this world who doesn't drop to their knees and worship Wyatt's every word is enough to lift my spirits. But then Garrett has to keep talking and douse my amusement.

"Look, she's different from the rest. Our usual tactics won't work on her. I needed to knock her off-kilter, throw her off-beat. Trust me, getting beneath her defenses will bother her way more than any pathetic hazing attempt." I sober in an instant. So that's the game we're playing here? Who can make Avery look like a fool the fastest? Movement shifts to my left.

"Dax, you going to come down and have some input in this?" Wyatt calls, no doubt seeing his friend over the bannister. Dax is staring at me, an unspoken question in his face.

"No thanks," he responds evenly. "I'm thoroughly entertained up here." Striding closer, he lifts a finger to his lips. Once in line with me, Dax grabs my arm and pulls me along, using his body as a shield to the end of the hallway.

"What are you doing here?" he whispers, opening a window. I look over the tree just beyond. A thick branch stretches towards the house, its leaves beginning to brown and wilt. On the trunk, a rope ladder presents an easy exit from the second floor into a line of bushes. I briefly wonder if the escape has been set up for the many women who stay over against Wyatt's knowledge, or if it's for the men prisoned inside themselves. Either way, Wyatt doesn't seem to have the control he believes and that makes me immensely happy.

"It's a long story. I have to go. The buses are hourly on a Sunday." I know this, because I carefully preplanned my route before I knew I'd be having a secret sleepover and feeling like I'd been hit by a truck.

"What-where?" Dax fumbles and then composes himself. His hand is still wrapped around my arm. "Don't worry about buses, I'll take you wherever you need to go."

"No thanks," I pry my arm free. Even if Wyatt hadn't so clearly warned me to stay away from his friends, twice, there's no way I want Dax following me around today. Lifting one leg out of the window, my second alarm pings from my phone. Shit, I've missed the bus anyway.

"What was that?" Wyatt calls, his steps ringing out on the stairs. Dax panics, shoving me out of the window and onto the low branch. I've almost crawled to the trunk when his heavy weight follows, causing the tree to wobble. Using the rope ladder, I hit the ground just before Dax drops down, grabs my waist and drags me into the bushes. We press against the wall, Dax's front to my back and his hand gingerly covering my mouth. "Dax?!" Wyatt calls from above. I still, closing my eyes as if that will help me become invisible. There's a grumble and a slamming of the window, leaving us in the clear.

"Let me drive you," Dax attempts again. He releases me and steps aside, running his hand over his short hair. "It's the least I can offer." I watch his blue eyes, accepting the sorrow sparkling within. True, Dax owes me, but he also doesn't know I won't let him off so easily.

"Fine, go ahead," I gesture out of the bushes. His rewarding smile is so similar to that first day in English Lit, when he was just a guy and I was just a new girl trying to find my feet. Dax leads me to the garage, careful to crawl beneath the windows. I do get a chance to appreciate his ass and glutes for a few minutes, his gym shorts riding high. Once inside, I stop short at the series of cars. Huxley's smashed-up SUV is in the corner, beside an orange Nissan. Dax walks towards a green Mercedes beside a small motorcycle collection. I glance at the time on my phone, not having time to hang around.

Opening the car door, I slide into the comfy leather seat and roll my palms over my knees. Dax settles behind the wheel, closing us into a confined space thick with tension.

"So...where is it you need to go?" he asks, drumming his fingers on his thighs. I smile sweetly, mounting my phone on his dash with the navigation set up for an OB/ GYN in the neighboring city. I wish I could have taken a picture of his reaction and mounted it on my wall.

Smirking to myself, I relax as Dax activates the rolling garage door and eases us out onto the street, out of campus and into the countryside. I wasn't prepared for the weight of stress to lift from my shoulders, as I hadn't fully realized it had settled there. Winding down the window, I let the wind brush over my face and work through my hair, breathing deeply for the first time in weeks.

Remaining quiet for the entire ride, I steal glances at Dax's unusual appearance. His blonde afro-style hair looks soft, despite being shaved at the sides and kept short on top. His powerful blue eyes stand out from his bronzed skin and his hands look big enough to-

"My mother is Latino, and my father is Brazilian." He answers the burning question in my gaze. I blush at being caught out, but only because my mind had started to drift. The Mercedes turns sharply into a car park beside the practice, the tall glass building looming above us. "I want to apologize," Dax swallows hard once we're stationary. I twist to face him fully.

"What are you apologizing for?" I cock one brow, my blonde hair falling forward.

"Well...um, for not doing anything I suppose. With the trunk, and then the cupboard..." Dax fumbles with his keys. I gently extract them from his hands to gain his focus.

"So not for trying to befriend me in the first place then?" I keep my face impassive. "You must have known who I was, the new girl in class who happened to start the same day as Wyatt's sister." It feels weird to call myself that but we quickly move on.

"I didn't know you were new. I was just transferred up to AP English Lit last week. I thought I was the new student and I just...I just wanted to talk to you. No strings, I swear." He watches me intently, no trace of a lie to be seen. The sharp lines of his jaw are close enough to trail my fingers over, his Adam's apple bobbing. The spunky attitude is stolen from me, my revenge scheme going up in flames. But he is Wyatt's best friend. He stood by while I was trapped in a confined space twice. He read my therapy transcripts. They all deserve my retribution.

Reaching for the handle, I look over my shoulder innocently. "Aren't you going to come in to keep an eye on me? They offer free chlamydia tests if you want to get checked out while we are here." Dax's shocked expression tickles me but I keep my face impassive.

"I'll wait out here." He states. Shrugging, I take my phone and step out of the car, walking straight through the rotating doors leading into an open reception area. Waiting in the line patiently to approach the front desk, I peer back to see Dax has gotten out of the car to lean against it with a cigarette in his fingers. I didn't know he smoked. The woman in front of me moves aside so I approach the receptionist. Thick rimmed glasses sit on her dainty nose, her hair is pulled into a tight bun with every strand perfectly in place.

"Excuse me," I lower my voice, "I believe the man by that green car outside is following me, so I ducked in here. Do you have a back door I could use?" The receptionist's brown eyes widen, quickly looking at Dax and back again. She nods quickly and directs me towards the fire exit. As I walk away, I hear her call for guards. The smile that graces my lips stems from pure evil. I start to run as soon as I reach the corridor I was pointed towards. Pushing my weight against the door release, I almost fall onto the street and continue running, laughing the entire way to my real destination.

The tattoo shop is set back from the high street, accessed by a staircase to the upper level. I inhale the sterile smell, a knot forming in my chest. The walls are adorned with designs, a showcase for the indecisive to choose from. Each glass unit has an artist's name printed on the plaque, so I can easily see who adopts each style. I'm already booked in with Ben, having seen his instagram and fallen in love with his delicate lines, dotwork and watercolor splash aesthetic.

I'm asked to read and sign a waiver and provide my ID, then I'm directed to the waiting area. The entire studio is alive with buzzing. Reclining leather chairs sit in front of each station, surrounded by bottles of ink and various supplies. The artists are covered in ink themselves, their arms and hands moving deftly as they work on their clients' skin.

"Avery?" A huge biker kind of guy, with multiple piercings, hundreds of tattoos and a long, thick beard approaches me. I raise my brows, a small laugh escaping me.

"I'm so sorry," I cover my mouth and take his gloved hand. "I was expecting someone a little more..."

"Less manly?" Ben's eyes sparkle. "Yeah, I get that all the time. These hands however," he holds them up, "are as gentle as a lover's kiss." There's a snigger around the studio, led by Ben himself. I'm immediately put at ease. Leading me to the back of the studio, to his table in the right corner of the room, Ben slides the dividing curtain closed to block us from public view. "I've got a stencil drawn up from the images you sent me. Let's get it placed and you can tell me what you think."

Shrugging the baggy t-shirt off, I turn in my bra and throw my hair up into a bun so Ben can line the stencil up with my spine. That knot in my chest lowers to a heavy weight in my stomach. I've been waiting so long for this day, but I never thought I'd be here alone. Ben guides me to a full-length mirror and asks my opinion. It's perfect. A thin arrow from mid-back to nape, a swirling line trailing the length to the feathered end. In the center, the rod stops short for roman numerals to fill the gap. Ben has put his own spin on the design, adding dots in additional swirls. It's delicate, feminine and meaningful. The best part is, it directly covers a scar in the center of my back I've grown to despise. I blink back the tears while I approve and lie on the lowered table.

"Now remember what we spoke about in the messages. Scar tissue is harder to tattoo over, so I'll have to press quite hard in some places." I nod, not trusting myself to speak. Once the business is out of the way, Ben is all kind smiles again. "It's a lovely design. Did you draw it?" Ben unpacks a fresh needle and sets up the gun.

"Yeah," I sigh into the leather. "My mom and I drew one each. We'd always planned to get them on my twenty-first birthday. It's the age she was when she got her first."

"Well, happy birthday! I'm honored to be permanently marking you for the occasion. And your mom? Is she on her way?" It's an innocent question and one I saw coming.

"No, she couldn't make it," I smile sadly. Ben seems to understand, wiping down my back in an overly caring gesture. Then the gun is powered up and I brace myself.

"Deep breath for me. We have sugary drinks if you start to feel dizzy."

"I'm all good," I respond bravely. I've been through much worse than this. The first stroke sets in. Soon followed by the next until they all blend together. Aside from my mom and Meg, Ben is the only one to have seen, let alone touch, one of the scars that litter my body from a previous life. Nixon is more of a 'pretend-it-doesn't-exsist-and-everything-is-okay' kind of guy. I bite down on my lower lip, resisting the urge to jerk away from the tattoo gun. Ben spoke of physical pain, but he can't know of the emotional affect his poking and prodding will have of me later.

I tense each time the gun lowers and relax each time he twists away. Mom promised to be here, to hold my hand. I have a moment of regret for coming alone. I don't know why I thought to do this by myself. If Meg wasn't away with her lacrosse team, she'd have been here. It's a harsh reminder that I have no one else in this world. My own fault really, I wanted to be a hermit. I thought if I only existed at the manor, the world would carry on without me. But now I've been thrust into it, and the only objective is to survive.

Breathing deeply, I desperately try to focus on the tattoo gun's pain, rather than the visions that filter into my mind from my damaged skin being touched. The sharp sting of the needle blends into that of a leather belt or the burning of a cigarette, my mind tricking my nose into conjuring the singed smell. Bile rises in my throat, shudders raking my body and tears leaking from my eyes.

I snap back into reality and realize the tattoo gun has stopped. Ben offers me a tissue, passing me the promised soda. I don't dare tell him it's not the pain that is affecting me.

"I'm sorry, I'll do better this time," I reassure him, sipping my drink. It might have been a good idea to eat before I arrived. Once he's satisfied, Ben sets back to work.

The vibrations of the tattoo gun reverberate through my upper back and I suck in a breath, waiting for the images to flood my mind again. However, this time they seem to hover on the edges and blur slightly, seeming to know that I'm on the home stretch to covering them from existence. If I can't see them, they can't hurt me – right?

Ben fills the cubicle with his voice, giving me another focus. I listen to his entire life story, from his various childhood homes to his cat, Beau. He's a softie for his kitty, treating him to a bowl of ice cream every Sunday afternoon. We run through the best ice cream combos for a cat, imagining all the favors he'd probably create if he had opposable thumbs. I hadn't realized how much time has passed when Ben announces he's finished.

The sting of an alcoholic spray is wiped across my back before I'm directed to stand. Ben opens the curtain and points to a long mirror in the hallway. The lighting is better out here, he informs me. I wrap my arms around myself, mustering some new-found confidence and step through the curtain. There are a few more scars to tackle on my ribs, smaller circular ones that are easier to hide with my arms. He promptly hands me a second, smaller mirror to hold.

"I added a little flair. I hope you like it." Ben steps away as I angle the mirror, my jaw dropping open. Like it? I can't form a coherent thought. Around the arrow, there are splashes of color in a watery effect. Pastels blur effortlessly around the feathers and arrow head. His dot work creates many pathways, I can't keep track. I knew Ben had talent, but seeing it on myself is something else entirely.

"Woah" I breathe when nothing else comes out.

"Nice job, Benny Boy," another tattoo artist catches sight of the piece in the mirror and comes closer to get a better look. A navy-blue cap sits backwards on his dark hair, his ears have large discs in the lobes and thick black tattoos cover his otherwise creamy skin up to his jaw. But it's the way he's looking at my back which makes me weak. I've imagined this moment many times, where the tattoo didn't quite cover my scar and all onlookers gift me a wince and a heavy dose of sympathy. But no, it's nothing like that. It's so much better.

More people come over, complimenting me, congratulating my first ink session. I'm a mumbling mess, promising I'll be back for more when Ben calls my name, drawing me away from the small crowd to get patched up. My head is reeling that I just stood out in the open in only a bra and no one is whispering things like 'oh, that poor girl'. 'How horrific'.

"So, this is wildly inappropriate, and I promise it's only with noble intentions." Ben helps me ease the t-shirt over my head. I adjust to the feeling, careful not to move too much. He then lowers onto his stool, choosing his next words carefully and quietly. "I recognise the demons you hold inside, and it doesn't seem like you have many people in your corner. If there's ever a time you feel trapped, don't hesitate to call me. I'm rather intimidating to those who don't know me." Ben winks, scribbling his number and address onto a scrap piece of paper and tucks it into the leg pocket of the sweatpants. I'm speechless by his offer.

I make my way to the main desk, where Ben shouts over to the receptionist that my money is no good today. Consider it a birthday present, which sets off every artist and client singing 'Happy Birthday' as I stumble out of the door and into Dax's hard chest. Large hands steady me, piercing blue eyes glinting with curiosity.

"It's your birthday?"

CHAPTER ELEVEN

"This really isn't necessary," I huff, my fist against my cheek all that's holding my head up. Dax sits across the table, planting down two tall milkshakes. One chocolate, one strawberry, both with cream and sprinkles.

"Just pick a damn milkshake," he grunts and I opt for the chocolate one. "I'm buying you dinner on your birthday because I'm a gentleman. *Not* a crazed stalker who follows you to the OB/GYN." I snort into my straw. Finally, I crack a smile since Dax half-dragged me into this fast food diner.

"What did the guards do to you?"

"Called the cops, who questioned me in the parking lot for an hour. Since you didn't stick around to back up your statement, they didn't have much to go on. That's the only positive I can think of right now." His brows are furrowed as he sips his drink. I quickly discover he doesn't like strawberry milkshake but he pushes it away instead of demanding mine back.

"Another positive is that I've thoroughly forgiven you," I wink.

"Oh well, it's my lucky day then." Dax rolls his blue eyes, sarcasm dripping from his tone. He swiftly changes the conversation. "What tattoo did you get?" With my inner voice satisfied Dax has been inconvenienced enough, I pull out my phone and show him the design.

"My mom and I designed them together. It started as an afternoon activity and ended with the promise to get them together on my birthday. Obviously, I didn't think I'd be going alone but I held up my side of the bargain."

"What was your mom like?" Dax finds a warm smile, encouraging me to open up. The fact he probably knows all about her means it's solely for my benefit but I suppose today is as good as any to reminisce. I tell him all about her; how she found me when I was ten years old, took me in and loved me unconditionally from day one. How every day she wasn't required to be on a film set, she'd fly home to spend the precious days with me. We had endless passion projects to fill our time. In the evenings, it was movies and popcorn. When Nixon was able to join us, it felt like my life was complete. It's all I ever wanted - the simplicity.

"You weren't a fan of the galas and award ceremonies I take it?" Dax asks his first question in twenty minutes as our food is placed on the table. Red plastic baskets lined with paper to soak up the greasiest burger and fries I've ever seen.

"That was always more of Wyatt's area of expertise. The spotlight, the showboating," I sneer. Deciding there's no lady-like way to eat the double-stacked burger between my fingers, I open my mouth wide and attack it. Dax makes a noise of disagreement.

"He wasn't as excited to go as you'd think," Dax points a fry at me. At my confused look, Dax sighs. "It was the only way he could get any quality time with his- your parents. Half of the time, he loathed the traveling and effort he had to go to for it." I don't need clarification to know 'quality time' means without me being there. If he felt any discomfort, I couldn't tell while watching the footage in high definition from the comfort of my sofa.

"Well he's a natural at bullshitting so," I shrug and go back to my burger. Dax frowns as if he wants to argue. Then a thought strikes me and I have to force it through the food in my mouth. "Anyways, ew. Can we not discuss Wyatt today of all days?" Thankfully, our conversation moves onto school and how I'm not going to skip any more of Mrs. Patrick's classes. Talking to Dax comes easily. He skates over uncomfortable topics and keeps the mood light. Once finished with our food, Dax clears up the table, stacking the trays neatly.

"If I offer you a ride back to your dorm, you're not going to have me arrested, are you?" he smirks, offering me his arm. I take it, withholding my answer. Let him sweat a little bit. The Mercedes is in a parking lot a few blocks away, and after such a heavy meal, I'm thankful for the slow walk. After a balmy day, an evening chill has settled. I shudder in the baggy sweats and t-shirt, and Dax hastily shrugs out of his hoodie for me. Maybe he is a gentleman after all. I wrap myself in his sea mineral smell, a lingering sadness settling in.

"We can't be friends, can we?" I keep my eyes on the sidewalk. Dax slides my bandaged hand back into the crook of his elbow.

"It's not advisable," he smirks. There's a playfulness there which I didn't expect. Wyatt seems to have a short leash on his men, but it doesn't stop them from rebelling. I put a pin in that thought for later.

"Can I ask one question before we go back to being strangers?" I lean into his side, playing along. Dax pulls me to a stop at a busy road, seeing me across safely before dipping his head to continue. "What's the deal with Axel? Are he and Garrett lovers or..." That smile instantly becomes twinged with sadness.

"Not exactly," he twists his lips this way and that. Reaching the parking lot, Dax pauses by a pillar. "As you know, abuse comes in many forms. Mental, physical, sexual...I can't speak for Axel. His story is his alone to tell, but I'll say that he requires a certain type of love. It's not easy to explain but Garrett understands him perfectly. Those two have saved each other time and again. I dread to think what would have happened if-" Dax seems to catch himself from rambling. My chest squeezes, desperate for him to continue. "The five of us are bonded like brothers but sometimes not even we are enough. If Axel were a ship at sea, Garrett would be his lighthouse. I know it doesn't make much sense."

Tears threaten to well in my eyes. It makes perfect sense to me. Some of us need that certain someone to be our anchor - Meg is mine. I didn't realize just how much I've been aching for her until this moment.

"I'm glad they have each other," I smile. An especially cool wind billows, whistling through the levels of the parking lot. We don't move. I'm content staring up into Dax's honest eyes, his warmth and cologne seeping into me.

Closing the last inch of space between us, I rest my head on his chest. Arms wind around my back, creating a stolen moment against the pillar which we'll not discuss here after. It's rare for me to admit when I need comfort. I've been so used to being wrapped in it, surrounded by those who understand me without needing an explanation. I don't know if I can add Dax to that list, regardless of the way his hands gingerly stroke my lower back, but at least for right now, I can pretend.

AVERY

CHAPTER TWELVE

"Then what happened?" Meg's smile leaks through the phone. I struggle to conceal my own.

"Nothing happened. He drove me back to the dorm block and I went to bed." Standing before my desk, I stroke a petal of my lilies. Kay took in the delivery yesterday, Nixon's scrawly writing on the greeting card. Each flower stands proudly, in full bloom in a range of pastel colors. Pinks, purples, oranges and yellows. I pause to smell them while Meg lingers on the other end of the phone line.

"Sooooo...you didn't hint at a birthday kiss?" she pushes playfully. I wish she could see my eye roll.

"Meg, seriously, the further I stay away from these guys the better. They make my head spin." I've withheld the closet ordeal with Wyatt. If people think I'm feisty, Meg would drive directly to his frat house and hang him with a belt. Lowering my hand from the lilies, I skate my fingers across to a manilla envelope.

"I got a card from Mr. XO," I attempt a chuckle. Meg goes instantly quiet, the silence stretching on.

"Aves...Are you-Did you open it?" she asks. I toss the envelope back onto the desk.

"No. There's no point, I already know what it'll say." On the front, my name is written in beautiful cursive, and in the corner, the signature

'XO'. I've received the same type of card every Christmas and birthday since I was adopted by the Hughes.

"Isn't that a bit scary? That he knew where you'd be?" Meg's demeanor has changed, concern lacing her tone. I know she means well but I didn't expect Mr. XO to just give up.

"Hardly. I have no doubt my relocation has been all over the internet. Don't worry, I'll forward it on as I always do."

Being wealthy and in the spotlight, fan mail is expected. My mom received so much, she had a PA whose main role was to sift through and pick out the ones she might like to answer. Typically, I only got this one. The contents don't seem to worry the cops, simple verses of staying strong and brighter days. Presumably a superfan of Cathy's who wanted to send some love my way too after the adoption and he has ever since. If it even is a 'he'.

"Okay, make sure you do. So what are you-" A flamboyant knock sounds at the door. I almost groan, dreading who's on the other side of it. Kay is out all day with her new girlfriend and I just wanted some peace and quiet.

"Hey Meg, I have to go. Love you."

"Don't forget I'm coming down next weekend! You'd better make a plan, biatch!" I laugh and end the call. Just before opening my door, I briefly look over my tiny shorts and t-shirt, the ends of my hair slightly dripping from its messy bun due to my morning shower. The knock comes again and I know I don't have time to change. Garrett is patiently waiting on the other side, holding a tray of coffees with the biggest and toothiest smile spread across his face.

"Why are you smiling like that?"

"Nice people smile."

"You don't look nice. You look crazed, and a little bit hungry."

"I'm always hungry," he snorts and pushes his way into my now crowded dorm room. In the spot he so recently stood, Axel is lingering a few feet behind. He meets my eyes very briefly, shakes his head and shrugs.

"Would you like to come in, Axel? Or shall I leave you moping out here in the hall?"

"I'm not moping," he mutters, taking my invitation. He seems tired today, dark circles ringing his eyes. I draw the door closed but not all the way, deciding that one inch of gap will prevent whatever is happening in here from escalating.

"What's this?" Garrett lifts the manilla envelope. I rush to snatch it out of his hand and shove it into a drawer.

"It's none of your business. What are you doing here, Garrett? I've got a very busy day," I lie. His eyelids lower as he tilts his head, calling me out on my bullshit. Regardless, I cross my arms and wait for an answer.

"I bought you gifts," Garrett instantly brightens again. Pushing a coffee cup into my hand, he then produces a small tub from his pocket. I recognise the brand from my morning of research into the best tattoo healing creams. I drop next to Axel on my bed. His thigh brushes mine and he doesn't move it away. Sipping the coffee, I sigh. It's perfectly sweet, how I like it.

"Dax told you then?" Garrett's brow raises at this.

"No," he beams. Like a kid who's just discovered where the best candy store in town is, Garrett's whole face lights up. I bet he's going to hold this over Dax's head when he gets back. In reality, the truth is much worse. "Wyatt installed a tracker on your phone the other night, while you were otherwise...incapacitated." He means locked up and having a panic attack, but I don't let that distract me.

"He did *what*?!" I jump up, my mouth gaping open. That bastard! I look to where my phone is sitting on the desk, Garrett standing in the way. I hand my cup to Axel, anticipating a fight.

"Never mind that for now." Garrett waves away my anger. "Let's see it then."

"No!" I shout a little too harshly. Putting them both in my eyeline, I retreat into a corner. "Thank you for the thought. I'll give it back to you once I'm all healed up." Holding out my good hand, Garrett sighs. He holds out the tub, letting me make the final decision to retrieve it. As soon as it graces my hand, he grabs and spins me. My front hits the wall, his knee pushing against my ass and his hands lifting my t-shirt.

"I hope for your sake you're wearing a bra," he chuckles. I thrash and cry out, hurting myself by tugging at the healing wound on my back. Luckily, I am wearing a bra as Garrett hitches my t-shirt up to my shoulders and lets out a low whistle. My heart twists painfully. Can he see the scar underneath? Is it raised and obvious through the ink.

"How the hell did you know where it was?!" I gasp, trying to shove his knee away with my good hand. Unfortunately, it's my left and I'm not half as confident fighting with that one.

"You backed yourself into a corner, not making any moves to conceal any other part of your body. Plus there's an ink line pressing against your t-shirt."

"He's surprisingly perceptive," Axel adds. I'd half-forgotten he was still here. Garrett tells me to hold still as two cold fingers touch my nape. I freeze.

"G-Garrett please. I don't-I hate having my back touched." His fingers halt on my neck, an uncomfortable pause ensuing. Is he looking closer now? Can he see what I've been so desperate to hide from the world?

"You're not going to be able to reach back here and you don't want this beautiful tattoo to scab and flake, do you?" His breath skates over my skin. He's close. Too close. But he is right.

"Fine, just...can Axel do it? Please?" The request catches all three of us off guard. Braving a glance towards my bed, those haunted hazel eyes are watching me closely now. Something Dax said stuck with me all night. Abuse comes in many forms. I almost passed out at the tattooist touching my scar, but if anyone has to do it again, I'd rather it was from someone who might understand. He nods once and Garrett finally releases me.

Pulling my t-shirt all the way off, because it's not like they haven't seen it all before, I return to my spot on the bed. This time, I face away, staring out of the window. All of the pleasant weather we've been having has finally caught up with us. Gray clouds hang low, the early drips of rain starting to beat against the glass. I love watching the rain from inside. I love the sound beating on the brick, pattering the ground. It's a comforting reminder that I'm safe and warm, that I have a roof over my head. For the first ten years of my life, that wasn't a given.

When Axel's hands touch me, I flinch. He's gentle, slowly drawing the cream in circles. Starting from my nape, he works his way down. I sense his hesitation, I feel what he's feeling. The raised scar tissue beneath his fingertips, the secret I've concealed. No one has touched it, not my mom nor Meg. He works cautiously, all the way down to mid-back and when I finally think it's over, his fingers spread out. Both hands stretch towards my ribs, encasing my sides. His fingers settle on the circular burn marks which await there and I stiffen. It would seem Garrett isn't the only one who is surprisingly perceptive.

"I'll have to come back this evening, and then twice a day going forward until it's healed," Axel murmurs. I almost whimper against his hold. I thought this would be enough to sate their curiosity. That they might be satisfied enough to leave me alone. Looking back over my shoulder, I stare into Axel's eyes before I concede.

"Okay." Across the room, Garrett watches on from his perch on Kay's bed.

"Well, that was hot." Axel remembers himself, withdrawing his hands. I don't bother with the t-shirt now, settling on my stomach and gathering the pillows beneath my chest. Axel shifts, laying a fluffy blanket over my lower back and ass. He takes the time to tuck in my legs, almost as if he wishes he could cuddle up beneath the blanket with me. Garrett steps in next, lowering to place a tender kiss behind my ear.

"Enjoy your very busy day, Peach." I suppress a shiver and wait for the door to click shut before retrieving my vibrator from the bedside drawer. The tension racking my body mingling with the longing twisting in my core. His softness, his touch. Emotions I've caged for so long start to unravel, the phantom touches skating across my back confusing me. I dip the vibrator between my thighs just as the rain starts to hit the window panes harder. The thunderous sound drowns out my moans as I chase that much-needed release. It comes fast and hard, crashing through me on a strangled cry.

In the aftermath of tremors, I reach for my coffee and flick open a dark romance novel on my ereader. Somehow, despite the years of trauma I've been faced with this morning, I manage to smile.

I suppose there are worse ways to spend a day.

AVERY

CHAPTER THIRTEEN

If I'd foreseen the connection my brain automatically made between Axel caressing my back and the intense urge to make myself climax, I can't say I'd have done anything different.

As promised, he visited each morning and evening, sometimes with Garrett and sometimes alone. I manage to keep a grip on myself while he's there, sitting on my bed and touching my skin. Around the time he started to rotate his thumbs on my shoulder blades and ease the kinks from my neck, my nipples began to harden. With each passing session, I grew wetter. To the point where I need to carry my vibrator in my backpack, not able to depend on Kay being absent from the dorm long enough. Pleasuring myself in the dance dressing room was my new low, but there was also something incredibly arousing about it too.

That's why I'm pointedly avoiding my dorm. I can't keep carrying on being horny all of the time. Neither can I allow myself to feel this comfortable with Axel touching me. He's unknowingly carving a path into my psyche. Regardless of how gentle he's been, he is still one of them. A Shadowed Soul. I can't trust him.

Tugging Meg's college sweater over my teal leggings, I point my feet in the dainty, pink shoes. We've been running through dances for the big showcase all week, testing pairings and letting each person get a feel of which role they'd like to aim for.

Despite having no plans to audition, I asked Theodore if he'd mind hanging back to run through the music with me. He was only too happy for the extra practice. I become distracted from my own movements, watching him become lost in his music. The passion he exhibits is the epitome of what dance means to me. Somehow, I've managed to dance my way closer, my eyes lingering on his hands. They're large, perfect for the piano, his manicured nails and smooth fingers stroking the keys. My breath hitches. What the fuck am I doing?!

Catching myself before I start drooling, I return to the back of the room and lean on the barre. In the floor-to-ceiling mirrors, I catch the blush lining my cheeks. My eyes drift to my backpack in the reflection, a familiar flutter beginning between my legs. Not now. I wait for Theodore's tune to loop back to a point I know and throw myself into the dance.

The choreography isn't like the classical style I'm used to. It's much more modern, combining tap and ballroom in some numbers. As unfamiliar as it may be, I find I'm able to shift between the styles without too much difficulty. Holding my arms out as if I were being led by a male, I spin back and forth, tracking the steps whilst on my tiptoes. My back arches as I dip backwards, tugging uncomfortably at my tattoo. It's in the process of scabbing now.

My leg extends to where my partner should be holding my ankle to turn me in a slow pirouette. Stretching beyond my natural reach, my leg suddenly seizes, as if a clamp has snapped shut around my calf. I crash to the floor, hugging the limb tightly into my middle, my eyes scrunching shut. My hand with the small bandage stings against the pressure but I continue holding my leg, crying out in pain. The piano has halted but when a body crashes into my side, it's not Theodore I find.

"I've got this, Tchaikovsky," Axel is on his knees. Lying me flat, he whips off my ballet slippers, takes my ankle in his hands and slowly rocks my foot back and forth. Each time the pain becomes too much, he holds for a few seconds and relents. Then, he does the same again. The agony shooting through my calf is unbearable, but soon my screams lessen. I find I'm able to take more and more of the stretch until the cramp begins to subside. I roll my head, noting the concern in Theodore's gaze as he collects up his sheet music.

"It's okay Theo," I wave him off, almost delirious myself. "Rain check until tomorrow?" He nods, not seeming comfortable in Axel's presence, and bolts out of the door. Swallowing, my throat scratches uncomfortably from the screams torn from me. Axel continues working my ankle, moving on to massage my calf. "What are you doing here?" I breathe.

"You weren't at your dorm. I didn't want to miss our... appointment." He's hesitant. It's only now I realize I'm lying on my tattoo. Pushing myself upright, I drag the sweater over my head. I'm too warm, my skin feeling too tight. Seeing myself in the mirror opposite, my hair has fallen free of its ponytail, my chest is flushed. But Axel's hazel's eyes look upon me as if I'm something better. Something precious.

"Axel, I don't think we should do this any more," I lower my head. My foot is still in his hands, subconsciously being massaged. I don't believe he even knows he's doing it, a genuine need for physical contact controlling his actions. Sighing, resignation passes across his features.

"It's okay if you don't want me to be around any more. I know I can be a lot." My heart plummets.

"No, that's not-" I start but it's too late. Axel releases my foot and begins to move away, the walls shutting down behind his eyes. Now the pain has ebbed, I shift up onto my knees to put us at eye level, grabbing his nape before he can move too far. A shadow of stubble is visible against his jaw, his cheekbones high and sharp. Axel's gaze shifts to mine, their coppery tint captivating me. He's beautiful up close.

With the back of my injured but healing hand, I stroke my fingers over his cheek. He responds as I knew he would, leaning into me. Lost in a trance where only he and I exist, tracing my finger along his strong jawline, my lips part. The fantasies I've been having while he tended to my tattoo return in full force. I shiver, despite the inferno raging within. I can't deny myself, nor can I let Axel think I don't want him around.

Leaning in closer, my eyelids flutter closed. The delicate softness of his lips press against mine as a throat is cleared in the doorway. Jolting away from each other, an amused-looking Huxley is standing in the doorway. His messy hair falls loosely onto exposed shoulders, a workout vest straining to cover his wide chest and failing to hide the outline of his six-pack. Heat flares to life in my cheeks as I half hobble upright, attempting to look casual as I push my feet into my trainers and head for the exit. I can't think when these boys are around.

"Avery, wait! Your bag," Axel jogs to grab my backpack. I turn suddenly as he crashes into me, my body acting as an activator for the device inside. The loud whirring of vibrations burst to life in the otherwise silent room.

"Is that..." Huxley raises a brow. My mouth drops open but only a squeak comes out. Never have I wanted to die a quicker death. Shoving my hand into my backpack, I search blindly to knock the damn thing off.

"No! It's my phone," I argue. While the entire contents of my bag is rattling, it's impossible to tell what's the vibrator, my deodorant, my water bottle. Why is everything I own phallic shaped? Axel, still holding my bag, gestures to the side pocket.

"You mean that phone?" he indicates to my cell sitting behind the mesh. Closing my hand around the vibrator, I attempt to switch it off and only manage to activate one of the thirteen settings. The rhythm beats twice, pauses and then judders, pauses and repeats. I finally manage to turn the damn thing off, pressing my injured palm to the center of my forehead. No one says anything as I slowly shoulder my bag, so embarrassed I might just throw up. Deciding something good might as well come from the most humiliating moment of my life, I look up at Axel.

"You thought I didn't want you around any more, but there's your truth. I want you around too much. I have to get myself off every time you touch me, so forget massaging my tattoo. You might as well just go down on me again."

"Again?" Axel frowns. My gut plummets.

"Yeah? You know...like before, with Garrett," I start to stutter. Huxley makes a strange sound in his throat, and it's his turn to go scarlet red. I watch him rub the back of his neck and stare instantly at the ground. "You?" I breathe in shock. Huxley's chocolate eyes raise to mine and he shrugs apologetically. "But...why?"

"Because Garrett's a meddling bastard, that's why," he chokes on a laugh. Axel mutters something to the same effect. I swallow, my pulse ringing in my ears. Concluding that I can't be here, sandwiched between these two gorgeous men, I blow out a harsh breath.

"Okay well. I'm going to go now. Let's not talk about any of this ever again." I take two steps when my backpack is tugged on. Huxley shoves his arm inside, a devilish smile on his face.

"You won't be needing this any more," he retrieves the hot pink vibrator and pauses to appreciate the girth and vascularity of it. I lied before - this is the moment I could die the quickest death. "If you want to cum, you'll have to find one of us," he directs his smirk to Axel. I've run out of air, my head starting to spin with all this to and fro.

"Wyatt will go crazy. You were there when he told me to stay away from you all." I don't know why I'm cowering behind Wyatt's rules. Maybe because I don't want to be locked in a fucking closet again, or maybe because it's an easy excuse. I can't go around screwing my stepbrother's basketball team within my first two weeks of school. Huxley doesn't seem to have the same reservations he had the other night, now he's feeling the weight of my vibrator in his hand and grinning as if seeing me in a whole different light.

"I know," he lowers to my ear and places a quick kiss there, "and that might be why you taste so delicious."

AXEL

CHAPTER FOURTEEN

"Axel honey, come on in. Don't be shy," my mother giggles into the microphone. I step into the room, picking at my bottom lip. As always, she looks incredibly beautiful, dressed in a black dress with a matching feather in her dark hair. Pearls surround her neck and hang from her ears. "Ahh, there you are." Her red lips smile over a champagne glass at me. Holding out her hand, I walk through the sea of women who gush and pawn at me as I pass.

An elevated stage has been fitted at the front of our ballroom for tonight, as it is every first Friday of the month. I shift my neck uncomfortably in the tight collar of the white shirt and navy tie mother insisted I wore tonight. I'm bulkier than the average teenager, having been forced into a vigorous exercise routine and strict diet. Navy slacks cover my legs and my brown dress shoes are freshly polished. Mother likes me to look older than my age of fourteen.

Stepping up onto the podium, mother embraces me in a tight hug that is only for show. She smooths her hand over my hair, pushing it over to the side the way she likes. Her pale brown eyes twinkle as they assess me, before turning me to face the crowd. This is one of the rare times I see her face lit with happiness.

"Okay ladies, take a good look and get those purses ready. We will start the auction at one thousand dollars." I try not to squirm under the

intense lighting and cat calls of the thirstiest and richest women around. Like my mother, most of the women here are widowed. But I don't think they have such financial strain as we do, which is exactly why mother forces me to 'be the man of the house and earn my keep'. My eyes prick but I clench my jaw to fight back the tears, knowing any weakness would earn me a swift slap and the auction would continue regardless.

"Five thousand dollars!" A gloved hand shoots into the air, the plump woman who owns it licking her lips at me hungrily.

"Ten!"

"Fifteen!" The lights are burning my retinas, my head beginning to spin. I fight against myself to keep my breathing even, focusing on inhaling through my nose for three seconds and exhaling via my mouth for five. Shouts and whistles for my attention fill my ears, mother's voice through the speakers saying the word I dread to hear each night in my nightmares.

"Sold!" Mother whirls around to kiss me on the cheek, her hands lingering a little too low on my back. "Can you believe it honey? Sixty thousand dollars! I can get that new Porsche after all." I try to join in her joy, wanting to be happy that I'm able to provide her with the luxuries in life father used to. But first, I have a night of misery to get through.

A woman hops onto the stage in tall red heels. She's fairly attractive, her wavy hair falling onto her shoulders and an extremely tight red dress pushing her chest up. Her long fingers stroke my arm through the shirt, a shiver running through me. I crave affection, but not like this.

"Why don't you go wait in your room honey? We will wrap things up down here." I step out of the woman's touch and half-sprint from the ballroom and up the staircase. Passing my room, I rush onwards to my father's old study. Even before cancer stole him from us last year, their marriage wasn't necessarily a happy one and he spent most of his time in here. Throwing the door shut behind me with a pained scream, I move into the bathroom and splash water onto my burning face.

My hair falls forward, which I automatically smooth back before catching sight of myself in the mirror. Rubbing the soft strands between my fingers, I stare at myself. Mother loves my hair; always running her hands through it and saying it's the best part of her that I inherited. A few months ago, a new hairdresser at the salon cropped my sides shorter than usual, and mother had her fired for it.

A stupid idea springs to life. Hastily opening the cupboard beneath the sink, I find a pair of clippers on one of the dusty shelves. Wiping them clean on a cream hand towel, I look back into the mirror. My hand is shaking slightly as I lift the clippers and flick the switch with my thumb. The powerful vibrations that meet my hand are a shock and almost cause me to drop it.

Mother's voice calls my name through the hallways, making my breath catch. She loves the idea of her little prince, the one who can maintain her rich lifestyle. Princes have to be handsome, desirable. I want to return to school with my friends, to play basketball and video games in the evenings. Not this. Never this.

That's the only thought going through my mind while I glide the clippers straight down the middle of my head as the door swings open. I won't be her whore. In fact, I never want to be desirable again.

Waking in a panicked sweat, I quickly run my hand over my scalp, relaxing to find it is shaved short. The echoes of my mother's cries when she found the basin filled with my brown hair ring inside my mind, soothing me. That scene replays in my dreams at least once most nights.

"It's Friyay!" Huxley shouts from somewhere beyond my window, drawing a smile from my lips. As long as I have my boys with me, I can overcome anything.

Rising from the bed, a glance at my phone tells me it's almost three in the afternoon. I planned to oversleep after last night's mix-up with Avery. The last thing I wanted to do is wake early and fidget, wondering if I should be creaming her tattoo or creaming something else. I enter the bathroom, glancing down at my raging erection. Garrett will be devastated he missed it. After a freezing cold shower, I drag on a white tee and blue sweatpants before heading out to find the others.

Stepping barefoot into the warm sunshine on the stone patio, Garrett chucks me a beer and I catch it at the last second. I move to join him on the wicker bench, eyeing the plate piled high with fried chicken wings on the table in front of him. I use the edge of the table to open the bottle with a hiss, surveying the scratch marks along the rim from where we've done it a hundred times before. Garrett offers me a half-eaten chicken wing in his greasy fingers as I rest my legs over his thighs.

"I haven't even had breakfast," I shake my head, taking a long swig of my beer.

All of us are close, but I often wonder if the guys know the extent of my mental state. They're my rocks, a constant presence I lean on at any given opportunity. I joined the Shadowed Souls as an angry teen who spoke with his fists. We all come from different walks of life, but it's never mattered. We accept each other for our sins, and their understanding has been exactly what I needed. They indulge my need for physical touch. They've never pushed me to speak when I don't have the words. Somewhere along the way, I was actually able to look in the mirror without grimacing at who I've become. Who my mother forced me to become.

Huxley appears from the house, volleyball under his arm, looking out over the lawn. Other than myself and Garrett, Wyatt is out here, stretched across a lounger in the sun and fast asleep. Shades cover his closed eyes, a blanket over his body which Garrett no doubt put there. Behind him, the net we erected for summer stands proud. Dax is next out, making a show of stretching.

"Last game of the year boys. Skins vs shirts?" Dax smirks, dragging his vest over his head. Huxley follows suit, much to mine and Garrett's amusement. Finishing his chicken wing, he wipes his hands clean on my sweatpants and pushes upright. *Thanks a lot, asshole.* We head to the back of the yard, leaving Wyatt to his nap. On the way past, I spot a whiskey bottle poking out from beneath the lounger and frown. Whiskey isn't usually Wyatt's vice, but I suspect Avery has everything to do with that.

We stretch out briefly, jumping on the spot to get our hearts pumping. Coach often imposes last minute basketball practices on us whenever his schedule has an opening, so we're used to warming up on the way to the court. Huxley notices that I'm taking an extra few moments to stretch out my neck and roll my shoulders. He saunters over.

"Maybe I should have left you to fuck Little Swan yesterday, and you wouldn't be so tense," he chuckles. My jaw drops and I shoot a look back at Wyatt, who is sleeping softly in ear shot.

We quickly took to calling Avery 'Little Swan' after we realized we're in way over our heads. Even when she doesn't know it, Garrett radiates towards her and watches on from a distance. Dax has taken an extra interest in English Lit and Huxley seems to disappear often, returning with flushed cheeks. Ironically, Wyatt's order to stay away from her has made her all the more desirable. I'm undecided where I stand on the matter.

Punching Huxley's chest, Garrett instantly appears with large, worried eyes.

"When was this? I thought you always shared with me," he whines. I roll my eyes and stride away, taking the ball from Dax's hands. I thought our threesome agreement was only beneficial to me, since Garrett goes home with women on his own all the time. I've spent too many evenings during my teens alone with women I didn't want touching me. Having Garrett there keeps me grounded, stops the memories from flooding back. So why was it so easy to be in Avery's company without conflicting thoughts getting in the way?

"It was nothing," I lie, tossing the ball between my hands. "I just got caught up in the moment. It won't happen again so keep it quiet." The three of them share a concerned look, knowing we don't keep secrets. Huxley and Dax slowly round their side of the net but I'm not hanging around, jumping high and slamming the ball down on their patch of grass. That seems to snap everyone back to reality as a round of chuckles fill the air.

"We'll let you have that one for free," Huxley scoops up the ball and gets into position. Batting the ball over the net, Garrett and I toy with them for a little bit. A friendly back and forth, the ball sailing through the air until I'm close enough to slam the ball home on their side once more. We're not bothered with keeping score or track of time, happy to lose ourselves to the afternoon.

Somewhere between my calves burning and Huxley taking a hard ball to the face, we call it quits. Garrett fetches more beers, Dax hands out bottles of water instead. His tanned body is coated in a sheen of sweat, his abdominal muscles shifting with each breath. Downing his drink, I watch his Adam's apple bob until he pours the rest of the water over his face and hair. Long fingers roam over his skin and come to rest on his neck.

"Take it easy, Dax," Garrett smirks, throwing an arm over my shoulder. "Our boy here hasn't been out to play for a while."

It's true. I've been missing practice and parties each morning and evening attending Avery's back, and I can't say I regret it. There are worse ways to while away the time than giving massages and stealing soft touches to feed my aching soul.

Dax smirks without apology and dries himself off with a hand towel. Even though I'm well aware only Garrett would cross that line with me, Dax and Huxley have no qualms being flirtatious teases. We settle into a stoic silence, the adrenaline flooding our systems. All eyes are directed at the Shadowed Soul who would usually be acting as umpire and calling ridiculous fouls. Wyatt would have kept score, and made sure the losers ran extra drills tomorrow morning.

"We need to get him out of here," Hux sighs. I nod in agreement as Garrett hums into his beer.

"Isn't there a grand opening for a new club in the city tonight? Eclipse or something?" Dax adds. I feel, rather than see, Garrett go tense beside me. Lowering his beer, his smile is horrifically wide.

"Fuck yes!" he shouts, rushing over to Wyatt. Without warning, he tips the lounger aside and then dives on our friend, shaking his shoulders. Wyatt is immediately on the defense, throwing punches and curses like wildfire. Whilst distracted, arms wind around me from behind. Dax rests his chin on my shoulder, his chest firm against my back.

"Are you okay? You seem quieter than usual." I lean into him, releasing a long exhale. What am I supposed to say? I'm having conflicting thoughts about my best friend's sister, who I shouldn't have gone near in the first place, despite everyone else in this yard lusting over her? Instead, I nod and force a smile. Huxley joins at my side, placing a kiss on my head.

"It'll be good for all of us to get out of here," he says. I couldn't agree more. The best way to get Avery out of my system is to replace her with someone else, someone *available*. Garrett drags Wyatt upright and somehow charms his way into a bear hug before leading him towards the house. We follow, arms and hands remaining tangled in mine.

I marvel for the hundredth time how I must be the most emotionally damaged of us, yet how I can be filled with so much love. These four men have saved me from myself time and again. We may not be conventional, or remotely functional at times but love is love, and I'll take it in any form.

AVERY

When Meg told me to make plans, she didn't expect more than ice cream and PJS. At a stretch, maybe a movie. Opening the cab door, and holding out my hand for her to take, she gasps at the nightclub front. The girls and guys in my ballet class have been gushing about the grand opening all week. So much so, I called ahead and booked a VIP table on Nixon's credit card. We spoke briefly on the phone last night, and since my real birthday was basically a write off, he agreed I deserve a real celebration.

The building towers into the starless night and appears to have a tilted front. 'Eclipse' is brightly displayed above the sleek, glass doors, framed by velvet rope. A red carpet trails the length of the sidewalk, already filled with people dressed in their finest cocktail dresses and suits, hoping to get in. The dress code is strict, as is the security. We approach two huge men dressed in black, kitted out with ear pieces and batons on their belts. I relay my name to the one with the clipboard, gaining us instant entry and a round of groans from those waiting in line.

Meg's arm winds into the crook of mine, her posture so much straighter than mine. I may be the one ballet trained, but my best friend has always exuded the confidence I've lacked. Since she only brought fluffy socks and silk pajamas with her, Meg has raided my wardrobe for a mini dress with long sleeves. The red lace exposes her cleavage and thighs through the fabric. Her brown hair falls back in loose curls.

"I still can't believe how scandalous you look," Meg gushes. Lifting a glass from an offered tray, her eyes dip to my dress. I did have time to prepare for our evening, which included a spot of online shopping. The black material cuts across the top of my thighs, affixed to my body via a double-ended zip up the front. From crotch to bust, the silver metal glints. I've pinned my hair up into a messy bun, leaving my upper back exposed between the dress straps. It's the first time I've ever shown this much skin in public, since my scar is artfully hidden behind the fully-healed ink.

I stop by a waiter in a bow tie, selecting a tall flute for myself. A raspberry has been slotted onto the rim of the glass. The club is already filled, the atmosphere filled with music and laughter. Exhilaration bleeds through me as we edge around the dance floor in our six-inch heels, spotting hundreds of couples grinding and dancing, lost to themselves. A soft glow illuminates the room, leaving sofas around the edges to fall into shadow.

The VIP area is on an overhanging balcony, closed off from the rest of the club but another bouncer and velvet rope we need to pass. Ascending the stairs, I'm on another level of excitement. This is my first time at a club like this, and I suddenly can't remember why I resisted venturing out to live my life for so long. The pink gin from the limo might have something to do with it.

Breaching the balcony, my smile is in full effect as I glance over the celebrities and influencers huddled in private booths, reveling in the privacy of this elevated sanctuary. Over the railing, I have an eagle-eyed view of the club, namely an empty circle in the center of the dancefloor cordoned off by tall barriers. The music is quieter up here, keeping the speakers across the far side of the club.

We're met by a hostess who leads us to our booth, although we don't make it all the way there. I stutter to a stop, dragging Meg to a halt with me.

"You've got to be fucking kidding me," I groan at the head of a table. The five suited men sitting around it, nursing a series of shot glasses and hands of playing cards, suddenly look up. Every damn one of them drops their jaws, their eyes raking down my body as if they have permission to violate me. Garrett is first to drop his cards and hold his hands up.

"I swear, this has nothing to do with me."

"What the hell are you doing here?" Wyatt scowls. Like the rest of them, his top button is popped open, shirt sleeves rolled to the elbows. There's a hint of black ink trickling across his collarbone and disappearing beneath the cotton. I mimic his narrowed eyes and clench my jaw, deciding he's not worth an answer. Moving towards the hostess, who is patiently waiting a few booths away with drinks menus in her hands, Wyatt shoots to his feet.

"I don't fucking think so. You really believe I'd let you walk around a club like this, looking like that?!" He gapes at me with open disgust. I give him a look that I can only describe as, '*Well, duh dickhead.*' I leave then, Meg at my side. We slide into our booth, finding a bottle of champagne on ice and a bouquet of red roses waiting. I slip the card free of its holder, reading the note inside.

'Happy Birthday, Angel. I'll see you soon. Love, Nixon.'

"Good, old Nixon!" Meg cheers. The hostess waits to pop the bottle and pour our glasses, instructing us to have a fantastic evening. I settle into the suede with my best friend, fully intending to. Sipping, tapping my foot to the music, the song has barely finished when we're invaded by huge bodies muscling their way into our space.

"Seriously guys," I moan, finding myself sandwiched between Dax and Meg. Huxley is on her other side, Wyatt nudging in on the end. Garrett and Axel bring stools, pushing them together as close as they'll go. On the table, the bucket is pushed aside for Wyatt to start dealing out two playing cards to each person, myself and Meg included. Once satisfied, he raises his hand to call the hostess back over.

"We'll have Frozen Daiquiris for these two," he moves his thumb between Axel and Garrett, "a Screwdriver for Hux. Whiskey Sour for me, and keep them coming," Wyatt drawls with his eyebrow hitching in my direction. "And alcohol-free ciders for the rest. You've got a board meeting tomorrow, Dax. I'm cutting you off for the rest of the night."

Dax nods while Meg launches herself towards the champagne bottle, snatching and clinging it to her body. I, too, hold my glass against my cleavage. The hostess closes her notepad, looking unsure but she leaves to fulfill Wyatt's ridiculous requests.

"Why do you let him boss you around like that?" I huff into Dax's ear. Every movement is tracked by all of them. His head tilts, a trace of his jawline passes over my cheek.

"He's obsessive because he cares. It's how he shows love." Dax's whisper brushes my ear. I release a bitter laugh.

"Well, thank fuck he doesn't love me." Breaking away, Garrett is giving me a strange side glance but for once, he doesn't say anything. He lifts a small, silver case onto the table, revealing stacks of colored chips which are handed out to each person. Somehow, we're entered into a game we didn't ask to play.

"You just carry around a poker set everywhere you go?" Meg asks jokingly. Wyatt's strict green gaze pierces her without a trace of humor.

"Courtesy of the club," he responds and flips the first dealer's card. Taking turns, they place bets until all eyes settle on me. Garrett grins, leaning forward on his elbows.

"How's your poker face, Peach?" I scowl at him. Peering at my cards, a five and seven of clubs, I raise the bet. Meg does the same, shooting me a coy look. The boys probably missed it, but I heard the message loud and clear. The testosterone around here needs a serious reality check.

By the time Garrett realizes just how much poker I've played with Nixon over the years, he's out of chips. He does offer to bet with items of clothing but Wyatt swiftly declines. Instead, Garrett is forced to watch, pout, drink, and sneakily tease Axel under the table until he joins the loser's club. Meg and I sneakily top up our flutes with champagne out of view, huddling together and giggling until it's her turn to deal. Meg's fumbling fingers shuffle the cards messily, much to the boy's dismay. She jerks around, laughing and fumbling, her breasts resting on the table.

Once we all have our hands, she turns into me, resting her head on my shoulder while she pushes two cards in between my thighs. I sit back, swapping out my hands while Garrett is begging to play, around unbuttoning his shirt. It's the distraction I needed. Now holding two aces, the first few rounds are typical, small bets being placed. On the table, the ace, two and five of hearts are glaring upwards. I can barely contain my giddiness, raising my chips. Everyone folds except Wyatt, his green eyes dark and boring into mine. Inclining my head, I take my turn.

"All in," I push my mound of chips into the middle of the table. He doesn't react, copying my move. Meg flips over the last card, the ace of spades. I don't know how she's done it, but she's a genius. Sitting upright with my chest puffed out, Wyatt holds up a hand.

"Before we reveal," he states, "I propose a forfeit for the loser." The champagne and adrenaline bolster my actions. In fact, this is the most Wyatt has ever said to me, and that in itself has a strange rush spiking in my veins. He turns his hand in a slow, calculated move. "That empty space down there has a very specific purpose, due to be revealed at midnight. If I win, you have to sign up to be a part of the reveal. If you win, I'll do it myself."

The following smile doesn't look at home on his face. I've never seen Wyatt smile aside from in photographs, but the goosebumps prickling my arms aren't alarming enough to deter me. Meg catches my eye, giving a little shrug. She's fixed the cards, I have nothing to lose.

"Fine." Gesturing for Wyatt to show his cards, he makes a show of insisting that I go first. Everyone sits forward in a tense silence as I place down my four-of-a-kind with a beaming smile. *Read 'em and weep, asshole.* Wyatt's brows raise. I've got him. For once, I have him right where I want him, squirming beneath the weight of his friend's gazes, rueing the day he ever-

Wyatt turns his cards and places them flat, revealing a three and four of hearts. A straight flush. My features don't shift but my cheeks set on fire, a blush creeping across my face and chest. His smug smile says it all.

"If you wouldn't mind following me," he stands and extends his arm to look at the Rolex on his wrist. "I believe it's almost time for your forfeit." Before striding away, Wyatt pulls a second deck of cards from his pants pocket and places them back in the case. His smirk is cemented in place, daring me to challenge him. The bastard cheated, and he knows full well I did too.

Huffing, I nudge Dax along to stand at my full height, plus the extra six inches of my chunky heels. There's one thing I promised myself all those years ago; Wyatt will never see me crumble. Despite the murmured objections from the others, I walk behind him down the stairs. He turns away from the dance floor, briefly speaking to a man in a fine blue suit against a hidden door, who then speaks in his ear piece.

The following events see me ushered through the back passages, down another set of concrete steps into the club's underbelly. It's dank, smells stale and looks grim, but there's a surprising amount of people milling around and the lights are bright. All the while Wyatt is close. Too close, when the corridors are narrow, the ghost of his hand on my lower back. I come to the conclusion I must be imagining it, shrinking away from his solid chest and arms when I can. He remains quiet, although the scent of whiskey on his breath is overwhelming at times. The bastard.

Suddenly, the room opens out and I freeze. In the center, a giant birdcage waits on a raised platform. A man rushes towards me, his blazer and beard fabulously sparkled, gushing that we're running out of time. I'm pulled into a throng of people, who attack me with hands and make-up brushes. My hair is adjusted and pinned higher, while a heavy brace is secured over my shoulders and across my ribs. Peering back, I spot a pair of huge feathery black wings. The make-up artist quickly jerks my chin forward to finish dusting powder over my forehead and down my nose.

Without notice, I'm manhandled into the cage's open door, someone announcing we're good to go. The music in the room overhead changes to a slow, steady beat and through it all, I spot Wyatt striding closer, his hands in his pockets. I near the edge, lowering slightly so we are face to face.

"Wyatt," I suck in a breath, bathing in the glow of his smirk. Then, I laugh straight in his face. The hysterics bubble out of me, a string of inebriated babble that force me to use the bars and steady myself. "You thought this would scare me. The sides are literally open, you absolute fucking moronic-"

As the ceiling opens up, the cage begins to rise. I stand in the center, bracing my legs wide. The music builds up to a steady rhythm, and I lift my arms above my head to begin to clap in time with the beat. The entire club, which has stilled for a moment, joins me. The sound is deafening, the purple lights are all directed on me as my body becomes visible. Cheering and wolf whistles break out all around, bolstering the confidence I found through the champagne.

The cage lifts high above the dancefloor, level with the VIP balcony and finally, the music shifts into a song I recognise. I smile, feeling Meg's eyes on me from somewhere within the shadows. *This is my jam,* I think as my body begins to move of its own accord. Wyatt sought to scare me once more, but he's done the exact opposite. He's given me a chance I never would have sought for myself. A platform to find out exactly who I could be if given the freedom. And that bitch is going to be fierce.

CHAPTER SIXTEEN

Watching Avery dance just became my newest infatuation. Blonde wisps fall free against her neck, the huge wings floating against her back. My eyes drag along the length of her body, a heady daze taking over my mind. I could stare at her for hours, my tongue thick in my mouth, desperate to lick every inch of creamy skin on show.

It's not the easy roll of her hips, the way her hands swirl above her head or how she somehow knows every time the beat is about to drop. It's her face. Eyelids closed, a simple smile on her perfect lips. She's in a state of complete serenity, lost to a world where only she exists. If I wasn't so enamored, I'd be jealous.

I grip the railing like a lifeline. A shudder rolls through my shoulders, the shirt across my back feeling too tight.

"Hey, do you want to-" Axel murmurs into my ear, his chest pressed against my back.

"Yes." I spin in an instant, cupping his jaw and spearing my tongue into his mouth. The same fruity taste lingering on my tastebuds explodes with his. I groan, pressing Axel back into the railing. He's trapped between my arms, our lips crashing. I chase him with desperation, not allowing an inch of space between us. Our cocks thicken against one another, as eager to connect as I am. Shifting my hips upwards, I swallow Axel's moan. He palms my shaft through my trousers, gripping tightly in a way only his large, strong hand can. I love it when he clenches me to the point of agony. In my mind, his head would dip to lick the bead of precum I have seeping into my boxers. And he wouldn't be alone.

"I was going to ask if you wanted to dance," Axel laughs when I break away, keeping his eyes closed. I pepper his cheek and jaw with kisses, licking a path behind his ear.

"Axel, I've never asked you for anything," I breathe, my hand cupping his nape. He snorts.

"That's a bald-faced lie."

"But I have a favor to ask of you now." Leaning back, I seek out his hazel eyes. His pupils are blown, enhancing the hazel flecks I've spent a long time memorizing. Just like the man they belong to, they're stunning and pure. Everytime I remember someone hurt Axel, incomprehensible fury fills me. He's too precious to be vulnerable all the time, and when he looks at me like this, I make silent vows to burn the entire fucking world down if it means his safety.

A figure shifting in the background catches my attention, a shifting pair of wings and the girl lip syncing to her heart's content. She, too, has experienced a darkness which should have never been allowed. My little Peach, who only wants to thrive. My delayed mind makes an unhinged connection between these two sweet souls.

"Please," I beg of Axel. His eyebrows shoot upwards. Our desire quickly subsides and when he grabs my face between his hands, it's with a tense possessiveness. I'm not the only one who'd go to war for what we have.

"What do you need, Gare?" His tone is thick and husky. Those words are enough to make me lose my fucking mind. Such a dangerous question, so many right answers. A smile grows across my face as I spin him, my crotch against the curve of his ass. We stare out over the blonde enigma in the cage.

"I need you to pursue her." I feel his sharp exhale as my fingers trail down his chest, slipping beneath the hem to rest on his hips. He's always been so receptive, so eager that he leans into my touch. "Before you panic, I know you still don't like being alone with women. I promise I'll be there every step of the way until you're comfortable." His labored breathing beats against me, his grip tightening on my arms.

"What would that scenario look like, even if Wyatt didn't cut our balls off for considering it?" Axel glances over his shoulder. Using my cheek, I nudge his jaw to face forward and speak directly into his ear beneath the beat of the music.

"It would look like her deep-throating your cock, staring up at you with those big beautiful eyes while she rides my face. It would be stolen kisses in hallways, forbidden touches behind closed doors. It would be you screwing her against the wall while I worship your ass, all of us covering our mouths to keep quiet while we break apart. It would be you covered in my cum and gripping her hair, forcing her to clean it all off with her tongue."

Axel groans, the pulse in his throat fluttering against my thumb. I stroke him gently, uncaring of those nearby giving us side glances. In the distance, the cage begins to lower, stealing the dark angel from our sight. Axel turns into me, his hands seeking reassurance in mine.

"Do I need her?" Those eyes knock me off kilter again, bearing the uncertainty he fails to hide on a daily basis. "Isn't it...aren't we good enough as it is?" His head dips and I gasp, sure my heart just cracked within my chest. Gently tilting his chin back upwards, I steal a kiss. It's different from the passion-filled, lust-crazed ones we typically share. Axel and I hide our true desires until alcohol is involved, then we can unleash them without repercussion. But this...this is a tender touch with all the words I would never dare say aloud. Ghosting kisses over his cheek, I sigh.

"You're everything, Axel. So pure, so fucking beautiful," my thumb traces his bottom lip. "She would understand you better than anyone."

"But you understand me better than anyone. All I want is you." A single tear runs the length of Axel's cheek at his admission. I catch it with my tongue. Fuck, I don't want to be thinking about all this heavy shit. I came out to get shitfaced and forget about the weight we all carry. But Axel knows me too well to let it slide.

"I'm not dependable, Ax. I'm in this for a good time, not a long time." The words taste like ash. Clearing my throat, I hunt for a fresh cocktail. Wyatt and Dax are deep in conversation at the bar, while Huxley has accompanied Meg downstairs to dance. On cue, the hostess stops by our table with a tray, replacing the empty glasses with filled ones.

"Come on, we're nowhere near drunk enough yet." Winking, and ignoring the pain behind Axel's eyes, I link our hands and draw him towards the booth. With each step, I mentally say all of the words that won't pass my lips. *You deserve love, Axel, but I'm too broken to give it to you.*

AVERY

CHAPTER SEVENTEEN

"Holy shit!" Meg throws herself into my arms the second I step through the side door. "That was incredible! You should have seen Wyatt's face when he came back." Grabbing my hands, she tugs me towards the dance floor. Huxley is standing off to the side, his arms crossed over his chest. Upon seeing me, his whole demeanor changes, a warm smile growing on his face. I feel that warmth spread through my chest as we pass.

"Was he pissed?" I ask once we've found a small space to declare as ours. Meg throws her head back and cackles.

"He was furious!" She sways slightly so I grab her elbows.

"Fuck, how much did you drink while I was gone?" I half-chastise. My smile ruins the sternness I try to push through my voice. Meg moves closer, winding her arm around my waist.

"There may or may not have been a stag-do doing body shots across one of the tables. I managed to knock a fair few back before your guard dog came and found me." Glancing over my shoulder at Huxley, I find him staring directly at me. His blond waves catch the purple light, which also makes his white shirt seemingly transparent. I swiftly look away.

"So, have you picked one yet?" Meg leans into me, using my body as an aid to help her dance without falling over. I sway with her, raising an eyebrow in question. "Oh, don't look at me like that. They're all lusting over you like a piece of meat. I couldn't get any of their attention while you were gone, and trust me, I tried."

"Of course you did," I laugh. "But they're not *all* lusting after me." My point sounds weak but it's true. Wyatt was sitting at that table and he hates my guts. Meg looks at me knowingly and bops my nose. I'm happy to let the conversation drop, dancing until my feet are throbbing. My hair has fully fallen free of its pins and my arms ache from holding up Meg.

"Come on, time for some water." Half-dragging her through the crowd, she protests that there's water in beer. Huxley meets us at the edge of the floor, swooping Meg into his arms like a feather. I hold his bicep, for a reason I can't determine. The stairs up to the VIP balcony are a mission as my heels drag but finally, I throw myself into the booth beside Axel. Huxley takes Meg elsewhere, but I'm not worried. For some inexplicable reason, I trust him.

"Having fun?" Axel asks. I toss my head back against the cushion and nod. It just occurred to me that I'll have to head all the way back down those stairs and through the club to make our way home. The thought has my limbs going weak. Garrett appears from nowhere, nudging into my other side.

"Don't react. We don't want to give him any more of a reason to hate you." His voice is in my ear, then he's gone.

"Don't react to w-" I start but Axel hushes me. Rolling my head, I look beyond him to see Wyatt at the bar with Dax. His body is angled towards me and though I can't see his eyes from here, I feel his gaze. It spears through my chest. The zip at the base of my dress is suddenly opened to my stomach. I gasp at Garrett throwing my thigh over his shoulder beneath the table. "Wait, what the fuck?!" Attempting to push at Garrett's shoulders, he stills and looks up at me from the shadows.

"Do you want me to stop?" he asks, echoing the night he pulled me into the garage and let Huxley go to town on my pussy. I clench at the memory, biting down on my lip as I gingerly shake my head. His smile is reassurance enough. Garrett doesn't waste a second, pushing his face into the apex of my thighs. He inhales, groaning.

"Fuck, you're so sweet," he mutters. Drawing my thong into his mouth, he sucks hard, his nose against my clit. I'm on fire, about to tense up when Axel grabs my other thigh and drapes it over his leg. His smile is lazy, as are his fingers against my skin. From knee to hip, he traces a pattern with delicate fingers until they trace my underwear. Gripping my thong strap in both hands, Axel snaps and peels it away, giving Garrett full, unrestricted access.

"Did you bring your vibrator with you tonight?" Axel asks with a small laugh. I melt into his side, moaning against his shirt. Garrett buries his face into my pussy, eating me like a man starved. His tongue dips inside my opening, his groans vibrating through my center. Licking intently, he moves to my clit, taking it into his mouth and sucking hard. Across the table, Huxley sits on one of the stools and braces his hands on the table. I shoot upright, tugging at my dress in an effort to cover my decency. All three of them laugh.

"Oh, please do continue." Locking his fingers, he leans his elbows on the table. Those chocolate brown eyes which watched me so carefully on the dance floor bore into me, his attention undeterred when Axel lowers the top zip on my dress. My black bra with lace trim is revealed to all watching. A flush skates across my skin but as Garrett's fingers enter me, I can't bring myself to care. My back arches, the flicks of his tongue too much to resist any more. Pushing my fingers into his long, brown hair, I grip his head and drag him impossibly closer.

"That's it, little Swan," Axel murmurs into my ear. His hand dips into my bra, rolling my nipple in his fingers. I grind into Garrett's face. "Don't let him breathe. Suffocate him with your glistening pussy." I gasp at Garrett's increased eagerness, his fingers creating a punishing rhythm inside of me. My skin is tight, my clothes suddenly too restricting. I buck and moan until Axel's hand slaps over my mouth. He silences my muffles but increases his pinching on my nipple. I'm laid back, a mess of sensations for Huxley to witness.

My orgasm builds in a rush of ecstasy I can't tamper. Between the low lights and the pounding of the music, between Garrett's licking and sucking and Axel's tormenting touch, there's no denying me now. I roll my hips, meeting Garrett's thrusts, my nails scraping against his scalp.

"You've got company," Huxley warns in a low voice. I barely hear it, fighting to glance sidewards. To the left, a pair are nearing. Collared shirts, flexing muscles. I shake my head against Axel's hand, my voice muffled. Garrett speeds up, adding a third finger and twisting with each thrust. I'm soaking wet, my juice glistening across his mouth as he finds my clit once more. He sucks so hard, I'm a goner.

Dax and Wyatt reach the edge of the table as Axel withdraws his hands, feigning innocence too late. A strangled moan escapes me, penetrating the club. It happens in slow motion and I'm heedless to stop it. Like a freight train heading directly for me, yet I'm frozen in place, forced to watch it approach with no way to avoid the impact. Wyatt's mouth drops, his eyes wide. The most intense orgasm crashes through me, causing stars to burst behind my eyes.

I don't hear myself moaning, or feel how I writhe until Garrett's pumping fingers slow. Gasping, I vaguely feel my legs being put back in front of me and the zips on my dress fixed back into place. When I crack my eyelids, Wyatt is all I see. His face is red, his eyes filled with a new level of fury. His nostrils flare as he grapples for a hold on himself, his throat bobbing a few times.

"I think it's time we left." He states coldly. Shame washes over me. I can hardly draw myself upright from the puddle I've wriggled down into. Garrett pops up on the other side of the table, wiping his mouth with his hand.

"Ooooh, can we hit the drive-thru on the way? I'm starving." He slings his arm over Wyatt's shoulder. The air around the table is thick with tension, everyone waiting to see how Wyatt will react. Instead of a huge show of aggression like I was expecting, he simply shrugs off Garrett's arm and walks away.

"Until next time," Huxley smirks and winks, pushing himself upright. Dax looks at me awkwardly, shifting his feet but ultimately, follows his master. Axel starts to move across the booth and despite knowing this was all one big game, my chest aches the most at his rejection. At the edge of the seat, he pauses and looks back.

"You coming?"

"Me?" I frown. I realize dully that Huxley left in the opposite direction to the others, until he reappears with Meg passed out in his arms. Axel reaches back for my hand, tugging me along behind him. Standing, he winds his arms around my waist and gives me a strange, yet open smile.

"Well yeah," he chuckles. "I'm not going to leave you here half-sated, looking for a stranger to finish you off." I can't even fathom a response as I'm whisked away beneath Axel's arm and left thinking, what the hell just happened?

AVERY

CHAPTER EIGHTEEN

A hand clamping over my mouth wakes me with a muffled scream. Thighs pin my arms by my sides, the rising panic in my chest burning in the back of my throat. I struggle, despite not daring to open my eyes. Reality merges with the nightmares plagued with forgotten memories. Another hand slips beneath my back and I jolt with a high-pitched scream, crying out for the fingers tracing my scar to get the fuck away from me. They feel the jagged line with intrusive interest. My writhing pays off, freeing me to lash out with my nails desperately. Strong hands grip my wrists, stilling my attack.

"Please...please don't touch me," I whimper as tears gather beneath my closed lids. The fight I so recently found dissipates as my voice cracks. Whiskey coats my face, the heated breath of my attack forcing me to gag. Still, I refuse to look upon the menacing gray eyes on the other side of my eyelids. His thinning dark hair and whitening chest hair. A thin gold chain that wobbles as he pushes me down under his beer-gut. The hands release my wrists, leaving me free to blindly punch out. My knuckles connect with a jaw and I open my eyes in shock I was able to hit him. Holy fuck, I actually hit him. But the person pinning me to the mattress and nursing his jaw in front of me isn't who I expected to see.

"And there I was thinking you weren't going to actually defend yourself," Wyatt's green eyes blaze at me from the light of the moon bathing the room through thin, netted curtains. He's still in his white shirt, although a few more buttons are hanging open and the tail ends are mismatched, as if he rolled out of bed and dressed in a rush. The black ink swirling his chest is visible, plumes of smoke blending into the wrath seeping from his pores.

Gripping the lower half of my face, he remembers himself, snarling that whiskey-infused breath over me once more. For that reason alone, I hate him. I hate how he taunts me, how he'll never let me forget. As long as I'm in Wyatt's vicinity, he'll never leave my past where it belongs. My body begins to tremble beneath him straddling my stomach as his knees painfully dig into my sides.

"I swear," he seethes, leaning over so our foreheads touch. "I'm going to break you."

"What the fuck did I ever do to you?!" I finally find my voice, shoving his head off me. First, he threw me into this room upon returning from Eclipse, locking me in and the others out, and now he wakes me the way he knows would scare me the most. He's read my transcripts, after all.

Returning to the same spot, Wyatt's forehead pushes forcefully against mine. His lips hover against my cheek. I lie still, watching the onslaught of emotions a very drunk-Wyatt is fighting against. His features switch from sympathy to rage and back to misery, conflict shifting his hands to ball in my hair and back out again.

"Why are you so resilient? Why can't you just leave me alone?"

"Me?! I didn't ask for any of this. I want to go home," my voice trails off. I don't need Wyatt's reply to see it written all over his face. Hughes mansion isn't, and never will be, my home in his eyes. Throwing his fists down into the mattress either side of my head, he shoves himself away. I track Wyatt to where he slumps onto the edge of the bed, his face in his hands. The soft light surrounding his frame is a direct contrast to the darkness radiating from him. It's the first time I've seen true emotion from him, and how much he feels aside from hatred. Despite myself, my chest tugs.

"You win, Wyatt. I'll back off." I whisper, flinching at the cynical chuckle that abruptly fills the room. Sliding myself up the headboard, I conceal myself with the covers.

"It's too late now," Wyatt sighs. His shoulders droop with the movement, a sense of defeat making him go limp. When he speaks again, it's quiet and I'm not even sure his words are meant to be heard. "I thought they loved me. All of them...I thought they genuinely loved me." Running a hand through his dark hair, it flops forward to cover his eyes. I've never seen Wyatt anything close to disheveled. I wish I could enjoy it more. He stands swiftly, his arms lashing out violently.

"Until you came along and proved once again, I've just been a placeholder. Everyone radiates towards you, they all treat you like some precious little flower. What do you have that no one can resist?" My mouth opens and closes again. Nothing I say would help, even if I could find the words. Wyatt needs to vent, and perhaps it's the alcohol in my system or the pity welling inside, but I'm feeling extra charitable tonight. Wyatt turns to look out of the open window, a gentle breeze shifting the curtain aside. "Why do you have to take everyone from me?"

In the boxers and t-shirt I found to sleep in, I slip from the bed. My feet are silent as I pad closer, cautious that I don't know him well enough to gage his reactions. Regardless, I'm not going to shrink beneath the covers while he prowls around like a wild bear. I'll face him on equal ground.

"I hear you," I breathe, tentatively lifting my hand. Aside from his recent aggression, we've never touched. I'm sure he'll spin and pin me up against the wall, but as my hand lowers onto his shoulder, he doesn't move. Now it's there, I swallow hard, undecided what I figured I would do now. Stroke him? Pat him? Wring his fucking neck for being so thick-headed? I can't decide. Instead, we stand, looking out over the back yard until I lick my lips and break the silence once more.

"I didn't seek them out on purpose. They all came to me." It's a weak excuse, but it's all I have. I don't want Wyatt's entire support system to abandon their years of friendship. I don't want to keep being the villain he perceives me to be. "This is stupid, Wyatt. Let's just call a truce. I'll leave your friends alone if you help me convince Nixon to let me return to my old life. I never wanted any of this."

If Wyatt heard me, he doesn't show any comprehension. Slowly, I withdraw my hand from his shoulder. It was worth a shot, attempting to find common ground. Turning back to the bed, he laughs softly.

"Do what you want, use whoever you want. I'm washing my hands of you," he stalks after me until my thighs hit the mattress. "But when

Garrett can't contain his demons, when Axel has another mental breakdown or Dax is in full panic mode and you can't reach Huxley because he's turned in on himself, don't you fucking dare come to me for help." Grabbing the bedside lamp, he hurls it at the wall. I yelp and squeeze my eyes shut as it shatters, anticipating an attack. I don't even try to defend myself, resigned that Wyatt will always look for ways to hurt me.

The door closes with a soft click. I slowly look around, fully expecting Wyatt to linger in the shadows, lulling me into a false sense of security. I'm seemingly alone, but safety evades me. I managed to catch a glimpse of Wyatt's layers beneath the bullshit, but the predator in him is back in full swing, prowling somewhere beyond my door. The sight of the large, empty bed unnerves me. What if he changes his mind? What if he comes back for round two of emotionally berating me in my sleep?

I hate that Wyatt has the power to send me straight back to being the scared, defenseless girl I've tried so hard to leave far behind. My trembling resumes, recent events replaying in my mind. Recent feelings that I haven't expected to surface. For a split second, Wyatt appeared exposed, raw and vulnerable. It's too bad he's so far past the point of redeemable in my mind, I can't find it in myself to feel sorry for him.

Instead of crawling beneath the sheets, I move towards the bathroom, remaining on high alert of the darkly shadowed corners. My breath hitches as I run the last short distance on tiptoes, needing to remove myself from the place he'd expect me to be if he returns.

Unlocking and slipping through the door across the opposite side of the room, I brace myself against the wood. Huxley is stretched out on his back, his long limbs covering most of the king size bed. His blond waves are spread across the pillow like a halo, and in this moment, I need him to be my savior. A white sheet pools at his waist, leaving his muscled abdomen and broad chest on full show. Slowly sinking myself onto the edge of the mattress, I pinch the edge of the sheet and softly tug it upward as I tuck my feet up. Huxley shifts, mumbling in his sleep.

"I don't want to work in a microwave factory."

I lower my head onto his bicep and continue to pull the sheet up to cover my body. Then, I lie perfectly still, pretending to be asleep as I feel Huxley's weight lift and twist over me. Ever so gently, he pulls on my shoulder so I turn onto my back, his arm beneath my head as I look up into his concerned chocolate brown eyes.

"What's happened?" he asks, his voice thick with sleep. My lip quivers and an unexpected tear leaks from my eye. I anticipated three possible outcomes from sneaking into his bed. Either he would remain asleep and I could escape before morning, leaving him none the wiser. He would kick me out for invading his personal space, or he'd try to fuck me. I hadn't been prepared for him to pretend to care. Regardless, I welcome the warm comfort of his embrace to keep nightmares and Wyatt away.

"I don't want to talk about it," I sob, twisting into his chest. Lying back down, Huxley simply holds me, one of his hands smoothing into my hair and the other stroking my arm. My tears soak his sheet until I begin to drift off, vaguely realizing Huxley is actively avoiding touching the scar down my back.

CHAPTER NINETEEN

I fly into Meg's arms the second she drags her feet out of her given bedroom for last night. She has a serious case of panda eyes and hisses when I squeeze her too tightly.

"I am never drinking again," she groans. I roll my eyes, leading her downstairs.

"Yeah, right. Until the next time," I smirk. I slept surprisingly soundly in Huxley's arms for the remainder of the night, waking without the hangover Meg is currently sporting. Unfortunately for her, I've already made plans for today. We've only got one weekend together until Fall Break, and I can't let it be wasted sitting in dark rooms in silence.

Entering the kitchen, I instantly smell coffee. Dax spots us in the doorway and smirks, grabbing another two cups. Garrett and Axel are facing away from us, sitting on stools to be hunched over the island. Axel is still, leaning on his hands, while Garrett's shoulders are flexing as he eats his breakfast. I approach, giving him a wide berth. Maybe, inhaling would be a better way to describe the way he's attacking a plate piled high with waffles, bacon rashers and a thick layer of syrup. Dax puts a cup in my hand.

"Do you have any aspirin for Meg?" I briefly take my eyes away from Garrett's knife and fork to address Dax. He's leaning against the counter, his biceps stretching against the cotton sleeves of his black shirt. His slacks have been pressed and shoes have been shined. Reaching for a packet on the window sill, Dax smiles when he catches me checking him out. That's right, he has his board meeting today. "Thanks," I pass the meds over to my best friend who has slumped over the island. "We'll be quick and get going."

Suddenly, Garrett's head shoots upright, his mouth full of food. "Where are you going?!" he muffles, but that's not why my jaw drops. Deep purple blemishes mark his beautiful face, his eyes black and nose busted. By his side, Axel looks over to me gravely, a sigh passing through his taut lips.

"Holy shit, Garrett!" I step forward and place down my cup. "Are you okay? What...wait, was it-"

"Totally worth it? Hell yeah." Somehow, through his bruises and split lip, he grins. Within the dark rings, his brown eyes glisten with mischief and he manages a wink, albeit a slow, painful one. It seems I wasn't the only one Wyatt paid a visit to last night. On cue, Huxley walks into the room, assesses his injured friend and rolls his eyes.

"One of us is going to have to straighten this shit out," Huxley mumbles, passing by me as if last night didn't happen. I'm thankful for it. Being vulnerable isn't something I like having advertised. The air around the kitchen shifts, unbeknownst to Meg. She swallows her meds, drinks her coffee and grabs my wrist.

"Come on then. Let's get on with this torture." I purse my lips, being tugged along behind her.

"It's called a hike, and it's good for you." Waving goodbye over my shoulder, I wriggle out of Meg's grip once we're free of the house. Resisting the urge to look back and see if my hunch that Wyatt is standing in one of the windows is right, I lead the way through side alleys and shortcuts back to the dorm block. Meg's bright pink BMW is shining in the morning rays, sticking out from the rest of the cars in the parking lot.

Kay is nowhere to be seen in our dorm, which is expected. Whilst waiting for Meg to perk up, I wash, change into my activewear and prep the picnic basket I had delivered through the week. It came pre-packed with dry snacks, but I figured we'll grab some pastries and drinks along the way. Rolling a blanket and stuffing it between the handles, Meg emerges from the communal showers, seeming much more herself. Her eyes have their intense topaz appeal back, her brown hair pulled into a high ponytail. I've done something similar to mine, leaving a few blonde wisps free at the front.

"For the record, next time - I'm planning the activities," Meg smirks. I concede, knowing they would include binging a romance series and doing face masks. Something we've done a thousand times, but with such an active life at college, Meg prefers the comfort.

"Deal. Although, you have to admit, it's nice to do something different for a change." Holding my phone high in the air, we pose with our tongues out for the camera. I send the selfie to Nixon, promising him there will be many more today. He won't believe I voluntarily opted to go for a hike, so photo evidence is needed.

We leave the dorm block, a skip in our step as we make our way over to Meg's car. Just as we near, three figures step around the side, playful smiles on their faces. I quirk a brow at Huxley's tanned boots and cargos, Garrett's sweatpants and backwards cap, then Axel's basketball jersey and the backpack he's shouldering.

"Um...what are you guys doing?" I ask, already anticipating the reply. Striding forward, Huxley plucks the keys from Meg's hand.

"You said we were going for a hike. What's the destination?" His chocolate-filled eyes hold me hostage.

"Well, I thought we'd head to Silver Birch Creek, but when I say 'we', I didn't mean..." It's too late. Huxley is entering the driver's seat, while Garrett slides into the back with a shit-eating grin and Meg giggles under her breath.

"I didn't feel like driving anyway," she half-shrugs. Taking the passenger seat, I don't miss her extra little laugh that I'm now left shimmying into the middle in the back. Axel and Garrett sandwich me in, their arms and thighs pressed firmly against mine. Neither actively touches me throughout the entire drive, and somehow, that's worse. After last night, the tension in my veins crackles with electricity, my mind reeling as I continually look over Garrett's hands. His fingers are long and skilled. At least Wyatt had the decency to leave them alone.

After a brief stop at a bakery, we eventually turn into an off-road parking lot. It's fairly busy, many wandering into the distance with trail maps and huge cameras looped around their necks. Hopping out in my Converse, I tie my pale pink hoodie around my waist and smooth down my tightly-fitted leggings in the same color. They do wonders for my ass, the high waist band sitting just beneath a white crop top. Once Garrett has finished stuffing our snacks into the picnic basket, Meg links her arm through mine.

Silver Birch Creek, as the sign states over the entrance, consists of over two-thousand acres, historic mill ruins and guided hiking trails. 'A Must-See,' the internet declared when I was searching for things to do after Waversea. Although, now we're entering with three gorgeous men in tow, I'm all too aware of the judgy stares we're receiving. Just a group of youths looking for a public gangbang, apparently.

We enter as a comfortable silence falls over our group. Each of us seems content to take in the wildlife, to appreciate the nature. It's a stunning time of year to visit, with the leaves turning into vibrant oranges and reds. Huxley breaks apart first, strolling a small distance back. Garrett and Axel share tender looks, despite the sight of Garrett's face. I'm still reeling over Wyatt's actions, and Garrett's too for that matter. Another reminder that I can't become complacent around this lot. I never know what they're thinking to do next.

Focusing on placing one foot in front of the other, we begin to climb a rocky slope. Trees line our path, birds tweeting from the branches and a perfectly blue sky visible overhead. Garrett's brown hair is swishing side to side as he dances to a song in his head, the basket swaying in the crook of his left arm while his fingers are intertwined with Axel's on the right. I smile in earnest, catching Axel's hazel gaze. There's a sweetness to their relationship which doesn't need a label. It just is.

We breach the tree line beside a wide, flowing stream. Thick boulders are scattered across the width, creating stepping stones we could follow all the way down the river. To the right is a raised outcrop the water pours from, creating a mini waterfall amongst the serenity. Craggy rocks protrude through the flow to form slippery ledges.

"First one to the top gets to make-out with Avery first!" Garrett suddenly shouts, shoving the picnic basket into Meg's arms. I try to shout after the three of them that I'm not some prize to be won, but they're already leaping across the boulders in a bid to reach the waterfall. There's no way they'll make it up there, but my heart thunders anyway.

Looking around the river, I notice a steep pathway winds alongside the mini cliff. A thin yet worn rope creates a barrier from the steep drops either side. Grabbing the basket, I'm shoving Meg in its direction with my teeth clenched.

"Bitch, move. You need to get to the top first," I grind out. She's still sluggish from last night but thankfully, the adrenaline starts to work inside of her. Pumping her legs in her little summer dress, leather jacket and biker boots, those years of lacrosse come in handy. We run as fast as the rocks crumbling beneath our feet will allow. A glance to our left shows the boys trying to drag each other down, too involved in their rivalry to notice us as we pass them. My calves begin to burn with the strain of a rushed climb but that doesn't stop the smile spreading across my face.

Nearing the top of the cliffside, Meg skids to a stop and I narrowly avoid slamming into her back. Between us and the grassy planes awaiting the boys, is a thin, rickety bridge. In the excitement, Meg must have forgotten how high we were rising from the ground. Now there's an open gap in the earth and a dark plummet awaiting underneath, she steps back into my arms.

"Hey, it's okay," I soothe her hair. "We don't have to do this, we can just head back to the car and get out of here. Leave the guys to make-out with each other." Meg laughs, despite the tremor in her voice.

"As if you wouldn't prefer to watch." We share a knowing look. Despite the figures scaling the waterfall nearing, I don't rush her. "Okay," Meg straightens and nods. I give a gentle tug on her hand, reassuring her we don't need to do this, but she's adamant.

As I watch her grip the flimsy rope like a lifeline and take tentative steps, I'm in awe of my best friend for the millionth time. She's always so tough, stubborn to a fault, but she never lets her fears conquer her. Since we first met as young girls, me in her mom's therapy office and her the free spirit sketching in the lobby, I've tried to model myself after her. I reckoned if I can have a scrap of her resilience, I would be alright eventually.

As her foot settles on the grass, she leaps forward and throws her arms in the air. I make quick work of the bridge, finding it's rather steady after all, and join her cheering. The view up here is incredible; dense forest on either side of the river stretching for miles, its lush autumn colors sparkling in the sunlight. Fresh air mixed with salt and pine fill my senses and a gentle breeze caresses my face. It's perfect.

Meg is quick to shrink down beside a tree, preferring not to stare out over the horizon. Axel spills over the ridge first, quickly followed by the others. They're soaked through, shirts sticking to their bodies.

"What took you guys so long?" I laugh, leaning down to touch the water. It's surprisingly warm trickling over my hand. Garrett stomps along the river in his sneakers, kicking a splash of water over me. I gasp and run over to the tree, ducking into Meg's side.

"Don't bring me into this," she smirks, shoving me away. The three guys stop before us, waiting patiently as I raise my brow.

"Come on then," Garrett gestures between Meg and I. "You owe us a show." I smirk, pulling my knees up to my chest.

"You first." Garrett pushes his hands into his pockets, not caving as easily, whereas the other two barely hesitate. Huxley and Axel grab their t-shirts and peel them off with delicious slowness. Meg's hand grips mine, centering us both in the heaven we've just tripped into. They're gorgeous, the sunlight at their backs appearing like halos.

Huxley holds more bulk, whereas Axel is leaner, but his abs and that sensuous V dipping into his waistband is no less defined. Skilled fingers drop to their buttons and zippers, and my mouth goes dry. Despite being in bed with Huxley last night, and waking with his solid cock pushed against my ass, watching them strip is something else entirely. They exude lust and confidence.

Dropping their trousers and shorts, they lay out their clothes in the sun to dry before laying out our picnic blanket. Axel pulls a second, albeit slightly damp, one out of his backpack and the three of them lie before us, questions in their gazes. I can't stop looking, the landscape of the creek suddenly losing its appeal. Dark ink is splashed across Huxley's thigh and Axel's shoulder, the same decayed skull as on Garrett's hand staring out. Each one is unique in how the shadows spread across the skin.

"Do you all have a skull?" I ask, reaching out to trace Huxley's. He doesn't seem to mind. Empty eyes appear hollow against the shaded bone, teeth open on a scream while thick black ink drips downwards in thick rivets. Tracing the image with my fingertips, his dick jumps behind his boxers and he quickly takes my hand in his.

"The Shadowed Souls," Huxley shrugs in answer. "We're bound for life."

"And what does it take to become a Shadowed Soul?" I quirk a brow in an effort to keep the conversation light. It doesn't work.

"You need to have suffered greatly and broken free," Axel answers, staring just past me and into the distance. As usual, his hazel eyes are haunted and I feel compelled to crack open his secrets. I want to understand the way the others do, to know how to comfort him. Garrett, laying in his soaking wet clothing, watches me carefully, his expression darker than usual amongst his bruised eyes.

Clearing her throat, Meg asks who's hungry and instantly, Garrett is back to his full, gleeful self. He takes a majority of the offered pastries, despite the size of the breakfast I saw him eat this morning. I honestly don't know where he puts it. We eat, my hand remaining in Huxley's for some unexplainable reason. Stretched across the blanket on his side, his long hair drips onto the grass. Luckily, the sun is warm enough to dry them off before they catch a chill. My mind wanders.

The view is beautiful, but I don't see it. The Shadowed Souls. Bound for life. Until recently, I thought I had a support system who would always be with me, too. I had the family I'd always dreamed of as a scared and lonely child. In a matter of months, I've had the life I loved torn away from me. My mom is gone, I can't see Meg as often, or the therapist I'm used to, and for the first time, I feel a twinge of anger at Nixon. Like me, he is grieving, but where I sought to remain close, he chose to throw himself into his work. He relocated me and left without even asking how I felt about it. A heavy sigh escapes me, my thoughts growing dark.

"Do you think Wyatt will ever forgive me?" I ask out loud. Confused gazes swing my way. Garrett leans his arms over his knees, the illustrative tattoos on his arms facing upwards. I take his distraction as a chance to investigate further, stopping between Bart Simpson and the Pringles man.

"Wyatt is our boy, but everyone knows you haven't done anything wrong. Even him." I snort at this. It sure doesn't seem that way to me. Garrett smiles sadly, running a hand through his brown hair. A trio of Mario characters flex on his bicep. "Hell, in another life, there's no doubt you would have been one of us. You've suffered worse than we have."

Meg tenses. We have an unspoken rule to leave the in-depth conversations for my sessions with her mom. She's the best friend I can rely on to help me forget my past, not remind me of it.

"It's okay," I laugh but the sound isn't convincing. "At this point, they know more about me than you do." I briefly dip my head into her ear to explain how Wyatt stole my transcripts. The pain that not only he, but all of them, read the documents burns with a betrayal I have no right to feel. These guys are a bit of flirty fun, but they don't owe me anything. Least of all, their trust.

"Anyways. From where I'm sitting, *on the outside,*" I emphasize, keeping that clear barrier between us, "it doesn't seem to be about who has suffered worst and least. You each have your own demons and pasts you've endured. Call me a hypocrite, but I just don't see where Wyatt comes into it. He had everything, and he gave it all up."

The silence that follows is damning. Either they secretly agree, or they know something I don't. When no response comes, I decide to wash my hands of this conversation. It was worth a try, to gauge the burning need for information I always crave. In my head, if I could just understand Wyatt a little better, maybe the events of the last ten years would make sense. But once again, I'm affronted with the truth that there's nothing redeemable about him.

"Okay, well, *moving on,*" Meg injects. She's scrolling through her phone, hunting for the song that starts to leak from the speaker. Don't Start Now by Dua Lipa. I instantly grin, remembering the corny dance routine Meg and I made up to this song on repeat in the dance studio back home. She jumps up with a grin and drags me with her.

"Oh no, no, no," I shake my head. Meg doesn't care, kicking my foot to bend it artfully. Our routine is a mix of my ballet and the breakdancing class she was taking at the time, never supposed to see the light of day ever again. Linking her arm in mine, she follows through the seven poses, our legs bent in a plié to start.

"Have you seen Avery dance? She's phenomenal," Meg raises her brows at our present company. I smack her for embarrassing me. Ignoring the blush in my cheeks, the guys lap up our stupidness as if it's addictive. I've never seen Axel smile so wide, or noticed how deep his dimples are. After a few small hops and some fancy footwork, Meg attempts to lift me. The move was much simpler when we were eleven and not fully-grown women, and definitely didn't end with me yelping as the ground nears. We collapse in a heap of laughter, slicing through the tranquil setting.

"I sure hope you don't do that during your showcase," Meg giggles, shoving me off her. Dusting myself down, I roll my eyes.

"I've already told you. I'm not doing the showcase. I'm just learning the routines so I can assist in the practices." It's a decent excuse and better than admitting I just want to be available if the other girls might want help. Making friends isn't easy when you've been introverted for the entirety of your teenage years. Besides, spending my evenings dancing is the perfect stress reliever and Theodore seems to enjoy the extra chance to play his compositions.

"Well, that's bullshit," Meg sighs, looking to Huxley for backup. "Tell her she's too good to sit on the sidelines." Hux freezes, torn between the two of us folding our arms and waiting to see which side he's on. Garrett barks out a laugh and saves his friend from choosing.

"No one can tell Avery to do anything she doesn't want to. But if you do decide to sign up, Peach, I'll let you borrow Axel for those massages you seem to like so much." My cheeks flame as Meg gives me a curious side glance. Axel watches me from where he's still laying in Garrett's lap, his haunted gaze not giving anything away.

"It would be selfish to hide your talent," he says in earnest. I scrub my hands over my face.

"Ugh, well it doesn't matter anyway," I wave them all off. "The auditions are today." Meg looks as if she might murder me.

"That's why you planned this hike in the middle of goddamn nowhere!" she shrieks. I exhale from my nose and purse my lips.

"I mean, it was recommended as one of the top attractions in the area," I start but Meg is already rushing to pack up our stuff. "Wait, no. It's a lovely day, let's just chill and enjoy the view for a while longer." Meg spins on me so fast, I thought she might slap me.

"Avery Hughes. This is your fresh start to live your life and experience things that never would have happened to you sitting in that manor. I can't get dressed up to support my best friend if you don't do anything. Now get your shit, get down that hill and get to your audition." She's a flurry of movement, throwing the guy's dried clothes at them. Just like that, our afternoon is packed up early while I stand around and whine.

"Seriously, this is ridiculous. We will literally never make it in time."

"Watch us," Axel walks towards me with focused intent. Being the object of his hazel eyes is unnerving, but then he scoops me up in his arms and starts the incline of the hill with long strides.

"I can walk, you know," I wrestle against him. This is just like when he tried to carry me across campus during my first week, except this time, I wasn't quick enough to decline. His broad shoulders and chest close around me, the embrace becoming filled with his salt-infused scent from the water.

"I know," he muses, his jaw brushing my hair. "But then I don't have an excuse to hold you." I shudder, keeping my mouth clamped shut. I can't trust what will come out. Melting into Axel's hold, Huxley soon runs past with Meg slung over his shoulder, squealing. Garrett is quick to join our side, his hungry gaze running over my body.

"I'm excited to see what our little Swan can really do," he and Axel share a secret smile, completely tuning me out.

"Your little what?"

AVERY

Thankfully, Mrs. Patrick has left us to work in pairs or small groups for today's assignment. After the audition yesterday, Meg finally got her wish to relax in our pjs and watch movies. Garrett let us use his bedroom for the flatscreen TV, but only because he spent the day also in the bed and stealing most of our snacks. I didn't mind, his interest in our chick flicks was adorable. We all had dinner together before Meg had to leave. It was pleasant, and even better because there was no sign of Wyatt.

"So, when do you hear back?" Dax asks in a hushed whisper. Our desks are turned into one another's, giving more room for my highlighters to cascade over the surface.

"By Wednesday," I half-shrug, not trying to seem too smug. Miss Nightingale was so pleased to see us fly through the doors just as she was packing away, that I saw her mark a large tick next to my name on her clipboard. The guys did stick around to watch, and Axel did give me that massage as promised.

Checking the time on the wall-clock, I return to our task. By the end of the week, we have to produce a 'Literary Analysis' essay from a provided list of novels. We'd quickly decided on To Kill a Mockingbird, as there is so much to work with.

"Okay," I sit up straight and poise my pen. "So I've divided the page into four parts. Literary devices, character development, overall structure and the relation of the theme to the time period. You start spitballing ideas and I'll jot them down." When I look up, Dax's blue eyes are shimmering, his mouth curving upwards. "What? Why are you laughing at me?"

"I'm not laughing at you," he chuckles and I raise an eyebrow. "I just think it's cute you're the only one in this room not using a Macbook." My eyes drag across the desks, indeed noting that everyone else is huddled over their devices. I frown, clutching the paperback to my chest.

"But I can't annotate the pages on a screen," I pout. Dax's smile spreads further.

"I mean, technically-" he starts. My eyes dart to the clock again. "Do you have somewhere else to be?

"Hmm? Oh no, not at all. Actually, I was thinking we should head to the library after and keep going while this is all fresh in our minds. I reckon we could write the entire essay in a couple of hours."

"As delightful as that sounds," Dax leans on his hand, watching me in an almost dreamy state, "I have practice after lunch and you clearly have plans you're avoiding. A common trait of yours, as I understand it." I look away. He's referring to how I tried to miss the auditions, and has just clarified that the guys do talk about me behind my back. I wonder how much they actually share, given the sticky situations I've been in with a few of them.

"Fine. Meg booked me an emergency appointment with the school counselor. It's meant to start-" The bell rings. "Now-ish." The room begins to stand and pack up, while Mrs. Patrick shouts instructions for our next lesson. Dax collects up my stationary while I make sure our notes are all neatly stacked in my notepad.

"I'll make you a deal," he says, zipping up my backpack. "I'll walk you over to the administration block for your session, and afterwards, we'll have that library date you are so eager about." I chew on my bottom lip, pretending to think about it. Quality time in Dax's soothing company rather than alone at the desk in my dorm; it's a no brainer.

"Only if you bring milkshakes," I concede with a small smile.

"Cream and sprinkles, right?" Dax steps closer and my face sets on fire. His tanned skin is flawless, his blue eyes searching mine. I forget to breathe when he's this close and looking at me so openly. Perhaps I've become too used to hidden intentions. Tilting my head back, my lips part. Pulling my bag onto his shoulder, he cups my jaw, tracing a small pattern with his thumb.

"Stop stalling. We have to go," he whispers, then smirks wide. Groaning, I stomp out of the room with him right behind.

Our luck with the weather has come to a sudden end. Rain thunders against the concrete courtyard, the sound of it covering those running between the buildings. I tuck my hair into the neckline of my gray sweater and pull the hem lower over my black skinny jeans. The Converse were a terrible choice, but they're my favorite. Just as I'm about to bolt through the doorway, a cover is held over my head. Dax holds his coat in place, urging me to run. We make it to the admin block, pushing through the huge rounded doors.

"Who taught you to be a gentleman?" I ask offhandedly. He nudges me.

"I've always been a mommy's boy, to a fault really." Wiping our shoes on the mat, we walk down the hallways. "I've done some things I'm not proud of, but I always try to be the man my mom would have been proud of. It sees me through the day-to-day." I don't miss his use of past tense and my brow furrows.

"Dax," I breathe. "I'm so sorry."

"Don't be. She raised me with love and compassion. You know what it's like. You have to find the good bits and focus on those."

Rounding the corner, his hand brushes the back of mine. Electricity runs through me. Stopping in the middle of the hallway, that same tension we narrowly avoided in class rushes back. Standing over me, I'm forced to look up. My neck is exposed for his fingers to trail over and slide around my nape. He doesn't pull back this time. The chemistry we've been dancing around is blatant, my eyes growing hooded. I want his lips on me, all over me. I want the touch of a man who would never cause me any harm, someone who yearns to keep me safe. Who puts my well being first and keeps me grounded.

A small smirk appears on Dax's flawless face as I close the last few inches of distance. From the first brush of lips, our mouths clash in a magnetic frenzy. Nothing like what I expected from the sweet Dax I've come to know. Those longing looks and lingering touches finally take over, charging the air between our bodies. Chests pressed together, hands seeking a closer connection, Dax takes my face in his palms. He tilts and opens me up to him, his tongue chasing mine. My fingers become tangled in his t-shirt, pulling him closer as if he'll disappear. As the world melts away, leaving only the lingering taste of desire on my lips, a body suddenly crashes through the center of us.

The hammering of my heart slams to a swift halt, my lungs constricting. The man standing in between us is equal height with Dax, but his focus is squarely on me. Reddened cheeks, green eyes blazing. Swallowing harshly, his nostrils flare. It's that same look from when he caught me with Garrett at the club.

"Are you able to go one day without whoring yourself out?" Wyatt steps forward. I stumble, preparing to fall until Dax catches me.

"Dude?!" he shouts, stilling Wyatt from walking away. I look up at Dax, still held at an odd angle in his arms. Those soft, open blue eyes are locked down, his jaw set. His entire face has been transformed, seeming unfamiliar from the man I'm beginning to know. Wyatt can be an asshole to me, I'm used to it, but Dax? I don't want to be the reason he loses his compassion.

"It's fine," I brush my hand over his cheek. Wyatt's head is turned, watching with a tick beating in his jaw. Taking my backpack, I straighten and square my shoulders. "I couldn't care less about Wyatt's opinions. He's always been wrong about me before." With that, I stroll away. Locating Counselor Lorna's room, I slam the door behind me and throw myself into an hour of moaning about my asshole stepbrother and his insistence on ruining my damn life.

HUXLEY

Things aren't right. In fact, they're swiftly taking a nosedive. Wyatt storms through the house, slamming every door in his warpath.

"Hey man, you weren't at-" I start, until another door is slammed between us, "practice." Shaking my head, I go back to my Sudoku book. One of these days, someone needs to get him and his kid sister into a boxing ring and let them hash out their differences. I don't see any other way, but I sure as shit won't be the one to instigate it. Currently, Dax is mysteriously absent, while the knucklehead twins are grooming each other in the dining-area-turned-beauty-salon. There's only so many pimple popping and plucking sessions I can sit through.

"I miss having people to talk to," I groan under my breath.

"We're literally right here," Garrett replies through the open archway. He currently has a green mud mask on his face, whilst pinning an apron around Axel's neck. Soon after, the electric shaver is switched on and my reply is lost into the air of ignorance. I try to finish my puzzle but soon give up, the repetitive buzz of the shaver grating on my last nerve. I know, deep down, it's not the shaver's fault I'm so irritable. It's so unlike Wyatt to miss basketball. Aside from us, it's his entire life. He's good enough to go pro if Nixon allows it.

We're used to Wyatt turning into himself, typically following trips to see his mom. It always had to be some big ordeal, some prestigious award ceremony where her perfect son had to be on her arm, parading in front of the entire world. He hated who he had to become in order to spend time with her, and I know from his drunken rambles, how jealous he was of the version of Cathy only Avery got to see. Now his mom is gone and there are no more chances for their connection to be fixed.

Yet, there was always basketball. Even when he was furious and refused to talk to anyone, he would be on the court, running drills until he couldn't stand. I should go and comfort him, but what is there to say? Sorry I'm crushing on your sister so hard, I've had to jack off in the shower twice a day since she trashed my car? I couldn't stay mad at her, and the guys down at the workshop had a good laugh at my 'scorned lover's' damage. Apparently, they get vehicles with similar affiliations brought in a couple times a month.

No, I sigh to myself once again. It's not my place to talk to Wyatt and convince him Avery might not be the villain he's always made her out as. That's something the two of them need to handle, and when they do, I don't want to be anywhere nearby. Shit is going to get messy.

Tugging out my phone, I opt for some doom-scrolling to pass the time. In the background, Axel and Garrett mutter and laugh quietly. Their fascination with each other has surpassed the simple need for comfort. I'd originally been skeptical of Garrett becoming so close to Axel once we moved into Waversea. Once we'd finally been about to free Axel from his gold digging mother. Garrett is well known across campus for his ability to be obsessive one moment, and act like you're dead to him the next. But with Axel, he's different. Considerate and patient.

Several reels and a fascinating documentary on knot-tying later, a notification appears at the top of my screen from the Student Message Board app. Across the room, chimes ring out and the freshly washed and pampered pair look at the same graphic I'm staring at.

*Join us for our Annual **Fall Ball**. Saturday, October 10th at 6:30pm.*
Main Auditorium.
Photo Booth, Autumnal Buffet and Disco until midnight.

My eyes slowly rise at the same time Garrett's do. Axel pockets his phone, turning his attention to setting the table. It'll be time for dinner soon but that's not what has Garrett on high alert - for once. His knuckles turn white around his phone, the appearance of a deer trapped in the headlights stuck between his brown eyes.

"Garrett," I warn in a low voice. Taking a step towards him, his eyes dart to the door and back to my face. "Don't you dare," I breathe. Then, he's gone. I curse, stuffing my feet in my Timberlands and taking off after him.

There's no way I'll let him ask Avery to that dance. She doesn't know him like I do. Today, she's a new shiny toy to play with, but tomorrow she'll be humiliated and confused when he's ghosting her.

For reasons I can't explain, which have nothing to do with how incredible she felt curled against me in my bed, I care. I want to heal her pain and eradicate her fears. I want her to come to me after every nightmare, to cry against my chest and permit me a glimpse into her soul. She's been through so much. Hurricane Garrett is something I can help her avoid. She's too special to become another notch on his bedpost, and if that means I have to piss off Wyatt even more by accompanying her to the dance myself, so be it.

AVERY

Stretching back, I lift my arms above my head and groan. Dax must be the only guy in the world who thinks a study date is exactly that; studying. The library chair has long since made my ass go numb and any attempt at jesting is immediately shot down. High above my head, a domed skylight shows that evening has fallen. I outstretch my leg, accidentally brushing Dax's. He quickly whips his back, keeping his eyes firmly on his textbook across the table. No one likes studying that much, I decide. This isn't about studying; this is about Wyatt.

"Fucking cockblock," I huff. Dax's brow raises and he peers up at me.

"Excuse me?"

"Nothing." Hunching over my book, I return to my highlighting. We decided to divide and conquer for our essay, which I reckon was Dax's excuse to sit on the opposite side of the table and ignore me. The yearning still lights his blue eyes, but he's keeping it under strict control. I wasn't sure if he'd even be there, at the end of my therapy session, with milkshakes as promised. He was, but none of the flirtatious touches were. Being interrupted by Wyatt's rage has really done a number on him.

Around us, the low hum of chatter picks up. I watch it pass through the tables, the excitement building and smiles growing. Whispers grow into giggles, flurries of students packing up and leaving. My curiosity grows as a pair of girls lean over the table, showing phone screens to their friends. Retrieving my own from my backpack, where it has remained on silent since therapy, I finally see what the fuss is about. A Fall Ball happening in a couple of weeks.

"Hey, have a look at this," I slide the device over to Dax. He glances over it, his shoulders remaining just as rigid. He makes a grunting noise and returns to his notes. I wait for a few moments, stewing over my options.

A ball could be fun. Part of embracing the experience and all of that, but I can't show up alone. I doubt any of the girls I vaguely know will pass up the chance to have dates on their arms. Dax would be the perfect date. He's thoughtful and sweet. He's never once touched me without an invitation, always happy for me to take the reins and when we kissed, it was purely unexpected chemistry. I want to see what else we can do, what else we could be, if he'd allow it.

"So...Do you want to go to the dance with me?"

Mid-sip of his water bottle, Dax chokes, his eyes wide and panicked. "But...I..." he seems stuck between confused and pained. "I thought you liked me?"

"I do," my cheeks flush. "That's why I'm asking."

"No, clearly you have a fucking death wish for me." Dax closes his book and swallows hard. "After this afternoon, if Wyatt saw me taking you to a ball, he would tear out my intestines and hang me with them." I slump back in my chair, lips pursed. Yeah, Dax is sweet and thoughtful, but he's not as bold as the others. Chewing on that thought, the tension grows thick between us. Suddenly, the two chairs either side of me are dragged backwards and I find Garrett and Huxley crowding my space.

"No need to pout, Peach," Garrett tucks my hair behind my ear. "Axel is already taking you to the dance."

"He is?" I ask at the same time as Huxley does. There seems to be more that the blond hanging over my shoulder wants to say, but I turn a quizzical gaze on Garrett. "Why?"

"Why wouldn't the hottest guy want the hottest girl on his arm? It's status quo," Garrett smirks and shrugs. I'm not buying it. Now most of the library has emptied out, the three men sitting around me hang on some unspoken truth I'm yet to know.

Garrett reclines, threading his hands on his lap. As his smirk falls away, the weight of his burdens finally show through. His eyes are still dark from bruising, but beneath that, there's the hint of sleep deprivation. His mouth tilts, worry framing his unusually stoic features. I feel an ache to bring the smile back, to run my fingers through his brown hair and ease his troubles, but hiding behind a mask isn't the answer. I need to know what's tumbling around his brain as much as I need my next breath. Finally, Garrett sighs, his dark eyes traveling to the window.

"Axel deserves love. Fuck knows, he deserves it more than any other fucker in this world. He deserves to be with someone who can flaunt him, kiss him in public, hold him through the night. He deserves it all."

I look around, finding neither of the other two will meet my eye. Reaching out, I push my fingers in between Garrett's to hold his hand.

"From where I'm sitting, he has all of that. With you."

Garrett's laugh is bitter, that smile returning to push everything else into the background.

"You give me too much credit, Peach. It's because I care for him, I won't move on without finding a suitable replacement."

"Oh, how romantic." I deadpan. "How did you know my lifelong dream is to become a scapegoat for someone too afraid to admit he's in love with his best friend?" My question goes unanswered. From the side glance Huxley gives me, it would appear I've summarized what everyone is thinking but would never say. As fun it is peeling back the layers to Wyatt's tormented friends, I have a hard enough time keeping up with my own issues. Packing away my books and planting my bag on the vacated chair, I lean on the back of it.

"If Axel wants to take me to the Ball, he can grow some balls and ask me himself." Arms instantly wind around my waist, a firm chest pressed against my back. Heated words are whispered into my ear, making me warm in all the right places.

"Avery, will you go to the Ball with me?" Axel breathes. I shudder at his unannounced appearance, wishing there weren't four sets of eyes watching me equally blush and melt. It's hard enough to remember we're still in public. Every day, these boys give me another naughty impulse. Very soon, something is going to have to give.

My lips part, a shallow breath escaping. Whiplash. That's what this feeling is. Chronic whiplash. Everytime I think I have a handle on my life, they appear to spin the world on its axis. It's impossible to understand what I can't control, and even more impossible to keep them away. I seriously need to get laid, I muse to myself, as the immediate available options stare at me, hanging on my response.

"Yes, Axel. I'll go to the dance with you."

AVERY

The only person loving the fact that I will be Prima Ballerina at the showcase is Meg. I have taken to late night practices, in a bid to keep busy, while she has taken to watching me through video call instead of studying.

"You need to extend your legs on the leap," her entire face fills the screen. I've propped my phone up on the piano so she can see the majority of the dance studio. Theo couldn't join me today, his musical talents were required at a bar mitzvah in the city. Letting my arms drop heavily from their poised position in front of me, I scowl at my best friend.

"You don't even know ballet."

"I know what looks good. You're leaping as if you're scared the ground might disappear beneath you. Let yourself feel the sensation of floating before you rush back down to earth." I snort a laugh.

"You're so full of shit. But fine." Running back the music in my head, I start the routine from midway through, drifting from one practiced plié into an arabesque. For now, I'm sticking to the solo numbers, not trusting myself to ask my partner Trey to join my late night sessions. He's six-foot of lean muscle, blond swoopy hair, impeccable posture and gloriously gay. All the best men are, but I don't trust myself to let that hold me back. I'm strung so tight, if he were to lift me above his head right now, I'd most likely arch down to try and suffocate him. My foot wobbles and I trip out of my rigid stance, grabbing the rail to stop myself from crashing to the ground.

"Woah, where the fuck did your mind just go?" Meg's voice echoes, ringed with humor. She knows exactly where it went. Ever since I accepted Axel's invitation to the Fall Ball last week, and avoided the Shadowed Souls like the plague ever since, my dreams have been more than vivid. I wake horny, I attend classes horny, I dance horny. Then, I made the mistake of drinking too much wine alone last Friday and spilling every confused, cunning thought that popped into my brain.

"So," Meg continues while I roll my ankle. "Who was it this time?" I throw her my middle finger, half hobbling over to my phone. Only when she sees me wince does she grow serious. Her pale blue eyes widen and she nears the camera. "Wait, are you okay? Where are your compression socks?"

"I couldn't find them in my bags. I think I left them back at the manor." I huff, swiftly holding up my hand to cut off her next words. "And before you lecture me, I haven't had time to order more. AP classes are hard, you know."

"Bitch, I know. I'm taking three of them. Get yourself some damn socks." I wave her off, bending to rub my ankle when Meg's sharp intake of breath sounds through the speaker. I raise my brow in her direction but she's looking off into the distance. "Avery, is there someone else with you?" My heart skips a beat as I stand back at my full height.

"No," I mutter quietly. Shifting my body aside, I watch the reflection of the camera rather than turn around to face the truth myself. I don't see anything at first. A large room of mirrored walls and an empty dance space. Until there's the tiniest of shifts by the rear door leading to the dark corridors and dressing rooms. I feel the blood drain from my face at the same time my hand lashes out, grabs my phone and runs like my ass is on fire. I don't pause to grab my bag and shoes, I don't dare breathe in case it slows me down. Throwing the main exit open, I slam into a tall body. Hands grab me, tearing a scream from my throat.

"Avery? Hey, what's wrong?" Theo gives me a small shake, his messy hair shadowed by street lamps. My brain works a mile a minute to comprehend what's happening.

"I th...I thought you were," I fight to form a sentence. "Not here.

You're not supposed to be here." Realizing he's still holding me, I wrench myself backwards.

"My gig was canceled so I came to see if you wanted to practice some more."

"Practice what?!" Meg screams through the phone in my hand. "Practice how blue Avery can turn if you strangle her?!" Theo's brows furrow, his mouth open but I still take a step away from him. Clinging my phone to my heaving chest, I sidestep around him.

"Avery?" Theo calls after me. "Shall I walk you back?" His desperation to stay close pushes my speed walk into a full-out run. My ankle screams in protest but I don't hold back, keeping Meg on call until I feel I'm a safe enough distance away. I slump behind a tree, my lungs crying out for a break.

"That was weird," I gasp, dropping my head back. Meg grunts in agreement.

"I was seconds from calling the cops. Are you nearly back at your dorm?" Peering at my screen, I bite down on my bottom lip. The outline of my face is dimmed, only reflected by the light of the window in front of me. "Oh shit, Avery. Where the fuck are you?"

"I went on autopilot," I hiss, shrinking down into a ball. "I didn't want to go back to the dorm, Theo might drop by to check I'm there. I'll be fine, trust me." Meg tumbles into a rant about me being untrustworthy right now as I pepper the air with kisses and whisper I love her, before ending the call.

Shoving the phone into my cleavage, I grab the rope ladder and climb the side of the trunk, shimmying along the thick branch Dax once shoved me onto. Reaching for the window, I find it unlocked and sigh in relief. Thankfully, my leotard and tutu allow me to climb inside with all of the finesse of a large feline. Music blares through the house, all of the lights on downstairs. I remain glued to the wall furthest from the railing, creeping past doorways. My hand wraps around a handle and I slip inside without incident, until a pair of chocolate brown eyes land on me.

Huxley stills mid-step, exiting his bathroom. Water drips down his body, from his long wavy hair, down his abs, to the towel held lazily over his dick. Either side, his thighs are thick and firm. The skull planted there, dripping in ink and shadow, seems to scream directly at me.

"Um, hey." I clear my throat, standing straight instead of creeping around like a hunchback. "Can I stay with you tonight?" His face doesn't shift, a long pause causing doubt to fester. Huxley's eyes track my skin-tight pink leotard and settle on my ballet shoes. They're ruined, caked in dirt. Now I'm staring at them too, the bruising around my ankle is starting to deepen, drawing all of my attention to the throbbing pain surrounding it.

"This is becoming quite the habit." Huxley's mouth turns down, but it's not my presence he's frowning at. Winding the towel around his waist and tucking it in place, his strides close the gap between us. Sweeping me off my feet, Huxley holds me close and carries me into the bathroom. I'm dropped onto the counter while he draws a bath.

As he tips bubbles into the swirling water, I watch the tattoo on his back shift in time with the corded muscle underneath. An angel sits central, her dress tattered and head turned downwards. In her hands, a sword lays horizontally, highlighted from the jeweled hilt to glint in all the right places. Her wings are the true masterpiece, sprouting from her back to cover the rest of his. The feathers, black with white tips, are spread wide and etched in such fine detail, I'm convinced I'd feel their softness if I were to reach out and stroke them. Curiosity gets the better of me, and I slip from the countertop. Tentatively brushing my fingertips over Huxley's shoulder blade, he stills.

"I wouldn't do that if I were you, Little Swan."

"Why not?" I breathe, continuing my exploration. He shudders.

"Because I can't be the first one to fuck you." Spinning, Huxley grabs my ass and hikes me up the length of his body. My thighs rest on his hip bones, our lips almost touching. "I've spoken with the others and we've come to an agreement. There are many things we're willing to sin for, but taking your virginity isn't one of them." My lips pop open, my cheeks flushing.

"What happened to seeking you out if I needed to cum?" I repeat back his words from the ballet studio. His resulting smirk is so cocky, I blush further.

"Is that why you sought me out?" I bite my bottom lip, preferring that reason to the truth. *My pianist freaked me out and I ran a mile on a twisted ankle.* Huxley takes my silence as an invitation to ravage my mouth, his tongue consuming my argument. His touch sets me on fire, his taste pushing me over the edge of inhibitions. Huxley may have made his agreement, but I've done no such thing.

My fingers sink into his wet hair, pulling him flush against my chest. The lycra of my leotard rubs in all the right places, tightening alongside my core. My nipples press into the fabric, brushing over Huxley's firm chest. He holds me as if I weigh nothing, his hands splayed over my ass and fingers tantalizingly close to my pussy. I roll my hips, hoping to shift his touch closer. In return, his dick tents the towel separating us and Huxley groans into my mouth.

"You're going to be the death of me," he mutters, sinking his face into my neck. Placing me on the edge of the tub, Huxley helps to strip me with the care and desire that contradicts his earlier statement. In the depths of his chocolate eyes, I reckon he is willing to sin for me. Once I'm bared, naked and openly wanting, Huxley lifts me into the bathtub. The water is delightfully warm and smells like him, apple perfuming the air. "Take your time," Huxley presses a kiss to my forehead. I try to reach for him but he's too quick.

"Where are you going?" I whimper like a desperate fool. Whatever happened to avoiding the guys and ignoring my libido just crashed and burned. Huxley palms himself through the towel.

"I'm going to beat my dick into a gym-sock so I don't explode all over you in your sleep tonight." Oh right, the pact against screwing me into next week. *Just fucking perfect.*

"And who said romance is dead?" I sigh. Once he's fallen asleep, I'll have to hunt for the pink vibrator he is yet to return and do the job myself. Huxley pauses in the doorway, his face growing stoic.

"Do you want me to romance you, Little Swan?" He stares at me so intently, I'm glad half of my face is covered by bubbles. The flush coating my cheeks underneath is something fierce, thanks to the sudden change of atmosphere. I can deal with sexual tension - it's practically second nature to me at this point - but romance? That's another ball game entirely.

The door across the other side opens, Dax stalling mid-step into the room. His blue eyes travel from me in the bathtub, my clothes on the floor, to Huxley turning away whilst squeezing his towel-covered cock. I expect him to do the same, but the longer he stands there, the more I sink into the bubbles.

The others, aside from Wyatt obviously, possess that wild streak which makes me want to tiptoe the edge alongside them. But Dax can't be painted with the same brush. He's sweet, attentive. He meets me for coffee during our breaks, arranges my highlighters so they don't roll onto the floor, duplicates his notes when I miss class. I find myself second guessing laying naked in his tub, worried about changing his impression of me. The silence isn't helping either.

"Vampires, bikers or stalkers?" he finally says after an age. My eyes widen blankly.

"Are we playing fuck, marry, kill while I'm in the bath?" Dax's brow tilts and the ghost of a smirk kisses his full lips.

"No. I'm going to read to you while you're in the tub. Pick your poison." Shifting to lean against the doorframe, the strong set of his jaw becomes more pronounced as he produces a full smile. If I weren't already in water, I'd have melted. Chewing on the inside of my cheek, I decide to test Dax's resolve.

"Fae," I raise my chin. He nods and retreats into his room without a trace of hesitation. Just how many romance books does he have in his arsenal?

AXEL

CHAPTER TWENTY FOUR

"Axel honey, come on in. Don't be shy." Stepping into the darkened ballroom, I'm shocked to find it empty. My mother is standing on the podium in a glittery black dress, diamond pendants hanging from her earlobes. Looking around suspiciously, I edge further into the room. "Ahh, there you are."

Pulling at the navy tie that is almost choking me, I shuffle forward in my polished brown shoes. Running a hand over my head, I feel the soft locks I've grown to fear. Mother's smile widens, the cherry red lipstick popping against her pearly white teeth. Beckoning me forward, she outstretches her hand, pulling me up onto the stage and hugging me tightly.

"I have a surprise for you," she whispers into my ear. Turning me by my shoulders, I face the vast space, my heart jolting at the sight of a vertical container that wasn't there before. Ten feet tall, the cell is made of glass and steel, filled to the brim with shimmering water. My fourteen-year-old self is looking back at me in the reflection of the glass, an unsure look in my hazel eyes. A splash at the top causes some of the water to spill over onto the marble flooring, and a panicked Avery appears inside. I rush forward on instinct, but my mother's hand grips my arm and yanks me backwards.

"You couldn't save yourself. What makes you think you can save her?" my mother laughs into my ear, her body flush behind me and her talons

sinking deeper into my flesh. Upon spotting me, Avery's eyes widen and bubbles leave her mouth as she tries to scream. Banging on the glass with her fists, her golden hair sways around her as a blood-red hoodie weighs her down to the bottom. It's Wyatt's, I vaguely realize. She pulls and yanks at it, but it's no use. And I can't do anything to help her.

A hand slides around my neck, tightening until I can't breathe but I don't take my eyes from Avery. She deserves a life free of misery and pain. To feel true joy without fear. As the last bubbles leave her lips, she begins to convulse and writhe against the burn of her empty lungs. A tear slides down my cheek as my own supply of oxygen runs out, but I refuse to fight against the hand holding me. I deserve this, but Avery doesn't. I could never be what she needs. My damaged soul is always going to drown her.

"Axel!" a voice screams into my ear. Those hands are still touching my neck and face, shaking me until I'm able to drag a full breath into my lungs. I shoot upright, directly into Garrett as he straddles my waist and grabs my nape. "You weren't breathing, you stupid fuckwit." He runs his hands over my shaven head, cupping my face and then drags me back into his chest. The reality of my nightmare settles on me like a ton weight. I'm used to revisiting my past, to watching my greatest fears play out behind my eyelids on a nightly basis. They're painful but predictable. This was different.

"It's okay, everything will be fine," Garrett soothes me, his arms stroking my back and shoulders. I throw my arms around him, our lips connecting as I desperately try to grab onto something real. Something worth living for. Returning my kiss, Garrett embraces me fully until I can taste the saltiness of my tears leak between our lips. My heart clenches as depression tries to tighten its grip. Garrett knows me. His soul is as damaged as mine, but Avery...she's too pure to be tainted. She's the epitome of what I've always wanted but can never have.

Sweet touches and tender reminders of him pull me back to the present. I retreat from his lips to cry into his shoulder, unable to help myself from being weak once again. Maybe Wyatt does have the right idea after all, to bury his emotions under an angry façade, because this touchy-feely shit isn't working for me.

Finally reigning control of myself, after soaking Gare's shoulder, I stare at the street lamp shining beyond the window. Gare attempts to arouse me, his fingers trailing my sides and dipping over my inner thighs. This is the routine. I dream, I panic, I cry and then I fuck out every ounce of emotion I don't want to feel. Garrett is always there, always willing to be that body for me to use. He believes he deserves it, but that couldn't be further from the truth. If I thought I could express the depth of our connection, of how I yearn to make love to him day in and day out, without him running scared - I would. He places tender kisses to my jaw, his fingers stroking a path along my dick. I barely feel it. All I feel is numb and completely useless.

"I need a drink," I gently ease him off me. Pulling on a pair of lounge pants, I scratch my head and leave the room. I'm reaching breaking point, and not even Gare's pity fucks are keeping the nightmares at bay. I need more. I need all of him. But instead of committing to me, he's found a blonde bombshell replacement to palm me off on.

My feet pad across the marble flooring, deepening the sour taste in my mouth. I hate Wyatt's taste in decor. He thinks money fixes problems, but to me, it's the cause. I'd take a tiny dorm room with twin beds. Dirty clothing piles in the corner, shelves overflowing with knick knacks I don't need. Anything to take me away from the mansion I grew up in, and the things I had to do to maintain it once my father died. But I also understand too well that people show love in different ways.

In Wyatt's mind, keeping us safe, secluded and secure is how he shows love. He doesn't let us worry about our next meal or how we'll fund our next semester. He takes care of us without words of affection. But at what cost to himself? Who has Wyatt's back when it all comes crashing down? The Shadowed Souls may surround him, but he won't let any of us in.

Turning into the kitchen, the refrigerator closes and I think I'm still dreaming. Avery turns her baby blues onto me, an oversized t-shirt just skimming her thighs. She's standing on one foot, the other tilted upwards like a flamingo. In her hand, she holds a bag of ice.

"What's happened?" I rush forward, my voice hushed. All of the mental berating I just gave myself about keeping my distance evaporates as I lean down to inspect her swollen ankle.

"It's nothing." Avery tries to brush me off. I extend her leg into the light and gently turn it. The blue and purple bruises conceal a lump, which is definitely not 'nothing'. "I went over on it at the studio, and then thought I saw something so I ran here. Stupid mistake, that's all. Huxley has already tended to it." Ignoring the stab of jealousy that strikes out of nowhere, I inspect the thin coating of cream he's applied. A rookie attempt.

"Okay well, this needs to be compressed and elevated. I've got some bandages," I rise to rifle through the cupboards. Avery sighs and stops me.

"It's fine, Axel. I can care for myself." Her words sound harsh, her hair rough from sleep. Did she have the same nightmare as me? Did she witness how I couldn't save her, how I'll always fail her? The next time she tries to wave me off and leave, I move forward quickly on instinct. Gripping her hips and planting her onto the counter harder than I intended to, I step between her legs and press my cheek against hers so those all-seeing eyes of hers can't look into my soul while it's vulnerable.

"That's the problem Avery. I do care. I just witnessed you dying in my dream so you can push me away all you like. I'm not going anywhere." My chest sinks at my confession. Despite the turmoil I've been putting myself through, despite knowing I need to stay away from her, I can't. She's an enigma. She's the light at the end of the darkened tunnel. I dare a glance at her expression. Glazed eyes assess me above a faint smattering of freckles over her button nose and her golden hair tickles my bare chest. A fucking angel.

"I'd rather the ugly truth than false promises Axel," Avery breathes. Another stab to the gut. It's too easy to forget Avery has her own demons. She carries her past with more grace than I will ever understand. Taking her hand from her lap, I link our fingers and bring our united fist up between us.

"I promise. Despite the fear that I'm the opposite of what you need, I promise that above all else, I will keep you safe." Leaning her forehead against mine, Avery parts her legs and hooks her arms around me so we are fully pressed against each other. The weight of my nightmare has lifted, but the underlying anxiety remains. My doubts will always be the driving wedge between myself and my happiness. Am I too tainted to be enough? Too broken to help fix her?

We stay like that, happy to support one another without judgment for the longest time. But it will never be enough. I need comfort like this to survive, gentle touches and soft caresses remind me of how it feels to be loved. To be alive. Garrett wants me to be with her. He's all but promised her to me. But I fear Avery alone won't be able to fill the void Garrett has created within me, and if she were to try, then I run the risk of losing them both.

CHAPTER TWENTY FIVE

I wake to a hand clamping over my mouth. With Huxley's snoring form pressed against my back, I don't panic like I did when Wyatt caught me half-drunk and cemented in a nightmare. This time, I open my eyes lazily, brow already cocked to see who is hovering above me. Garrett is the answer.

"Get dressed," he whispers, removing his hand to chuck a pile of clothes onto my midsection. I groan, my voice slurred as I roll over.

"I have English class."

"I know you have an edible ass. Now get it downstairs." He rushes out of the room on tiptoes like a sneaky little nymph, while I push my head further into the pillow.

"Just go," Huxley huffs, shoving me out of the bed. "He keeps things interesting." I roll onto the ground, landing on my hands and one foot. The other is high in the air while the clothes topple onto my back. After Axel bandaged my ankle and grabbed two sofa cushions, he tucked me into Huxley's bed with my leg elevated and a kiss pressed to my temple. It was an experience to say the least.

I emerge dressed in a mixture of girl's clothes which were no doubt left over from wild frat parties. At least they've been laundered. The t-shirt sits short above my navel, a huge pink heart in the center. On the bottom, the ripped jeans are a good fit and after stealing an additional pair of thick socks from Huxley's drawers, my ankle feels much better in the high-laced boots. I recall waking a few times in the night to my ice compact being swapped out for a fresh one, but that could have been in my dreams. I was all over the place after Theo surprised me, Huxley bathed me and Axel held me as if I'm precious.

On the landing at the top of the stairs, I stop as Wyatt ascends in his basketball jersey and shorts. His hair is damp, his green eyes are tired. He sees me at the same time as my hip leans against the railing, staying well out of the way. By the glare he gives me, I half expect him to toss me down the stairs. Without breaking his stride, he comes directly towards me, stopping on the step below.

"So you just stay here now?" he asks with bitter acceptance. My brows hit my hairline. Is he actually talking to me? Wyatt doesn't talk to me - he talks at me. He lords over me like some big bad wolf with more money than sense.

A thousand replies toy with the end of my tongue. Should I just say yes and make it official? Rooming with Huxley beats communal bathrooms and ties on doorknobs. Although, he'll probably grow bored and want his personal space back soon. Perhaps I ask Wyatt if there's a spare room for me, since apparently we're trying out this open communication thing. Unfortunately, years of anger and loathing don't disappear so easily.

"Get over it, Dipshit." Pushing past him, our shoulders lock in a battle of wills before I win out and manage to move forward. Garrett appears at the bottom of the stairs when I reach the lobby, directing me to the garage. Huxley's white SUV stands proud, all fixed and shiny like new. The orange Nissan and green Mercedes sit either side, but Garrett ignores all of these.

Tossing me a helmet and leather jacket, there's a silent instruction to mount the Ducati at the back while the garage door lifts. Garrett takes the front, zipping up his own jacket. There's a challenge in his brown gaze which I refuse to fail. Hopping onto the back, I pull on the helmet and wrap my arms around Garrett's middle.

Twisting the throttle, we shoot out of the garage, skidding hard onto the street. I'm glad I didn't have time to eat breakfast. The stench of burnt rubber surrounds us as Garrett's laughter vibrates beneath my palms. Thankfully, once we hit the main roads, he morphs into a very competent driver. We reach our destination with all of our limbs intact. Our destination being a shopping mall.

"You woke me up early to go shopping?" I ask once free from the helmet. Garrett takes it, chaining the pair of them to the bike.

"Not just shopping. Dress shopping."

"Dress shopping?" I echo back, delayed when he takes my hand and tugs me through the empty parking lot. "What do I need a dress for?"

"For the Ball, you silly goose." Garrett laughs at some internal joke. "I need to make sure you're looking good for my boy." I sigh. Our fingers are intertwined as we walk through the automatic doors.

"I'm so confused by the dynamics here."

"They don't need to make sense. If you wanted conventional, you probably shouldn't have a crush on your step-brother." I stop still, a gasp torn from my throat.

"I do not!" I shout in outrage. Garrett rounds on me, his arms folding over his chest.

"You're telling me, you've never used that cute little pink vibrator Axel was telling me about while imagining it was Wyatt's tongue?" My eyes widen further as I look around for anyone nearby. Luckily, the mall just opened and no one else thought Wednesday morning was an ideal time to venture out. Provoked by Garrett's smug smirk, I square up to him, prodding my finger into his chest.

"For the record," I growl and narrow my eyes. "My vibe is bigger than what you're packing." Garrett leans back to laugh, attracting the stares of shop clerks and a curious security guard. Winding an arm around my shoulder, he urges us to keep walking and drops his mouth to my ear.

"They don't make molds girthy enough, Peach." I'm left with that mental image as we seek out a spot of breakfast first. Garrett urges me to pick out whatever I want, even though I have to get my own tray. There's no room on his amongst the pile of bagels and pastries. Once we reach the cashier, he produces a credit card and flashes it at me. I just about make out Wyatt's name before Garrett pays. We sit in the middle of the food court, surrounded by empty tables and eat until we can't stomach another bite.

"This is literally the worst thing to do before a dress fitting," I lean back and stroke my food baby. I can't remember the last time I've felt so full. Not that Nancy, the manor's cook, would let me gorge on so many syrup-soaked waffles at the start of the day.

"I'm in no rush," Garrett holds up his coffee. I tilt my head at that, looking beyond the mask.

"Avoiding something?" I ask. Garrett's interest in his cup suddenly becomes forced. He pries off the lid, swirling the steaming liquid inside. I wait patiently, knowing out of the two of us, Garrett is the one who will break the silence first. Finally, he groans and drags a hand down his face.

"I'm avoiding Axel."

"Why?"

"Because I'm a fucking coward." Downing the rest of his coffee, Garrett lets every last drop patter his outstretched tongue before coming back to me. "I went looking for him last night and I saw you both... having your moment." He fakes a gag and I roll my eyes.

"So what?"

"No, it's nothing. Just...I mean, Axel usually relies on me after a nightmare but this is perfect actually. He needs to start moving on. It's best you see him at his lowest. Make sure you know how to handle it before I..."

"Before you, what?" I lean my elbows on the table. Garrett is at a loss for words for once, so uses his fingers to mime himself running away. Exasperation puffs out my cheeks. "You are the most ridiculous person I've ever met."

"That is deeply offensive," Garrett touches a hand to his chest. Stacking our plates, I busy myself with clearing away. I reckon I've figured out what it means to be a Shadowed Soul. You have to be stubborn to a fault, unable to see past your own damage and a terrible judge of character. Sure enough, the entire lot of them have misjudged me in one way or another. Typically by underestimating the strength I've spent years building brick by brick.

"You're so certain you're going to fail Axel. Maybe instead of pushing him away, you should pick out a suit and take him to the Ball yourself." I twist my lips. Garrett chuckles, preparing to move on from this conversation.

"You'll be a better match for him. We have shopping to do," Garrett pushes to his feet and offers me his hand. I accept it, but refuse to leave just yet.

"Last question," I state. A glint returns to Garrett's brown eyes as he stands close enough to force my head back. "Why does it have to be me or you? Why can't we just...see what happens?" With my hand in his, Garrett's smile turns sad. His thumb strokes my wrist.

"That was two questions, Peach. Come on, I'm ready to see you strut around for me." I drop the topic from then on. Whatever Garrett is working through with himself, a brief chastising over breakfast isn't going to change his mind.

We carve a path through the mall and up the escalator, Garrett seeming to have a destination in mind. A beautiful shop tucked away in the corner. Behind the window displays, thick blinds have been pulled down between the glass panels and the interior. I've barely stepped inside when a cheery sales assistant pops up.

"Good morning," she beams with a wide smile. Her hair is swept back, not a strand out of place. In a simple button down uniform, her name tag labels her as 'Tasha'. "Can I help you with anything today?"

"Please," Garrett smiles that mischievous smile which means I'm going to hate what he's about to say. "This lovely lady needs a dress to take my boyfriend on a date." I call on every shred of inner strength to remain impassive. To her credit, Tasha's smile only dips for a second. I step between the two of them, gesturing to the store.

"Ignore him. He chats shit to shock people. I need a dress for a ball at our university. Nothing too dark, it washes me out." I throw a pointed look at Garrett, daring him to disagree. He finds a low suede sofa and sits with a flourish, his leg crossed over the other knee.

The boutique specializes in ballgowns at first glance. Sorted by color, rails poke out of the walls with long, glittering gowns resting on their hangers. Between each set, sits a stand of coordinating shoes, bags and jewelry. Tasha asks a few questions about my usual likes and dislikes, takes several measurements and ventures off to select suitable dresses. My fingers trail the sequin and lace gowns, a flurry of butterflies coming to life within.

"I've never done this sort of thing," I confess to Garrett. He's watching me casually, but I've come to know he sees more than he says. My movements are being cataloged, so I might as well be upfront. "The galas and award ceremonies were always Wyatt's thing. I much preferred staying home and watching through the TV screen."

"Sounds lonely." I snort a laugh.

"You haven't met Meg's friends. During spring break, we had a group come and stay while Nixon and my mom were out of town. Gowns and galas may not be my thing, but apparently booty shorts and beer kegs are."

"Really?" Garrett sits forward, his face alight with curiosity. Tasha returns with her arms filled with special garments she keeps out back. Every single one is exquisite, and a one-off she assures me. I shift through the selection, unsure where to start.

"What color will Axel's suit be?" I try to approach the selection process from a logical standpoint. If Meg were here, she'd have already picked out my entire outfit with matching accessories. Garrett laughs, verging on bitterly.

"You won't get that man in a suit and tie. He's triggered by tight collars around his neck. He'll wear a very expensive t-shirt and jeans though." I peer back but Garrett's attention is on the images littering his arms. No doubt he's looking for space to squeeze in something else. Affronted with Tasha's curious gaze, I think back to the frat house party. I hadn't noticed it at the time, but where the rest of the gang wore shirts and slacks, I now remember Axel in a fitted tee. Interesting.

"So I'm matching denim. Navy blue is it." This immediately whittles the selection to two dresses. A much more manageable choice. Tasha leaves to set up the dressing room while I browse shoes and bags, cursing myself for being so shit at this type of thing. Although, maybe it's not that I'm shit. Maybe it's that I don't really care for it. Gowns, diamonds; it's all so frivolous. I've never been interested in being dressed up and paraded around.

Arms wind around my waist, fingers prying a clutch from my hand. Garrett's head drops into the crook of my neck. He inhales, my eyes flutter closed. The press of his body, the steady rise and fall of his chest. A rare moment of stillness takes place and my mind drifts. How long has it been since Garrett was still? Since he took the time to quiet his mind? Warmth spreads through my entire body, my back molding into him. I feel light and weirdly safe, despite knowing Garrett of all people could switch personas and leave me in the dust if he wishes.

"I knew you'd be perfect for him." The whisper brushes my collarbone. My gut churns. As much as Axel is a gorgeously haunted man who I could see myself connecting with on a deep level, there's something similar within Garrett. We stand in our embrace for a while. Long enough for the small voice in the back of my head to grow from an equally tentative whisper to a shout, overpowering all common sense.

Maybe I want to be perfect for you, too.

AVERY

At precisely six o'clock, a light rap sounds on my dorm room door. I briefly glance at Kay, who is curled up in bed on her phone.

"Well, it isn't for me," she grumbles. Her on-off girlfriend invited someone else to the ball, prior to officially calling it quits with Kay via text message. She's been in moping mode all week, and watching me twirl around in my ball gown hasn't helped.

Checking my face and teeth one last time in the small desk mirror, I brush down the navy satin skirts. My phone is tucked into an invisible pocket, beside the thigh-high slit. Along with a low dip between my cleavage, the bust held in place by thin spaghetti straps, I can see why Garrett chose this dress before I'd even tried it on. Meg wouldn't have believed I was going out with so much skin on show, which is why I sent her a dozen photos before pulling on the satin shawl.

My heels click across the room and I open the door. Axel is leaning against the hallway wall, standing promptly as he looks me over. His hazel eyes sparkle, his features slack. I hide my blush by tucking the free blonde tendril from my updo behind my ear. He steps forward and untucks it again.

"You're stunning," Axel breathes. So is he. Garrett mentioned he'd be in jeans, but Axel's swagger is evident in his styling. The denim is dark, the fit tight and akin to slacks. His t-shirt is also fitted and mostly hidden beneath a blazer. His brown belt matches his dress shoes.

"You don't fix up too badly yourself," I smile back. From behind his back, Axel produces a corsage. A singular rose, the petals a flurry of rainbow colors.

"I figured you didn't have an official prom." My smile falls away as Axel eases the band around my wrist. Amongst the flirtatious fun, I hadn't expected such a considerate thought. My eyes float over Axel's shoulder, watching others being accompanied from their rooms to the stairwell. No Garrett in sight. My chest tightens, a feeling I can't describe bubbling beneath the surface. I push it aside and find my smile once more. I vowed to myself to enjoy this night. Like Axel has already pointed out, putting myself out in the real world isn't a regular occurrence.

Axel offers his arm, guiding me from the dorm block to the parking lot. A limousine awaits. I tip my head to the chauffeur who opens the rear door, revealing the rest of the Shadowed Souls. Garrett looks at me over the rim of a glass, his smirk blocked from view. As I take a seat, the slit in my dress opens wide. Huxley's eyes drop immediately while Dax acts the gentleman and looks away. Across the far end of the seats, with a bottle of whiskey in hand and a girl in his lap, is Wyatt. He's the only one who seems to have brought a date.

"You guys seriously hired a limo for a four minute drive?" I scoff. "Why am I even surprised?" Axel slides into my side, winding his arm around my waist and tugging me close. Apparently, being his date tonight means he gets handling rights over me. Garrett downs his drink, a brightly colored cocktail of some kind, and raises a brow.

"Economy needs rich fuckers like us to do reckless things," he half shrugs. Axel leans into my ear.

"What he means is - we paid the chauffeur for the entire night. After this four minute drive, he's grabbing takeout and going home to his family. We had a nice chat while waiting for you to get ready." I blink a few times, trying to concentrate while Axel's thumb brushes my cheek. Everywhere he touches me, I'm alive. It's the first time his fingers have graced my skin since creaming my tattoo. At odds with this recent behavior, he's no longer holding back. The drive is quick and before I know it, we're stepping into the main hall.

Instantly, the rich, earthy scent of fallen leaves and cinnamon strikes.

Garlands of vibrant orange, red, and yellow leaves are strung along the walls, interspersed with twinkling fairy lights. The ceiling is draped with gauzy fabrics in shades of hazel and gold, creating a canopy that bathes the room in a warm, golden glow. My arm is in Axel's as we pass through the curtained archway, a slow smile spreading across my face. It's busy, but for once, I couldn't care less.

We stand in line for a photo op, the red carpet trickled with more leaves and pumpkins. I stand in the center of a roped area, a camera facing the autumnal backdrop. Pausing, I glance back at the four guys giving me their thumbs up. Wyatt decided not to enter with us and I'm not mad about it. I chew on my bottom lip when the assistant calls for my smile, my hands wringing the strap of my clutch bag. I've never really been the 'look at me' type, and I'm certainly not comfortable alone in the spotlight, but I give it my best shot for the flurry of flashes which follow.

Suddenly, a rush of bodies slam into me from all sides. Hands claim every inch of my waist and hips, the guys grinning goofily. Someone tickles my ribs and someone else grabs my ass. My own laughter is caught on camera several times over. Two photo strips are handed over, one going into my bag and the other in Huxley's pocket. We move on, letting the rest of those queuing have their turn.

The main feature in the center of the hall is a large dance floor, its polished wood reflecting the overhead lights like a mirror. At one end, a stage is set up for the band, adding a lively backdrop to the chatter and laughter filtering throughout. Around the dance floor, tables are set with burgundy tablecloths, littered with gold flakes and adorned with centerpieces of carved pumpkins. Across the far side, a long buffet is announced as open.

"Food!" shouts Garrett. He barrels through a nearby crowd, causing drinks to spill. Axel chuckles, his mouth dropping to my ear.

"He literally just ate before we left."

"I do like a buffet," I shrug, tugging him in the same direction. We graciously sidestep around the group now wearing their apple cider and I offer a pack of tissues from my clutch. They decline.

Dax and Huxley hang back to grab a table, although I've lost sight of them amongst the women who took their cue to shoot their shot. I have no right to be jealous. We all deserve to enjoy the evening, but I opt to not look back and regularly assess their choices in women either.

The buffet is laid with serving platters, ladles and bowls, the main option being a pumpkin chili.

"Should we grab some for the others?" I ask Axel, claiming myself a bowl. He snorts and shakes his head.

"Wyatt can't handle spicy food, but you didn't hear that from me." I look away swiftly to hide the intrigue in my expression. That's a note I'll save for later. Dishing out my soup and taking some bread slices, Axel has already moved onto the far end - the desserts. They range from caramel apples and spiced cookies to a chocolate fountain with skewers of fruit and marshmallows ready for dipping. Garrett easily has one of each piled on his plate and Axel soon has the same. I roll my eyes at their sweet tooth, carefully holding my steaming soup. I starved myself all day rather than look bloated in my ball gown, and now I'm ready for a proper meal.

Reaching the chosen table, happily finding Wyatt is nowhere to be seen, the squad of beautiful girls instantly move away. I make a show of smelling my pits and checking my breath.

"It's not you," Huxley laughs. His fingers twitch as he resists the urge to pull me into his lap. Instead, he stands to pull out my chair. "I sent them away," he mutters against my neck, the brush of a kiss lingering there. I sit with a skeptically-raised brow.

"You didn't have to do that. I'm sure we all want to get laid tonight. " Dax chokes on his drink just as Garrett sits on my other side. He slaps Dax's back roughly, and the smile doesn't leave his face.

"True that," Garrett agrees, shoveling chips and guacamole into his mouth. It's lucky he's cute. "But we don't want to get laid by any old piece of ass. Cheerleaders may be flexible but they never fail to have an attitude problem." He points a chip at me. I lean on my fist, playing along.

"And you think ballerinas are any better? I hear we all have an ego complex." Garrett grins, his dark eyes twinkling with mischief.

"But they have the stamina to make up for it." He winks. Dax is still spluttering as he leans forward.

"What he means to say is, we're not about that other woman drama."

"Same thing," Garrett shrugs and keeps eating. I laugh until my sides hurt and gulp down my punch. It feels good to be in public and not feel anxious. To be present and in good company, rather than hiding in the back and picking at my cuticles. I eat my soup and tap my feet to the music, watching those dancing. On my fourth punch refill, I become convinced it's spiked. The warmth in my belly and carefree lightness to my head is enough evidence.

"Dance with me?" Axel asks. I lean against his shoulder, my smile stupidly wide.

"I thought you'd never ask." Axel takes my hand and leads me to the center of the dancefloor. The music slows, causing the sea of bodies around us to either couple-up or slink away. As the lights dim, I eye Axel suspiciously. He pretends not to notice, but I see the dimple deepening as he tries to hide his smirk. Nothing surprises me with these guys any more.

His hands rests on my waist, firm but gentle, and I place mine on his shoulders, feeling the strength beneath his jacket and t-shirt. I'm hyper-aware of every point of contact between us. I'm not sure who initiates it, but soon we're closer, our bodies swaying together in perfect sync. I feel the heat radiating from him, smell the faint scent of his cologne mixed with an underlying layer of citrus. My breath hitches as his hand slides a little lower on my back, pulling me closer until there's hardly any space between us.

I look up into his hazel eyes. They are smoldering with intensity, causing my pulse to quicken. Suddenly, the air feels thick with unspoken desire. His thumb brushes against my side, a subtle, almost teasing motion that leaves a trail of fire in its wake. A shiver rolls the length of my spine.

"Avery," Axel murmurs, his voice husky. I still, forgetting how to move. How to breathe. The music plays around us, enveloping us in our own bubble amongst the masses. "I can't describe how beautiful you are." His words send a thrill through me, and I can't help the smile that tugs at my lips.

"You don't clean up too badly yourself," I whisper back, my voice barely audible. T-shirt or not, Axel looks, smells and feels amazing. He leans in, his lips brushing my ear, and it takes everything in me not to shiver.

"I didn't just mean tonight in that dress. You're so fucking beautiful, Avery, sometimes just looking at you knocks me off kilter. You're so pure," he breathes, and then he pulls back just enough to look at me again. "So accepting. Do you think you could be with someone like me? Someone broken who will never be whole enough for you, but wants to try anyway?"

Our eyes lock, and for a moment, the world fades away. Axel's expression is open, those cracks in his armor on full display for me to either patch up or tear to shreds. And it's evident he doesn't care which. He's so willing to jump off the cliff with me and see what happens. I can't deny wanting to do it too.

Drawn by an irresistible force, my lips find his. A slow, almost tentative movement that burns me from within. I lean into him, putting all of my weight into his strong arms. His hand slides up my back, cradling the nape of my neck, and I melt into him, losing myself in the sensation of his warmth, his mouth slow and seeking. Axel isn't looking for hot and heavy, he's giving me a deeper connection I'd usually run from. I'm not running this time.

When we finally pull apart, I'm breathless, my heart pounding. He rests his forehead against mine, and I can feel his breath, warm and ragged, mingling with mine.

"That was so hot," a voice trembles slightly at my back. I shift, noticing Garrett is close behind, and that it's his hand on my nape, guiding me into Axel. "Mind if I cut in?" Despite asking the question, Garrett doesn't wait for a response. His hands grip my waist and he physically sets me aside before stepping into Axel's personal space. Winding his arms around Axel's neck, Garrett sways, twisting them both away from my eyeline. A light tap on my shoulder announces Dax's arrival.

"I'm not quite sure what just happened." I blink a few times. Dax laughs, holding out his hand for me like a gentleman.

"Garrett does what he's best at. He pushed the two of you together and then decided he was jealous. He's fickle, you'll get used to it." Spinning me in a ballroom-style twirl, Dax draws me close into his body, but keeps his hands in the proper places and our bodies properly distanced. I smile up at him.

"There's a lot of people around. Shouldn't I be worried about the rumors I'm creating here?" I half-tease, but also notice the side glances I receive from switching from one Shadowed Soul to the next.

"It depends," Dax half shrugs, smirking all the while.

"On what?"

"On if you care about what people think, or if you would rather chase what your heart wants. You can be respected and admired by those who don't know you, or you can be happy." My brows lift as I'm caught off-guard by Dax's honesty. I don't know why, he's never given me any half truths or false fantasies. Stepping into his body to avoid his stare, I rest my head against Dax's shoulder. He takes his cue to tighten his arms around my back and just hold me, swaying to a rhythm that is completely off-beat and totally our own.

My thoughts drift to my mom. There's no better example of public opinion. She was admired by the entire world, always in the news for her charity work and generosity. She spent her entire life living for others, myself included. But now I think back to the times she thought I wasn't watching. To when she'd play melancholy tunes on the piano or forget to sit properly when watching a movie. In those moments, I saw a woman who gave all of herself to others, and I'm starting to wonder if there was anything left for herself. Living that way is exhausting, and I've never really given a shit about respect.

"I choose happiness." I declare. Those large hands on my lower back tighten.

"Good girl," Dax brushes the ghost of a kiss against my cheek. I gasp softly at his playfulness, my thighs clenching. When so many other big personalities live under one roof, I can see how he might be easily discounted. But a gentleman who opens doors and then whispers dirty things in my ear? Dax is ticking all of my boxes.

Smiling into his shoulder, inhaling his sea mineral body wash, I could remain like this all night if it wasn't for the hand that roughly grabs my arm, tearing me away. I wobble in my heels until I'm spun to meet Wyatt's green eyes. Eyes in which the pupils are blown wide and there's a stupidly weird smile on his face.

"Ahh fuck," I mutter under my breath. Brooding Wyatt, fine. Glaring Wyatt, no problem. High-as-shit Wyatt? Yeah, I can't call that.

That same hand on my upper arm drags me into his personal space, his fine suit brushing against the front of my dress. I shove at his chest as Dax grabs his wrist, but Wyatt's sneer only gets wider.

"I wouldn't if I were you," he chuckles with an ominous undertone that gives me pause. There's nothing more unnerving than his seemingly-kind smile when I know the blackness of his heart. Or lack of, in this case.

"It's fine, Dax. Give us a minute." After a lengthy side glance, Dax nods and backs away, taking a lingering Huxley with him. Stalling my shoving, my hands remain on Wyatt's chest. One arm slides around my back and in a smooth movement, he jolts me closer as a cold object presses against my thigh. It's metal and at the hilt of my skirt's high slit. The dimmed lighting causes shadows to fall over Wyatt's sharp features, yet I still watch intently, trying to gauge his next move. He starts to sway us side to side.

"Not going to scream for help?"

"That would imply that I was scared," I reply instantly. It's all bullshit, of course. I don't think I've ever sensed Wyatt so volatile. I also don't want to become too comfortable with the Shadowed Souls coming to my rescue, which is why I don't pay any attention to Garrett and Axel waltzing around in the background.

The cold metal inches higher, tugging at my satin. It's a blade of some sort, a pocket knife maybe. Either way, the thrill of desire that slams through me is completely unwarranted. Wyatt, despite his inhibited state, doesn't miss a beat. His green eyes sharpen, his head slightly tilted.

"You like this, don't you?" he smirks. To test out his theory, Wyatt presses the knife closer, its sharp edge taut against my skin. It's not so easy to feign indifference this time. I swallow thickly, my lids lowering. My mind slips. The world fades away. Nothing exists except Wyatt's solid chest beneath my palms and the press of metal against my thigh. I try to predict the moment the blade slices my skin, a warm trickle of blood creeping south.

Wyatt's mouth is beside my ear then, his breath heated. "Holy shit. You're just as fucked up as I am."

"No one is as fucked up as you are," I mutter back. Yet I'm not moving back. Between the bulk of his outline, the dimmed lighting and the loud music, I don't pull away. It's the longest Wyatt has given me his attention and I'm seriously questioning my life choices as to why I care. Why, after everything, I want more of it. Because I hate myself, I quickly decide.

"You know, I've been dreading this stupid dance," Wyatt is grinning again. Ear to ear, like the Joker. Every sway we take, the blade creeps up towards my thigh.

"Then why are you here?" My nostrils flare, the only tell that I'm affected. His chest is hard beneath my palms, long and steady breaths causing them to rise and fall. His suit is designer, I now realize. His dark hair is impeccably swept back and the cologne. That goddamn cologne which invades my senses and makes me dizzy. My lungs seize as Wyatt leans forward, his mouth against my cheek. I shiver and internally curse Garrett for putting this fantasy in my head.

"I figured since slutting around was your thing, I would just give you a helping hand." Then he strikes. The blade moves effortlessly, gliding through the satin of my dress, over my hip and across my waist at a wonky angle. I suck inwards to avoid being cut across my abdomen, and finally his arm releases me. He's torn away before I've even gathered the remains of the fabric together, just about concealing the black thong I'm wearing underneath. Wyatt must catch a glimpse anyway, his barking laughter ringing out over the music.

"Who exactly are you dressing up for, little sis?" he calls out, gaining everyone's attention. My cheeks instantly flame. Anger boils my blood, sending me over the edge. I've changed my mind. Fuck this asshole.

Standing tall, I let my dress fall in its tatters. Huxley and Dax are dragging Wyatt away as I storm after them. They stop on the edge of the dancefloor, all three watching me tentatively. I grab Wyatt's tie, wrapping it around my fist and yank him towards my face.

"I don't give a fuck who you think you are. You don't get to slut shame anyone." No thought process happens beyond that, just the jerk of my leg as I knee Wyatt squarely in the balls. Whatever drug Wyatt is on infuses a trickle of laughter with his screaming, his legs giving out and body crumpling onto the floor. He's a mess of howls and whooping, a sad sight for the men who come to stand around him.

In some silent conversation I'm not a part of, Dax and Huxley attend to carrying Wyatt out, while Axel's arms swoop me up. Our exit is swift but not quiet, as Garrett holds his hands high and shouts, 'there's nothing to see here!'. It's too late anyway. I glance over Axel's shoulder to the sea of camera phones and flashlights pointed at me. The one and only time Wyatt has acknowledged me in public, and it's been caught on camera for the world to see. So much for not giving a shit about outsider opinions.

CHAPTER TWENTY SEVEN

Gritting my teeth, I rise from yet another stumble and glare at myself in the mirror. My feet are killing me from last night's heels and this morning's grueling dance practice. The sun has yet to rise, but sleep wasn't an option. Every time I found enough peace to drift off, startling green eyes were waiting for me. All encompassing, bordering mesmerizing. They swallowed me whole, luring me into a whirlpool I couldn't surface from. Wyatt's laughter pounded against the inside of my ears until I woke in yet another cold sweat. I hate him. I hate that still, after all this time, he won't let me grasp a trace of happiness.

So here I am. Focusing on all I have, all I can depend on. Dancing. It may prove a little tricker this morning, but eventually, I will find my zen. Theo had the good sense to record his piano mastery so we can practice without him being present. Perhaps our run-in spurred him to think twice about stalking around the studio in the dark. Strolling over to my phone, I restart the piece again and take it from the top.

I dance for hours, pushing myself through the entire showcase from start to finish. In the parts I'm supposed to have a partner for, I fill in the lifts with leaps and moves which fit the music better. I might have to talk to Ms. Nightingale about some transitions which don't flow as easily as they should. During these short breaks where I'm jotting down notes, I roll my ankles and stretch. I've pushed myself far beyond the typical length of practice and now I'm starting to suffer for it. I can't pretend it's not exactly what I wanted - the excuse to shower after everyone else has left for class and return to bed for the day. I won't be surfacing until I can sleep soundly enough not to dream.

"From one monster to another," I mutter to myself. I can't pinpoint when my fears changed from my birth father to Wyatt. They're at different ends of the scale in terms of physically hurting me, but Wyatt's insistence to exploit my weaknesses and prey upon them is taking precedent. My birth father was a bastard. Just a bad man who did bad things. Wyatt? He's a privileged fuckwitt who never learned to share and blames me for it.

Light pierces the high windows above the mirrors. I hear the rumbling of chatter before the door opens and a crowd of dancers leak inside. All smiles and fresh faces. It seems everyone had a much better night at the ball than I did. Grabbing my phone from the piano, I head across the studio to pack up my stuff. I change out my shoes and tug Meg's baggy sweatshirt over my head, keeping my back to those setting up around me. I don't need any questions and at worst, I don't need the pity. Lifting my backpack, a padded envelope sits underneath with my name on. I frown, tentatively picking it up.

I pry open the seal, pulling out a pair of compression socks. My ankles throb on instinct, welcoming the sight whilst my hand trembles. There's a note inside, a ripped piece of paper with rushed handwriting.

'You wouldn't get them for yourself.'

A kind thought, I suppose, if the two letters at the bottom of the page didn't have my heart lodged in my throat. XO. My eyes fly around the room at everyone setting up and stretching against the rail. They all greet my suspicion with raised eyebrows and frowns.

Shoving them back inside, I crush my belongings to my chest, envelope and all, and rush out of the studio, crashing into multiple shoulders as I go. For the second time in (two weeks?), I fly across campus with huge strides. My heart is pounding, the last of the energy I reserved for a shower quickly waning. Dashing across a road, narrowly missing being hit by an oncoming car, I make it to the frat house. There's no time wasted on climbing the tree today; I throw the front door open and burst inside unannounced.

The first person I find is standing in the kitchen, leaning his hip against the counter. Workout gear clings to his muscled body, a protein shake in hand. Green eyes lift to mine, hickeys littering his neck. I can barely breathe, my grip cramping around my backpack.

"Is there something I can help you with?" he asks after a beat. His casualness is a red flag to my anger.

"You know what," I throw my bag down onto the ground. Upending the envelope onto the island, Wyatt's eyes slowly trace the note that floats against the marble. "Yeah, you can fucking help me. You can do your damn job!" Slamming my fist down on the counter, I instantly regret it but refuse to let my face falter from its glare. Wyatt doesn't react aside from the dip in his tone.

"Excuse me?"

"You are most *definitely* not excused. You were told to watch over me. Nixon ordered you to keep me safe." My shoulders are so tense, my neck will snap if I shift too quickly. Finishing his shake, Wyatt toys with his tongue against his teeth. Again, he looks at the note with a lack of interest. Maybe fan mail is a common occurrence for him too, but I certainly have never received one without a postage stamp. Without an address. As far as I know, this is the first time Mr. XO has hand delivered a message. It means he was *here*. He is here, somewhere in Waversea. At a loss, I grip the socks and toss them across the room. They hit the refrigerator and drop to the floor.

"What's happening in here?" Huxley appears. His presence brings the others from wherever they were hiding. Wyatt sighs, slowly walking to leave and pausing when he's looming over me.

"I believe it's the definition of a bitch fit." Forget the red flag. I lunge at him, grabbing fistfuls of hair and skin. I fight dirty, my nails digging into anything I can find, hanging on with all my might when someone else tries to drag me away. Using one hand to grab the back of Wyatt's hair, I punch him with the other. His head whips to the side, an instant welt blooming across his jaw. A hand catches my arm before I can do it again.

"How's this for a bitch fit, asshole?!" I scream as I'm finally pried away from him and into the cage of multiple bodies. No one attends to Wyatt, who's massaging his jaw and checking his teeth with his tongue. My mind is screaming. Now I've had a taste of his pain, I want more. He deserves more. I attempt to dodge those holding me, my fist clenched and ready. Maybe I can liberate a few of those perfectly straight teeth as well.

"Avery, stop." A voice finds me amongst the bodies. Hands cup my cheeks, tilting my face upwards to Dax's. He pleads with his blue eyes, his concern palpable. I scrunch my eyes closed, refusing to let go of the rage. Wyatt will never take me seriously. He'll never listen to me, and I don't know why I still care. The anger twists bitterly inside, turning on myself. He's part of the problem, but this desire for his attention is what will always haunt me. Why do I want him to accept me?

"Breathe. Talk to me." Dax tries again, his thumbs stroking across my skin. Wetness pools there, the first hint that a tear has escaped my eye. Tiredness wins. My limbs drop, the tension ebbing away.

"I have a...I don't really know. A fan, I think." I open my eyes. The others are crowding me, but it's Dax I talk to. He's the one I know is always listening. "He...I mean, I think it's a he. Meg and I call him Mr. XO. He's been sending me birthday and christmas cards for the past ten years, sometimes other letters and flowers. My favorite chocolates," I shrug. "It's all been pretty innocent, but I forward his notes onto our private investigator anyway."

"Okay," Dax nods. Slowly, he shoulders his way through his friends to guide me to the sofa. Huxley is at my back the entire way, until we sit and he nestles into my other side. I keep my attention on Dax's hands stroking mine. "Then what?"

"I received a note and a gift this morning in the dance studio. He was here, in person. He's never felt this close before, and I kinda freaked out."

"The night you came to me with your ankle twisted," Huxley breathes. "Something spooked you then too." I can only nod. Garrett reappears, sitting on the coffee table with his long legs crossed and a bag of chips in his hands. His loud crunching earns him scowls from everyone, but he couldn't care less.

"Stop struggling," I hear Axel huff. He's moved away to attend to Wyatt's jaw, muttering that it needs ice. I can't hide my smirk at that.

"Dax and I will head to your dorm, pack up your stuff." Huxley kisses the top of my head. I grab his thigh to stop him from getting up.

"Wait, what?!" Looking at Dax, he seems to be in agreement.

"You're staying here until we find out who this Mr. XO is. Maybe

Wyatt doesn't care about protecting you, but we do." His eyes remain soft, his touch lingering. I swallow thickly, watching them don jackets and shove their feet in their sneakers. Huxley's jaw is set, his back rigid as he swings his keys around his index finger.

"Wyatt, ice your own fucking jaw. Axel, attend to Avery's hands. Garrett, share your snacks." He dishes out orders in a tone I've yet to hear but instantly find attractive. My eyes lower to my hands, finding my knuckles red and pulsing. My nails are cracked, and a few half-crescent moons in my palms are prickling with blood. The three of them stalk out of the door, Wyatt's glare promising revenge. It doesn't have the same appeal with a pack of frozen peas pressed against his face.

Before Axel gets close, I jump over the back of the sofa and seek out my phone, sending a quick photo of my hands to Meg. She's going to love this.

CHAPTER TWENTY EIGHT

In retrospect, this is the last place I should have run to. The police station would have been a better option, considering I've ended up in jail anyway. Despite his broken nose and general foul mood, Wyatt has finally taken my safety seriously - and I hate him even more for it. I'm certain the huge planner now situated on the kitchen wall, detailing every aspect of my life, is more to taunt me than aid me.

For the past week, seeing us through to fall break, Dax has escorted me between classes. Huxley drives me anywhere else, whilst rotating with Axel to watch me during ballet practice. Garrett is my lunch-time buddy. I've grown morbidly fascinated by the way he swallows without chewing. It's like watching a colorfully-tattooed pelican who's never tasted carbs before. Wyatt has been...around, unfortunately. We haven't had any real interactions, but I've been forced to watch every basketball practice and suffer his presence at meal times. I do have my own bedroom though, so that's eight hours a night without being loomed over.

And there's now. A Sunday study session for everyone ahead of assignments due next week, mine and Dax's included. Five additional chairs have been set up around Wyatt's large desk in the study, with him in the large leather chair in the center. I tap my purple highlighter aside my head, proofreading through Dax's half of our essay while he does mine. Then we'll swap back and amend where needed. I'm halfway through a yawn when my phone buzzes in my pocket. Sneaking it out of my sweatpants, I peer at the screen beneath the table.

Meg: 'Got them to break their pact yet?'

I suppress a sigh and a smile, shooting back a message that says I'm working on it. Two damn weeks in this testosterone-filled house without my vibrator and some dumb pact they decided to make without consulting me. Sure, I could look elsewhere but I essentially have four cockblocks surrounding me at all times. And let's be honest, no one else in the vicinity can compare.

"No phones during study time," Wyatt remarks in a clipped voice. I roll my eyes and pocket my phone.

"I can't help it when some guy decides to slide into my DM's, and ignoring his dick pic would be plain rude." Shrugging, I put on my best puppy-dog eyes. Wyatt's nostrils flare. The other pens and fingers typing at laptop keys around the table have gone still. After a beat, Wyatt dismisses me.

"Sure," he returns to his macbook screen. The light illuminates his annoyingly handsome face. "After you've left the study, message whatever simp you like. I just figured you had a little more tenacity than that." My blood starts to boil, the way it always does around Wyatt. Oh, I have tenacity alright - the bruising lingering on his jaw is a testament to that.

"You don't know anything about me," I huff with unspoken weight behind my words. Wyatt catches on though, his gaze spearing me in an instant.

"I know enough. Perhaps whoever is distracting you from your studies will entertain your fanciful ideas of candlelight and flower petals, but they won't get your ass to graduation. That'll take hard work. A lot of hard work," he drawls the last part. I don't let him rattle me in the way intended. Instead, I chuckle into my drink, tipping my head back to take a long, refreshing sip from the can. When my gaze returns to the table, five sets of eyes are glaring intently at me.

"What's so funny?" Wyatt says through clenched teeth. I raise a brow, feigning innocence and go back to my work. Usually, if you ignore idiots, they leave you alone. Not here, apparently.

"Speak your mind," Wyatt demands and slams his fist on the table. I blink up at him from beneath my lashes. "You don't think this imaginary guy will actually care about you, do you? He'll take your virginity and brag about it to the world. Then what? I'm left to face the cameras and press while you tuck your tail between your legs. I don't fucking think so."

My highlighter pauses mid sentence, bleeding through the paper. Why would Wyatt choose now, of all times, to decide to be a brother? I look at the others, curious as to whether they all think the same. From the desperation and pity in the rest of their eyes, apparently they do.

"Now isn't the time to stay silent. Go ahead and tell me you're waiting for the one or something equally pathetic." Wyatt closes his macbook and interlinks his fingers over it. He thinks he has been backed into a corner of his own creation. Ironically, this is the longest Wyatt has ever spoken to me, and he's never been more wrong.

"I don't..." I let my voice trail off. Everyone leans in, although I don't think the rest are hoping for the same answer as Wyatt. Either way, neither are getting it. I lean back in my chair, chilled as a freaking cucumber. "I don't know how I'm supposed to lose my virginity twice." Garrett whimpers. Full-on whimpers like a caged animal while Axel's eyes close briefly. Across the table, similar reactions on biting knuckles or rubbing napes are taking place. And then there's Wyatt. The only sign he gives that he actually heard me is the cracking of his knuckles.

"Who?" His voice is dangerously low, his head turning to assess his friends. I wrinkle my nose.

"Why the fuck do you care?"

"I care because, as I was led to believe on the weekly calls from my mom, you never left the manor. So that means you've been screwing around at my college. Potentially, my house." He picks up my purple highlighter and snaps it in half for dramatic effect. The others are now looking at each other accusingly. The air grows tense while all I can think is, this is quickly becoming ridiculous.

"Not that I need to explain myself to you, but I was often home alone and Meg would bring friends over sometimes," I purse my lips. My omission is for the rest seated at this table, blowing their bullshit pact to smithereens. The vein at Wyatt's temple looks like it's about to break free and punch me in the face, while his jaw ticks and I figure I've come this far. I might as well hammer the last nail into the coffin and finish this with the final say.

"Don't worry, *Bro*. I never fuck where I sleep. I used your room for my sexcapades. You always did have the best mattress. Did, being the operative word - it's rather dented now." Dax clears his throat, trying to catch my attention. His hand is slyly cutting a line over his neck in a '*Stop. Stop now,*' gesture. He clearly doesn't know me very well.

"So," Wyatt rolls his neck as if trying to choose the right words. He fails. "You're not the frigid little introvert I was led to believe." Perhaps that was supposed to hurt me. I raise one shoulder, putting my notepad into my backpack. Zipping it loudly, I grab the strap and stand.

"At least I'm not living up to my cliché. You, however," I smile across the table. "You are exactly the spoiled-"

"Do. Not. Finish that sentence," Wyatt growls. I lean forward on the desk.

"Selfish-"

"I'm warning you, Avery," he pushes to his full height. The shiver I get at the way he growls my name is too good to deny.

"Arrogant," I over pronounce every syllable. Wyatt's hands are fisted on the mahogany wood. I lick my lips, allowing him to break eye contact and track the movement. Parting my lips for an entire breath, the room falls still.

"Brat."

Wyatt moves before I can track him, vaulting himself onto the desk. I squeal, dashing for the door. A body beats me to it and I freeze in shock, blinking up at Dax. Pale blue eyes hold a hint of frustration. His hand closes around the handle, twisting and throwing it open. Grabbing my nape, he all but shoves me into the corridor and slams the door just as Wyatt collides with him. I stall, stunned by the commotion taking place inside the study before I remember I need to move.

My socks slide on the marble flooring, causing me to crash into a wall. Footsteps thunder behind me. I use the bannister to slide down to the lower level, making it all the way to the front door. Throwing it wide, I'm two steps out on the porch when hands simultaneously clamp over my mouth and around my throat. I'm dragged inside kicking and struggling, then turned sharply towards the coat closet. The firm body behind me is forceful in shoving me inside.

"I've got you. Trust me." The deep rasp of Garrett's voice mutters in my ear. I stop struggling, knowing he should be the last person I trust - but he isn't. Garrett may be reckless, but he's never given me a reason to be wary of him. Yet. Pulling the door mostly closed, a strip of light streams inside. I fall still as figures rush through the lobby, temporarily stealing the light. They race outside, Wyatt's commands fuelling the stampede.

"They can't be far. Find them!"

Garrett chuckles at my back, slowly releasing my mouth. "I love it when he uses his angry voice. Don't you, Peach?" To prove his point, he pushes his hardening cock against my ass. "Be a good girl for me and cum before we're discovered." I don't get any other warning.

Garrett strips my sweatpants and panties down to my ankles and his tongue dives into my pussy from behind. My hands fly out to grip the door frame, a silent gasp on my lips. Garrett's large hands cover my ass, my ankles locked in place by my pants. I arch, eagerly trying to guide his tongue to the bundle of nerves fluttering for attention at the front. The more I tilt and direct, the more Garrett pulls back.

"You're infuriating," I mutter.

"He really is," a reply comes, but not from inside the closet. I realize the light streaming in has been blocked permanently, the outline of Axel's shaved head standing beyond the door and facing the lobby. He's guarding us. Listening to us. The thought makes me wetter as Garrett's fingers toy with my ass, his tongue running a smooth path to and fro. He strokes me languidly, teases incredulously, but never enters. I groan and he laughs.

"Don't you like my punishment of choice?" he murmurs against my inner thigh.

"No," I huff and he suddenly bites down. I jerk, the pain shooting directly to my g-spot. Kissing the same spot, Garrett moves towards the other side.

"You have no idea how hard your attitude makes me." This time, I'm ready for his bite. He's marking me. Staking a claim. Returning to my wetness, Garrett doesn't hold back any more.

His arm winds around my hip, fingers seeking out my clit. I part my legs as much as I'm able, allowing his tongue to spear me. I lose all sense of gravity, my entire existence based on the tongue thrusting in and out of my cunt, the fingers vibrating over my clit and the man beyond the door intently listening in. There's no being quiet now, the moans flood from me as I grip the door frame like a lifeline. I break apart, arching my back in an attempt to suffocate him. Something tells me this is Garrett's ideal way to go, consuming my cum as I shatter into a million pieces. I grow limp from the force of it, my forehead pressing against the wood. Vaguely, the fabric of my panties are eased up my legs and pulled high over my hips. I gasp at the tightness against my throbbing pussy, Garrett's clenched hands holding the straps in place.

"Wait, I thought..." I gasp, my mind catching up with me. They know I'm not a virgin. Surely these games no longer need to be played. Garrett chuckles, his jaw leaning on my head as he apparently reads my mind.

"Not yet, Peach. Not like this. I may not be bound by Dax's stupid pact any more, but I've waited this long. When the time comes for me and Axel to fucking destroy you for any other man, it'll be strung out over an entire day and night with intermittent naps. You'll wake to a cock sliding between these pretty lips and fall asleep with one buried deep inside of you." I shudder as Garrett's index finger brushes over my mouth and briefly dips inside. "When you go to bed tonight, I want you to touch yourself thinking about us."

"Okay," I breathe, my voice husky and eyes unfocused as I lean against him. "But I've taken to crawling into Huxley's bed when I'm lonely, so he might get the wrong idea." I'm spun so fast, if he wasn't holding me, I'd have toppled over. Axel moves for the crack of light to reappear over Garrett's face. His smile is so wide, so predatorial, I feel the physical burn within. I'm playing with fire. But then he kisses my neck and moves his mouth towards my ear.

"Let him."

CHAPTER TWENTY NINE

Slamming the door to the study closed, my chest heaves. The constant buzzing of my phone starts in my pocket again. I grab the device and toss it across the desk. Until tonight, I thought there was hope that my men were still with me. That their fascination with Avery was a passing fad. But not after they shut me in the room, held me back from teaching her a lesson. They defend her, protect her, hide her. They've chosen their side. After all these years, after all I've confided in them. Everyone chooses Avery in the end.

The vibrations of my cell quiet, and then start back almost immediately. I kick the sideboard before opening it, grabbing out a bottle of whiskey. I down a hefty amount before dropping into my leather chair and hitting the answer button, putting the call on speaker.

"What?" I growl.

"You'd better try that greeting again, boy," my father threatens. I can hear the clench in his jaw, but he rarely speaks to me without it these days.

"What, sir?" I drawl, mockery dripping from my tone. He huffs and I take another long drink.

"When I call, I expect you to answer. And when your sister is threatened, I expect to hear it from you. Not in passing conversation from Megan." Slamming the drink down, I frown at my phone. Why

199

the hell is my father speaking to Avery's best friend? Then I remember, I don't give a shit.

"She's not my sister," I mutter beneath my breath. I know it will spark another round of the same argument, so I quickly move on. There's only so much I can handle before a headache settles in. "Avery wasn't threatened. She was gifted a pair of damn socks. And trust me, she's got a comfortable little set up here in my house. She's untouchable." *Even from me*, I keep to myself.

"I'm not surprised you're not taking this seriously. Avery and your mother have been receiving messages from this *Mr. XO* for years. Any contact needs to be reported back to myself or our PI." A yawn pulls at my mouth, the tiredness I feel settling deep into my soul. I'm so tired with all of this bullshit. Avery is a pampered princess who the media have always been desperate to capture on camera. Of course she received interest from external sources; my mother and father effectively turned her into a hidden, untouchable treasure.

"If you're so concerned about her, why don't you move Avery into your New York penthouse? Or would your little whore have a problem sharing her sugar daddy?" There's a pause on the other end of the phone and I know I've shocked him.

"Wyatt. I'm warning you," the growl comes through the receiver. I prop my feet up on the desk and cross my ankles. I wish he could see me, the king of my own castle. Not the senseless rich boy I'm perceived to be. Information is power. Nixon has his PI, and I have mine. His affair started long before mom was killed. I bet that would rock Avery's perfect image of her perfect father figure.

"I told you I didn't want her here." I repeat like a broken record. Every phone call is the same.

"I also told you, I would cut your cash flow if you don't take care of her," my father quips back. I roll my eyes, swirling the whiskey around its bottle.

A sudden flare of loneliness hits me hard in the chest. Another reminder that no one, not even the Shadowed Souls, really knows me. My bestest friends in the entire world, the only family I really have, also believe I'm motivated by money. More often than not, I'm mulling over ways to disappear after graduation. Leave this life behind and start fresh, somewhere I can be who I really want to be. Respected for my degree, liked for my personality - not the size of my pockets.

The only plus side to being rich is that I've been able to fund Dax's schooling, remove Axel from his toxic mother, give Garrett the stability he craves and help Huxley become emancipated from his parents. They've got everything they need, everything they could want, and I've kept myself guarded in the process. When I eventually vanish overnight, they'll be glad they don't have to deal with my moods any more. Until then, we're all stuck in this misery together.

"Hire someone else. Send her somewhere else, but she can't stay at Waversea. I'm done being your lackey. You can't control me anymore." I push away from the table and pace the room. It's the first time I've dared to speak to my father this way, but I have no reason to keep up pretenses any more.

My brothers have chosen Avery. I no longer have a place in their day-to-day lives. My mom is dead. I no longer need to be the model son to parade around on camera while the real favorite child sat safely behind the mansion gates. Maybe I should be thanking her for freeing me from all of my roots, but I'd rather hate her for it. The bitterness tastes better alongside the whiskey pouring down my throat.

"It's the best place for her," my father sighs after a moment. "She's meant to be untouchable there." I pause mid-step and mid-swig at the defeat in his tone. Returning to the phone, I lean on the desk to hang over it.

"What's that supposed to mean?" A few beats pass for Nixon to clear the emotion from his voice.

"I'm passing through a nearby state in the next few days. You're on fall break now, I believe. Meet me for dinner and we'll talk in person." My head falls forward. It's on the tip of my tongue to say no fucking way, but something holds me back. My father is keeping something from me, and I need to know what it is. Secrets fester and destroy. I should know, I have one decaying me from the inside out. Sighing my acceptance, my father perks up. The joys of getting my submission, I suppose. "I'll text you the details. Oh and Wyatt, don't even think about not bringing Avery with you."

My phone shatters through the window before the line goes dead.

AVERY

CHAPTER THIRTY

I wake to a commotion beyond the door. Stretching out like a cat, I lean against the length of Huxley's body. A part of me came here last night to test Garrett's resolve. Would he seek me out? Want to keep watch? The answer to both is no, and without his recklessness to spur me on, I keep my hands firmly tucked beneath the pillow. Another round of shouting sounds from the hallway, feet running from one length to the other. I elbow Huxley in the ribs.

"But I don't want teeth like a walrus," he whines and I thump him again. He begins to stir when the door flies open. Wyatt leans in, keeping his eyes on the ceiling.

"We're traveling. Pack your shit. Cars leave in an hour." He leaves without looking at either of us, probably already discovering my bed empty and fearing what he'd find. The door is left open and I drag myself to sit upright against the headboard. I quickly discover the 'commotion' I heard is Garrett.

"Axel! Grab the toothbrushes. I'm on road-trip snacks!" He rushes by in a flurry, hugging a backpack to his chest. Axel strides by next, unhurried and sighing. His eyes are shadowed and I reckon the steaming mug in his hand is the only reason he's awake at all. He pauses mid-step, glancing over the room. "Ahh, fuck," he sighs again and turns his head towards the hallway. "Who's on Huxley duty?"

"I'll do it," Dax appears. I instantly melt at his warm smile, his muscles caged in a tight fitting t-shirt. He approaches, winks and rounds the bed. Axel also enters, handing me his coffee and pressing a kiss to my cheek. The fact I'm sitting in the same bed doesn't phase anyone. I sip and watch the pair pin down Huxley's arms before Dax shouts in his face.

"Hux! The bacon's burning!"

"I'm vegan!" Huxley jolts, his arms bucking against their hold. It takes a few seconds for his eyes to focus and breathing to relax enough for the others to let go. "Wait, I'm not vegan," he shakes his head and rolls his neck.

"But you are awake," Axel smirks. "Wyatt's ordered a road trip. You need an overnight bag, apparently." Dax heads over to Huxley's dresser, pulling out folded clothes and placing them on top. I marvel at the ease with which they all work together without need for words. They truly are family.

"Where are we going?" Huxley groans, laying back down.

"Your guess is as good as mine," Axel shrugs. "Nixon has requested his presence." I straighten, placing the empty mug on the bedside table. Axel returns to my side and sits next to my legs. "You too, little Swan." His fingers seek out mine, that need to be touched controlling his actions. My chest clenches.

"I'd rather stay here and watch this unfold," Huxley leans on one arm, smirking knowingly. A thin blush coats Axel cheeks, his hazel eyes slowly waking fully. Extracting myself from beneath the covers, I crawl into Axel's lap. All eyes fall to my small vest and shorts combo. In the mirror, I catch the light in my own eyes. My blonde hair is a bird's nest, but there's a smile spread wide across my face. I'm going to see Nixon. The ache of missing him hits me stronger than ever, spurring my feet to run through the opposite exit and start packing.

A short while later, we're bundling into the garage. Bags are thrown into the trunk, excitement thrumming through us. It's amazing what a change of scenery can do, even if none of us know where we're going. Wyatt enters last, purposely slamming his shoulder into mine. My strap is dislodged and he catches it, dragging the backpack away from me.

"Avery rides with me. The rest of you take the SUV." He grunts, tossing both of our bags into the back seat of his Nissan and deeming it out of use. I freeze, the rest of the Shadowed Souls creeping closer.

"No way. I'd rather be leashed and dragged along behind," I cross my arms. Wyatt scoffs.

"That can be arranged."

"Dude, you haven't wanted to be near her. I'll ride with you," Huxley attempts. His hand lightly wraps around my wrist as the weight of their anxiety settles on my shoulders. Wyatt waves off their concern, opening the passenger door. Grabbing my nape, he all but drags me into the seat. My skin burns beneath his touch. Wyatt is touching me.

Slamming the door closed, I peer out with huge puppy dog eyes. Wyatt's words are muffled, but no doubt delivering a threat alongside our destination. Four sets of eyes watch me longingly as Wyatt drops into the driver's seat and the car flies forward. I smack my forehead on the window.

"Why can't I ride with them?" I try not to sound whiny, and fail.

"Nixon was clear. You are to be at this dinner. Do you really trust them to not take you somewhere discrete and finally give in to the desire that's been destroying everything I've built? The battle of testosterone in my house is suffocating."

I exhale through my nose. *His* house. *His* rules. Grumbling, I pull my phone and headphones out my bag, curling up and keeping my back to Wyatt.

Me: You'll never guess what this asshole has just done.

Meg: I doubt it will surprise me, but go on…

I wake as the Nissan comes to a stop, the engine dying out. My ears ache from the headphones but I'm glad I managed to drift off. It saves sitting in awkward silence with unwanted company. Wyatt is already out of the car, slamming the door. I rub my eyes, groaning at the stiff neck I've acquired. He's staring at his phone in front of the gas station, waiting for me to peel myself from the car.

"Fill up. I'm going to stretch my legs," he jerks his head to the pump. There's an aura of annoyance around him, but for once it's not directed at me. I half-watch him constantly checking his phone, the tick in his jaw beating as he paces the gravel nearby. Finishing with filling up, I head into the small store and busy myself picking out snacks. A grin grows across my face as I pick out chili heatwave potato chips and jalapeño-infused jerky. The bottles of flavored water I pick out are solely for me. Paying, I exit with my blue carrier bag and smile sweetly when Wyatt returns.

"I got snacks." Shaking the bag, Wyatt's lips pinch as we re-enter the car. I couldn't sleep any more if I tried, too wired and more than a little bored of his company already. Instead, I link my phone up to the speakers and hit play on Theo's classical piano pieces.

I've put the thought of Theo being Mr. XO aside, after a basic online search showed he grew up in a rural part of Asia. His family relocated often and always to places off the grid. As a ten-year-old boy, I doubt sending me welcome letters to the Hughes household was at the top of his priority list.

Wyatt is easing the car out of the gas station when he skids to a stop. "Not a fucking chance," he dives across me for my phone. I purposely drop it down the side of my seat.

"It's for the showcase! Since I'm missing practice today, I need to play through the dances in my head." A lie. I know those dances back to front now, it's just a matter of perfecting the transitions. Something I can't do from the passenger seat while flying down a lengthy road with no civilization in sight, but it serves to irritate Wyatt. Sweeping a hand through his brown hair, he throws himself back in his seat and speeds onward. Being a good road-trip buddy, I pop open the potato chips and offer him one, keeping the packet concealed in the bag. Wyatt, not wanting to lose face, snatches it from me and stuffs it into his mouth. A moment later, the chewed remnants are spat all over the dashboard and the car briefly swerves.

"The fuck?! Drink!" Wyatt holds out his hand. I stare at it.

"Aww, I'm sorry. These drinks are only for people with manners." I keep the bag out of his reach. He's panting slightly, his cheeks turning red. Wow, Wyatt really doesn't handle spice well.

Suddenly, he turns the wheel and we fly onto the roadside, the tires kicking up a shitload of dust. I scream as he launches himself at me, forcing the plastic bag from my hand. His fingers are tightly gripping both of my wrists, his shoulder pushing me back into the seat. He takes the water and gulps it down. Anger festers within me as he drinks. Typical Wyatt, taking what his wants. Getting his own way.

Feeling helpless and trapped being a toxic combination, I lower my head and sink my teeth into his shoulder. Through the t-shirt, I bite as hard as I can, uncaring of the consequences. Wyatt is on me in a second, ripping his shoulder from my grip. Flicking a lever, the chair flips backwards and his chest is covering mine. His green eyes are on fire, mirroring the blazing sunlight coloring the sky outside. His breath comes in ragged puffs of air, a testament to his fury. The silence that follows is suffocating.

"You're the worst kind of person," I breathe out of need to break the tension. I'm choking on it, unable to inhale beneath his weight. Slowly, too slowly, Wyatt's hand comes between us and settles around my throat. I lie immobilized, too intrigued as to what he'll do to stop him.

After a beat, his grip begins to tighten. His emerald gaze doesn't leave mine for a moment, even as his thumb presses into the tender flutter of my pulse. He's not choking me, not yet. It's a warning, a promise of what could come. A shiver rolls through me, but the cold touch of fear doesn't follow. I swallow beneath the heat of his breath fanning my mouth. My hands subconsciously touch his ribs, faintly holding him in place. I want this. Wyatt touching me. An inch separates our lips and as much as my mind is screaming this is wrong, oh so wrong, it makes me want it all the more.

"Say it again," he growls, his voice barely above a whisper, but carrying an undeniable edge that makes it seem much louder in the stifling silence. "Remind me why this is the opposite of what I should be doing." I swallow hard, trying to suppress the tiny tremor in my voice.

"You're...the worst kind of person." I repeat. I can taste defiance in my mouth, dancing on the tip of my tongue with words that could ignite a wildfire. A ghost of a smile tugs at one corner of his lips, and there's something terrifyingly thrilling about the way it doesn't reach his eyes. Caution masks itself as fear, but I'm not scared. The glint in

Wyatt's eyes has never seemed steadier, and I've never been so sure he won't hurt me.

The silence stretches on again, warped by the strain of new territory between us. His figure looms over me; heavy and intimidating. And then, much to my surprise, Wyatt does something I didn't expect – he laughs. It's not a hearty laugh, nor a particularly delightful one - it's a broken chuckle filled with bitterness and disregard. It echoes inside the car before being carried away from existence.

"I've never pretended to be anything else," he remarks dryly, before he slowly unwinds his hand from around my throat and pushes himself off me. He moves back to his side of the vehicle, straightening himself up as if nothing happened. My heart is hammering in my chest.

"What the hell was that?!" I gasp, finding the lever to bring my seat back upright. Wyatt ignores me, staring forward but I refuse to drop it. "Hey, I'm talking to you. What just happened there?" Gripping Wyatt's arm, his head turns and those eyes consume me again. His pupils are blown, the intensity within not only from hatred. My lips part.

"Don't," he growls thickly. Skidding sounds come from behind and I spot the SUV in the rearview mirror. The emotion in Wyatt's features shuts down immediately, his hands gripping the wheel. My door is opened and I'm helped out by Dax.

"My turn to ride up front," he explains with a kind smile. "Garrett's whining is driving me crazy." Subtly, Dax turns my hips and nudges me in the direction of the vehicle waiting behind. I walk on numb legs, confused and conflicted. Huxley slides out of the driver's seat, a frown pinching his brows together. He looks over my throat and clenches his jaw.

"What the fuck did he do to you?" Trying to push past me, I gently place a hand on his chest. Huxley stills instantly.

"It's fine. I deserved it," I say. My voice is hollow and my eyes are looking into the distance until Huxley cups my cheeks, bringing my attention back to him.

"You never deserve it. You're innocent in all of this."

"Am I?" Huxley's chocolate eyes widen to match mine. Something about Wyatt's reaction has thrown my mind into turmoil. Something happened in that car and I have no idea what it was. Huxley guides me to the backseat where Garrett and Axel are waiting. I'm enveloped in their touch, cuddled from both sides. Huxley's gaze continues to drift to mine in the rear-view mirror, the frown tugging at the corners of my mouth remaining.

Hating Wyatt because he hates me is easy. But when he slips up and lets another emotion break through, I struggle to reflect it back. Especially when I don't know what that new emotion is.

AVERY

CHAPTER THIRTY ONE

We arrive at our hotel as the sky becomes blemished with rays of a muddy sunset. Perhaps my mood is dulling the colors, but I'm hardly focused. Garrett fell asleep on me hours ago, my shoulder long gone numb. Axel is lost to his own world, staring out of the window while tracing patterns over my hand and arm. Huxley glances at me often in the rearview mirror, his expression unreadable. I'm too trapped in my own mess of thoughts to be able to answer his scrutiny with reassurance.

"We'll stop here tonight. There's another six hours to go tomorrow. I've got the key cards," Wyatt says through the driver's open window as the vehicle comes to a halt. Huxley nods and steps out to attend to the bags, leaving me with Garrett drooling on my shoulder and Axel's absent-minded touches.

"I'm going to wake him," I whisper, nodding towards Garrett. I'm done with being stuffed in a car for today, heightened emotions and unspoken questions filling my head.

"Mmmhmm." Axel acknowledges, his eyes never leaving the sight of the hotel outside. There's something distant about him and my heart tugs that I don't feel comfortable enough yet to outright ask him. Maybe if I had realized sooner in the journey, I could have distracted him with some small talk. Patting Garrett's arm lightly, he snorts and grunts.

"Garrett. We're here."

"Ugh," Garrett blinks awake, rubbing his eyes and looking around blearily. He struggles upright, stifling a yawn with the back of his hand. Axel still doesn't move, lost in a world of his own. Garrett notices instantly.

"Hey Peach, would you mind attending to Dax?" Garrett gestures out of the window. Dax is leaning against the Nissan a few spaces down, a cigarette between his lips. "He only smokes when he's stressed. Riding with Wyatt must have been...interesting." He proceeds to crack open the door – a polite way of telling me to give him and Axel some space.

"Did I...do something?" The words float out of me before I realize there's concern churning in my chest. Garrett's eyes drop to my neck and return to my face so quickly, I feel the truth like a punch to my gut. The bruise growing on my throat has triggered something for Axel. Nodding, I maneuver myself over Garrett's lap and exit the SUV. I have no right to feel the ache at being excluded. Axel has his demons; I know that. As much as I know that Garrett is the best to deal with them.

Approaching the Nissan, I lean next to Dax and hold out my fingers. "May I?"

"You smoke?" he raises a brow.

"On days like this." I accept the cigarette and take a long drag. What I really want to say is, one summer I took a bad turn and Meg's friends hooked me up with a large amount of weed.

It followed the release of a new documentary made of my birth father and on a whim, a group of us thought it would be an interesting watch. Seeing how the media portrayed me was often comical; some rapunzel style character who got her happily ever after. But I hadn't been prepared for the amount of interviews this documentary featured. The amount of people involved, those who knew of the abuse I suffered and did nothing to save me. And then there was him. He gave graphic recounts of what he did to me from the safety of his jail cell. He was almost proud. The glee in his eyes as he described my sickening memories became a recurring nightmare I couldn't shake unless I was sated and high enough to empty out my mind.

Huxley returns, slightly breathless and juggling key cards. "You and Wyatt have rooms to yourselves, Dax and I, and Axel and Garrett will share," he explains, handing out the key cards before offering mine. "I figured you might need some time alone."

"What have I missed?" Dax frowns further. I stop myself from pushing the creases out from between his brows. I wish we could go back to this morning, where excitement was high and the day held so much potential. I'm not sure being alone is what I need, but I also have no words to offer for otherwise.

"Nothing. Let's head in for the night." I shoulder my bag and walk through the hotel's lobby, although sleep is far from my mind. I'm still reeling from the interaction with Wyatt earlier today, and everything else seems insignificant.

For a roadside hotel in a small town, the floors are shiny and polished, a scent of lemon cleanliness in the air. Potted plants line the walls, adding a touch of greenery to the otherwise beige space. The front desk is tall and wooden, and there are flushed sofas and armchairs scattered around for guests to relax in. It's more than pleasant.

Our rooms are all located down the same hallway, five floors up from reception. I opt for the stairs, eager to avoid any awkward silences such as the cramped elevator ride. Garrett and Axel spill out of the elevator at the same time as I emerge. The smirks back in full force, as if there's a naughty joke only the pair of them are in on.

"If you need tiring out later, we'll be awake. Just give us a little time first." Garrett gives me a lazy wink before disappearing into their door with Axel trailing behind him. His head is down, the image of submission. Dax and Wyatt enter their rooms, leaving me alone with Huxley who's leaning against the wall with his arms crossed over his chest.

"You should've let me go after Wyatt," he says eventually. There's a quiet anger simmering in his voice that makes me shift uncomfortably on my feet. My stomach slowly turns to lead.

"He didn't hurt me. Not really," I counter, rubbing my throat subconsciously.

"It doesn't matter." Huxley pushes himself off from the wall and edges closer to me, his face taut with tension. "You don't have to protect him."

"I'm not protecting him," I retort quickly, too quickly perhaps because Huxley raises an eyebrow at me.

"You sure about that?" Before I can respond, Dax pops his head out of their room.

"Hey, I'm ordering room service. Come choose what you want." Piercing blue eyes land on me, set alight by the contrast of his tanned skin. His blonde afro is starting to grow out and I imagine what it might look like long, and if I have enough influence over Dax for him not to cut it. By his willing gaze, I know I do. "You feel like joining us for dinner?" I smile kindly, my heart fluttering the way it always does for Dax. Whoever said good guys finish last didn't meet him.

"I'm good," I reply regretfully. I'm not in the frame of mind, and if I allow him to, Dax would do whatever it takes to fix my sour mood. As it stands, I need time alone to mull over things.

Letting myself into my room, I find my bag already on my bed. Digging through the pockets, I realize too late that my phone is still lost in Wyatt's car. I guess Meg won't be talking me down from the ledge of stupid ideas tonight. Instead, I strip and shower, standing beneath the scolding spray until my skin is a vibrant shade of red. With a towel fixed around my bust and my hair clipped high up on my head, I spot the mini bar. Fuck yes.

If you've ever wondered how many tiny wine bottles it takes to get tipsy enough to confront your broody stepbrother, the answer is all of them.

My knuckles rap on the door, my back straight with confidence. I'm doing this. When an answer doesn't immediately come and I worry about being caught at Wyatt's door, I knock again. *Harder.*

"I swear, Garrett, if you ask me for a threesome one more time, I'll-" Wyatt swings the door open and stills. He's briefly distracted by the wet patches which have dripped from my hair onto my t-shirt. I sway slightly, a silly smile on my face as I mentally praise myself for putting a bra back on. The short shorts may have been too much. "What are you doing here?"

"I want to talk."

"Then call your therapist." Wyatt attempts to shut me out but my foot is already in the door jamb. Raising a brow, I stand my ground.

"I can cause a scene out here if you'd prefer." Currently, there is no one else in the hallway. No one to see me entering Wyatt's room when he sighs and strides away. A thrill of trepidation filters through my chest. I close the door with my back, taking a steadying breath. I'm in the viper's nest. A place I've avoided for so many years, and built up into something I thought I should fear. Now I've jumped the first hurdle, I blink rapidly to clear my vision.

Wyatt sits on the window sill, putting as much distance between us as possible. Looking out at the night's sky, pierced by lit buildings, the shadows cling to him. I shake my head, my brain sloshing against the sides of my skull. It doesn't help. The darkness shrouds him, like the grim reaper. Or maybe just someone who's so incredibly lonely. He's the eye of the storm. Surrounded by the whirlwind of his reputation, yet inside, he's still sad and all alone.

I spot my phone on his bedside table. Jolting forward, I trip on the leg of a desk and the world tilts. I hear the thud on the floor more than I feel it, and steadily drag myself to the bed. Flopping onto it, I reach for my phone but the battery is dead and my head is starting to swim anyway. Trying to drunk text Meg would have only served to bring on my headache sooner. The whole time, Wyatt says nothing. I roll over on his bed, laying my head on my arm.

"Do you want to screw me or something?" I blurt. Wyatt's head whips to me, his green eyes ablaze. I twist my lips. "Something happened in that car. If you wanted to hurt me, kill me, dump my body on the side of the road, you had your chance. But you didn't, and I can't understand why."

Wow, that was much easier than I thought. Hours of confusion all summed up in one drunken babble. I knew this was a fantastic idea. Wyatt, with his jaw tight enough to crack and hands fisted, doesn't seem to agree.

"Not everyone wants to screw you, Avery," he says my name without the usual disdain. Exhaling, his hand is released from its clench and he returns to look out of the window. "I'd rather cut my fucking dick off than touch you with it."

I make a hum in my throat and roll onto my back. Staring at the ceiling, I sigh. I came here for answers, but it's clear I'm not going to get them. I'm stuck, stuttering over the same thoughts.

Somewhere along the way, Wyatt's perception of me has become part of my persona. I'm the charity case. Adopted and hidden away. Sometimes I think if Cathy wanted a companion for when she was home from filming, she probably should have just gotten a cat.

"I don't know how to do this," I mutter.

"It's easy," Wyatt turns to face me, his elbows resting on his thighs. My head rolls to the side to watch him. "Whenever you get sentimental over time lost, remember that you destroyed my childhood. You've taken everyone I thought cared about me, and now you rock up in here asking if I want to screw you?! Stop looking for something that isn't there, and get the fuck out of my room."

And there it is. What I wanted...right? My body sets alight with fury and my delayed brain decides I wanted answers, but apparently not that one.

"Oh, change the fucking record, Wyatt!" I sit up way too fast and bile rises in my throat. "It's not my fault you didn't get enough of mommy's hugs as a child. It's not my fault you were so easily replaceable!" I scream. Wyatt visibly flinches. I gasp through my hoarse throat. That wasn't my imagination, I saw the pinch of his brows, the look of pure despair break through before he locked it back down. Climbing off the bed, I approach him in a flurry of babbling.

"Shit. No, I'm sorry. I take that all back." My hands hesitate from touching his arms. The weight of regret on my shoulders threatens to buckle my knees. I can't stoop to his level. I can't end up like him, hating for no reason. Wyatt's head is turned slightly, his sunken green eyes staring at the wall. He's waiting for me to retreat, to leave like he's asked. But fuck it, I've come this far.

Pushing him back against the window, I jump into his lap and wind my arms around his head. I hold Wyatt against me, consumed by every inch of his heat seeping into my body. What was it Huxley once said about forbidden fruit?

"Get off me," Wyatt growls but makes no move to remove me from his lap. I bury my head lower into his neck, my arms tightening.

"No."

"Avery, I'm warning you." I inhale his expensive cologne and slip from the reality, and the timid girl, I once knew.

"I don't care. Do your worst."

Wyatt moves so fast, a shriek escapes me. His arms crush me into him, all sense of gravity failing me. My back hits the wall, trapped beneath his muscle. Unable to touch the floor with my tiptoes, I wind my legs around his waist on instinct, and Wyatt's hands on my thighs hold me there. Shorts were a terrible choice, after all. My core clenches.

"Wyatt," I say too breathlessly. He refuses to look at me.

"I can't have you like this." His reply is spoken directly into my ear. I phase in and out, bringing a hand between us to trace the ink at his collar bone. It dips into the neck of his t-shirt, barring me once again from seeing the full tattoo. Fuck, I want to know what it is so bad. "I'm not allowed to have you like this." Despite his words, Wyatt's thumbs stroke my thighs. The belt on his jeans pushes against my center, giving me a false perception. I've had this dream; Garrett has all but forced it upon me.

Grabbing a handful of messy brown hair, I drag Wyatt's head back to look at me. The hatred is still present in his green glare, but there's more there. I can see it clearly now. His full lips are pressed together, his jaw ticking, but he's not withdrawing.

"This..." Wyatt looks over my face. There's no indication of him liking what he sees, but it strikes me fiercely with how much I want him to. "This will never happen again." His hands retract as quickly as they lifted me. I drop to the floor, evidently sliding down his body. My hands don't get the memo as they settle on his hips and my head presses against his chest. A harsh pounding beats against my ear, causing me to smile. Well, look at that. Wyatt has a heart after all.

Everything from then on is a blur. The punishing grip on my wrist, the room spinning. My bare feet grace the rough carpet of the hallway, a loud banging causing me to wince. Words float through the air as I'm thrown forward into another hard body.

"Deal with your mutt."

Arms envelop me, just as muscled and firm as the last. Dax places a finger beneath my chin, bringing my face up to meet his.

"Oh, what did you do, Swan?" His piercing blue eyes are an anchor to the storm I got swept into. I was so close to breaching the center, to seeing Wyatt's true intentions. On reflection, I didn't need to see it. I felt it. The biggest grin spreads across my face as I sway into Dax's hold.

"I got answers."

Avery

CHAPTER THIRTY TWO

I haven't seen Wyatt all day. Well, to be honest, I've barely seen anyone beyond the silhouettes through my cracked eyelids, passing me meds and water while we traveled the last leg of the journey. I spent most of the car ride spread across Dax's lap with an eye mask on. To my credit, I only threw up on him once. Without him caring for me, there's no way I would currently be sitting upright in this busy restaurant, just about ready to stomach food.

The restaurant is in the heart of a bustling city, and thankfully is packed tonight. Every table is filled with smartly dressed people of all ages, chatting and laughing over their meals. Amongst the masses, and given the table's position off to the side, I'm visibly invisible to all who don't know I'm there. Servers rush back and forth from the open kitchen, balancing plates of steaming food on their trays. The chefs work at a furious pace, and I welcome the distraction whilst wringing my hands in my lap.

"Darling," Nixon's voice rings out amongst the clinking of cutlery and noisy chatter. I smile at my adoptive father, standing to accept his hug. His salt and pepper hair is pushed back and his blue eyes hold a startling amount of clarity for his age. The waistcoat of his three-piece suit rubs against my cheek as our embrace lasts a few more desperate seconds, then I'm swiftly ushered back into the high bench seat. Nixon opts for his back to the door, his neck slightly hunched as if trying to shrink into the cushion.

With less caution and a whole load of new curiosity, I settle back in my comfortable jumpsuit. Sea blue and cinched at my waist by a fabric belt, the floaty material swishes around my legs. There's a teardrop cutout in the bust, held in place by a halter-neck strap. Around my neck, I've taken great care in applying concealer to hide the faint bruising that lingered.

"You look beautiful." Nixon attempts a smile. It falls flat. "Where is your brother?" I use the distraction of a waiter taking our drink order to hide my blush. Especially after last night, I don't want to think of Wyatt as my brother ever again.

"He'll be here soon," I attempt to answer casually. As I meet Nixon's searching gaze, I can only hope my voice doesn't betray the fluttering sensation in my stomach. The sound of Wyatt's words play on repeat in my mind, his searing green gaze as heated as the touch that had lingered on my skin.

I'm not allowed to have you like this.

"So, how is business?" I ask after clearing my throat. A feeble effort for some normality, but Nixon isn't truly present. His eyes are darting everywhere, looking at everyone who passes. In the dimmed lighting at the back of the restaurant, his skin appears gaunt, cheeks slightly hollowed.

"Business is as fine as it can be," Nixon responds, his gaze sweeping back to me. His smile is tainted with a hint of melancholy that had not been there a minute ago. "You know how cutthroat the corporate world is. But enough of that, tell me all about your schooling. Have you made some good friends?"

Opening my mouth, I close it again. My gaze travels over Nixon's shoulder, over the booth's high back. And there he is. Wyatt confidently navigates through the restaurant as if he owns the place. Brown hair gelled back, sharp jaw freshly shaven. The black ink swirls around his open top button. Deftly unhooking his jacket button with one hand as he walks, Wyatt slips into the role of the millionaire's son with ease. This is why he was always asked to attend the award ceremonies and charity events. Being a cocky, charming bastard is second nature to him.

"Father," Wyatt holds out a sharp hand. Nixon stands and shakes it, briefly patting his son on the shoulder. Seats are taken and I hold my breath, tightly pressing my ankles together beneath the table. Wyatt's attention stays on Nixon, not bothering to even acknowledge my presence. "Did I interrupt anything?"

"Avery was just about to tell me how school is," Nixon nods for me to continue.

"Um, yeah. It's good, I suppose." I sip my water. I hadn't planned to get to the point so quickly, but the opportunity has presented itself earlier than expected. "But I really think I would be much better off returning to the manor. There are so many...distractions at Waversea. My education isn't progressing anywhere nearly as quickly as it did with the tutors. And then there's Counselor Lorna who doesn't know anything about me and I have reason to question her client confidentiality."

I shoot Wyatt a look but he's only interested in the menu. Lowering my gaze to my own, I quickly decide I can't stomach any of these rich dishes. Soup it is.

"You're in the right place, Avery." Nixon states, leaving no room for argument. Clearly he forgets how headstrong I can be.

"Can this be open for discussion?" The waiter approaches again, delivering our drinks and producing a small tablet in his hand. Wyatt asks for a whiskey, to which Nixon swiftly says no. Instead, he orders a bottle of red wine and my stomach rolls. Chewing on the inside of my cheek, I order my soup and wait for him to leave before placing a hand on Nixon's arm.

"Please Nixon. I spent a long time carefully constructing a cage around myself in the manor. It's where I feel safest." I try once more with a gentler tone. Nixon's blue eyes soften, his hand covering mine. I know from the small incline of his head, I've got him.

Sure, I'd miss the guys, but their fleeting interest in me hasn't changed anything. I'm a shiny new toy, something to play with. I still envision a future for myself where I can work from the study, dance in the ballroom, and be in total control of who enters my life and when. Besides, they could visit, if they wanted to.

"That's a shame," Wyatt comments, the hint of a smile at the corner of his mouth. "You're supposed to be the prima ballerina at the Winter Showcase."

"Oh, that's wonderful news!" Nixon releases my hand and his posture instantly straightens. The smile he gives is one full of pride. "You'll have to let me know the date. I wouldn't miss my little girl's first public performance for the world." The scowl I give Wyatt should be enough to set his hair on fire. Starters are served; Wyatt's smelling so strongly of fish, I know he's toying with me. I chew on a bread roll, trying to ease myself out of the remnants of my hangover. Once Nixon has poured and drank half a glass of wine, I huff and try again.

"*Please Nixon.*" I try again, tucking my long blonde hair behind my ear and lean in closer. "I don't...I would feel safer at the manor. Let me return home."

"I'm afraid that's not an option," he shakes his head. I feel the anger tears building up behind my eyes. "You're not to return to the manor. Not even for Thanksgiving break."

"What? Why?!" My cheeks redden at the attention I attract and I quickly lower my voice. "I was planning to catch a flight in the morning and spend the break with Meg." I turn whiny and I don't care. Dropping my bread roll onto the plate, I cross my arms. I can't understand why Nixon is punishing me like this. Wyatt is there with a quip to seal the deal.

"I'm sure you and Meg had some more of those wild parties planned. What was it you mentioned about screwing guys in my bed?" His face cracks into the most cunning grin, while my eyes prepare to pop out of my head. Nixon has gone still, his wine glass halfway to his mouth. The waiter who comes to retrieve our small plates cleverly does so without making any fuss. The restaurant is buzzing with noise, whereas our table couldn't be more silent. Finally breaking the tension, Nixon moves on.

"The manor is having renovations done." He eyes myself and Wyatt in turn. Wyatt's smile falls away, his eyes narrowing. "There is asbestos within some of the walls and ceilings. I've commissioned a full repair to clear it out. Neither of you are to return there until I tell you it is safe to do so."

"Why are we here?" Wyatt suddenly interjects, his face tight and body turned towards Nixon. I shrink back, feeling like a fly on the wall. I've heard of the screaming matches the two of them can have, but usually only from Nixon's end of the phone call. I can only imagine how venomous Wyatt can be when the mood strikes.

"It's important that we talk. There are matters the three of us must discuss." Nixon swallows hard and it's the sight of his nervousness which causes my stomach to twist.

"Out with it then," Wyatt rolls his eyes. If I could pulverize him with my stare, I would. Nixon doesn't have the same notion, his head lowering for his hushed tone to be lost beneath the restaurant's clamor.

"It mustn't have gone unnoticed that I've been distant lately," Nixon begins. Wyatt snorts and I kick him under the table. "After Cathy's death, I started receiving...letters. Threats. And there were photos."

"What kind of photos?" I frown. Nixon touches his jacket, as if those very images are burning a hole through the cashmere, but he doesn't remove them.

"Pictures from the crash. Angles I haven't seen in any of the police reports. I believe they were taken before."

"Before the police showed up? What are you saying?" I shake my head. The ground is slipping away beneath me and when I look around the table, I have nothing to cling onto. Not the man delivering me news he's kept hidden, and definitely not the younger man who's gripping his knife too tightly. A shrill ring bursts from Nixon's pocket, and he promptly excuses himself to take it. More like rushes out of the booth and slips into the back of the restaurant.

"What is he saying?" I ask Wyatt, expecting some sort of answer. In the spiraling confusion, I'd forgotten how much of an asshole he is.

"Don't tell me you nearly fell for that?" He chortles, reaching for his wine but I saw the effort it took to unfurl his fingers from around his butter knife. How white his knuckles were before they disappeared until the table. "Nixon has other interests, and he's willing to create any fiction in which to make himself feel better."

I blink once, my brows raised. Wyatt searches for patience on the ceiling and finds none.

"He's got someone else, you moron. He's moved on, probably even before my mom died, and now he's palmed you off onto me so he can run away into the sunset. He's always been a selfish bastard obsessed with appearances. He wanted to be the charitable foster parent, and when the novelty wore off, he found another focus." Spearing a piece of his fish, Wyatt pops it in his mouth and chuckles to himself. "You really can't keep anyone's attention for long, can you?"

I sit back, opting to tap my foot in irritation rather than launch myself across the table and gauge Wyatt's eyes out. No one so cruel should have eyes so beautiful. My jaw aches with the telltale sign that I might cry, so I push all emotion aside. Wyatt will not get the satisfaction of seeing me hurt.

"What the hell is your problem?" I whisper-shout across the table. "You say I'm this terrible burden in your life, yet you've done everything to ensure Nixon won't let me go home. I don't care who he has or what he's doing, I just want to leave you as far behind as possible." Wyatt rests his elbows on the table, his shirt sleeves stretching against his biceps. He's so brutally handsome, it's hard to look at him.

"Nixon was never going to change his mind, although it is comical watching you try. I figured I'd knock you down from your Golden Girl pedestal instead." Wyatt's shoulder raises in a shrug as he drinks from his glass. His throat bobs, his fingers toying with the glass's stem when it touches back down on the table. All the things I don't want to notice, and shouldn't, I do. "You're not the only one who can fuck with people's heads."

A small laugh bubbles from me. Oh, so this is a twisted type of punishment. I want to leave Waversea, and as much as Wyatt wants the same, he's willing to suffer at my expense.

"This isn't part of the twisted game you like to play." I retort, my eyes rolling as I cross my arms again. "This is my life." Wyatt continues to toy with the glass stem, his gaze flickering between the wine and me. He smirks, but there's no kindness behind it.

"Isn't this life we've been thrown into together just one grand circus act? Sure feels like it most of the time." I frown at him across the table. Around us, one table starts singing happy birthday and a round of cheering follows, glasses clinking, hands clapping. At our table, it's more akin to a funeral. Death glares and unspoken words. Nixon reappears in a flurry, his eyes wild and cheeks puffed out.

"I'm sorry, I have to go. It's urgent." Collecting his jacket from the chair, he hastily puts it on.

"Already? We didn't even get to catch up properly." I stand, trying to still his arms. He drags me into a quick hug and presses a kiss to my head.

"I know, darling. Stay and enjoy the meal. It's nice to see the two of you together for a change." There's a sudden feeling of churning in the pit of my stomach.

"Wait, what about Thanksgiving Fest?" I complain. Fuck, I'm really coming off like a whiny bitch, but I can't help it. Thanksgiving Fest is an annual tradition for the Hughes' to celebrate their staff. Every year has a different theme and is outsourced from external companies to give every employee at the manor a lavish night off. Mom always planned it months in advance, meaning this is the last time we would get to enjoy one of her dinners together. My last chance to feel like she's still with us in spirit.

Nixon simply shakes his head. Wyatt steps forward and takes his turn to be stonewalled.

"You were supposed to be explaining some invisible threat of Avery's that I was supposed to care about. Not running back to your-."

"Shut your damn mouth, Wyatt," Nixon spits so harshly, I flinch. All of the tension around our table rushes into Nixon's posture, the worry in his blue eyes turning glacial. I reckon if we weren't in public, he'd have throttled Wyatt and thrown him across the room. "I expect you to take Avery's safety seriously. Her wellbeing is paramount. Do you understand?" Nixon's voice drops to a threatening level. Wyatt doesn't miss a beat, his eyes narrowing once more.

"What aren't you telling us?"

Nixon's phone rings in his pocket again. There's only time for him to throw me one more sympathetic look before he leaves, leaving us staring after him. I follow several steps into the main restaurant, watching his dash through the tables. Not to the main entrance, but off to the side and out of sight. At the restaurant's exterior, a crowd of paparazzi have gathered, flashes capturing a celebrity who is entering. The noise is deafening in the short time the door is open, a phrase leaking through. *Look, it's the Hughes siblings!*

I quickly spin and duck into the booth, keeping my back to those now spilling across the restaurant's window front. Security do their best to usher them along, but the cameras keep flashing and my head starts to pound. There has never been a photo of myself and Wyatt together in any tabloids. No proof we have ever stepped into each other's lives really.

The waiter returns, placing three meals before us. Wyatt is back in his seat, fully focused on his steak salad and intent on ignoring me. What's new? I sink lower, a mixture of emotions clashing within my chest when a hand touches my shoulder. I flinch for the second time as a row of figures appear at the table. The four of them have opted for less formal clothes, slacks and fitted t-shirts or sweaters. My mouth waters more than it has done all evening.

"Sorry to impose," Huxley brushes his thumb over my bare shoulder, "but we've been sitting at a table in the back and saw Nixon leave."

"And we figured you might prefer some more enlightening company," Dax adds, eyeing Wyatt who's now ignoring everyone. It must be a really good salad. As the others nudge me to shimmy around the table, Garrett drops into Nixon's empty space and picks up the knife and fork.

"And it's a huge shame to waste such good food." He's already shoveling dauphinois potatoes into his mouth and eyeing up my bread basket. "You gonna eat that?" I push both of my bowls over to him and sigh.

"Can we just get out of here? It seems totally pointless coming all this way for nothing."

"Not for nothing," Axel leans over to speak in my ear. His hazel eyes are alight with mischief, a small smile on his lips. He strokes my arm languidly, instantly melting my insides. "We spotted a club down the road. Silk and Satin," his brows bob playfully.

"What kind of club is called Silk and Satin?" I snort. Garrett's grin grows.

"A sex club," he announces around a mouthful and loudly enough for anyone nearby to hear. Wyatt falls deathly still, his focus centered on the tablecloth. Pushing my bowl of soup back towards me, Garrett winks. "Eat up. You'll need some energy."

GARRETT

CHAPTER THIRTY THREE

My fingers twitch with giddiness. Hux went ahead to make sure we could leave the restaurant and enter Silk and Satin via back exits to avoid the cameras. I was more than surprised to see Wyatt tagging along at the back of our small group.

Listening to the orientation speech by Trixie, the receptionist, I can't help but gravitate to put myself between Avery and Axel. I was supposed to be pulling back, leaving them to it by now, but I can't bring myself to miss an opportunity like this. Selfish bastard I am and all that.

"Once you're inside, you'll find a bar on your right. We encourage you to open a tab; staying hydrated is key. Feel free to wander around and look at all of the rooms before deciding where you'd like to start. Every room has a discrete viewing area which can't be seen from inside. Please familiarize yourself with the color-coded wristbands throughout the club. We use colors to gauge whether you're here to play or watch. Consent and protection is imperative at all times. Make sure to discuss your safe words. There will be staff members throughout if you have any specific preferences which aren't already accommodated for." Trixie finishes up.

Wyatt is strung so tightly, she mistakes his glare for interest. Trixie winks his way, then permits us into the main club beyond an electronic barrier. We find small baskets lined across the bar, holding a multitude of condoms in various sizes and rubber wristbands in a range of colors.

Wyatt puts his card behind the bar for us all as I pick out two baby pink bands for Avery and Axel. *Pink means Play*, the poster on the wooden surface states. *White means Watching*. There are more colors, for those who have come alone and are open to any partner, as well as those for dominance and submission.

Wyatt passes out shots, a strangled curse on his lips as he downs his. Something along the lines of 'what the fuck am I doing here?' I'd provide him with the answer but I don't think he's ready to hear it. Avery quickly follows suit, then grabs my hand and squeezes it tight.

"Let's get you out of that modest jumpsuit," I say into her ear. Beyond her head of golden hair, I spot the sign for the dressing rooms. Inside, rows of outfits have been hung for every sexual fantasy. My eyes fall on the one I want immediately and I lift it from the hook.

"No way. Seriously, out of all these choices, Garrett?!" Avery starts backing up and bumps into Axel's firm chest. I raise my arm, flashing my wristband and Axel, as usual, instantly understands.

"Do as he says. He's our master tonight." Circling my wrist is a rubber band in Dark Purple, announcing me as the Dominant tonight. Well, every night but that's beside the point. Avery takes a beat to comply, dropping her head and taking the hanger from me. I catch her chin as she tries to pass, turning her head to look at me.

"Surrender control to me, Peach. I'll show how refreshing it is." My heart skips a beat as those huge, blue eyes blink up at me. So pure and innocent. So fucking willing. I release Avery before I give into the voice in my head and take her right here and now, turning my attention to Axel. "Your turn."

We emerge into the dimly-lit foyer. Myself, Avery in a skimpy ballerina's leotard, crotchless and complete with tutu, and Axel topless in loose fitting trousers which are already tented. Around both of their necks, matching black collars are connected to the leash in my hand. The power thrumming through my veins is a heady feeling I won't tire of anytime soon.

"Aren't they perfect?" I grin, presenting my new pets to my closest friends and brimming with smugness. Everyone in the vicinity wants Avery, and there's something to be said for diving in at the deep end.

Dax takes in Avery's lithe body, her nipples puckered against the thin fabric, her cheeks twinged with a flush. Huxley openly appreciates both of them, his chocolate eyes hungry and lustful. Reaching for the small baskets, he puts back the white band and dons a pink. I smirk, resisting from calling him a good boy.

From his stool at the bar, Wyatt tries to hide his interest, and fails. His hooded gaze floats back to Avery's face, his breathing shallow. Turning back before anyone notices his mask has slipped, his hand sneaks out and he grabs the white band Huxley just put back. I chuckle, walking away.

Behind an unassuming door, the main hall is divided between glass windows with benches and portraits of naked figures debasing each other. I make a mental note to find out who the artist is, planning on having my own commissioned. The sound of moans and low chatter greets us as we step inside, hit by a wave of warm, moist air heavy with lust and sweat.

We pass the windows, peering into the rooms with interest. Each is a different scenario, fully equipped with toys, restraints and the likes. Every once in a while, we'll pass a window restricted by black curtains pulled around the benches. If the light above is green, we're able to peer in. If it's red, there is a private show happening which we can't interrupt. I still in front of an empty room depicting a standard classroom. My grin is wide enough to ache. It's perfect.

"Ready?" I purr into the hollow of Avery's neck while she looks on.

"As I'll ever be," she exhales. I raise a brow and she quickly ducks her head. "I mean...yes Garrett." I bite my bottom lip to stifle a moan. Usually, I'd opt for a different name. Something to make me forget who I am and how I came to be like this, but when Avery says my name, it's pure sin. I shoot a sideways glance at Axel for his compliance. He is already scanning the room with bright eyes.

An employee steps forward to unlock the door for us while Dax draws the black curtains around the bench. Wyatt slams his fist onto the button on the wall, switching it to red. Then, he leans against the wall facing the curtain, acting as if he's not going to watch. I know him better than that.

"You not coming?" I ask Huxley when he lowers onto the bench. His mouth hitches in a smirk at the double meaning to my words.

"I'll have my turn with Avery when you've finished with her." Her sharp intake of breath sounds as I laugh.

"I'll try not to wring her of pleasure completely, but I can't make any promises." The door locks behind us as I unhook their leashes and pull Avery into my arms.

"Axel. Sit." He obeys in my peripheral. Beyond Axel and the classroom set-up, the darkened glass has been made to look like a chalkboard. There's nothing to see but the dim reflection of myself peering back while Avery patiently waits for her command. Her breathing is ragged, her chest pressed close. I can't deny those huge pleading eyes, or our audience.

Grabbing either side of Avery's face, I drag her in for an explosive kiss. She's frantic, crazed with the need to touch me. Fingernails drag down my chest, her breaths coming in short pants between my lips. She chases my tongue across her lips, and in turn, I swallow her contented moans. She's more than ready, the timing couldn't be any more perfect.

Sliding my hands into her hair, I hold her tightly in place. There won't be a single movement in this room that isn't ordered or overseen by me. When her urgency becomes too frenzied, I drag Avery's head back.

"Your safe word is *'brother'*," I whisper. "Although depending on the context, I might think you're begging for a certain someone to come join us."

"Asshole," Avery tries to turn her head away to hide her blush. I don't allow her to.

"Watch that sassy mouth of yours. I'm in control here, and I might decide you deserve punishing."

I lead Avery to the teacher's desk, skirt swirling around her thighs. Her willingness makes me instantly hard, her barely concealed arousal intoxicating. Sitting her on the edge, I push her to lie back and follow. My mouth traces heated kisses across her throat and jaw. "Lift your skirt," I growl in her ear. She does so without hesitation, revealing her glistening cunt. Even I have to stand back and appreciate the view for a moment.

Gripping her hips, I position Avery's legs over the desk's corner, making sure she's splayed open for those viewing through the blackboard. The only person I can hear is Axel as he palms himself through his trousers, his eyes glued to the place where my fingers spread Avery open.

"Axel, be a good boy and feast on our Little Swan until I tell you to stop."

He doesn't need to be told twice, his tongue lapping at her entrance with enthusiasm as I watch. His cock strains against his pants, seeking release even though we both know it won't happen until Avery's at least two orgasms deep. Pulling up a chair, I alternate between lazily circling two fingers around her clit and muttering in her ear.

"It goes without saying, you can't come until I tell you to." She whimpers. Axel isn't going easy on her, causing her back to arch and hands to grip the desk's edge. "Do you think Wyatt is watching Axel eat your cunt, Peach?" I whisper. Her eyes scrunch closed. "Na ah, open those beautiful eyes. You'll want to be present for every second. How else are you going to dream about me dominating you every night?"

Her moans are music to my ears, and I have to adjust my cock in my jeans to avoid giving into the urge to take her right then and there.

"Look at me," I command. Avery responds immediately, turning her head to stare into my eyes. She barely so much as blinks while I stroke the hair aside from her beautiful face. I drink in the way her brows pinch, her nostrils flare. She's a gorgeous girl, but like this? She's fucking stunning. I watch her writhe, battling against her own will and the control I've set.

When her whimpers become more frequent and high pitched, I turn my attention to Axel. "Take out your dick," I order. "Stroke yourself to the beat of Avery's moans. When she stops, you stop." Axel complies, dipping his head back between her thighs. I can tell he's picked up his pace by the sounds filtering through the room. Raising his free hand, hazel eyes peer up at me for permission. I nod once. Axel pushes at least two fingers into Avery from her shocked gasp. I take pity on her nipples, straining for attention and draw patterns over them in turn.

Within moments, Avery screams a mixture of mine and Axel's names, shuddering around his tongue and fingers. Axel looks up with hooded eyes, stilling the hold on himself despite the precum pooling at the tip. He looks pained and I pout for him.

"Tsk, tsk. I didn't give you permission to come, Peach. Poor Axel has to wait longer now. Turn onto your stomach." I give her thigh a push when she remains panting on her back. Slowly, Avery flops onto her side and then her front, the tutu sticking up in the air. Gripping the crotch hole, I tear them open to reveal her perfect ass. Laying across a nearby desk, amongst an assortment of sex toys, I pick out a ruler. It's made of bamboo, thirty centimeters long and fitting with the theme. I hand it to Axel.

"You can spank her as many times as you see fit for stealing your pleasure." Axel's eyes darken. This is where his true pleasures lie. Sweet, gentle Axel who seeks comfort in the form of simple touches. But when he's given the chance to release his true desires, another side of him comes to life.

I nod at Axel, giving him permission to begin. Running his fingers along the smooth wood, he brushes the wood over Avery's ass. A soft stroke, a hint of what is to come. Avery wriggles in anticipation. I'm considering tying her down when Axel raises the ruler and brings it down with a sharp crack on the edge of the desk. Avery cries out, her body jolting at the sound, but no mark blemishes her skin.

"Not her." Axel shakes his head, dropping the ruler to the floor. My brows shoot into my dark hair.

This isn't the first time Axel and I have played this game, where he puts me in control of how much punishment he can dish out. When a teenage boy has his consent and control taken away by his mother's friends, he doesn't stand a chance at ever enjoying normal sex again. It started as a ruse, and at first, I was barely involved. I was merely on hand in case Axel ever lost touch on reality and needed me to reel him back. Then, it evolved into more. But today is the first time he's refrained from exorcising his demons.

"Okay," I concede. Axel's shoulders relax but there's still the issue of Avery disobeying my command. My hand spanks her ass so quickly, no one in or outside of the room could have seen it coming. I kneel next to Avery, caressing the red handprint burning into her flesh. She flinches but soon relaxes into my touch.

"You're lucky Axel is taking pity on you tonight. I'd have let him go twenty lashes if that's what he needed." Avery's eyes widen, although they remain unfocused. I look over at Axel, his chest heaving and hazel eyes wild. He can't go much longer without a release. This time when I lay my hand on Avery, it's what I'd consider a love tap.

"Push up onto your forearms and tuck your knees beneath yourself.

Ass up for me." Avery complies, the lust filling her blue gaze once again. Remaining beside her head, I take a foil packet out of my pocket and toss it to Axel. He catches it, rips it open with his teeth and sheaths himself with the rubber. I make a slow show of stripping out of my jeans, leaving my t-shirt in place. At the bulge in my boxers, Avery licks her lips.

"I want to see all of you," she breathes quietly. "I bet you're a beautiful sight." Axel, mid-fisting his cock, looks up at me in an instant to gauge my reaction. It takes everything in me not to cover my chest with my arms. Instead, I twist so the blackboard is no longer in my sightline and reach for a blindfold.

"You're the beautiful one here, Peach." I force a small smile as I ease the blindfold over her eyes. She bites her lip, leaning into the game I'm setting up around. A brief, relieved breath escapes me as I slip back into my dominating role.

"I think you've earned your reward, Axel. Show Avery how good you can make her feel." Axel moves behind her eagerly as she adjusts her hips, presenting herself to him. He enters her in one smooth motion, causing Avery to cry out in pleasure.

I stand back, stroking myself lazily as I watch them move together, finding their rhythm. Avery's back is taut, her grip on the table telling. Axel is in just as much turmoil, his face clenched and pinched as he withdraws and re-enters her with painstaking slowness.

Between her slender curves and his defined abs, I become frenzied just watching, and I know my own release is coming. Unlike our friends, who are watching every moment from a distance, desiring what we have. The power we wield over the enigma between us. I don't know where the fuck Avery came from, but damn if I don't regret the years I sat listening to Wyatt's bitching rather than meeting her. The years we all suffered. Sure, Avery couldn't have prevented the torment we've been through, but her light could have brightened our days.

Taking myself out of my boxers and reaching out for Avery's chin, I open her mouth and slide my cock all the way inside. The acceptance of her warm throat draws a long groan from me. Her tongue flattens, allowing me all the way inside where I still. She bucks but I hold myself there for a moment longer. A simple reminder that her pleasure, pain and life are currently held in my grasp. It's the ultimate submission.

Accepting her fate, Avery goes limp and I smile, pulling back. She chokes in a breath, which turns into a moan when Axel slams back into her.

Allowing her to recover, I tap my dick against her mouth. Avery opens immediately, taking her turn to punish me. She sucks hard, swirling her tongue around my tip and deep throating me in turn. I shudder, clawing at her hair. When Axel slams into her gorgeous cunt, she jolts further down my shaft. I become lost in their ecstasy. Our reality slides into a fantasy where only chasing pleasure exists.

"Don't forget, I can be whoever you want me to be, Peach." I reassure her, holding her hair back in one fist and cupping her cheek with my other hand. I let my fingers trail south, stroking the faint bruising around her neck she's tried to conceal. My balls draw up and tighten as I grab her throat in the exact same place and squeeze. "Is this how he held you? Is this how you wish he'd fill you?"

My words are strangled, so it's only fitting she is too. At the sensation of my cock filling her throat, I pump faster. Thrust harder. Axel and I fuck Avery across the table and just when she screams a gargled sound and tenses against the wood, I explode into her mouth.

"Drink every drop," I demand, riding out my pleasure. Avery is too limp to refuse, taking my cum like such a good fucking girl. Withdrawing, I stumble to the chair and drop down. My cock is painfully swollen, a deep shade of purple. Straightening my t-shirt, I watch Axel drag Avery into another orgasm in quick succession, and drowns in it with her. Their sounds fill the room, panting and moaning until he collapses over her. Instantly reaching for me, Axel pulls on my hand until I stand on shaky legs. He turns his head, licking the last drop of cum beading at my tip. I gasp and jolt, steadying myself on his shoulder.

"Cheeky." Our movements are sluggish as I finish dressing and Axel moves away to clean himself up. I turn Avery over on the table, smirking at the wet patch coating the front of the torn leotard. Someone had fun. Removing the blindfold, her baby blue eyes squint through the markings left on her face by the mask. Her blonde hair is a mess, her lips swollen. Utterly fuckable, I think to myself and my dick jumps once again.

"You did so good," I praise, peppering her face with kisses. "You took us so well." Avery murmurs something, the words a mess of sounds. Something vaguely similar to, *'Garrett, thanks for this. I needed it.'* My smile widens further and I stroke her hair. She leans into my touch, angles her body into me and my thoughts stutter over themselves. She's perfect for Axel. Exactly what he needs. But now I'm starting to wonder...how the fuck am I going to be able to let her go?

A buzzer signals the opening of the door. Axel leaves without saying a word, and Huxley takes in his place, a fluffy robe in his hands. I smirk triumphantly.

"Sorry mate. Maybe next time." He barely registers my presence, his attention on Avery's slack body. She cracks an eye as he approaches.

"It's okay. From what I've just seen, she's worth the wait." Huxley eases Avery out of her costume with care, slipping the robe along her arms. She watches him care for her, tying the cord at her middle before scooping her up into his arms. Their blond hair messes together, the clash of their blue and brown eyes meeting with adoration. I hope we look that good together. Moving towards the exit, I come to my senses and bound after them.

"Hey," I catch Huxley's shoulder. "How long did Wyatt stay?" His eyes are thoughtful as he contemplates answering, but when it does, it's to Avery's questioning gaze.

"Too long to be considered polite."

CHAPTER THIRTY FOUR

Zipping my bag closed, I sit on the bed, staring blankly at the wall. Garrett and Axel were integral in distracting me last night, but now the truth has hit me. I can't go back home. Possibly for the entire time I'm at Waversea, Nixon seems determined for me not to return to the safety blanket I knew.

Gripping the edge of the mattress, I force back the tears. It's as if Hughes Manor was being held in a protective bubble, just out of reach but always there. Nixon has taken a pin and burst it into pieces, taking the last of my resolve with it. I have no fallback. When the Shadowed Souls have finished having their fun with me, I'll have nowhere to go.

A rap on my door signals it's time to go. I shoulder my bag and slink into the hallway, forcing a false smile for those waiting. Wyatt and Huxley are deep in conversation by the elevator, Garrett and Axel are looking at me like I'm sex on legs and Dax offers to take my bag. I have no fight in me, so I let him.

We settle into the two cars; Wyatt and Garrett in the Nissan, Huxley driving the SUV with Axel up front, and Dax in the back with me. I take comfort in knowing Garrett is going to drive Wyatt crazy all day long. Otherwise, I don't pay much attention to anything aside from the music leaking from the speakers. It's a throwback session on the chosen radio station. It's only when a low flying airplane briefly steals the sunlight does my foot stop tapping and I sit upright.

"Where are we?" I ask, but it's obvious. We turn onto a tarmac strip lined with hangers and a plane landing in the distance.

"Surprise," Huxley catches my gaze, his wide grin and chocolate eyes glinting with excitement. I narrow my eyes but it goes unseen as we enter a hanger. There's a whole team of people waiting for us, most of them uniformed. The car doors are opened and a hand offered for me to step out. I thank the man in his forties, who then moves to the trunk for our bags.

"You chartered a private jet?" I hiss-whisper as Huxley rounds the SUV and slides an arm around my waist. I attribute his touchy-feely vibe to the missed opportunity between us last night, and leave his hand to rest on my hip.

"It's not exactly chartering if you own it," he says beside my ear. I gasp, my eyes turning wide. Huxley owns the jet sitting before us being checked over by a team of people? I look closer now at the man who assisted me a moment ago, noting the logo embroidered onto his purple and yellow uniform. HV. Huxley Vaughn.

Unable to formulate a response, I go through the motions of being led to the metal stairs and guided into the jet. I'm used to Nixon's show of wealth, but somehow knowing all of this belongs to Huxley feels different. He's so young, yet he has it all.

"Why are you even attending Waversea? You could be anywhere in the world, living the dream," I comment whilst running my fingers lightly over the plush leather seats and polished metal accents. The interior is outfitted with first-class-style reclining chairs, a small bar stocked with all types of drinks imaginable, and even a private bedroom visible in the back.

"I suppose my dream isn't the same as most peoples," Huxley tilts his head in thought and then takes an aisle seat. I opt for the one beside him so I can look out of the window.

"What is it then - your dream?"

"I'll let you know when I find it," he replies nonchalantly, but I feel the intensity of his stare at the back of my head. When the heat of his eyes lingers for too long, I look over my shoulder and raise a brow. Huxley chuckles. "You think I'm full of shit don't you?"

All around the seats are filled across a wide table and to our left. Wyatt is quick to kick back his recliner and push a set of headphones into his ears. Up front, the cabin door is closed and the attendants give us privacy.

"No, I just..." I look around at those watching me closer than I realized. Is this some sort of test? "I don't know what could possibly be left to want?" Thankfully, Axel is on drink duty and he slides me a can of soda. Something to busy my hands with as a flush coats my cheeks. "Obviously, you have all the money and power you could ever want. With that comes a lot of female interest. I just don't get what Waversea holds for you."

I also don't get why the thought of Huxley leaving school to be a playboy bothers me. I can see it flashing before my eyes; his sandy blond hair beneath the strobe lighting of a club, a drink in one hand and two girls balanced in his lap. He could easily be the type of guy I can't stand, and even if I don't understand it, I'm extremely grateful he isn't.

We buckle up as the engines roar to life and I allow myself to sink into the leather seat, closing my eyes for a moment to process this sudden change of events. I should be used to the twists and turns of my life by now. Everytime I think I'm settled or I know what I'm doing, a curve ball comes and blows me out of the water. I don't realize the silence that has settled until it becomes heavy, and I peek back over at Huxley. His hand is toying with the armrest between us, on the verge of dropping onto my leg but he's holding back.

"Of all people, Little Swan, please don't underestimate me," he says quietly, and I glance up in time to see the flash of vulnerability appear in Huxley's features. "My whole life, people have only cared about my looks, my parents included. I'm always being judged for what I'm wearing or who I'm hanging out with. No one cares to know that my desires run deeper than materialistic things. I want the things money can't buy - experiences and knowledge. I want to be more than a cliché."

I exhale sharply and take Huxley's hand in mine. Shit, I know better than to judge people and I went and did it anyway. Huxley pulls my hand up to kiss the back of it and grins.

"And the adventures this fugly lot take me on aren't something I'd pass up for the world."

"Hey!" Garrett kicks Huxley beneath the table. At his side, Axel rests a soothing hand on Garrett's thigh, but he still pouts. "I'm not fugly."

"You're drop dead gorgeous," Dax reassures him from across the walkway. The following laughter bounces around the plane, cut short by our ascent into the sky. Beyond Huxley and Dax, I catch sight of Wyatt's sleeping form. A frown pulls at my mouth and I turn back to the window before anyone notices. Is he genuinely tired, or is Wyatt taking himself out of the conversation because I'm nearby?

For the first time, I have a niggling feeling that I shouldn't be here. I shouldn't be taking Wyatt's friends away from him. It's become apparent they're all he has, and until this past weekend, I didn't care because I knew he didn't deserve them. Now though, I'm starting to see the effects of his withdrawal and I can only imagine the mental turmoil he's going through. His own fault - yes. But still, I'm becoming more and more invested in a place where I don't belong. It's ultimately going to be me or him that stays, and the way my fingers are knotted with Huxley's speaks volumes.

Our plane ride doesn't take more than an hour and a half, and the conversation has long since moved on. The boys discuss politics, news, tv shows, all of which I quietly listen to. Then they talk sports and I tune out completely. Garrett has the flight attendant running back and forth with snacks every five minutes, while Axel plays footsie with me under the table.

Once landed, we're escorted by more of Huxley's staff into two Bentley's. I don't miss how all of the others pile into the rear car, leaving the front one for just Huxley and I. When I question him on it, he simply smiles.

"I've waited patiently for my chance with you. I'm done waiting." My heart flutters at his words so I settle into the backseat and stare out of the window. If I think too much about the large arm thrown over the back of my seat, of the warmth seeping into my nape, I might do something stupid out of desperation. Huxley's right; he's waited so patiently. He deserves more than an overload of rash decisions on my part.

We're driven through a stunning city where the rich must thrive. We pass expensive retail stores on busy streets and fountains in public rose gardens. Winding up a hillside, each house grows further apart from the last and is harder to spot behind walls of greenery and huge iron gates.

Pulling up to a set with the 'HV' logo branded into the center, I crane my neck in awe.

"Holy shit," I breathe, spying the whitewash walls through the bars. Windows dazzle in the midday sun, framed by carefully coordinated floral displays. The sheer volume of balconies and wings visible from the front have my eyes bulging in my head. "This is your place?!" Beside me, Huxley inclines his head, his long wavy hair tickling my shoulder.

"Last night, Wyatt mentioned you're not allowed to return home. I figured the least I could do is lend you mine." My head turns into his face. Chocolate eyes filled with earnestness stare back. As we roll towards Huxley's mansion, his fingers press beneath my chin to tilt my lips the rest of the distance to meet his.

Everything Huxley is - overwhelmingly warm, dependable and solid - hits me all at once. His kiss is gentle, but it settles deep within my core. His mouth brushes over mine, unhurried yet fuelled by passion. By the time his tongue slips past my lips, I'm a quivering mess beneath him. I melt into the firmness of his chest, my hands settling on his biceps. He flexes, a show of power that mingles with the intoxicating scent of his cologne. It's taken the longest to carve out this moment with Huxley, and it's over far too quickly.

We stop in front of the front entrance, a member of staff opening the Bentley's rear door. My cheeks are flushed red. Huxley's knowing, cocky gaze doesn't leave my face as I scoot out without a moment to compose myself. Two massive doors are opened from the inside before we've reached the top step.

"Where are the others?" I peer back at the empty driveaway. Huxley's hand is on the small of my back.

"I may have sent them on a little detour." His brown eyes sparkle with mischief. "Come on, I have a surprise for you."

The house is every bit as grand on the inside as it is on the outside, with high ceilings, marble floors, and priceless artwork adorning the walls. Huxley leads me up a winding staircase, his touch gentle but firm enough at the same time. Butterflies burst to life within me, tenfold from when he pushed me up against the bathroom mirror after the frat house party. A night I refused to think about before, which is now branded at the forefront of my mind.

When Wyatt shut me in the cupboard, Huxley came for me. Huxley cared for me, as he has every night since; whenever I climb into his bed for comfort. He's never once pushed for more than a cuddle, he's waited until I was ready.

I'm ready right now.

Tracking the potted plants along a network of hallways, we head towards the back of the mansion and stop at a closed door. There's a rounded bay window to my right with a bench seat underneath to look out onto the gardens.

"I've given you the room overlooking the pool. Just in case you want to watch my midnight swims." He winks but I'm too flustered to be flirtatious. I lean into Huxley, my eyes hooded as I tilt my head back.

"I'll be watching every night," I mutter, pushing up onto my tiptoes. Huxley's responding grin is equally stunned and smug. He lowers his lips to mine, his hand sliding up my back to cup the back of my neck. The other settles on my waist, crushing us together. Huxley's palm seeps through the thin material of my t-shirt, the heat of him searing me like a branding iron.

"Don't you want to see your surprise first?" He asks against my cheek. I feel the effort he's putting in to restraining himself, but there's really no need. I shake my head, winding my arms around his neck, and haul myself upwards. Huxley's chuckle rumbles against my chest as he catches me, pressing me against the wall beside the door. Crashing my mouth against his, I claw at his shoulders and roll my hips. I can't help myself, as if my next breath depends on shifting the overwhelming desire flooding my veins. I'd do anything he wanted in this moment, including let him take me in the hallway.

"Huxley," I moan into his ear before biting his earlobe gently with my teeth. "I want you." His groan reverberates deep in his chest. The look in his deep chocolate eyes is enough to set my world ablaze, but still he's holding back ever-so-slightly. Gripping his hair, I drag him closer. "Please."

Huxley's hand trails up my bare thigh, bunching the material of my skirt. He's everywhere, his mouth on my neck, his tongue tangling with mine, his hands dancing across my skin one moment, and in my hair the next. It's like a dam has burst between us, and now there's no containing it. Broad shoulders ripple beneath my fingers, the shudder that rolls through him ending with his hips pressing further against mine.

"Wait, wait, wait. Let's press pause on this real quick," Huxley tears himself away from me breathlessly and plants me back on the ground. The air between us is cold, so I automatically step back into his body. His neck is marked by my nails and his blond hair a tangle mess of fucking hot. "I really think you should go in and see your surprise."

"Fuck the surprise. It can't be better than what's out here." Both Huxley and I are stunned by my revelations, but it's too late to play coy now. I step forward, palming his dick through his jeans. The door to the guest room flies open.

"Bitch, fuck you!" A female voice cuts through my haze of desire. Cocking her hip with both hands fixed on her waist, a long brunette ponytail slips over her shoulder. Releasing me, Huxley slowly backs away.

"Surprise," he says with a sideways slant to his bruised lips. My brain stutters to a stop as I look from him, to her blazing blue eyes and button nose.

"You...How...Meg!" I come to my senses and throw myself at my best friend. She catches me in a crushing hug. My heart breaks then, as her telltale vanilla and honey shampoo clears my mind and I realize just how much I've missed my best friend. How much I've needed her. It suddenly makes sense that it wasn't the manor I was feeling so heartbroken about not seeing - it was her. Meg is home to me. Standing back, I take in her cute pumpkin skater dress and the suitcase on the bed beyond her shoulder. "How the hell did you get here?!"

"I got the call last night to say our fall break plans have been relocated, and I was flown in this morning." Linking our arms, she walks us inside the room. It's huge, infused with deep purples and golds, complete with the promised balcony and more than big enough for the two of us to share. I look back to the hallway but Huxley has already disappeared. "Apparently, you're not allowed to isolate yourself from the world any more. You need company at all times."

"Huxley said that?" I smirk to myself, dropping onto the bed. Meg stays standing, her face incredulous.

"No, Wyatt did."

AVERY

I smile at Meg for the hundredth time as we get ready for dinner. I still can't believe she's here at Huxley's home. Hell, I can't believe I'm really here. A uniformed butler brought my bags up to our room a while ago, and not just the one from the plane. Apparently, while we were in the air, Huxley had his driver heading in the opposite direction to pack up our belongings from Waversea and bring them here.

"I couldn't pass up the chance to join in this crazy adventure you've got yourself on." I try to hide my smirk but her hold on my hair doesn't give me anywhere to go. I'm sitting at the vanity table in the expansive en-suite bathroom as Meg braids my hair down the back of my head and over my shoulder.

I've caught Meg up on most of what I've been up to lately. The ball, the note for Mr. XO, my awkward dinner with Nixon and the sex club. Divulging anything non-emotional and non-confusing is easy. It's the rest I'm struggling to put into words. I wouldn't even know how to explain that I drunkenly invaded Wyatt's hotel room and *hugged* him. Meg would think I've lost my damn mind, and I'd be inclined to agree.

"You're oddly quiet," Meg raises a brow. "Before we head down, it would be helpful to know where your head is at. Spill the tea, Aves. Is Huxley officially your new man?" We share a knowing, mischievous look.

"Well, I mean, they're all holding my attention. It would be detrimental to select just one," I bite down on my bottom lip and my cheeks flame for the second time today. Meg's hands still, her blue eyes flying to mine in the mirror.

"Slut!" She grins wide. "I love this new you. You're so confident."

"For the record, none of this was orchestrated by me. It's all on them. They seem sort of obsessed with sharing me. Except for Wyatt, obviously."

"*Obviously*," Meg echoes. I drop my gaze to my lap. The more I think about Wyatt, the more blurred the lines become. My memory is tricking me, creating emotions and seeing expressions that weren't there. I never thought I would prefer him hating me for the sake of it. It was safer that way, but at least Meg is here now to keep me from doing anything stupid.

Finishing my braid with hairspray to keep the fly-aways in place, I join Meg by the door in a pair of dark, skinny jeans. There was much debate on what we should wear to dinner, and settled on causal. Up top, I have a simple white t-shirt beneath a pale pink blazer. Meg opted for a black jumpsuit. Then sparked the shoe debate and ultimately, I'm not ready to be slip-sliding around in bed socks. Pushing my feet into a pair of ankle-boots in the same blush pink, we make our way to the bottom level. I can hear Garrett's laugh and decide if I follow that, I'll either find the kitchen or the dining room.

Everyone is already seated when we approach the vast mahogany table. Despite the six other chairs down the far end, the guys have all opted to sit close together. A space has been left either side of Huxley at the head of the table. I automatically walk to the one between him and Dax, putting Wyatt out of my eyeline on Dax's other side. Meg sits beside Axel with Garrett on the end. He's the only one already eating.

"Wine?" Huxley offers. I nod, basking in his relaxed smile. The ends of his blond hair are curled more than usual, as if he's taken the time to dry and style it. A black t-shirt hugs his chest and biceps, the swirl of black ink dancing across his arms. Even his breathing seems more focused than I remember, a steady rise and fall of his chest distracting me from the menu being placed in my hands. He's so at ease here, not a care in the world as he asks the butler to fill my glass. A true King of his castle.

"A menu?" Meg snorts, peering at me over hers. "Is this a home or a five star restaurant?" Huxley's brown eyes slide from me to Meg, a hint of amusement in his half-shrug.

"I don't stay here often so I called in a chef to feed us for the next week. He brought his own team and a whole range of menus."

"Thank fuck for disgustingly rich friends," Garrett says around a mouthful of soup and bread. A few murmured laughs sound around the table, one radiating from Huxley himself. Everyone falls into a comfortable silence to glance over the food choices, but I can't stop myself from frowning behind the laminated card. If we weren't here, would Huxley be sitting alone? Is that why he doesn't stay here often and prefers to spend his time at Waversea?

Once we've placed our orders with a pretty, young waitress dressed in black and white, Meg decides one glass of wine is enough to start voicing every question she has burning inside.

"So, the Shadowed Souls, huh?" She says to no one in particular. "What makes each one of you worthy of the ink and title?" I gasp at Meg's audacity and kick her beneath the table.

"Megan! You can't ask that outright!"

"Maybe you can't," she rolls her eyes and crosses her arms. "I don't think anyone really cares what I do and as the only member of your chosen family present, it's my job to vet these guys out. See who's worthy of you."

"Can't argue with that," Dax tilts his head towards me. I can't share his smile, my eyebrows are too busy pinching together.

"You really don't have to indulge her," I warn. A large, warm hand slides over my thigh in an effort to reassure me it's okay. Dax turns his attention to Meg.

"I was raised by the most incredible woman, but I don't have a single memory where she wasn't sick. Everything we had went on her healthcare, and ultimately her funeral. I already had my scholarship before she passed, and Wyatt pulled some strings for me to board at the school rather than be lost in the care system. He's been covering any shortfalls in my funding ever since so I can stay at Waversea."

My breath is held in my chest, my jaw beginning to ache as I hold back the desire to cry. I didn't know any of that, but words are useless when everyone is present. Instead, I place my hand on Dax's beneath the table. He automatically links our fingers. Even when his heart is bleeding, Dax refuses to let his small smile drop away. Meg thanks Dax for his honesty, and turns her eyes on Huxley. He huffs a laugh, widening his legs to touch my knee.

"I became emancipated from my parents when I discovered they were stealing from me." My eyebrows hit my hairline and after a moment of surprise, Huxley seems to remember I've been rather sheltered. "I was a child model and played a few small parts in various shows and movies." Further down the table, Garrett coughs the word 'modest' into his fist. Huxley ignores him again, keeping his attention on me.

"Anyway, I won this residence in court since it was my money that paid for it. Wyatt helped me along the way, lent me your family lawyer when I didn't have access to my own. Without him, I would have been stonewalled every step of the way."

I barely have time to register as the other two chip in their stories in quick succession, starting with Axel.

"Pops died of cancer when I was fourteen. My mom whored me out to pay for her luxurious lifestyle." Axel rushes out his words, as if that wasn't the worst two sentences to have ever been muttered. Sighing deeply, he fidgets with the table cloth. "Wyatt was the first to notice, and banned me from going home in the holidays. In all my times of weakness, he always remained the strong, stoic one."

I wish I had the guts to lean forward and read Wyatt's expression right now. As it stands, I'm ramrod straight, frozen in my seat and it appears to be Garrett's turn.

"My parents were travel enthusiasts," Garrett carves a pattern through his soup with his spoon. For the first time that I've seen, there's food in front of him and he's not devouring it. "They loved traveling so much, sometimes they were gone for months. Sometimes they forgot they'd left their son at home to fend for himself."

My stomach turns to lead. Garrett without a smile and a joke at the ready is a travesty, but his expression right now is enough to convince me he's never truly laughed before. The sharp lines of his face are taunt, his brown gaze haunted. Garrett lets the curtain on his dark hair fall forward to avoid looking at me.

"When the money they'd left ran out, I grew too weak to go to school. That's when people started to ask the right questions and the police came to visit. I was removed from my home that day and I haven't seen my parents since."

"You've never wanted to confront them?" Dax asks, joining the conversation. I presume this isn't a usual discussion for the five of them. Garrett rolls his neck until it cracks, further stressing that he's uncomfortable.

"I won't waste a minute of my life on those people. They're getting what they deserve, locked up behind bars." Spearing his forgotten bread roll with a steak knife, Garrett's smile returns as he looks at Wyatt, but there's no kindness behind it. "Nothing that a couple years of the best therapy money can buy to heal paternal trauma, right Riot?" Tipping his glass towards Wyatt's, Garrett downs his wine in one gulp. I read between the lines.

"I see there's an interlinking theme in all of this," I breathe to myself. Our conversation is paused by the arrival of our food, the plates lowered in complete, stale silence. Garrett picks up his fork but pauses, staring at his salmon. Whatever caused him to hesitate passes within a second, his boyish grin finding me across the tableware.

"Bon appetit," he winks and dives in. Personally, I've lost my appetite but I try to smile back. Axel's attention is elsewhere, aimed at the far window. Meg has yet to move, her skeptical eyes watching the only person present that I can't see.

"And you, Wyatt?" she asks, twisting her lips. I know that look, she's re-evaluating. "What did you need the Shadowed Souls for?" His answer comes immediately, with the same pissed-off tone I'm used to hearing.

"My family replaced me, so I created one that wouldn't."

Beneath the table, I briefly grip Dax's hand harder. I need strength. After everything I've just heard, of how Wyatt was everyone's saving grace except mine, a cold tendril of misery carves through my chest. If only he accepted me, our lives could have been so different. In another universe, he could have been a rock for me to lean on too. Puffing out my cheeks, I try to dislodge this overwhelming feeling that will inevitably make me cry.

"For what it's worth," I angle my head around Dax, "I am sorry." I see Wyatt's outline shrug and his fork clatters against his plate.

"Don't be. I wouldn't trade the men at this table for the world."

Garrett's smile turns genuine at this, like a puppy who's just been praised. It's too cute not to enjoy, but Wyatt isn't done yet. "I never would have tried to run away from them like you did."

Meg's eyes snap to mine like a laser, all-too-knowing.

"What's that supposed to mean?" Huxley queries first, his legs tensing as he sits upright.

"Our dinner with Nixon. Avery was begging to leave Waversea."

"You want to leave Waversea?" Axel asks, his presence back with us at the table. I try not to wriggle under his hazel gaze, although inside, I'm scrambling for the words.

"No. I mean, I want to go home, yes. I never wanted to leave Hughes manor in the first place, but it's not as black and white as Wyatt is making it sound."

"Her actual words were that she wanted to be alone again. That there are too many distractions at Waversea."

"Distractions," Dax murmurs to himself. He retracts his hand from my thigh. I wasn't prepared for how deeply such a simple act could cut, but it hurts. The ache in my chest is amplified when he pushes away from the table and leaves. Now Wyatt is in my eyeline, and I would give anything to wipe the smug smirk off his face. He was looking for a way to get his friends to turn on me, he's been biding his time, and here it is. Huxley's eyes are full of pity as he skids his chair back too.

"I'll go after him." Garrett is next, but not because of Wyatt's revelation. He's simply finished eating and gestures for Axel to follow him. I try to reason with myself that he just needs some time, that discussing his childhood is a sore spot that he needs Axel to soothe away again. That leaves myself, Meg and the asshole glaring at me as if this was all my fault.

"Couldn't help yourself, could you?" I scrunch a napkin in my hand and toss it at him. Without waiting around for what is sure to be another dig at my personality, I storm away. Taking the stairs two at a time, my chest heaves. Why is Wyatt so convinced I'm the villain in his mind? He's created a version of me that doesn't exist, and twists everything to fit his narrative.

Turning a corner, I skid to a stop, realizing I have no idea where I'm going. Shadows move within a room down the hall, the door just ajar. I sigh heavily, hoping to catch Dax before Wyatt appears to hammer the final nail in the coffin. He wants me gone, and this is the closest he's come to succeeding so far.

Tentatively, I push the door open. My breath catches in my throat.

AXEL

I feel her there before I see the door shift. Regardless, I don't stop. Relaxing my jaw, I take Garrett deep, relishing in the velvety feel of him in the back of my throat. He's too lost to his pleasure, head thrown back on the armchair and a hand pressing firmly on my shaven head. I massage his balls, pulling back, then lowering down again, taking as much of him as I can. It's a slow sensual torture, my tongue swirling around the head of his cock in between. There's no more movement at the door and I'm sure Avery has left. It's for the best. Garrett doesn't discuss his past for a reason, and now he needs to forget again. Something I understand all too well.

Garrett's mewl makes me smirk around his shaft. He stiffens, but doesn't come yet. I won't let him. Whenever I wake from a nightmare, he's always there, nudging my legs apart. In those moments of fear and confusion, it's not the climax I need, but the grapple on reality. That's exactly what Garrett needs right now - to remember who he is, and what he has to live for. It's become a dependency for both of us, blurring the lines between trauma and pleasure.

The sound of knees dropping onto the wood floor next to me is enough to break my rhythm and I gag. Garrett curses as he grabs my head again, but it's too late. I cough and sputter, pulling back with haste. Avery's large blue eyes are blinking innocently, a question in her knitted brows. She's shed her blazer and shoes, having discarded them on the way over. Slowly, her hand wraps around mine at the base of Garrett's cock. He's roused, staring down at us with dazed eyes. His hair is a dark mess from dragging his hands through it.

"You have no fucking idea how perfect the two of you look kneeling in front of me." Garrett eases further down the armchair, widening his legs to permit us both access. Avery's attention is focused on me, her movements tentative as if she's waiting for permission.

"Start slow," I lightly push Avery's head forward. "Make him wait for it." Her lashes lower for a moment, fanning her freckled cheeks as she obeys. Her small pink tongue pokes out, swirling around Garrett's plump head. Tightening her grip around my hand, we stroke him together until I can't hold back any more. I drag my tongue up one side of Garrett's cock while Avery mirrors me on the other, her beautiful blue eyes blown and on me. I breathe harshly, a desire I've never known developing.

Without need for strategic discussion, Avery kneels up higher while I drop lower. She swallows Garrett's dick whole, while I attend to his balls and gooch. Sliding a finger to his ass, I circle Garrett's pucked hole. The noises escaping him are a whole new level of yearning. He grips the edges of the armchair, shuddering beneath us. When my finger pushes inside, I gauge how he pushes down onto me. What was meant to be a simple, quick blowjob before dessert has become something entirely more delicious. I slide my mouth up his length one last time before I can't handle the throbbing in my own jeans any longer.

"Bed," I grunt, jerking my head in the direction of the four-poster beside us. Garrett nods, his brown eyes glazed over with lust. I help him to stand on shaky legs and guide him to the mattress. Avery moves to follow but I stop her with a hand on her shoulder.

"I want you to watch this time." Her eyes flicker with confusion so I kiss her quickly and harshly, sharing the taste of Garrett's precum between our salty tongues. Sitting her back in the armchair by the window, I level her with a stern look, making sure she's going to watch our every move.

Once beside the bed, I push Garrett backwards, his cock bouncing with anticipation. I undress his lower half, leaving his t-shirt in place as his jeans and boxers join Avery's discarded clothes on the floor. Standing at the foot of the bed, I motion for him to roll over. Garrett moans but obeys without hesitation, presenting his ass for me to see.

I bite down on my knuckles at the sight of him perfectly puckered and aching for me. I don't often take advantage of being a Switch, but it's my turn to show Avery what I'm capable of. Up until now, she's only seen me as the submissive Garrett uses to bolster his need for control. However, I have my own needs, and they run much darker. Garrett stills as I run a single digit along one side of his ass, then down the other, teasing him mercilessly.

"Relax," I murmur, pushing that finger inside him again, adding another before circling them both in and out in a delicious rhythm. He moans louder now, his hips rocking back against me as he begs for more. "Easy, Gare," I chuckle, spanking his ass lightly before reaching for the lube stashed in the drawer beside us. I packed the essentials, whereas Garrett packed for this exact moment. I bet in his imagination, he thought he'd be the one on top. It's fun to spice things up once in a while.

"Axel. I can't wait any more," he grunts out as I take my time undressing for Avery's eyes and coat both of us in the slippery substance.

"I know," I soothe, lining myself up with his entrance and slowly pushing in. His walls clamp down like a vice grip as he arches into me. "Relax, Gare." I kiss each knot of tension from his back before righting myself and looking over to our spectator. And what a sight she is.

Avery is leaning against the wingback chair, her hand tucked into her waistband, rubbing herself to the rhythm I set. Flushed cheeks, wild blue eyes. Her hair is falling free of its braid, the friction giving her the appeal of a wild lioness.

She watches intently as I pick up speed, bottoming out in Garrett's tight heat. His ass slaps against my stomach with each thrust, his whimpers fueling my desire. I grind against him, hitting that special spot I know has him seeing stars and moaning my name.

"That's it," I say, coaxing Avery on. "You like watching Garrett being vulnerable for a chance? It's such a beautiful sight, if I do say so myself." Trailing my fingers along Garrett's skin, he shivers for me. Avery's cheeks flush a darker shade of red, but she doesn't tear her eyes away from the erotic scene in front of her. Garrett's moans grow louder and more desperate as I continue to pound into him relentlessly.

A low whimper escapes Avery's lips as she also increases her pace, her hand flattening to suggest her fingers have entered herself. The sight of Garrett submitting so willingly to my touch is arousing and liberating to all three of us. It's taken me a long time to finally shed my inhibitions and embrace my truest desires without restraint or judgment. A long time to admit to myself in the mirror that this is how I was always meant to be and I actually like it.

Meanwhile, Garrett's nails dig into the sheets as he submissively takes everything I give him. At this rate, he's handling the feeling of being stretched open and filled by my cock far better than I am. I'm on the verge of exploding, having reached a new height of pleasure I didn't know existed.

Knowing that Avery is watching only makes it more thrilling, our eyes locking half-mast and filled with lust. Feasting my eyes on her perfectly rounded tits pushing against the fabric of her top and the flush spread across her chest and neck, I feel myself start to spiral and by the tension in Garrett's shoulders, he knows it too. I slowly withdraw and nudge Garrett to roll onto his back.

"Get over here, Little Swan," I breathe through clenched teeth. Avery pauses, her hand falling still in her panties as she seems unsure but I gesture for her to come closer. Like a puppet caught by the strings, she saunters over to the bed. Her long legs are too restricted by those tight jeans, the white sheer top revealing her taut nipples. The long, blonde braid still hangs over her shoulder with strands falling free to frame her delicate face. When I become too impatient, I wrap that braid around my fist and tug her the rest of the way.

"Take care of Garrett for me. He hasn't stopped asking me how tight your sweet cunt is all day."

Avery looks uneasy, causing me to smile. In all of the time she's been around us, she's refused to let her mask of steel slip. But at this moment, she looks vulnerable and a twisted part of me has never wanted her more. I slip from the bed, my dick bobbing with each step to the bathroom. Bracing my hands on the counter top, I collect myself before cleaning up.

I re-enter just as a stunningly naked Avery lowers onto Garrett's cock. The curve in her waist, the fleshy roundness to her hips, her creamy skin. I have to lean against the door jamb and enjoy the view, committing it to memory. Whenever I would cream the tattoo on her upper back, I'd imagine her like this. Bouncing in my lap, looking over her shoulder with a coy smile.

Sensing me watching, she does just that. My feet are moving until I'm crawling up behind her, tilting her head back and crushing my lips against hers. I'd almost forgotten the softness of her lips as they move against mine, pushing my tongue inside her hot little mouth. Garrett rubs my thigh with the hand not fisted in his hair. I know exactly how close he is. We've shared women many times before, but nothing compares to when we're with Avery.

Lowering my mouth to her neck, I suck and lick every inch of her skin like a man starved. Her gaze rolls from Garrett's dangerously dark eyes to mine, no doubt the sensations making her light headed. I move my hands to Avery's waist, lifting and lowering her onto Garrett. Her moans are like the sweetest music as Garrett bucks beneath her, his hands stroking over mine as he runs them up her curves. Sitting upright, Garrett's fingers find her hair tie, teasing her golden locks around her shoulders before he pulls it over one side. I watch his lips skate across her exposed neck, planting feather light kisses and licking a trail up to her ear in the same manner I just did.

Her soft moans have me at war with myself, my fingers twitching to throw her down roughly and bury myself inside to the hilt, but I have to savor this. Sliding my hand around Garrett's head, I pull him over her shoulder to kiss me instead. I didn't fully believe Garrett until this moment, but he's right. This is where Avery belongs, sandwiched between us. My grip on her waist is painfully tight as I grind her down into the man I love, rolling her to draw out their pleasured groans. Avery leans in to suck on Garrett's neck as I duel with his tongue and her fate is sealed. She's ours now.

Arching back into me, I feel the urgency of Garrett pounding into her from underneath. Breaking our kiss, I tilt my brow with a knowing look. I've always been able to take my time whereas Garrett has to battle for control against the monster within. He needs to devour men and women as quickly and savagely as his food, and I already know that one taste of Avery will never be enough.

My hands are on their own journey, seeking out Avery's breasts as my teeth sink into her shoulder. Overloading her with sensations so she doesn't know where Garrett ends and I begin. Drifting my palms across her skin, I halt over the small scars littering her ribs. Avery remembers herself in an instant, her body tensing.

"Shhh. I'm never going to hurt you." I speak into her ear, pressing my chest against her back.

"I know," Avery replies in a small voice, but glances back with concern in her bright blue eyes anyway. Using it to my advantage, I capture her lips with mine again, not shifting my hands until she relaxes beneath my touch. We're all scarred here, whether physically or mentally.

Reaching back, Avery holds my neck as she grinds her ass back against my shaft. I stroke my aching erection slowly, settling in for the ride. Her nails scrape over my scalp as I pinch and tease her nipples between my forefingers and thumbs.

"Switch," I tell Garrett as Avery's climax nears, testing my stamina to the max. He moves to the left as I pass on the right, a move we've done many times, reversing the roles. The second my back touches the mattress, Avery grabs my cock and impales her mouth on it. I gasp in response as she works my shaft like the world's tastiest lollipop.

Garrett plunges into her from behind and fucks her with the same vigour as before, causing her to moan with my tip at the back of her throat. The vibrations reverberate down to my balls and I can't hold back any longer. My load shoots into her throat which she swallows greedily, spurring me on for longer. Avery finishes sucking every single drop out of me before coming up for air with a 'pop'. She's smiling triumphantly, but she doesn't realize that was part of the foreplay. I'm not done with her-not by a long shot. Garrett's hands slip under her thighs, lifting her high so she is straddling me.

"Have you ever taken two cocks at once before, Peach?" Garrett drags Avery's head aside. His lips are on her neck but his eyes on me with a clear message. His dominant side is back in full force. I smile back. Thank fuck for that - I hate it when he's mopey.

Reaching up, I pull Avery down to meet my mouth, pushing my tongue into her mouth on a gasp as Garrett thrusts into her forcefully. Kissing a path down her neck, I take one bouncing nipple in my mouth whilst massaging the other with my hand. Sucking powerfully, she whimpers and pulls my hair. Repeating the same process on her other nipple, I can tell how close she is by the trembling of her body against mine.

Garrett pauses his movements as I line myself up with her pussy, and ease in alongside him. I practically see the stars burst in Avery's eyes as soon as I've entered, our cocks sliding together in her wetness. She cums so hard, I'm almost forced back out.

Her teeth find my neck, biting down as she screams through her orgasm and I push her head down to ensure it leaves a mark. Her fingernails scrape down my chest and I'm hard for her again, thriving on the pain as much as the pleasure. There's no pretending we'll be able to last, the combination of our girth and her tight heat too much to resist. With coordinating thrusts, we push Avery further than she's been before, stretching and claiming her.

Somehow, we manage to see Avery through to her next climax, out of sheer stubbornness. The slide of Garrett's cock next to mine is too much, as is listening to his praise calling Avery a good girl. She's not just good, she's fucking perfect. Slumping over me, I hold her delicately, relishing the lengthy moans beside my ear. On his own strangled groan, Garrett pulls out and moves Avery aside. Grabbing my dick, he jacks us off in unison until we're both shooting cum onto my stomach. I'd usually complain about being used as a splash pad, but it was better than the alternative.

"Fuck, that was amazing," I breathe, scraping my nails through his hair. Garrett walks into the bathroom before returning to throw a damp towel over my torso and flops down next to me. Avery stands to pull her panties and jeans back on straightaway. Frowning, I wonder why she isn't trying to stay and snuggle with us. Garrett would have let her be the big spoon. Probably.

"I suppose you're done avoiding whatever brought you into this room," Garrett says. There's no question of judgment in his tone. Just the understanding that we all need to escape sometimes.

"I need to apologize to Dax. I just don't know how." Avery chews on her inner cheek and drags her top back on. The blazer is next but she makes no move towards the door just yet. Garrett stretches out across my side of the bed like a cat.

"I tend to send him a bunch of sunflowers when I'm in the doghouse. He can never stay mad at me after that."

Avery pauses mid-fixing her wild hair to eye him suspiciously. "You send him flowers?"

Garrett was ready for such a reaction. "It's only weird if you make it weird. Men like receiving flowers too." Avery nods to herself, pushing her feet into a tiny pair of boots.

"Well, I don't have immediate access to a florist. I'll have to try using my words." Heading towards the door, she's stopped by Garrett's rough laugh.

"Your choice. One of those magical blowjobs would probably work too."

"He'll be by the fountain," I try to offer some helpful advice instead. "Pass the pool, take the steps down into the gardens and turn left. He always goes there to think when we stay here." Cleaning myself off, I lie back with my arms behind my head. Avery stills in the doorway, opening and closing her mouth a few times.

"Thanks, both of you. And about what Wyatt said-"

"Don't mention it, Peach," Garrett waves her off. His eyes are no longer open. "If we worried about everything Wyatt said, we'd spend our whole lives crying. Or fucking. Or cry fucking."

With a last small smile, she disappears and I sigh, staring at the ceiling. It's not long before Garrett's breathing has evened out. I wish my mind could turn off so easily.

"Gare," I say as he's just falling asleep. "Can I ask you something?" He turns into me, tucking himself into my side and pressing his mouth against my ribs.

"If it's to question whether we're getting that girl on some contraception before we ruin her, I'm way ahead of you," he yawns widely. "Although, it would be one way to ensure she doesn't try to run off again." I blink a few times, deciding to leave that thought for another time. No, that's not what I was going to ask. Licking my lips, I rub my head and then my jaw, finally sighing and just going for it.

"Are you still planning on leaving me?"

Garrett's head pops up so fast, my eyes widen. The neckline of his t-shirt gapes, revealing the colorful artwork spilling over his chest. In the gaps between the random assortment of images, he has patches of skin colored with the rainbow. I've realized along the way that Garrett will have anything and everything permanently marked onto himself in a bid to cover what he hates the most. His body.

I turn onto my side, sliding a hand up the hem. I'm the only one Garrett will allow to touch him like this. My fingers skate across his washboard abs, not resting until they settle over his heart. The harsh thumping reverberates through my palm. The heart I long to claim as my own. The man I wish would love me as thoroughly and unconditionally as I do him.

The entire world can discard Garrett as a joker, only suitable for mild entertainment, but to me, he's prince charming. He has what it takes to save me from the abyss of my nightmares. He knows me better than anyone else, so when he sees the sincerity in my eyes, he knows I mean it. Swallowing hard, Garrett's hand raises to cover mine and his forehead dips towards mine.

"As if I ever ever could."

CHAPTER THIRTY SEVEN

Trudging through a muddy patch, I curse my shoe choice under my breath. What Axel neglected to say when giving me directions is that I'd be going on a magical mystery tour through a mile of greenery. The hedges are too high to see that I'm not going in circles, and I'm sure I took a wrong turn because the paved walkway came to a sudden stop three rose bushes ago.

Coming to a halt, I look back, contemplating leaving Dax's apology until tomorrow. He might not want to see me anyway. After all of the effort he's put into our joint assignment, into accompanying me to my counseling sessions, even just to help me get through each day, and I called him a distraction, I begged to live alone once more. Well, I've had a cold dose of what that would be like and it's clearer than ever, the grass isn't always greener on the other side. A tender pressure between my legs and a heavy heart show I can't go back. I'm ruined. I just hope I still have a choice in the matter.

Through the moonlight leaves, a rustle catches my attention. I didn't see it at first, but now it's moved, I can make out the silhouette. Tall and clearly a man's. It moves again, darting away.

"Hey!" I call, taking chase. No doubt Axel followed me to make sure I went the right way. So why not just reveal himself? Unless this is part of a game, in which case, it's much more likely to be Garrett stalking around in the shadows. I thought they'd thoroughly tired themselves out. My heels slow me down, my blazer whipping against the wind I create. Pumping my arms, I spot a gap in the branches ahead.

"Sorry about this Hux," I mutter, throwing myself through the hedge. Twigs claw at my hair but I make it to the other side in one piece. Putting myself ahead of whoever I seem to be chasing, he haphazardly collides with me. I'm spun away, forced to face the paved path. A hand clamps over my mouth. Oh, we're playing this game.

I wriggle, but there's no real fight in my jerky movements. Hot breath fans over my ear, the low sound of a rattle just underneath. A smoker, I'd hazard a guess. Unease trickles through me, sending a shiver down my spine.

Suddenly, I don't want any part of whatever this is. I kick back, struggling with earnest now but the assailant's grip tightens, immobilizing me. I twist as much as I'm able, releasing a scream against the large palm covering my mouth. My head turns inward, hoping to get a clue of his identity in the dark when it hits me. The unmistakable, overpowering and sickening scent of whiskey.

That fucker.

I squirm harder, adrenaline passing through my veins. Like fuel to the fire, my unbridled hatred for Wyatt spurs me on. I suppose he sat at the dinner table, having a good laugh at my expense whilst drinking himself into oblivion and thinking up new ways to torture me. From the pounding of my heart, he'd be glad to know he's succeeded.

I continue to struggle, refusing to let him hold this over my head at the breakfast table tomorrow. As his grip on my mouth loosens minutely, I seize my opportunity; it's now or never. With a muffled scream, I bite down on the hand covering my mouth as hard as I can. There's no holding back, years of frustration crashing down between my teeth and the fleshy part between his thumb and index finger.

He barely grunts in pain, grabbing a fistful of my hair in his other hand and dragging my mouth free. I cry out too late, my body free falling as I'm flung to the ground. I hit the ground with such force, a flash of light bursts behind my eyelids. His feet beat against the pavement as he flees, taking the pussy's route back to the mansion. I grimace after him, vowing to get my revenge later. Meg will help me think of something far more creative and malicious than I would come up with on my own.

Licking my split lip, I push myself upright. I'm utterly lost now and my only hope is to follow the way Wyatt fled. The path seems longer this way, curving around to finally give me an open view of the gardens. An outcrop framed by a low stone wall looks over a multitude of garden sculptures and in the center of them, exactly what I've been searching for. I can't contain my sigh of relief.

Illuminated by lights, the fountain stands tall and proud, water pouring from the mouths of intricately carved mythical creatures into a large basin. Its white marble gleams in the moonlight. In the center, the figure of a woman stretches her arms upward, as if reaching for the stars themselves. I rush down the stone steps, following the sound of bubbling water. A shadow sits on the edge, a hand lowered to tease the water with his fingers. I'm so thankful Dax is still here, that my steps quicken and I don't realize until I'm almost upon him that he's not alone.

"Oh shit," I skid to a stop. "I'm sorry, I can leave." Both heads turn my way and Huxley stands.

"Avery?" He frowns at me. "What the hell happened to you?" I follow his eyeline to see my white top is caked with mud, and the distinct taste of blood lingers in my mouth from my lip. I fake a smile, waving off his concern.

"I'm fine. Nothing I can't deal with later." Huxley looks like he wants to argue further but allows me to pass him and settle next to Dax. My body is angled away from the fountain, whereas his is facing inwards. The lights flood his face, picking out the sharpness of his jaw and adams apple against his smooth tanned skin. His blue eyes are intense, tracking the marble carvings with intrigue. I may be biased, but I think my view is better.

"Dax..." I breathe, now unsure of what to say. He's not like the others. He can't be distracted by physical affection until he forgets there was a problem to begin with. On the flip side, I can't just tell him what he wants to hear. Dax deserves the truth, even if it's not pretty or simple. Tentatively, I take Dax's hand in mine and at least he doesn't retract it.

"It's not you," Dax says without looking at me. I stutter, looking to Huxley for context. Instead, the blond sits behind me, his large hands resting on my waist. His fingers rub soothing circles into my back, transporting me back to a time before all this. Before confusion and emotional territory, when I could convince myself this was all just a bit of fun.

"I-I don't understand."

Dax turns to face me. "The problem isn't you. It's me."

"How is the problem you? Wyatt was right, I did beg to go back home."

"Which you have every right to do. The problem is what I felt at the thought of you leaving. I shouldn't feel so cut up when I don't even have any sort of relationship with you." I can only blink at him, wading through the swamp of emotion swimming in his gaze.

"Dax, I..."

"It's okay, Avery." Dax cuts in, pulling his hand back to rub his neck. "You see me as a friend and nothing more. And that's okay. I just..." he trails off, looking towards the fountain again. "I know things aren't easy with you and Wyatt being under the same roof, but it's not all been bad. I guess I got my hopes up that you might want to stick around for a while longer at least. I thought there was more time." He stops short, jaw clenching as if to rein in further words.

"Come here," I reach for his shoulders and turn him to face me. Taking his face in my hands, I force Dax to get out of his head and focus on the words I'm saying. "Let me explain before you start jumping to your own conclusions." Huxley pushes closer too, his chest against my back to listen in too.

"I love hanging out with you guys. No two days are the same, and I enjoy the calm ones as much as Garrett's batshit crazy parades. But...I'm also confused by what's going on here. There's only one of me and four of you. I just can't be enough for each of you, so it's difficult not to feel expendable. Like a passing fad to be dropped when someone better comes along. I was merely protecting myself."

Dax's expression slips into something akin to devastation. Huxley tenses behind me, a sigh dropping his forehead onto my shoulder.

"Ahh fuck, Little Swan. If you don't know how we feel about you, then that's on us." The dynamic changes in an instant, my body being pulled and eased into a Dax and Huxley sandwich. Their heat seeps into me, chasing away a chill I didn't realize I had. My mouth lowers into the curve of Dax's neck, stinging from the cut I forgot was there.

"None of us do anything conventionally," Dax whispers to me. I inhale him, savoring his sea mineral smell, his touch. He holds me so gently, whereas Huxley is glued to my back. The arms around my waist squeeze tight as if I might disappear.

"You're not a passing fad. We all saw how special you were the moment you pepper sprayed Garrett, and we've been falling ever since," Huxley mutters. I suck in a breath. I know they're trying to soothe me, tell me what I want to hear but it's having the opposite effect. All I feel is more sure I can't be enough.

"Look, I know it's fun competing with each other for my attention but...falling?" I try to pull back. Neither let me so I sigh and melt back into their hold. "How am I supposed to deal with this without hurting anyone? I don't want to hurt anyone." Tears spring to my eyes, the fight fleeing from my body. Why am I always in fight or flight mode? Turning to an emotion I prefer, my nostrils flare. "Except Wyatt."

"I wouldn't worry about that," Huxley chuckles into my hair. "Wyatt hurts himself. We love the guy, but once he chooses a standpoint, he won't budge. No matter how much begging, bloodshed or money is thrown his way."

We fall into contemplative silence, the sound of water cascading beside us filling the empty night. I can see why this is Dax's favorite place; it's ideal to sit and think. Everything seems a little less muddled all of a sudden, but that might have more to do with the arms shielding me from the cold than the fountain. They make it seem simple - all I need to do is stick around. Give it a little more time before I try to run back to the life I knew.

"We're not asking for forever," Dax says into the quiet, "but you don't have to worry about being expendable. As long as we hold your interest, you'll be the center of ours."

"Okay," I concede. A weight lifts from my shoulders as I surrender control. I'm not steering this ship, and if Dax says I'm not going to be tossed overboard, I believe him. A yawn tugs at my mouth, the turbulence of the day finally settling in. Huxley laughs, swinging my leg over the lip of the fountain.

"Come on, time for bed." Understatement of the century. I dully remember Meg is patiently waiting for me . This was supposed to be our fall break. I can't let her down. Huxley guides us back to the mansion in under half the time it took me to venture across the gardens, and Dax's hand remains in mine the entire way. I keep leaning into him, reminding myself that I can be comfortable with just this. The here and now.

Passing the pool, we step through the open french doors to find only one person is still awake. Wyatt is reclined on the sofa, feet up and a book in his hands. I push down the overwhelming urge to dive on him with my fists swinging, and instead I smack his book so it hits him in the face.

"You're absolutely pathetic. I hope you know that," I raise my chin and walk away, Dax's hand still in mine. Wyatt yells a string of curses after me, causing my smile to deepen as I climb the stairs.

"What was that about?" Dax asks, then catches himself as we stop on the top landing. "Actually, don't answer that. Sweet dreams, Little Swan." His lips press against mine in a light caress, careful not to cause any pain to my busted lip. Dax never pushes for more, further cementing that everything's going to be okay. I smile as we break apart.

"Goodnight Dax."

Huxley leads me the rest of the way to my room, where Meg is passed out across the bed, a bottle of wine tucked into her armpit. With a snort, I peck Huxley on the cheek and head inside. Meg mumbles that I have some serious explaining to do when I adjust and tuck her into bed, before heading into the bathroom. I undress, flicking on the shower. Just before the room fills with steam, I lean on the counter to stare at myself in the mirror.

My cheeks are pink, my lip split down the left side. My hair is a rat's nest and my neck has mud splattered across it. Yet I'm smiling, and I feel whole. How the hell is my life this crazy?

DAX

CHAPTER THIRTY EIGHT

Drumming my fingers on my thighs, I can't take it any more. I push out of the car, preferring to pace outside. It's been over an hour since I text Avery to meet me here, and with each passing second, I have the dreaded feeling she failed to get out of the mansion without any attention. I don't know what came over me when I woke up this morning. I lay in bed all of last night in a half-dream state, imagining ways I can get closer to Avery. Of how I can put myself more in the forefront. I love my brothers, but when competing for attention, they've got the charisma and confidence I sorely lack.

"Would you like me to take you back?" Huxley's-borrowed driver lowers the window and leaned over the passenger seat to ask. I twist my lips, staring at my phone's screen. She said she'd be here.

"Give it a little longer," I sigh, tapping my foot. He nods and retracts, leaving me to question if I should have done something simpler. A walk around Huxley's estate or a leisurely morning swim, maybe? But no - that wouldn't have been surprising enough. I want Avery to see there's more sides to me than the geeky guy who wants to carry bags and open doors for her. She told me last night that she doesn't feel good enough, and I've never resonated with her so much.

I'm about to call it quits when a dark town car races past the street, before backtracking and coming to a screeching halt just beside me. My heart hammers against my ribcage as the backdoor flies open. Axel and Wyatt scoot out, as Huxley abandons the passenger seat. His knuckles are painfully white and when I look past him, I can see why.

"You let Garrett drive?!"

"No one lets Garrett do anything. He just...*does*." Huxley doubles over, ready to dry heave. I hide my irritation, crossing my arms in an effort to remain calm.

"Where is Avery?"

"She's riding with Meg," Axel answers, joining my side to face the road. "They were supposed to follow, but Garrett thought shaking them loose around town would be equally as fun." I pinch the bridge of my nose. I should have known better than to think just because I'm patient, waiting my turn to have Avery's undivided attention, that the others would extend me the same courtesy. There's a reason good guys always finish last, because the nosey fuckers in the way are easier to placate than ignore.

"So, what's the deal, Daxy?" Garrett slings an arm over my shoulder. "I was just about to have second breakfast when your distress call came in."

"Distress call?" I frown, looking out at my phone. I'd sent a message in the group chat that I was busy this morning and I'd be back later.

"Yeah, you're never busy. Wyatt should know, he controls your calendar. We were worried you'd been kidnapped and half of your organs would have been listed on the black market by now."

"Not worried enough to forego showering," I roll my eyes as his soapy smell washes over me. Garrett's grin is infectious and I shrug him off before he sees that he's got through to me.

A second town car appears in a much calmer fashion, pulling up smoothly into a parking space beside the building's entrance. Avery and Meg appear with wide smiles and a carton of drinks each. They've dressed similarly in tight-fitting leggings and oversized college sweaters, their hair in high ponytails. Meg calls out the random assortment of drinks they've brought, from coffees to bubble teas, while people snatch up their preference. Slipping away, Avery approaches me last with a sweet smile.

"Sorry we're late. We couldn't be bothered with Garrett's detour, so we took one of our own." She hands me a plastic cup with a straw. Strawberry milkshake with cream and sprinkles. Grinning, I accept it whilst winding an arm around her waist and tugging her closer.

"Couldn't get out undetected, I take it?" I say into her ear. She leans into me, brushing her nose along my jaw.

"Not a chance." Her hands slip underneath my t-shirt, trailing over my abs with sensual slowness. "But don't worry about them. I'm here for you." I smile genuinely then, skating a quick kiss over her temple. Garrett starts to get bouncy, thanks to the mini cup in his large hand. Ahh fuck, who let him have an expresso? Leading Avery towards the building, I can't find it in me to be angry. This is how it's going to be, all of us orbiting around her. I should get used to it and still find a way to stand out.

The warehouse is on the outskirts of town. If it weren't for the music leaking through the high windows, anyone would think the old structure was derelict. Graffiti covers the exterior shutters and the main entrance is boarded up with wooden planks. A simple sign with an arrow indicates the side door is to be used for attendees, which creaks as I open it for Avery to pass through. She doesn't hesitate, trusting me to follow right behind.

Strobe lighting bounces against a polished wooden floor filling the center, sectioned off by red ropes. The back of the warehouse has a small diner next to an arcade, every machine switched on. Random popcorn and candy floss machines are scattered amongst empty tables and chairs. Ed's Roller Disco is said to have once been the place to be on a Friday night. It might not be in its prime any more, but it's perfectly secluded for us. After putting a call in to the owner and mentioning Huxley's name, I managed to get the place stocked and fully staffed to ourselves for the entire day.

In one bundle, everyone barring Wyatt runs over to the skate hire booth like a bunch of children. He lingers back, keeping himself removed from the fun as he always does. I wait my turn, before requesting my required shoe size from the punky girl behind the desk. I also notice an on-hand arcade assistant, as well as kitchen and serving staff present in the diner. Accepting my skates, I sit in a nearby chair to pull them onto my feet and tie the laces.

Avery and Meg are already on the rink, hand in hand while they skate and sway to the music. I had no doubt they'd be naturals, even if I was hoping to be the one holding Avery's hand. Music bleeds from the speakers, one heavy bass tune blending into the next. Lifting her arms above her head, Avery's sweatshirt rises to reveal the top of her skin-tight leggings leaving nothing to the imagination. Her ass is a testament to all of her dance training, her thighs and calves something to be both jealous and proud of.

Axel passes by, his fingers lingering on my arm and a question in his hazel eyes. I let him pull me to my feet, steadying myself on his arms before he leads the way onto the rink. "You all good, Axe?" Instead of answering, he looks over my shoulder to where Wyatt has taken up position in a booth on his own. With the table dividing us, he can safely watch from the shadows and pose no risk of being invited to join in. I sigh, patting Axel's bicep.

"He'll come around eventually," I say without really believing it. Wyatt hasn't been this distant for this long before. Axel's expression doesn't change and not for the first time, I wish he didn't wear his heart on his sleeve. Empathizing with all of us takes a toll that I worry he won't always be able to handle. I tug us over to the rink, offering out my hand. His resulting smile is heartwarming.

The first glide of wheels shifts something inside both of us. The stress that's been weighing on my chest lately begins to lift with the anticipation of having some fun. One look around and I know having everyone here was for the best. We deserve to cut loose.

Skating around the oval dancefloor, I bump shoulders with Gare to start a race. He's visibly vibrating with energy, breaking through the hold Axel and I had on each other. Hux is quick to join, the four of us speeding around with no finish line. The girls dance in the center, cheering and whooping like cheerleaders. We push ourselves until our calves are burning, not a care in the world. This feels good, right even. To be free, to live the life I've been gifted.

The latest tune by Charlie XCX that has been all over the radio starts to play, gaining our shouts of approval. Moving my shoulders in time with Axel and Hux, my cheeks begin to hurt from smiling for this long and I don't plan on letting it drop any time soon.

Avery joins us as we dance side by side, overtaking and showing off her moves. I whip my phone out to catch a video of her moonwalking backwards, then turn myself to grab a couple of selfies. Garrett's face is right there, taking up most of the screen as if I don't already have a camera roll full of his photo-bombing. Pocketing my phone, a pair of small hands slide around my waist. Avery turns me to face forwards, her smile lighting up her whole face.

"Thank you for this," she beams despite her split lip. I kiss the tip of her nose, avoiding hurting her mouth. It looks angry and sore, but Avery won't let that stop her from having fun. She lightly tugs my arm, pulling me to the side of the rink. "I'm sorry it's not what you were hoping for." Garrett chooses that moment to yee-haw above the music, and I can't help but laugh.

"It's fine, Little Swan. Seeing you happy is all I wanted."

"Not true," Avery raises a brow knowingly. "You wanted us to spend some alone time together - outside of campus." I nod, not prepared to lie to her. Drawing her into my arms, Avery leans on me for stability.

"We'll get our turn. I'm a patient man. I can wait."

"Oh, Dax," Avery sighs, laying her head on my shoulder. "You shouldn't be so quick to put yourself at the back of the line. Not when your friends are so eager to push in front."

I snort. Story of my life, but I also know patience pays off. Today is a good day. Not all of them will be, and who Avery turns to in her times of need will be telling. Garrett and Axel can be loud and playful, and even Huxley can bolster his way in when he's done with waiting. But not me. I'll be here, stoic and ready. I'll catch Avery when she falls.

"Go have fun," I press my lips aside her forehead, resisting the urge to call her '*my love*'. On cue, Meg grabs Avery and drags her away laughing. I watch her for a short while longer before seeking out a drink. Once my skates are off and my milkshake is all gone, I stride into the arcade in my socks. Pushing some loose change into a pinball machine, I feel a presence at my side as soon as I release the first ball.

"Bet I can get onto the scoreboard before you can," Gare whispers into my ear, licking my lobe to put me off. I misjudge the flipper and the ball plunges back into the machine. I shove Gare away playfully, spotting another pinball machine across the space and directing him to it.

"Loser buys lunch," I shout across the space between us.

"Perfect, I've already ordered!" he replies with an evil laugh. Starting up the next game, I somehow lose on repeat for the five rounds until Garrett's hands shoot into the air and he roars in victory. Motherfucker. Running over to me, he rubs his knuckles against my hair and bounces into the diner to collect his re-heated prize.

Looking around the room, I fail to spot my brothers until I notice a pair of legs hanging out from one of the booths. Wyatt's booth, to be exact. I exhale deeply, heading over to join. Huxley is lying on his back, his head in Axel's lap who is absent-mindedly playing with his hair. Garrett scoots in, nudging me closer to Wyatt, with a trayful of enough food to feed all of us if he permitted it.

"They'd make a cute couple, don't you think?" Garrett asks, gesturing to the girls with his chin. They're still in the rink while a slow song plays, dancing together sensually. Avery's arms are around Meg's neck, whose hands are planted on Avery's hips. Spinning in slow circles, the two of them joke, smile and giggle together. Gare starts chanting 'kiss, kiss' loudly, pumping his fist in the air and shattering their moment. Happy to put on a show, Meg turns to twerk against her friend's crotch. Avery spanks her while biting her lip before they start laughing and return to skating side by side.

"No way, those two know their way around a cock," Huxley replies from his horizontal position without even looking. His statement bothers Wyatt and everyone sees it.

"No need to be jealous, Riot," Garrett says around a french fry. "I'd happily play spin the bottle with you if you need some action." He chuckles, but his attempt to lighten the mood falls flat.

"Things are never going to go back to how they were, are they?" Wyatt says stoically. Huxley sits up, the humor in the air dying a cold death.

"Different doesn't have to be bad," Axel attempts. Wyatt's eyes are squarely focused on Avery and Meg, the tic in his jaw beating profusely.

"While I watch my best friends trip over themself to fuck my-" he catches himself and clears his throat. "Avery. That doesn't sound like anything I want to be a part of."

"What are you saying? Are you going somewhere?" Huxley raises a brow. I'm sure beneath the music I hear Axel whimper. Garrett tuts, pushing his basket of fries away.

"Or you could pull the stick out of your ass and admit you want to fuck her too." I wasn't prepared for Garrett's brashness. Sucking in a breath, I divert my eyes to my lap, preferring not to see if there is any truth lingering in Wyatt's green eyes. If what Garrett just said is true, not only have I been blind to everything going on around me, but our lives just became much messier than I anticipated.

"Who's fucking who?" Meg asks, the girls appearing. They pull up small stools to sit at the table and help themselves to the discarded food.

"No one, yet," Garrett winks at Avery. She smacks him upside the head before snatching a pickle from his plate. Tension returns to the table as the majority of us watch them eat in silence. The lack of conversation doesn't go unnoticed.

"Okay, well what do you say we leave these losers to their angst?" Avery asks, nudging Meg with her elbow and grabbing their skates. They head to the booth to swap out for their sneakers, waving goodbye. "We might go catch a movie or something. Don't wait up," Avery calls.

I watch my idea of a dream date get flushed away as she leaves. Once the door swings closed, Wyatt stands up abruptly, shoving his hands in his pockets and stalking off without a backwards glance. Huxley is hot on his heels and Axel follows with pleading eyes.

Leaving me alone with Gare and the aftermath of their departure, I huff at the side of his face. He pauses with a half-eaten burger hovering in front of his face.

"What? Did you want a bite?"

"Don't play dumb. Did you really have to taunt Wyatt like that?" Garrett rolls his jaw as he finishes his mouthful and places the burger down with added care. When he turns to me, there's a starling amount of clarity in his dark brown eyes.

"The way I see it, there are three outcomes of the tightrope we're all treading. We lose Wyatt, we lose Avery, or the pair of them stop pretending they don't feel the attraction I've seen since the start and we all get to live happily ever after." My mouth drops open and my eyes dart around, grappling for something to say.

"They're step-siblings, Garrett. It's never going to happen." He scoffs, waving me off as he stands. Beneath his mess of dark hair,

Garrett's eyes cut through me with more seriousness than I thought he possessed.

"A piece of paper doesn't negate the fact they've never spent more than an hour in each other's company. They're strangers, not siblings. Give it a little more time and a little more nudging from yours truly. You'll see that I'm right. I always am."

AVERY

CHAPTER THIRTY NINE

The week slips by at an alarming rate. Whenever I check the time, hours have passed and the larger the knot of dread in my stomach becomes. Life is simple here. Days are spent in the pool or lounging around indoors. One day, Meg and I had a reading marathon and the next, we had a spree of watching corny drama series' back to back. I was a good girl and made sure all my assignments were completed and I'm up to date on the reading syllabus, but aside from that, I've been happy to forget Waversea even exists.

Today, Meg and I are venturing out for the second time only since arriving, deciding we can't face another stroll around Huxley's estate. It's beautiful, but I don't want to run the risk of finding Wyatt reading in a random corner or jogging through the gardens. Everywhere I go, he seems to be there. I swear he's doing it on purpose. At least there haven't been any more awkward silences or insufferable dinners, but the vacation is coming close to an end and I don't want to jinx it.

Meg links her arm through mine as we saunter down the driveway, a picnic basket hanging from her other hand. We're both wearing jeans and light raincoats, undeterred by the gray clouds. Tomorrow, Meg and I have to part ways. She's heading home to Brookhaven to spend the weekend with her mom and I'll sulk here, pretending Thanksgiving isn't happening.

"So, what's the plan for tonight?" Meg asks once we're on the main road.

I shrug. "There was mention of a movie marathon in Huxley's home theater."

"Ooh, which movies?" Her face lights up. "Horror ones I hope."

"Nope," I grin back at her, "Axel has a list of rom coms he wants to binge." Meg groans dramatically but doesn't protest as we traipse down a gravel path off to the side, diverting around the back of the iron gates. Despite being overcast, the air is humid, a gentle breeze rustling the leaves and bringing the promise of rain this afternoon. I love the rain, particularly the sound of it beating against a window or rooftop. That's the one memory I have gladly brought with me from my childhood; being inside when it rained was the only time I felt protected and safe from external dangers.

We follow the heightened wall surrounding Huxley's property, sticking to the directions he gave us. There isn't another house for miles, only the sound of crickets chittering in the undergrowth cutting through the silence. We walk for a while without talking, content to be in each other's company. It's not easy to tell the time of day with the sun being hidden and we made the conscious choice to leave our phones behind today. No tech, no distractions. There's something wholly freeing about being uncontactable. Just where Huxley said it would be, we find a small clearing beside a gently babbling stream.

"This is it," Meg says with a flourish, setting down the picnic basket and spreading out the checkered blanket. I grin, dropping down next to her and eagerly digging into the food. Although, food may be a very loose term, as we only packed desserts.

"It's perfect," I mumble around a forkful of chocolate cake. The stream is crystal clear, allowing me to see all the way to the bottom where small fish swim between rocks and plants. The water ripples gently as it flows over pebbles and creates small whirlpools where leaves and twigs get caught. The air around us is fresh and crisp, with hints of damp earth and wildflowers.

"Are you going to be okay when I leave?" Meg says just as my mind was drifting to a thousand other places.

"Of course. Why wouldn't I be?" I twist towards her, a frown creasing my brows. Meg fumbles with her small, paper plate.

"Oh, no I didn't mean anything by it," she rushes to say. I raise a brow, knowing her better than that.

"But?"

"But...I just worry." She exhales loudly and puts her cake aside. Damn, she must be serious. "I know the guys are good to you, for now." Meg avoids my gaze but I instantly understand her concerns. I had the same ones myself a week ago. "I just don't want you to get hurt. It's not quite...normal for them all to be so focused on you. What if you wake up one day and it doesn't seem quite as endearing any more? It could easily become suffocating."

I ponder on that for a moment. I've been so worried about me being enough to keep them interested, but Meg's mind sees the opposite. Although, the real question isn't whether I'll become suffocated by the guys always being around, but if they will back off should I ask. And the answer is unequivocally yes, and that's what's important.

"I love you for worrying about me," I smile, leaning into Meg's shoulder. Her head leans on mine.

"Just try not to get swept up okay. Don't let them push you into anything you don't want to do." My eyes widen but I remain in place. Meg doesn't know the Shadowed Souls like I do. Aside for asswipe Wyatt, they wouldn't hurt me. Even then, his taunts are verging on childish now.

"They're a group of basketball players, Meg. Not a cult." I try to laugh off her concern. She nudges me upright and whips around, pinning me with a serious stare. I hold my hands up. "Okay, okay. I promise I'll stay in control and keep you in the know."

"That's all I ask." She finally smiles. Relaxing back into our surroundings, we lay back and the chat falls to other things. Like a boy she's been flirting with at her college, how she's taking a break from the swim team to focus on being Captain of her lacrosse team now they have passed qualifiers.

The stream's constant babbling is soothing, a repetitive sound that blends harmoniously with the rustling of leaves in the trees overhead. Occasionally, I can hear the splash of a fish jumping out of the water. I could sit here all day and night, if it wasn't for the first raindrop that touches my cheek. Beyond the trees, the clouds have grown darker, and a thick black sheet now covers the sky.

"Time to go," I sigh. Meg helps me to lift and fold the blanket, stuffing it back into the basket. A sudden breeze skates down my spine and I shiver, goosebumps erupting over my skin. Lifting the picnic basket and looping the strap over my arm, we start the ascent back.

As if conjured by us leaving the safety of the trees, a sheet of rain falls from the heavens. We squeal and laugh, running along the gravel path which instantly becomes muddy. Holding onto each other, we make it to the top, back on the road that has water droplets pummeling off the tarmac like bullets. I picture the steaming hot shower I'm going to have when I get back, the fluffy warm towel and silk pajamas. It's what keeps me moving.

I don't slow as we approach the iron gates, barely thinking twice about the van pulled up on the opposite side of the road. Pressing the buzzer repeatedly, we wave at the camera watching overhead for someone to let us in. Meg's arm grabs mine, roughly yanking me. I frown at her, then follow her eyeline to the person approaching. It's just a UPS delivery man who hands me a cardboard box and retreats. I stuff the box in our picnic basket as the gates open and we run up the driveway. Two butlers are waiting with towels, swapping them for our soaking wet sneakers and coats.

"Still love the rain?" Meg asks, roughing up her hair with the hand towel.

"Yep," I beam. The guys are in the kitchen playing a card game across the island. I plant the picnic basket down on the counter, turning to leave. "You had a parcel delivered, Huxley. It's in the basket." Then I head upstairs and help myself to his shower. I've finally started to find my way around the mansion, unable to resist sneaking into his bed just once this week. There are few things a cuddle from Huxley's strong arms can't heal.

Once washed and smelling like his apple shower gel, I pad back to my room in a towel to dig out those pajamas I've been dreaming of. Lilac satin with fluffy bootie-style slippers. Meg braids my hair down my back, leaving her own in a messy bun and we head back down to join the boys' card game. Only once we reappear in the kitchen, Garrett, Axel, Dax and Wyatt are standing and staring at me gravely.

"What's wrong?" I ask, dread forming in my chest. On the island, the parcel is torn open.

"That box had your name on it, Peach." Garrett gives the cardboard a quick side glance. "I thought you might have ordered some sexy underwear for us, so I opened it." The frown lines framing Garrett's mouth don't sit right with me. Meg moves first, peering into the box. The stiffness to her shoulders is enough to tell me this isn't some kind of joke, and she turns to hand me a note.

I thought your mother would have taught you some self-respect, but it appears you're as much of a whore as she was. I'm watching you, Avery. Make better choices.

"What the fuck is this?!" I toss the letter as if it's burned my fingertips. Approaching the box on swift feet, I forget how to breathe. Stacks of photographs are spread across the base, all featuring me. All with one of the Shadowed Souls. All from inside Huxley's boundary wall. I can't track the images through the tears blurring my vision.

Me kissing Huxley in the pool, walking hand-in-hand with Dax through the gardens. And they aren't limited to outside. Through a window, I'm bent over the snooker table with Garrett's crotch pushing against my ass. In the living area, I'm reading while Axel massages my feet. Fuck, I really do look like a whore.

"Mr. XO?" Meg questions. I scrunch up my nose. The note was different, the tone not seeming right and the typical signature missing, but I can't be sure. I'm not sure of anything any more. My hands start to shake as I sift through the photos.

"He's never sent photos before. He's...pretty harmless." My voice grows small. He *is* harmless, right? A superfan who has sent me gifts, poems and little check ins across the years. On some dark days, his letters were a saving grace. A reason to remember that someone else might care about me. I've had more communication from him than my supposed brother. But now...it's all so sudden, it's all too much. "This just seems too creepy."

"That's what stalkers do, Aves." Meg holds up a photo, her cheeks turning red. "They escalate. You weren't at the manor or Waversea, where he expected you to be. He's found you, followed you and now he's acting out." My ears switch off. I can't hear through the buzzing as I really look at the photo she's holding up. This one is different to the rest, framed by a white border.

"Holy fuck," I gasp. Garrett is there to support me when my legs are preparing to give out.

"I know right. Who the hell uses polaroids any more?"

"No," I shake my head, fighting the urge to elbow him in the ribs. "This was last week. Here, in the gardens. I thought...I was so sure..." My eyes float up to Wyatt. He's yet to show any emotion, but now his eyes narrow and he snatches the photo from me. Captured in time, the image shows me sprawled across the floor of the rose garden, mud caked over my pink blazer. I absentmindedly lick my lip where the split was, remembering the flash of light when I fell. I thought I'd just hit my head too hard, but now...Now nothing makes sense. "I thought you attacked me," I whisper at Wyatt. His green eyes bulge in his head.

"You were attacked?! Right here under our noses, and you didn't think to tell anyone?" Squaring my jaw, I grab the photo back.

"No I didn't, because I thought you were being the asshole you always are and trying to scare me. Telling people would warn them that I was planning to stab you in the eye with a pen while you sleep." Wyatt scowls, trying to step up to me but Dax puts himself in the way.

"This isn't the time for this," he grits out, turning a warning look on Wyatt to back up. Huxley enters then, his phone clenched in a tight fist.

"Police are on the way, the surveillance team are scanning the camera footage for the last week and searching for the UPS van's plates. Chances are, they're fake. I've called in extra security to surround the property."

"It's not the delivery guy's fault," I shake my head, feeling woozy. "He was just doing his job." Huxley's expression is filled with pity as he approaches, reaching over me to flip the lid of the box.

"There's no postage stamp or address, baby girl. This was hand delivered, most likely by the man responsible."

My world tilts on its axis. Strong arms catch me as I fall, scooping me up against a firm chest. I can't see for crying, the weight of the truth crashing down on me. He was right there. Within reaching distance, showing me how easy I am to access. If Meg hadn't been there, would he have attacked me again, stuffed me in the van and driven away? It's all too much, too many what if's and I can't stop the tears from falling.

Gripping Huxley's t-shirt in my fists, he sits on the sofa and cradles me until I have nothing left to give.

I don't realize I've drifted off to sleep until the police are being shown into the living area. I blink up to find the curtains are all closed, secluding us from the outside world. Wyatt escorts Meg to the dining area with a detective to give a separate statement, leaving me with the rest of the guys while I try to help the sketch artist conjure up a face I barely saw. He shows me a few versions and I feel completely useless that none of them feel right. It was pouring with rain and I didn't pay enough attention.

It's late into the night by the time we venture back upstairs, exhausted and stressed. I curl up beside Meg, apologizing for ruining our last night together.

"Shhh, Aves. None of this is your fault." She soothes. I snuggle my face into her neck, holding her hand in both of mine beneath the covers.

"I want to go home," I whisper. Nothing like this ever happened at the fortress that is Hughes Manor. An idea strikes me, the wording of that letter still bothering me. "I want to see the other letters. Maybe I overlooked something, or maybe there's a clue to whoever this guy is that I didn't notice before." Sitting upright, I stare into the darkness. Meg joins me, her arms rounding my shoulders.

"You know what, Aves. I think that's a fantastic idea."

AVERY

CHAPTER FORTY

Meg and I are up and dressed at the buttcrack of dawn, silently slipping our belongings back into our bags. There's really no need to creep around, given the rooms are so large and spread so far apart, but it feels necessary. My heart has been tripping over itself all night, my mind playing out all the scenarios that could happen instead of letting me sleep.

We could be followed back to the manor. The builders doing the restoration work could call Nixon on sight and I'll have to explain myself to him too. The Shadowed Souls could decide I've betrayed them and refuse to speak to me again.

Placing an envelope on my pillow, I step back, chewing on my sore lip. I owe them the truth, but if I do it in person, they'll convince me to let them tag along. The photos were a clear message. Whoever has been watching doesn't like me with them. If this stalker sees Hughes Manor as of much as a sanctuary as I do, taking five guys back home might aggravate him even more.

"Ready?" Meg whispers. I nod, slipping my strap over my front. We hold our shoes, careful not to make a sound whilst tiptoeing through the mansion. The sun hasn't risen beyond the bay windows, the wait staff yet to rise. Aside from the ticking of an old grandfather clock at the base of the staircase, it's eerily still. Meg goes ahead while I pause on the top step, looking back the way I've come. I'm stalling. Hoping someone has the intuition to come stop me. Then I shake my head. I need to do this. I need to know if I've overlooked something from Mr. XO. Were there signs? Clues?

Clicking her fingers, Meg brings me back to the present. I rush down the stairs to join her. We only pause long enough to push our feet into our sneakers, moving quicker now. We're halfway to the front door when I hear the soft but unmistakable creak of leather from an armchair. A light switches on a second later and we freeze, Meg's hand already on the handle.

"You two really are as stupid as I thought," Wyatt groans. Pushing himself upright, he grabs a duffle bag which was sitting at his feet.

"And where do you think you're going?" Meg pops her hip, failing to keep her voice down.

"I'm driving you idiots back to the manor. Or did I misinterpret the sneaking-out plan?"

Wyatt emerges from the darkened corner, one eyebrow raised. He's dressed in black slacks and a white polo shirt that hugs his broad chest, complete with leather jacket. His dark brown hair is swept back, his green eyes dulled due to the lack of real lighting. If he's been awake all night, waiting for this moment, there are no dark circles under his eyes to show it. My stomach plummets as he saunters over to us, taking in our attire and demeanor.

"You're not coming," I hiss.

"Correction - I am, and I'm driving." Jingling a set of keys in his hand, I stutter, at a loss for words. Meg nudges me, silently urging me to come up with something plausible to change his mind.

"For what possible reason? You hate going home."

"No, I hate being around you. But I also don't like being lied to." Unlocking the front door, Wyatt pulls it open and waits for us to pass through first. I half-expect some sort of alarm to go off, sensing Wyatt is leading us into one trap or another. But it doesn't and I'm left scowling at the side of his face.

"I've never lied to you." In truth, I've barely spoken to him in all these years. It's a pity really, but of his own creation. Wyatt's face is illuminated by the Bentley's headlights briefly flashing.

"Good to know, but I'm talking about Nixon." Wyatt clenches his jaw, popping the trunk for our bags. Once inside, he slams it closed, making no effort to be stealthy. He looks at me briefly, but no less filled with irritation than usual. "There's something going on at the manor, and I plan on finding out what it is."

With every mile put between us and Huxley's home, the less sure I am that this was the best idea. My unease is doubled by the figure in the driver's seat, one hand on the wheel and tapping his thumb to the music of his choosing. Meg and I took the back seats, keeping our distance. For all we know, Wyatt could speed off the edge of a cliff, putting us all out of each other's misery.

Spotting the sun just about to crest on the horizon, I press my lips together. It won't be long now until my phone starts blowing up, and then I'll be the one begging for that cliff roll. But no phone calls come. Not as much as a message. I decide then that I've cut my ties for the last time. Dax won't forgive me twice. Whether it's a curse or a saving grace, my sleepless night catches up to me. I barely register my head dipping onto Meg's shoulder as images take over, plaguing my mind.

Dark rooms, flickering candles. Eyes blazing red with their anger. More people I've drawn in like moths to a flame, just to push them away and create heartache that never needed to exist. The figures talk to me, echoing back thoughts I've struggled against for too long.

Why do you do this to people? Can't you help yourself from causing pain? Why can't you just disappear? How are you so unloveable?

I wake some hours later, stretching my legs and filling my appetite at a small diner before we get back on the road. So it goes; sleep, stretch, refuel and carry on. Wyatt doesn't speak unless necessary. He pushes the Bentley to over a hundred miles an hour at any given opportunity, eating up the distance to Brookhaven. It's not the most exhilarating thirteen hours of my life, but at least Meg is there for small talk and comfort.

For a good, long while, we discuss the murder mystery party my mom had planned for Thanksgiving Fest. The characters are already assigned in brown envelopes, the matching attire in a box in the attic.

One last extravaganza in her name. I sigh, falling back into a fitful sleep as I remember the parties from previous years, when everything seemed so simple.

Finally, I peel my eyes open to shades of gold and pink coating the sky. We're no longer on the open road but instead, we're navigating through the urban jungle of towering buildings and blinking neon signs that is the Manor's neighboring city. Beyond the tinted windows, the streets are alive with people heading out to start their weekend off the right way. Risqué outfits and beaming smiles, high heels and tiny handbags. Women line the sidewalk, all the way to the Ambassadors Theatre where a dance group similar to the Chippendales are performing tonight. Meg's face lights up as her hand squeezes mine, and Wyatt snorts in the front.

"Not a chance." Instead, he slows and turns in the opposite direction, confusing me by the back streets he takes. The car comes to a stop in an empty parking bay, adjacent to a tall building of brick and wire terraces. Five floors high, flowers potted along repetitive windows. Wyatt turns to face us, his green eyes cold and unreadable.

"We're here," he says simply before exiting the car. I frown as I climb out onto numb legs, just in time for Wyatt to throw my bag into my chest.

"What are we doing here?" Meg asks, looking up at her own home building like a stranger. The light on the third floor is on, signaling her mom is home.

"I thought we were going to the Manor?" I stomp towards Wyatt. Tossing Meg her bag, he closes the trunk and tries to return to the driver's seat. Meg is waiting on his other side so we can close him in. Wyatt sighs dramatically.

"It's too late to go snooping around in the dark, especially with a stalker on the loose. We'll go in the morning, during daylight hours when the cops are more likely to respond should anything go wrong."

"You're not staying at my place," Meg reels back as if she's been slapped. Wyatt leans back against the Bentley with a bored expression and folded arms.

"Obviously. I'll be camping out here to keep an eye out."

"You think we could have been followed," I gasp, suddenly looking all around. The street is quiet, a lamppost every twenty feet to light the road. It all hits me at once and I could roll my eyes at my own naïvety. That's why Wyatt has had the pedal to the floor during most of the journey, why he passed popular service stops in favor of deserted diners with stale food, why he's been on high alert. Although that goes against everything I know to be true - Wyatt doesn't care enough to be protective of me.

At his silence, Meg and I slowly walk backwards to her steps, watching him slip back behind the driver's seat. Her shoulder leans against mine.

"Do you trust him?" I breathe clutching my bag to my front in the same way she is.

"Not in the slightest. He's probably waiting to meet your stalker so he can shake his hand and welcome him into the building."

A tentative smile crosses my lips and I relax a little. "Thanks for that."

"Anytime," Meg says, leading me up the stairs to her front door. Her mother is sitting at the small dining table when we enter, doing a jigsaw puzzle with a glass of wine and some old school dance anthems playing on the radio. Her hair is pinned up by a claw clip, brown frizzy curls exploding from the top. Cotton pajamas and fluffy, bunny ear slippers are a far cry from the pantsuit and briefcase therapist who used to visit me every Thursday for our weekly sessions.

"Hey mom," Meg kisses Keren's bobbing head, breaking the trance the jigsaw and music had over her.

"Hi sweetheart. I expected you home hours ago- Oh, Avery! It's so lovely to see you," Keren sees me and shoots up from her chair. There's an awkward pause where she morphs between an overjoyous smile and then tries to reign herself in, shakily holding up her hand. I knock it aside and drag her in for a tight squeeze. There's no need for polite pleasantries at this point. This woman knows more about me than anyone else on the planet.

"Nice to see you too, Keren. I'm loving the vibe going on here." I wave a hand over her outfit and the table. "Is there space for two more to join in?"

"And wine for two more to enjoy," Meg hastily adds, heading for the kitchen. "We're going to need a shit load of wine tonight!" Keren's brow twitches and mouth opens, most likely to chastise Meg's language, but a huge grin breaks out instead.

"There's a few bottles in the refrigerator!" she calls out. "Get yourself comfortable, Avery. I want to hear all about that new school of yours." Picking my bag up from where I dropped it, I turn away as Keren's hand touches my arm. "As your friend, not your therapist," she feels the need to add. I smile warmly, jumping over this blurred line with both feet.

"Of course," I agree, seeking out Meg's room. I find it easily, marveling that I've never been to Meg's apartment before. She's always insisted on coming to the manor, and being a hermit, I've never thought to insist otherwise. Slipping into the room, I opt to leave the light off as I approach the window overlooking the street. The white Bentley sticks out sorely against the night. Inside, Wyatt has reclined the driver's seat, his arms underneath his head. Through the shadows, I trick myself into thinking he's staring directly at me. My heart skips a beat as I jerk backwards.

"Make mine a double measure!" I shout to Meg, placing a hand on my chest. Whatever it takes to get my mind off stalkers, shadows and watchful eyes.

CHAPTER FORTY ONE

Two figures stumble out of the main doorway, hissing at the brightness like a set of vampires. I lean against the car, wondering how I'm the one who had the most uncomfortable night's sleep, but they look like zombie versions of the girls who entered the building last night. Holding a hand over their darkly-rimmed eyes, they almost crash into me whilst hunting for the rear handle.

"Heavy night?" I raise a brow. Meg grumbles something incoherent, while Avery blurts out one word.

"Coffee." I roll my eyes. Waiting for the pair of them to be seated, I slam the door as hard as I can. Their cries from inside bring a smile to my lips. Silver linings, and all that. Despite my plan to get to the manor early, I do detour for drive thru coffee like the hospitable escort I am. Nursing their takeaway cups, I slide a glance to the rearview mirror.

"Happy now?" I sigh. Daggers are glared back at me from the backseat.

"Fucking asshole," Meg seethes. Avery tilts her head in agreement.

"We know you can't be nice to save your life, but you didn't have to keep braking so sharply every ten seconds," she scowls. To prove a point, I slam my foot on the brake and the car jumps to a hastily stop. The girls cry out and curse, bringing a slither of joy to my cold, dead heart.

"Thought I saw a cat," I grunt, making a show of peering over the dashboard. Finding some Xanax in the car door, I toss it into the back, ensuring that by the time we eventually reach the manor, my passengers are semi-personable. Ditching the car a street over, we walk to the gates, which are oddly slightly parted. We enter, walking up the driveway to the house I once thought of as home. I hate being here. I hate the feeling of time lost, of memories faded.

On approach, there is nothing out of place to be seen. No scaffolding, no sign of any restorations taking place. Avery strolls for the front door until I make a sound in the back of my throat. Jerking my head to the side, we amble around the outside of the manor first. My gut tells me something isn't right, starting with the open gates.

Everything seems normal; the sliding doors are locked, the pool is covered over for the winter. There are no lights on, no one anywhere to be seen. Until we get to the rear, I'm starting to believe there's no reason Avery couldn't return here after all. Fantastic news for me, I think, but then I see it. The window to my father's study is covered with wooden slats, remnants of glass still littering the trampled bushes underneath.

"What the hell?" Avery takes a step back. My hand flashes out before I can stop myself, spying a shard of glass just behind her heel. As soon as she's stable, I retract it and then push past, shoulder barging her for good measure. I wouldn't want her to get the wrong impression.

I lead the pair to the kitchen door, finding it also locked. Avery shoves me aside as payback, and reveals a lockbox between the shrubs. She knows the code to release the key, and once inside, she attends to the alarm. I push my hands in my pockets, leaning against the counter with nonchalance. Maybe then she won't realize I wouldn't have known what any of the codes were. It won't be my birthday and I sure as shit refuse to acknowledge hers.

From the inside, my father's study looks like a bomb has exploded. A weapon has smashed through his desk, cleaving it in half. The drawers are strewn across the floor, papers and files upended across every inch. His sideboard is in similar condition, although the bottles of drinks have been left untouched.

"What do you think happened in here?" Avery holds a hand over her chest. Meg doesn't spare her much of a glance, her face grave as she assesses the mess.

"Seems like someone was looking for something. The real question is, did they find it?"

"Not likely," Avery scrunches up her nose. "Nixon only kept work files in here. Anything of personal importance is in the safe." I still, on the verge of stepping into the study. Keeping my face impassive, I half-turn my head to acknowledge the outline of her face.

"We need to check if the safe is intact." My words are crisp and sharp, hopefully not revealing that I have no idea where this fucking safe is. The girls both lead the way, allowing me to fall behind and keep watch. Meg's reassured swagger is a visual reminder that she knows my own home better than I do. Up the stairs and along the passage, we enter a nondescript room containing a random assortment of furniture and artwork, all covered with dust sheets. At my curious gaze, Avery rolls her eyes.

"We call it the auction graveyard. Mom often came home with random pieces she couldn't resist bidding on, although many are from charity events. There's the odd memorabilia piece she was gifted from the set of her latest film and a couple of awards dotted around too."

Making a beeline for a covered cabinet, Avery tugs the dust sheet free. The wooden piece presents as an antique, but the hinges and screws are too new. A set of double doors containing glass showcases mini trophies and picture frames within, whilst Avery pulls out the large bottom drawer to reveal a face of steel. The safe faces upwards at the three of us crowding around.

"Open it," I demand. Avery looks ready to elbow me in the face.

"It's a finger scanner," she glowers, leaving off whatever name she just wanted to call me. "I don't have access to it. You wanted to check it's intact, and it is." Staring down at the armored box, a swirl of curiosity and frustration wars within. A burning sense of needing to know what my father is hiding flares to life.

"What use are you?" I huff, walking away. The girls don't pay me any mind, taking the time to recover the cabinet. I'm on my way back to the stairs when I hear a click and the sound of footsteps from below.

"Darrell?" a gruff voice leaks through the lobby. "Did you turn the alarm back on last night?" A shuffle comes next as I plaster myself to the wall and with a flick on my hand, urge the girls to do the same.

"Yes, 'course I did. I know I did," another voice replies, this one more nasally. The first man grunts.

"I'm calling it in." *Fuck*. Within seconds, my father is going to know we've disobeyed him by coming back home, calling him out on his bullshit restoration lie. He's covering up a break-in, and I have the uneasy sense that this is all relating to Avery. "Ay Boss, we're back in the house. There's signs of tampering with the alarm system. What are our orders?"

My feet are retracting, an arm outstretched to push the girls back into the auction graveyard room. After a beat, the gruff one comes back with the swift command to search the manor. My jaw clenches. I knew we should have gotten here earlier. Urging Avery to move, she stands firm and grabs my wrist.

"This way," she barely whispers, tugging me along the hall. Meg is right behind, ushering me along. Despite my instinct to stay still and be stubborn, I have to relent to the fact that Avery knows these walls better than I do.

She speeds along as quickly as she's able without making a single sound, into my parent's room and to the left of the four-poster bed. Releasing me to grab either side of the bedside table, the whole unit swings aside with a click to reveal an open hatch in the wall behind. Avery slips in first, Meg following straight after. It's a tight squeeze, one not made for any type of muscle, but I manage to just about fit. Behind the bedside table, there's a rope handle to pull the hatch shut, sealing us in the dark space. Lithe footsteps echo around the hidden walls and a moment later, a light appears at the top of a slender staircase.

"What the fuck is this place?" I frown as I make it to the top of the steps and enter a rather spacious room. Peering around the size of it, the crease between my eyebrows deepens. "Where the fuck is this place?"

"It's a safe room," Avery gives me a wide-eyed, mini head shake kind of action which infers I'm a fucking idiot. "And we're just below the attic. It's a minor extension that was put in years ago, only really visible from the outside if you know to look for it."

Unlike the dim steps leading up here, the room is bright and airy thanks to a vent system in the top corner. Avery moves past me to close the door with a push of a button, which I now notice is made of a heavy duty metal as it seals us inside. There's a matching one across the far side, separated by a computer desk on the left and a set of bunk beds on the right. Bedding sits neatly in vacuum-sealed bags on the end of each mattress, which is also covered in a protective plastic. A pink, fluffy rug stretches out in the center of the room, filing the space between fully-stocked shelving units.

"I'm..." I glance between the pieces of paper tacked to the walls, displaying shaded sketches or vibrant colourings. "So confused."

"I was an abused child who refused to go back out into the real world," Avery states so plainly, it's as if she's said it a hundred times before. "Mom had this room put in for me. If I was ever scared while she was away, I'd come here to feel safe."

Avery sits at the desk, powering on the computer. It's old and clunky, but comes on immediately. She loads up a splitscreen of security cameras I didn't know were dotted through the manor, skipping through the screens until she finds the men loitering around. There's easily ten of them, six inside and more visible through the windows. They wear dark polo shirts with a logo I can't make out, their uniforms and steel-toe boots suggesting they are here to replace the broken window. If only they were doing that, and not helping themselves to the contents of the kitchen and dropping onto the sofa to watch TV. It seems their sweep of the house was short lived.

Swinging around in her chair, Avery's blonde locks fall over her shoulder as she sits deep in thought. "Although, in the last year or two, mom started joining me in here. We would hide out sometimes."

"I didn't know that," Meg looks over to Avery from where she's retrieving a bottle of water from a mini fridge. "What did you do in here?"

Avery shrugs. "Play card games, read, sketch. Sometimes we'd watch the cameras and spy on Nixon and the staff."

"And that didn't seem weird to you?" I cross my arms, not stepping any further into the room. I feel weird being here, like this space was crafted for Avery alone and I'm intruding. Not that I'd usually give a shit, but this isn't my turf. I don't belong in the manor, never mind a place where the demons of Avery's past are meant to be firmly on the outside.

"I mean...not until now...It was just meant to be a game." Avery's gaze becomes hazy. I watch her whole world rearrange behind her blue eyes. Meg kneels beneath Avery's legs, stroking her jean-clad thighs.

"I don't think it was a game, Aves," she says softly. "I think your mom might have been scared of something too."

My eye twitches. The tension and the onslaught of guilt that hits me becomes all too much. "Stop calling her that," I hiss, clenching my fists by my sides. Two heads swivel to me, their accusing expressions adding to the weight crushing my chest from the inside. I do what I always do, blocking out the bullshit and focusing on the hatred. It lays dormant inside until I need to call on it, forcing the rest of the world to still. "She wasn't your mom," I seethe through clenched teeth.

"We're really going to do this now?!" Avery shoots to her feet, stepping to me with her chest pushed out. She's ready to swing, and I'm ready to block it when Meg pushes between us, her head upturned to the ceiling.

"Both of you stop acting like twatmuffins," Meg sighs. "If you don't want to seem like siblings, stop bickering like a pair of them." Avery steps back, strolling towards the bunk bed. From underneath, she pulls out a plastic box and places it on the mattress, her attention focused on what's inside. Meg drops down at the desk, so I head to the shelves to busy myself with being nosey.

The top half hold necessities like long lasting food and toiletries. I shift through with sparked interest. Clearly my mom thought Avery might be holed up here for long periods of time, with the need of portable toilet bottles and crystals, cleaning soap that doesn't need water and shampoo caps. I decide the lower shelves are reserved for forms of entertainment, as Avery stated. Arts and crafts, pencils, watercolor paints. Boxes of DVD's for the computer and books that have extremely worn spines. I opt not to look through the box labeled clothing.

"How often did you come here?" I ask, deciding my curiosity beats my desire to not speak to Avery ever again.

"In the early years, sometimes nightly. Once my biological father was incarcerated, it was only when the nightmares hit. That door leads to my bedroom," she jerks her chin across the room. "But recently, I only came when Mom asked. She just wanted to escape sometimes and I thought I understood." She frowns, continuing to shift through the papers holding her attention. Now she's speaking, I can't get her to shut up again. "These are all of my letters from Mr. XO. He never missed a single Christmas or Birthday. I kind of thought he was my friend."

I kind of think that's the saddest thing I've ever heard, but I keep it to myself. It's never been so apparent to me as when standing in this room, how lonely Avery was. From outside the manor, I thought she had the perfect life. Hell, I wholly believe she convinced herself she did too. Now it's all crashing down around us both.

"Aww, I remember this one," Avery smiles distantly. Meg crosses the room to sit by her side, plucking the crumpled piece of paper from her hand.

"This was when we'd had those awful storms and all the power cuts," Meg also reminisces, clearly remembering too. "*Amidst the wind that fiercely blows. In the eye of the storm, your spirit still glows. You shine brightly, providing light. Guiding me through the darkest night.*"

I cringe so hard, my stomach rolls. Turning away I hang over the computer, preferring the view through the screen. Although, these jobsworths still aren't doing what they're being paid for. Most linger around, almost lying in wait, while two have finally entered the study.

Crouching over the broken drawers littering the floor, I expect them to start tidying the mess. Instead, they're carefully sifting through the papers, occasionally taking out their phones to capture a photo and move on.

I lower into the chair, enlarging the camera footage of the study only. Another man enters, this one twice the size of the others. His polo shirt appears to cut the circulation off around his biceps, his trousers too tight fitting to actually be his. The veins in his neck bulge as he shouts something, kicking the armchair over with his boot. The crash reverberates through a set of headphones sitting on top of the computer tower. I slip them on.

"*This is a huge waste of time! It clearly isn't here!*"

"*Boss wants every inch of this room scoured before we sign off on it. If he deems the study clean, then we'll fake another break-in for the next room and move on.*"

"*There's no one here. We could ransack the whole house and be done with it.*"

"*You know we don't operate that way. Keep it clean and contained. That's the deal.*"

"*Catherine Hughes kept secrets from her husband for decades. She wasn't going to leave the evidence of it lying around in his own office.*"

"*Nixon must know by now. He'd have had people looking into her*

The wireless mouse in my hand clatters to the ground. I push the headphones off as if I've been burned, my entire body shaking. My jaw aches from its tensed position and my spine is rigid enough to snap.

"Wyatt? What is it?" A gentle hand settles on my shoulder. I jerk out of the seat, as far from her touch as I can get in this room. The walls don't seem so wide apart any more, the darkness closing in around me. "Wyatt?" She calls for me again. What did that stupid poem say? A light in the darkness, the eye of the storm. Avery's pale blue eyes fill with concern, offering me exactly that. A lifeboat, if only I could let myself accept it. Twisting away sharply, I face the steel door containing me in this claustrophobic lock-box.

"When they've all left, give it an hour before you come out. We're taking Megan home and then we're getting the fuck out of dodge. No fucking arguements." I press the release button and exit, lowering myself onto the wooden steps halfway outside the safe room. Avery takes her cue to shut me out, shrouding me in darkness. I tremble, placing my head into my hands. Silently, I cry into my palms, stifling my sobs into nothingness.

She didn't just die in a car accident. My mom was killed. A sickening feeling turns my stomach. The memories I try to call on are twinged with shadows. Tainted with guilt and paranoia. Her bright smile which might now seem forced. Her lingering hold in the crook of my arm that may have been tighter than I realized. I was so distracted by my own anger. What secrets was she keeping that she couldn't tell anyone?

Cold air sweeps past my hunched frame, yet I'm on fire. Words echo through my ears on repeat. This is all my fault. I should have been there. I should have seen more. I could have saved her.

AVERY

CHAPTER FORTY TWO

"You know he's going to be pissed," Meg states as if I'm supposed to care. I shrug, opening the opposite door to the one he left through. Wyatt can sulk on his own all he likes. The repair guys must have decided they didn't have the right tools for the job, since all of them packed up and left pretty soon after Wyatt's episode. I waited as instructed, but in that time, I realized I'm done waiting. I'm actually home, exactly where I wanted to be.

Pushing through the wall, I appear in my bedroom. Decorated in soft pastel pink and gray, the room hasn't changed since I left. The king size bed in the middle of the space, the desk and walk-in closet across one side, and a vanity mirror on the other. I drop the box of Mr. XO letters down on the bed, leaving the rest until later. From those I did look through, there wasn't anything worth noting. No hint at who this person is, or what they want. Just innocent letters, not the ramblings of a psychopath. Of that, I'm fairly certain.

Collapsing onto the plush duvet, I stare up at the ceiling fan steady and unmoving above me. Meg heads over to the door leading onto a thin balcony. Just big enough to stand on and lean over the railing to see the driveway. Whatever spurred her to do just that is quickly followed by an 'eek'.

"The fuck was that?" I crunch my neck upward. Meg rushes back in, her actions all flappy and panicked. My own chest leaps, a sense of unease brewing as she grabs my wrists and drags me upright. Dragging me to the balcony, her hand on my nape twists my head to peer at the large gates.

"I think you've got a problem."

"Shit," I gasp, my eyes wide. Then I'm running, through the manor, down the stairs and rushing to open the front door as a convoy of white Bentley's pull up. Huxley, Dax, Garrett and Axel all file out of the first, followed by streams of Huxley's uniformed staff out of the rest. The guards take up stations beside the front entrance and main gates, while butlers, maids and the chefs start to unload the trunks.

"I can explain," I blink widely, holding my hands up to Huxley's chest. He pauses in front of me, gently placing his hands over mine and smiles.

"No need. We anticipated as much. I'm just surprised Wyatt agreed to accompany you." Placing a kiss on my temple, he eases me to step aside and allow his staff to start filing through the lobby. Meg directs them to the kitchen.

"Where is the shitbag anyway?" Garrett hops up the steps, sweeping me into his arms. I gasp, and not from him swinging me around.

"Oh shit, I left him trapped in the walls." Garrett's responding laughter bleeds through the manor, instantly lighting the place with his humor.

"I wouldn't expect anything less." He sets me down just as Meg swings back around, stating that she'll attend to freeing Wyatt. I'd happily leave him there, but my attention is swayed by Axel's stunning hazel eyes. He lowers his head with tantalizing slowness, placing a tender kiss on my lips.

"Did you at least find what you were looking for?"

"I have more questions than answers," I sigh. "What are you guys even doing here?" Releasing me, Axel guides me into Dax's embrace. He was patiently waiting on the sidelines.

"Last weekend of Fall Break," Dax smirks. My heart melts at the warmth in his blue eyes, thankful that he isn't mad at me for sneaking out. "We've come to have the Thanksgiving Fest you wanted." My mouth drops open. They've driven all this way just for me? With a rush of excitement, I push up onto my tiptoes; giddy, throwing my arms around his neck. Dax shifts his head back when I try to plant a huge kiss on his mouth. "Before you thank me, it was Wyatt's idea. He called from the car last night."

Like a douse of cold water, I step back skeptically. Dax chuckles, reading my mind.

"Don't worry, we won't let him ruin it. With any luck, he's the character we kill off in the first five minutes and we don't have to suffer him for too long." Dax winks and I splutter a laugh. I'm not used to Dax, of all people, being conniving.

There's a rush of bodies in the manor, all moving with a sense of purpose, and it hasn't felt this much like home in too long. Meg and Axel help me dig out the box from the attic, containing all of Mom's plans. We won't be putting the party on for the staff like usual, but there's something much more intimate about celebrating with the Shadowed Souls. I think she'd approve of me having fun with a group who aren't being paid to attend for once.

Dishing out character sheets and outfits, we all find a space in the various empty rooms to freshen up and get ready. The time to learn our given persona is imperative, as is for the murderer to discover who they are. Meanwhile, the cooks adhere to the menu provided for the dinner and the housekeepers sort decorating and hiding the clues. The theme for this evening is the nineteen-thirties, in the height of the Guys and Dolls era.

Meg dresses with me in my room, transforming herself into Isabella Sinclair - the glamorous and mysterious ex-wife of our host, Victor Blackwood. Her navy blue dress is covered in small white flowers, cinched in all the right places at her waist and bust. The V is lower than I imagine it would have been back in those days, although the fabric does reach her knees in a tight-pencil skirt fashion. Bouncing her hair with tight curls and a gold pin to move the strands away from her face, she finishes off with black kitten heels, a tiny handbag and dainty leather gloves.

I offer her the crook of my arm, signaling I'm ready also. I emerge from my room as Lucy White, Victor's loyal and efficient personal assistant. My dress is a deep purple, covering me wrist to neck and down to my shins, the satin gilding over my body like rippling water. At my throat, a large cream bow drapes over my chest. A mauve fascinator is positioned in my loosely curled hair and I hold a small clutch bag.

We're first into the dining room. Name cards indicate our places, as well as small character sheets between the cutlery in case we need prompts. In my clutch, I have the opening manuscript to start the game.

"Oh yes," Huxley waltzes in approvingly. "You two look fantastic." I warm inside as the hunk in a suit takes the time to kiss Meg's cheek as well, before finding his place at the head of the table.

"Victor Blackwood, I assume." My grin is doubled by the effect Huxley has put into styling his long hair back and tied a cravat at his top button. He bows with a flourish as Wyatt and Dax join us. I half expected Wyatt to bow out, or turn up in sweatpants in protest, so I'm incredibly surprised at his olive green army attire. Medals shine against his chest pocket, a badge number pinned across his shoulder. His dark hair is impeccably in place, there's a cane in his grip and as always - he's scowling.

"Colonel Edward Grey," he sticks out a rigid hand to Huxley-I mean, Victor. "Retired military officer known for my strict sense of duty and intimidating presence." Huxley shakes his hand with a prim and proper 'how do you do' while I'm snorting with laughter inside. There couldn't be a more perfect role for Wyatt if it was written just for him. Dax is in the seat beside me.

"Lucy White," I briefly curtsy. Dax takes my hand and kisses the back of it, the white lab coat hanging from his arms ruffling in the process.

"Dr Henry Henderson, resident physician," he smiles kindly. I snort a laugh. *Henry Henderson*, really? "Calm demeanor, sharp intellect, so on and so forth." For some reason, Dax's character has donned a British accent and I'm here for it.

Covering my laughter behind my hand, he pulls out my seat for me. Wyatt does the same for Meg, his movements tight and precise. Meg's bemused expression mirrors mine for her place diagonal to me. With Wyatt on her left, that leaves the space between her and Huxely, and the one to my right. On cue, clipped footsteps enter the room.

"Professor Alexander Green, at your service," Axel tugs on his jacket to straighten out the non-existent creases. His slacks are brown, as is the leather briefcase strapped across his chest. He takes the time to greet each member of the party with a clammy, rushed handshake and takes his seat beside me. I grin at his face, waiting for him to break character.

The most I get is a shy sideways glance and a hushed rehearsed spiel. "I'm a scientist, working on a rather private invention as funded by Mr. Blackwood."

"It's lovely to meet you," I greet back. Looking around at everyone seated, we share knowing glances, just waiting for-

"My darlings!" Garrett calls as he saunters into the room, accompanied by a rhythmic click-click-click. I twist in my seat and I swear, I almost die at the sight before me. His dress is scandalous, red glitter and frayed around his muscular legs. He's stuffed his bra cups, roughed up his brown hair and somehow found platform heels to fit his huge feet.

"Miss Felicity Rose is here and ready for her close-up!" Puffing on a fake cigarette in an eight inch holder, Garrett poses against the door jamb, holding a gloved hand up to his forehead. I can't contain my laughter a moment longer and as I descend into hysterics, everyone else joins me. Even Wyatt cracks a smile before remembering his no-nonsense persona. Garrett clip-clops across the marble, blowing dramatic kisses to everyone in attendance.

"I'm so sorry I'm late, my darlings. I was just performing at the theater stage and I couldn't deny the audience an encore. Hopefully I didn't miss anything?" Garrett bats a huge set of fake lashes on his eyes and pouts his red, painted lips. I decide no one is leaving this room at the end of the night before we've got a group photo.

"Just on time," I announce, sliding the manuscript out of my clutch bag. Around us, the wait staff step in to fill our champagne flutes while I read out the introduction. "As Mr. Blackwood's personal assistant, he would like me to welcome you all here this evening. However, I must regretfully inform you that this is not a simple dinner amongst friends and colleagues. There has been a murder."

"Ohhh!" Garrett gasps and clutches the pearls around his neck. Axel's jaw clenches as he tries and fails to resist laughing.

"Indeed," I raise a brow, attempting seriousness. "This morning, Mr. Blackwood and I discovered the body of the housekeeper in the larder. We have invited you all here, not only to help identify the killer, but also as our prime suspects. Anyone of us at this table has the connections, motive and means to pull off such a feat. It's our job to figure out who."

Withdrawing a handful of small, square cards and miniature pencils, I pass them around to each member at the table. For one brief, selfish moment, I cast a glance over those present, finding myself overwhelmed. Just a few months ago, I only had one person I could rely on. Now, with all the effort they've put in, enjoying this night with the Shadowed Souls suddenly means so much more than they probably realize.

The card fits into my palm, listing seven rooms and seven objects. These aren't the large, laminated sheets my mom had printed and prepared, but an adapted version whipped up this afternoon by pen. I make a note to thank Huxley's staff, not lost in the irony that this celebration was meant to be for my own, yet they're nowhere to be seen. Plastering on a small smile, I find everyone waiting for their next instruction.

"The rules are simple. Between courses, we will look for these weapons in these rooms. If you find a weapon, you can either share it with the group, or attempt to hide it but it can't leave that room. The murderer wants to throw people off, so be on high alert for sneaky behavior. You can ask each other any questions to deduce motives. Once you think you know who killed the housekeeper with what weapon, you can declare your suspicions at the dinner table and peek at the sealed envelope. If you're right, you win. If you're wrong, the game continues."

And with that, the first of six courses is served. Huxley assumes the role as head of the table with as much ease as his own. His chest expands within the suit, a glass of champagne in his hand. He doesn't always drink, often swirling the hazel liquid and peering at me over the rim of the glass. His gaze is magnetic, affecting me even with Axel between us.

"So, *Professor*," I attempt to distract myself. "Tell us about this invention you're working on." Axel straightens his shoulders, wincing slightly as he tries to read his character sheet. He's not a natural at acting, bless him.

"Well, if you must know, it's an advanced radio communication device. A cutting-edge portable radio device which has been designed to transmit and receive messages."

"Such a device would be revolutionary for military use," Wyatt raises a brow, his colonel's badge glinting beneath the chandelier. He, unsurprisingly, does not have any issues acting. I reckon his whole life is an act.

"How far along are you in terms of prototypes?" Dr Henry Brown asks, aka Dax. He leans across me, his fresh scent of sea minerals brushing over me like a caress. I can't help but catch the crystal blueness to his eyes, or how the blondeness of his short afro hair contrasts with his tanned skin. Sharp lines and pointed features, and he's beautiful. Truly beautiful in a way I can't fathom. Catching me staring, he gives a quick wink and moves back into his seat.

"Actually, I have produced a working set of prototypes," Axel admits. "I provided Victor with a sample on my previous visit. Do you have any feedback?" All heads twist to Huxley, who's entire focus seemed to be on me.

"Huh? Oh, yes. Um...," Hux taps his jacket pockets. "I seemed to have misplaced it."

"Misplaced it?!" Axel gasps, getting into it fully now. "That was the only working pair I have. Without the receiver, mine is useless." Taking out his smartphone, he tosses it across the table. I have to bite my lip to suppress a bark of laughter. Huxley waves his hand in the air.

"I'm sure I can throw money your way and have you whip up another one."

"That doesn't resolve the issue of where the other has gotten to," Meg suddenly interjects. The ex-wife pops a piece of fish into her mouth and chews slowly, forcing us all to wait for her to continue. "Seems to me something of such expense and importance would have been ripe for stealing. How vetted are your staff these days, Victor? When you're not screwing them." She leaves Huxley with such a glare, I can feel the frostiness across the table. But she has a point.

"You're insinuating the housekeeper could have been involved?" I frown, tapping a finger on my chin. "Definitely seems like a motive to me."

"We will have to see what turns up," Dax pats the sides of his mouth with a napkin. "If you'll excuse me." Pushing his chair back, he stands, indicating the first course is finished. I didn't even touch mine, too engrossed in the plot to eat. As the others take their exit to go hunting, I quickly dig into my starter. There's nothing ladylike about my movements, but when I peer up, Huxley is still seated and watching me.

"What?" I ask, narrowing my eyes.

"Oh nothing," Huxley plays with the stem of his glass, his fingers stroking a repetitive pattern. I reach for my glass, suddenly needing a drink myself. "I'm just enjoying watching you." Butterflies flutter deep down, my cheeks heating slightly. Huxley in his fine suit, his long hair styled, his jaw freshly shaved. But I've seen that all before. No, it's the hunger in him tonight which is drawing me in like a moth to a flame. He seems to be insatiable, and it's not the dinner he's looking forward to. I duck my head, removing the napkin from my lap.

"Because that's not creepy at all. We should investigate before you try to stab me with a butter knife."

"I'm not the murderer here, Lucy White. Are you?" Huxley's chocolate eyes sparkle with mirth as he leaves the dining room, leaving me alone with my racing heartbeat and thoughts. Why did that sound so hot, and what the hell is wrong with me for thinking it did?

CHAPTER FORTY THREE

I should be hunting for clues, ticking weapons off the checklist in my pocket. Instead, I'm too busy watching Avery. Moving from the study to the kitchen, I don't want to be anywhere she isn't. Her wide blue eyes and even bigger smile. She's stunning, and I can't take my eyes off her. The slinky satin hugs her body, not leaving a millimeter of skin. I wouldn't put it past Cathy Hughes to have had the dress made just for Avery, just for this occasion. The same goes for Meg. From my understanding, the girls were always together, always present, and Cathy treated them both like her daughters.

Once inside the kitchen, she drifts from countertop to appliance, searching low and high, pulling out drawers, opening cupboards. The island is littered with covered food, divine scents filtering from underneath. It seems the chef pre-made all of tonight's food and left small cards with heating instructions.

Avery's small 'aha' is endearing, coming up behind her to see what she's found. Beneath the basin, a candlestick stands tall and proud, out of place against bottles of detergent and cleaning fluid. Avery is crouched, marking an X on her sheet, then looking over her shoulder at where I'm lingering.

"Our little secret," she winks, closing the cupboard door. I don't know what comes over me as she stands, except for a surge of need.

Gripping Avery to my body, I nudge her back against the counter. Her curves mold to me, her lips popped open in surprise.

"Dr Henderson!" Avery gasps and giggles. My hands land on her hips, gentle, seeking. The satin helps the glide of my palms to the small over her back and upward, holding Avery to me like the most precious woman in the world. I've never been a fuck-and-run kind of guy. My mom raised me with respect.

"Our little secret," I breathe, pressing my lips against hers. She smells devine, vanilla and honey overwhelming my senses. Her lips are so soft, smudging lipstick over mine. I reach for her chin, tipping her head aside to allow my tongue to dip inside. There's no rush, no reason we can't savor the moment alone we've managed to carve out for ourselves. Avery pushes into me, every part of our bodies touching, all the way down to where her leg intertwines with mine. My hand slips into her hair, carefully holding her. Delicately worshiping her.

A shuffle by the door interrupts us, members of the wait staff arriving to prepare our next course. Avery's eyes are bright, her lips seeking more as I reluctantly move away.

"Where's next?" I ask, reaching for her with one hand and rearranging my stiffened cock with the other. I don't need fast-paced and heavy to get me excited; Avery's body resting against mine will do it every time. Avery opts to head back to the dining room, muttering conspiracy theories. One of which is based on Wyatt's military presence, given Axel's communication device and its potential.

"It has legs, I'll give you that." We break apart as we re-enter, finding both Huxley and Wyatt lounging by the large window. "They do look mighty suspicious." Avery nods in agreement, narrowing her eyes and making an I'm-watching-you gesture. Huxley mimics it back, Wyatt looks bored.

"My darlings!" Garrett swans in, his heels clicking lazily behind me. I keep my focus forward, noticing Wyatt's curiosity suddenly peak. It's the most animated I've seen him all night, but not in a good way.

Sauntering past, Garrett is throwing his hips from side to side, making a show of his corset-given curves. I roll my eyes. Nothing Garrett does surprises me any more. On one gloved finger, he's swinging something that looks identical to a gun, the black metal catching the lighting. On second thoughts, maybe he can surprise me after all.

"Garrett," Wyatt is tense and still. Deathly still. "Put it down."

"It's Miss Rose to you, hot stuff." Garrett bats his ridiculous lashes, not sensing the shift of atmosphere in the dining room. Huxley, although seeming confused, holds up his hands and edges closer.

"Seriously, Gare. Do as Wyatt says. Put it on the table and step back."

Moving to the head of the table, Garrett leans over the high-backed seat. "This old thing?" He grabs hold of the butt and extends his arm, closing one eye while the other is trained on Wyatt. "It's just a prop." A shift of movement puts Avery flush against my side, her hand desperate and seeking. It wraps around my wrist, her breath skating over my neck. I spear her a glance, our blue eyes meeting with unease. It's not common for Wyatt to be spooked.

"Garrett, what the fuck?!" Axel walks into the dining room with Meg, the first sight being his lover pointing a gun at Wyatt's head. It's wrong. Everything about it feels wrong. After a tense moment, Garrett sighs loudly. His shoulders slump, causing the dress' bust to curve away from his body.

"Fuck's sake guys. I thought I was the one meant to be wearing panties. It's just a game." His arm jerks aside, his finger pressing on the trigger. No one truly expected the crack of gunfire to explode from the barrel, a bullet lodging itself in the wall. Two inches over and it would have sailed through Wyatt's head. Garrett freezes, his mouth dropped wide open. He shakily tosses the gun onto the table and trips over himself in an attempt to scramble away. "How...how did you know it was real?" Garrett is sheet white beneath his make-up, finding himself trembling in Axel's arms.

"The red stripes on the grip. It's my father's. All of his guns are modified, back from when he used to take me shooting as a kid." Wyatt replies gravely, the vein in his head pulsing. He hesitantly reaches over to click the safety on. "Where did you find it?"

Instead of responding, Garrett skitters on his stilts and with Axel's help, guides us to the games room. Dark oak paneling blends into rich, leather armchairs flanking an empty fireplace. In the center of the room, a pool table takes up most of the space. Shelving units stand tall, overstuffed with books and knick knacks. A vintage jukebox in the corner adds a nostalgic touch, if the side panel wasn't lying on the wooden floor. Garrett points towards it, one shoulder offering a half-shrug of apology.

"If I was going to hide something, I'd choose the jukebox."

"Apparently, so would someone else," Huxley comments. He lowers, pushing his hand into the jukebox's open cavity. He withdraws a padded brown envelope, packed with stacks of money, the holster that the gun came from and an old, dusty diary. The cover which was once red, is now peeled and a shade of suntouched pink. The strap holds a keyhole which I believe has been pried open, given the limp status of the bronze clasp. Avery's grip on my arm turns bruising, her breath sawing out in a rush.

"I've seen that before." Releasing me, she edges forward and accepts the diary from Huxley's large hand. "It's my mom's." The spine creaks as she opens the front cover, revealing 'Property of Cathy Hughes' just inside. Snapping it shut, Avery hugs it to her chest, taking a step back. Her gaze is firmly, intently squared on Wyatt. No words are needed to portray what she's thinking, that he'll storm forward and snatch it from her.

A bell rings, indicating it's time for us to take our seats for the next course of dinner. No one moves, except for Meg stepping closer to Avery.

"Why would your mom hide money and a gun?" she asks the question we're all wondering.

"And what was she scared of?" Wyatt adds. He looks distant again, lost in his mind. With that, the fun and games are over. Wyatt strides out with clipped boot-steps, indicating we're done here. We follow as I draw Avery under my arm, protecting her while she hugs the diary like a lifeline. A tangible connection to her mom, something she long thought was lost.

Stepping off to the side, Axel draws Garrett into a hug, soothing hands stroking his mass of brown hair. "I nearly killed him," Garrett whispers into the crook of Axel's neck, visibly shaken. Using one hand, I unbutton the lab coat, mid-sigh when I crash into Huxley's back. He's just done the same to Wyatt, in the doorway of the dining room.

"Garrett!" Wyatt roars. I peer around Huxley's huge frame, struggling to see the cause of Wyatt's standstill. But that's the point - I don't see it. The gun, from the table, is missing. I drag Avery aside, keeping her firmly in my protection as Wyatt wheels around, seeking out his target. His boots eat up the space between them, where he tears Garrett from Axel's hold. "Where the fuck is it?!"

Garrett's eyes lock down immediately. Any sense of regret and vulnerability vanishes. He shoves Wyatt a step back, before coming chest-to-chest with him.

"I don't know what you're talking about," he grinds through his teeth, but his fists are no less clenched. Garrett may be a six-foot man in a red dress, but he stands up to Wyatt, unwavering in his heels. Foreboding ripples through me, pre-empting Wyatt's following shove and the swing of his fist. He clocks Garrett in the jaw, and the air is sucked out of the lobby. We've never fought. We help beat on others, defending our brothers even when they're in the wrong. But we don't fight each other.

"I'm giving you one chance to step away from me, Riot." Garrett tries a last ditch attempt to diffuse the tension in Wyatt's shoulders, despite seething with anger himself. I release Avery, tucking her back beside Meg. Hux is with me, chests puffed out and ready to break them apart. It's only Garrett's quick glance over Wyatt's shoulder and a miniscule shake of his head that keeps us back. Then he moves. Garrett's hand is around Wyatt's neck, the movement too swift to track. Spinning him, Garrett forces Axel to dive out of the way so he can pin Wyatt against the wall.

"Give me the fucking gun," Wyatt chokes out, his hands clenched around Garrett's arm. His green eyes wander, looking over the lack of places Garrett could hide the weapon. It doesn't deter him from kicking out, hitting Gare's shin hard. Garrett is unaffected, his hand on Wyatt's throat tightening. Veins bulge, Wyatt's face turning an unhealthy shade of red. I inhale sharply. Garrett isn't backing down.

"Come on man, that's enough," I break free of those watching and tap Garrett on the shoulder. I'm not foolish enough to use force, not when Garrett's face is taut and his posture stiff. Like a feral animal, it's always best to proceed with caution, or we'll all be the subject of his rage. "We know you don't have the gun. Let's look for it instead, it can't be far." My reasoning falls on deaf ears.

Slowly shaking his head, Garrett mutters something under his breath. Wyatt's struggles fall limp, his face stubbornly tense until the light goes from his eyes. Garrett releases him the instant he passes out, his limbs crumpling in a heap on the marble floor. Huxley is right there, scooping Wyatt up into his arms.

"Was that really necessary?" he huffs in Garrett's direction. Finally stepping back, Garrett rubs his jaw, a bruise already starting to appear.

"Yes." And with the dramatic flare I would have expected, Garrett swishes his skirt and sashays up the stairs, one hand on his hip and the other floating through the air like some sort of queen. My attention falls to Axel, a bystander in all of this.

"Never a dull day," he sighs, and heads in the direction of the dining room. At least someone is going to address the actual problem, now that Wyatt's mini-suicide mission is over. Huxley carries the limp man in question to bed, and I'm left turning back to the girls watching on with wide eyes. As I approach, Meg's miniature bag begins to vibrate.

"Shit, Aves. I told my mom I'd update her. I promised I'd head back home tonight, spend some time with her before I head back to school. But I can stay, you clearly need me," Meg's hand extends towards the diary still clutched to Avery's chest. Avery shakes her head, tears on the edge of her blue eyes.

"It's fine. I'm just going to go to bed and read for a while. I'll call you a car," Avery steps away, actively distancing herself. I step in then, seeing where I can actually be of use in this shitshow of a night.

"I'll drive you home," I nod to Meg, then address Avery. "As long as you're sure you'll be okay?" Avery nods, finding a small smile to reassure me.

That's how I find myself in a white Bentley, following Meg's directions through a city I don't know, and have never had any desire to drive in. I find a cigarette box in the door and ask Meg to light for me, while I puff and abide by a ridiculous amount of traffic lights.

"I didn't know you smoked," she comments, then lights one for herself. I spare a look that says *'ditto'*.

Luckily for myself and all of those around me, I don't have an addictive personality. I can take or leave smoking, but in times of heightened stress if there's one available, it's something to do. A brief distraction, then back to the problem at hand. What am I stressed about tonight specifically? Stupidly, it's that Avery didn't get the party she'd hoped for, not the fact the staff must have misplaced a gun, probably thinking it was a prop to our game like Garrett did.

Turning into a long street, Meg directs me to a parking space beside a tall building. It looks the same as all the rest, mounted by stone steps and a metal railing. Five floors high judging by the repetitive windows. She doesn't immediately thank me and leave as anticipated, so we sit there for a while. I sense her watching me each time approaching headlights illuminate the car and then plunge us back into darkness. After a while, I can't simply listen to the low beat of the radio any more.

"What is it?"

She twists her lips, still fully dressed as Isabella Sinclair from the nineteen-hundreds. To that effect, I'm in a lab coat and if we were to have been pulled over, I can only imagine what the cop camera footage would have looked like. Finally, she sighs.

"I think I like you." I tense, dropping my hands from the wheel.

"Is this a test? If so, I believe I'm spoken for."

"No, it's not a test," Meg laughs to herself. It was definitely a test. "I mean, out of all of them, I think I like you the best. You're different with Avery. Protective, yet subtle about it. I just want to make sure when shit hits the fan, you'll do your best to handle the fallout."

"What makes you think there will be a fallout?" I ask, catching Meg's incredulous look. Her raised brow says it all.

"You saw what happened tonight. Wyatt is a loose cannon. He's just arriving into this world of mysterious letters and items going missing. But not Avery. She's used to the secrecy, and has developed the ability to look past it. There's been things happening in that manor for a long time, if only she'd let herself acknowledge it."

"Do you know something?" I breathe, my lungs locking. The atmosphere in the car shifts, weighing me into my seat. My heart beats for Meg's next words.

"Perhaps. The real question is, can I trust you to keep her best interests at heart? Even when Wyatt starts to realize he's been lied to all this time? Even when your group starts to choose sides and fracture from within. Even when it comes at the risk of losing Avery all together?"

She's wrong. The Shadowed Souls are too strong, have been through too much shit to let anything come between us. In times of strain, we don't break down or split up, but come together. It's what we've been doing for Wyatt since Avery arrived on campus, although he refuses to acknowledge it. He wouldn't have survived his hatred for her, spotting her in the halls or seeing her in the bleachers at our games. He'd have lashed out, become reckless. We unintentionally brought Avery in, allowed him to exorcise his demons with us nearby to keep him contained. We let him work out his troubles and start to see a way through them, that light at the end of the tunnel. And in reality, we didn't do it for Avery. We did it for him.

But that doesn't change the fact that Meg is staring at me, her eyes guarded. She's holding the strap of her bag tightly, chewing on her bottom lip. She's scared, and believes everything she just said to be true as if it's already been set in motion.

"Fucking hell, Meg. What do you know?"

AVERY

CHAPTER FORTY FOUR

An affair? Twenty one years ago...

A lump has formed in my throat as I snap the diary closed. If anyone had been unfaithful, I might have believed it of Nixon. Wyatt has suggested as much. He has always traveled for work, and I'm accustomed to his lack of communication whilst away. A little out-of-sight, out-of-mind. Although when he was home, we were the center of his universe. But my mom? There's no way.

Yet she wrote about it. Detailed it. Does Nixon even know, or was this a secret mom took to her grave? Now I know too, and I can't unsee the words echoing through my skull.

I'm pregnant.

Fuck, I hate to even think it, but poor Wyatt. He already feels so hard-done by. Like he doesn't belong. This would break the rocky foundations he still stands on, even though I know he would rather sink in his ship of denial than admit he's affected. More than that, if he isn't Nixon's son, what would happen to the trust fund Wyatt lives on? The same trust fund he uses to pay for Dax's tuition. It's that thought alone that cements my decision to keep this secret to myself. It's what my mom wanted; it's what I'll honor.

Numbness takes over my entire body. Despite the decision I've made, I lie still in bed, shaken to my core. There will be no sleeping for me tonight. I've yet to change out of the sweatpants and t-shirt I threw on after my shower, my hair crinkling at the ends from air drying. I couldn't wait to start reading mom's diary; now I wish I hadn't bothered.

Slipping out of bed, I rifle through my bags and find my ballet shoes. It's been too long since I've danced, since I've escaped from the reality I've been thrust into. I take the compression socks as an afterthought. I'll relish the burn of exertion in the morning, but I can't be sloppy now. When I return to Waversea, my schedule will be overrun with practices for the showcase. For one last time, for tonight, I want to dance for the escape.

The manor is still. Quiet. I've taken this route a thousand times, probably more. Too many nights of broken sleep needing to be soothed away. On the bottom floor of the manor, I take the hallway tucked behind the staircase, permitting myself entry to the last room on the left. The dance studio.

A figure inside shifts quickly. My body jolts. Braced on a smattering of foam mats with his back to me, I hold a hand over my own throat, stifling the scream that almost escaped me. Counting his sit-ups in harsh whispers, his lightly tanned skin glistening. Sensing me, he suddenly stills in an upright position and twists to glare over his shoulder. The one person I could have done without seeing tonight and he's right there-brooding expression, clenched muscle and all.

"Wyatt, *fuck*," I curse before I can catch myself. A tidal wave of guilt hits me, knocking the breath from my lungs. He stares at me, crystal green eyes narrowed in question. I have questions too, like how much would he hate me if he knew Nixon chose to adopt me, but would probably disown Wyatt if he knew the truth. It's too much to bear. I turn away, stepping back into the hallway. Wyatt snorts.

"What? One blow-up with Garrett and you're suddenly wary of me. You haven't been deterred before." I peer back as his attention moves away from me. Kicking his legs out beneath him, he alternates to push ups. The definition of his muscle is something else, each outline deeply ingrained. I find myself staring, clenching the ballet shoes in my hands. I can't go back to my room. I can't be left to stew in my own thoughts for that long. A distraction is what I was seeking, and I've found one.

"I can't sleep," I announce in way of explanation. Closing the door with myself inside, I lick my lips, unable to satisfy my wandering eyes.

The shorts on his lower half are baggy, slipping haphazardly up his beefy thighs. He's naked otherwise, only coated in sweat and ink, the decayed skull on his calf. Finishing his set, he's suddenly up on his feet and facing me.

"Holy…dragon," the air rushes out of my lungs. Covering Wyatt's front, a dragon sprawls from chest to groin, its mouth open in a roar and impressive detail carved into every scale. Smoke encases the beast, trickling over Wyatt's collar bone where I've noticed it before. The only color is a starkly bright yellow in the eyes, otherwise the entire piece is hauntingly monochrome and exquisitely shaded. Wyatt clenches his jaw, looking anywhere that isn't my face.

"You couldn't sleep," he parrots back, his gaze dropping to my hands. "And you thought you'd prance about in the dead of night? Didn't you know the shadows in here can't be removed so easily." Tapping his temple with one finger, I'm jarringly reminded of his disdain for me, and of all the reasons I should feel the same. Jutting out my chin, I adopt a stronger posture.

"Well, you've never seen me dance."

Wyatt huffs through his nose. "How about a proper outlet?" Holding his arms wide, he gestures to the mats he's spread across the studio floor. I stare blankly. Wyatt is undeterred from whatever is happening here, bracing himself in a fighting position with his fists raised. It's my turn to snort.

"You want to fight with me? I thought that's what we've been doing this entire time."

"I want to see what skills you actually possess when not catching me off-guard with a rogue swing." He's referring to the jaw punch in his frat house kitchen. I wouldn't call it anything but a decent punch personally. I tilt my head back and forth, mentally weighing up the pros and cons. Eventually, I settle on the knowledge that if I leave here with even the tiniest bruise, the Shadowed Souls would come down on their leader like a ton of bricks.

Sounds good to me.

Dropping my ballet shoes aside and kicking the bootie slippers off my feet, I join him on the mats. "Aren't there gloves and pads in the gym?" A strange, sideways smirk sits upon his mouth, and that's when I decide he's either high, drunk or still starved of oxygen from Garrett choking him out. The Wyatt I usually get on a daily basis would have rushed forward with a hard jab to my ribs, raining pain down until I was left crippled on the floor with no less of a broken leg. But apparently, this Wyatt doesn't do that.

I throw the first hit, a tap really on the inside of his raised arm. A test for how he'd react and the result is disappointing. Wyatt starts a dance of his own, sidestepping until we're slowly circling. The studio is brightly lit but that doesn't prevent darkness lurking in every corner, the scent of dust thick in the air. No one has been in here, whether to clean or otherwise. I move on silent feet, every muscle tensed, every sense on high alert for his next move. For the moment he stops seeing this as a cute little game and decides to attack. My heart pounds with a mix of adrenaline and something else—something I refuse to acknowledge.

A smug smirk plays on his lips. He's as infuriatingly handsome as ever, his dark hair tousled, his green eyes glinting with a challenge. The sight of him like this, looking at me this way, sends a jolt of electricity through me, an undercurrent which heightens my senses. It's all so wrong, so foreign, but I'll be damned if I lose his attention now.

Wyatt lunges, and I sidestep, our bodies brushing for a split second —a flash of heat that I feel down to my core. I counter with a swift strike to his abs, but he blocks it effortlessly, briefly bringing our faces inches apart. I can feel his breath on my skin, so close it's almost suffocating.

"You're holding back," he taunts, his eyes locking onto mine, daring me.

I growl, pushing him away with all my strength, creating a few feet of distance. "I'm just getting started." I launch another attack quickly, our movements fluid, almost synchronized. Every strike is a clash of wills, each touch not aimed to hurt but to send sparks flying. My mind is unfocused, confused.

He catches my wrist, twisting me around and pinning me against his hard chest. I struggle, but his grip is like iron. His face is so close to the curve of my neck, his warmth colliding into mine with a mix of anger and something else, something darker, more primal.

"You're infuriating," I hiss, but my voice lacks conviction.

"And you're irresistible," he counters, his lips brushing my neck with the faintest touch. I freeze, stilling all protests. Perhaps Wyatt will assume my rigidness is fear, not spurred by curiosity. Why is Wyatt giving me his attention now? What's changed?

"Why do you always have to make things so difficult?" he murmurs, his voice husky. My heart hammers against my ribcage, the irony of his words igniting a fire within me. Sure, I'm the one making things difficult, when Wyatt's temper runs from scolding hot to ice cold, the trigger unknown.

I use his momentary distraction to my advantage. Spinning into his body, I bring my knee up sharply, aiming for his side. He grunts, the hold loosening just enough for me to slip free. I spin around, my fist sailing through the air, but he dodges, catching my wrist again. This time, he pulls me close, our bodies colliding.

Our faces are inches apart, both stunned to be so close. For once, the clench of Wyatt's jaw isn't present, leaving his face slack and lips slightly parted as he pants. The tension is unbearable, a magnetic pull. Inside, I'm screaming for the door to open. For someone to interrupt and knock some sense into us. This shouldn't be happening, but I'm too weak to stop it. Wyatt's eyes, beautifully green and blown to shit, flick to my lips, and for a moment, everything else fades away. There's only the two of us, locked in a strained embrace, both fighting for control in more ways than one.

This isn't right. If Wyatt doesn't hate me, I don't know where I sit in the world. Worse than that, if Wyatt isn't being an asshole, I have no reason to dislike him. What am I supposed to do then? Make small talk in passing, send him a christmas card, sit for awkward family photos? I wish I knew what he was thinking. What possessed him to not take one look at me and storm away like usual. It's easier that way. Simpler if we both know where we stand, and in the times Wyatt fails to uphold his side of our decade-long war, I suppose I'll have to.

Shoving him away again, I snap us both back to the cold reality we've created. He dances around, taunting me like a bull with a target. I duck low, using my knees and fists at his core while he twists away, rarely putting his hands on me. It's different now—charged with an intensity that goes beyond the physical. Every move, every fleeting touch, is laced with an undercurrent of desire. I hate him for it, hate the way he gets under my skin, hate him for the fire he ignites in me.

"Your self-defense teacher needs firing." Wyatt's lips curl into a damnable smirk, his body thrumming with confidence or recklessness. I've yet to decide.

"I could hurt you in so many ways if I deemed it worthwhile." My voice is too breathy, too affected. Coming to a standstill, I know this can't go on any further, despite the playfulness I wish I saw in Wyatt more often.

"Ha!" he laughs, striding towards me. His dragon tattoo seems to breathe in time with the rise and fall of his solid chest, his abs tight and that deeply engrained V leading to his waistband - nope, not going there. The image of a cocky asshole who loves dangling that carrot of hope in front of me, he makes the mistake of sliding his hands into his pockets. "I would pay millions to see you try."

"Suit yourself." I half shrug, snapping my arm out. No flourish, no big swing for him to see coming a mile away. My fist smashes into Wyatt's nose, the crunch of bone beneath knuckle ringing through the studio. I swiftly stand back, out of arm's reach, awaiting the fallout.

"Will that be cash or card? I don't trust your cheques not to bounce." I flutter my eyes innocently. And there it is. The line is redrawn. Wyatt holds his nose, blood pouring in thick rivets down his arm, following the network of veins pulsing there. His eyes grow hard, the clench of his jaw returning. A tremor of fear that I should have felt all along finally sparks to life, causing a shiver to ripple down my back.

"Do you feel protected now?" Wyatt asks through bloodied teeth. My brows knit together, the makings of a trap closing in around me.

"What?" I swallow hard.

"Your wellbeing is paramount. That's what my father said, and then left you in my care. You can run back and tell him I've done my job."

"So that's what this was? A way for you to score points?" Wyatt moves suddenly, closing the distance between us while I force my feet to stay grounded. Grabbing the hem of my t-shirt, he tears the fabric in two large hands, spraying blood over my chest in the process. Freeing the material from my abdomen, he holds it over his nose, glaring at me with furious eyes.

"Do I look like I give a fuck about scoring points?!" He's in my personal space, looking down on me. The white fabric in his hand quickly becomes blood red. "My men can cuddle you, stroke your hair and tell you that you're safe. But who is actually helping to train you?

To keep you on edge, aware of the dangers lurking nearby? Wake the fuck up Avery."

Shoving past me with the full weight of his shoulder, I stand stunned. Speckled with blood, left confused, conflicted and with the sinking feeling of heartbreak weighing me down. I can't tell him. It's not my place. In his own warped, twisted mind, Wyatt thinks he's following his father's instructions. All the while, that man may not even be his real father.

CHAPTER FORTY FIVE

"Ahh!" I bellow, scaring the nurse half to death as she repositions my nose. I snuck out at dawn this morning to seek professional help, in fear my nose would heal crooked and I'd have to look at myself every day in the mirror knowing I was sucker punched by *her*. The fake sister I should hate even more now, instead of feeling semi-impressed.

I backed her into a corner, wanting her to plead me for her life. Wanting her to cry my name in fear and when that didn't work...Well, I'm not going to dwell on that. What was supposed to be a test of her defense, or an attempt to appease my curiosity, became something I couldn't pull back. And she punished me for it.

Whether I like it or not, Avery has changed. Not like the pathetic girl who flinched too hard and held sadness in her huge, blue eyes. She's braver now, and I have my own brothers to blame for it. She's learnt to thrive under pressure and I'll never be able to break her now.

"Okay, Master Hughes, it's straight again now. No strenuous exercise for at least two weeks and please be careful with who you anger in the future." I'd spun her a line about getting into a fight at a party. Hopping down from the medical bed, I pull my leather jacket on and catch a glimpse of the purple bruising beginning to line my nose and seep under my eyes in the mirror on the opposite wall. Turning to the silver haired nurse, whose wrinkling leather hands are deceivingly strong, I thank her and accept the painkillers she hands me.

Driving back to the mansion in Huxley's Bentley, I use the time alone to ponder what the fuck I'm doing with my life. I was on track, so focused on what mattered. My schooling, my degree, playing in basketball matches and keeping socializing to a minimum. I only fucked girls out of necessity, to rid enough testosterone to not let myself become distracted by it. Well look who's fucking distracted now.

I'm running behind schedule on my coursework, my gang is splintering and I'm sinking further into the fractured child I've tried so hard to leave behind. Foresight has always been something I pride myself in, but my options are quickly dissolving all around me. Avery isn't backing down. She isn't making any attempt to separate herself from us, and my men don't seem inclined to let her.

Pulling into the underground garage, I park next to the Rolls my father has left here. Usually, it would be paired with a driver on speed dial to escort Avery wherever she'd like to go. Assessing my nose in the rear-view mirror, I exit the car with a heavy exhale and make my way into the manor. An elevator separates the garage from the main lobby, tucked beneath the staircase for discretion. Striding into the kitchen, I find Axel making omelets with an eager Garrett sitting at the island with a fork in hand. The large, mounted clock shows an ungodly early hour, so I eye the topless chef with suspicion.

"Why are you awake so early?" My voice comes out all nasally, so I decide to keep talking to a minimum. Sitting beside Gare, Axel leans over the island to pass me his half-drunk coffee since we take ours the same way – milk and two sugars.

"Couldn't sleep, and this one's stomach growling didn't help matters." He points his spatula at Garrett, who flashes his best hazel puppy dog eyes at him. I roll my eyes. Typical that there should be twelve guest bedrooms and these two decide to cling to each other.

"Ooh, what smells so good?" Avery walks in looking as fresh as ever, completely unaffected by her sleepless night. Her blue eyes fall on me and she overacts a gasp, raising her hand to her mouth. "Oh, how insensitive! I didn't see you there Wyatt. Do you need me to describe the smell to you?"

Huxley bursts out laughing as he walks in behind her, guiding her over to the table with a light hand on her shoulder. I should groan, noticing the way everyone is looking at my nose. She probably ran through the halls with a banner, alerting the entire household to her mini victory. Her golden hair is slightly damp, dripping onto a fitted white t-shirt as she swans further into the kitchen in gray sweatpants. I force myself to stare into the mug I'm nursing. Dax also appears to help Axel serve up six plates of omelets as we all take our seats at the table.

"Anyone else need coffee?" Axel asks, hovering behind his chair.

"Tea for me but I'll make it," Avery hops up and they both return to the counter. Failing to listen to the conversation happening around me, the whispers and giggles from behind keep drawing my attention over my shoulder. Axel fiddles with a strand of her damp hair as she leans into his muscled frame, all the while making her tea. Growling, I turn my focus back to trying to eat my breakfast, having to chew slowly to ease the strain on my already-tender nose. By the time the pair have returned, I've finished and leave my empty plate on the table, needing to put space between me and *her*.

I spend most of the day in my father's office, cleaning up the mess left by the contractors who showed no interest in actually fixing anything. Dust and debris from the shattered window cover almost every surface. As I sweep up the remnants of their negligence, I can't help but feel the weight of frustration and disappointment settle over me. The workspace feels like a battleground, and I am the lone soldier tasked with restoring order. Story of my life really. Me in charge, making the decisions others don't want to and rely on me for.

Running a hand down my face, I jerk and hiss at the pain I cause myself in forgetting about the broken bone. My brain is fried, so I take a break. Finding a few of the guys playing the PlayStation in the living room, I stride around the huge sofa and place myself right in the center, between Dax and Hux. As much as I want to be alone, I know I need to put myself in the comfort of my boys. Otherwise, I might as well not even be here.

"Where's Avery?" I have to ask, ignoring their side glances. I'm not in the frame of mind to torment her right now. I don't feel angry. I feel empty.

"She's booked a last-minute appointment with her old dance tutor. There's something she wants to perfect for the showcase and doesn't think Nightingale is up to the task," Garrett answers without looking my way. On the screen, Axel's character is killed off by Dax's, so he tosses the controller into my lap to take over. He rises, stretching his arms high above his head. I notice then that Axel, and all of those lounging around, are kitted out in their basketball jerseys and shorts. My heart leaps.

We haven't played together in too long, considering we're supposed to keep up our daily practice sessions, even in the breaks. A physical release is exactly what I need. The video game is set up for another round, between myself and Garrett before I can say otherwise. One game won't hurt, I reckon, as we start to tap the controller keys frantically.

The elevator door pings further within the mansion, which I ignore. Avery must be escorting her tutor in from the garage. Suddenly, the chandelier above explodes like a firework, the crack of gunfire hindered by the shattering of glass. I dive onto the floor as the metal frame smashes into the coffee table, splintering my arms with tiny shards as I frantically try to protect my head. My eardrums produce a high-pitched ring as I scramble across the floor, glass cutting into my palms and feet as I somehow make it into the kitchen. Pushing myself upright, I grab for the widest and sharpest knife from the utensil drawer before returning to just inside the archway.

Peeking around the corner, Dax is still lying flat on the floor, using the sofa to hide him while Garrett has leapt to hide behind the piano. The ceiling from the hallway into the living room is punctured with bullet holes and the empty socket that held the chandelier is swinging back and forth eerily. Three figures dressed all in black stand in the living room, their stances confident. My heart stutters. Axel peeps around the far wall, catching my eyeline whilst remaining hidden from the intruders.

"Find Avery," I mouth, to which he nods and disappears. The moment stretches as I stand, unsure of what to do. I don't stand a chance at attacking; they have a multitude of guns strapped to their hips for fucks sake. Dax catches my attention, his body shaking as he holds his hands over his ears.

"Hand over the Hughes child," the biggest of the men states loudly. "No one else has to get hurt." The deep voice booms throughout the room. No one dares to move, frozen in place by fear. Garrett's wide eyes find mine as he vigorously shakes his head beneath the piano, but what choice do I have? All of my closest family are in this house, and Avery. After a few deep breaths, I step out into the living room with the knife clutched tightly at my side.

"I'm here," I sigh, resigned. "Just leave everyone else alone." My voice comes out more nasally than I'd have liked right now. Staring into the dead eyes peering out from under a ski mask, a flash of confusion passes through them as the lead thug begins to laugh. The two men flanking him join the condescending crescendo, pointing at me and nudging shoulders. Aware of the pistol pointing right at me, I stand perfectly still, my jaw clenched.

"Not you, obviously." He finally manages to compose himself enough to say. Keeping my features schooled, I fight against the panic gripping me. *Obviously*? "Find her," he says to the guy on his left. Striding towards me with the gun pointed on my chest, he gestures to the knife with his chin and I drop it to the floor with a clang.

There's a look of betrayal in Dax's eyes, his face hard. If I could, I'd throw my arms out and scream, *'what the fuck do you expect me to do?!'* Am I supposed to fight a gun with a knife with the idea of saving Avery while I bleed out on the floor of a house I loathe? How is that the better choice, than being led back to the sofa with a barrel pushed against my nape?

Dax resigns to being found and pushes himself up next to me, shaking his afro out of the shards stuck in it. The other masked man drags Gare up by the back of his vest and tosses him our way.

"Is this all of them?" The larger of the two, who I've dubbed the leader, asks as they both circle the coffee table, glass crunching under their boots as they keep pistols trained on the three of us.

"There's another two somewhere," his blue-eyed friend answers, confessing he's done his homework. They knew we were here and they've picked their moment carefully. Where the fuck are Huxley's guards? Wait, where the fuck is Huxley? Both men are huge, bound in matching black cargos and tight, long-sleeved shirts showcasing their muscles. Their military style boots tie in with the tactical vests that hold multiple pockets bulging with more bullets.

The leader lifts one foot onto the frame of the table and rests the firearm on his thigh as he assesses me. His head cocks, a mocking tone to his voice. "You don't know, do you?" He questions, catching me off guard. Gare and Dax look over to me but I can't answer their curiosity, since I'm as much in the dark here as they are.

"Know what?" I ask back. His only answer is a chuckle. My eyebrows crease as I stare at him, trying to place his deadened eyes from somewhere but coming up empty. But then I shift my focus to his shape and size, wondering if he was the man on the surveillance camera. The one who was sifting through my father's papers and spoke of my mother's death as if he knew exactly what happened. He has the answers I need.

"Found this one trying to sneak in through the window," a gruff voice sounds as Axel is pushed along by a gun in his back. His hazel eyes find mine, an apologetic look painted within. I try to give him a small smile to tell him it's okay, but I don't know if I manage it. Shoving him down onto the sofa with us, the third masked intruder darts off again in search of Avery. My gut twists with worry, not for any reason other than I genuinely hope she is somewhere safe. In her hidden room, watching on, I hope. I can be the monster who keeps her up in the middle of the night, but not this. Not to be used for ransom and fuck knows what else inbetween. I taunt her but even I have my boundaries.

Growing agitated, I try to probe the leader without much direction in mind. I just hope if I keep him talking, he might reveal his intentions. Accidentally spill a secret which could provide some clarity as to what the fuck is going on.

"You're doing this for the money, right? State your price. Whatever it is, I'll get it. Just leave us alone." Out of the corner of my eye, I spot Axel's shaky hand seeking out Garrett's. The leader notices it too, a sneer crinkling the edges of his eyes. Terror bleeds through me, the need to protect my family has never been more present. They're here because of me. I chose them to be my brothers. I can't have any more guilt on my hands.

"Money means nothing to my boss," he finally shakes his head and returns to his full height. His lackey eyes him with a type of warning, but he continues anyway. "Your dear mother stole something from him years ago. She didn't keep her promise, and the time has come that we repaid the favor."

AVERY

CHAPTER FORTY SIX

I haven't heard a noise from anywhere in the house for the longest time, but I still remain hidden in the airing cupboard. Perched uncomfortably on a pile of folded towels, I cradle my knees up to my chest and bury my face into them. The boiler behind me is hot to the touch and the air in here is stifling, almost too thick to breathe as I rack my brain to understand what happened.

I had been sitting in the dance studio, tapping my foot impatiently waiting for Elena to arrive. Being an ex-professional ballerina, she's usually prompt for every one of our dance sessions, even given the late notice. As the clock above the door stated, she was an hour and ten minutes late. I'd given up waiting. Midway through typing out a text to Meg, asking if she's recovered after last night, I walked the corridors when the ping of the elevator sounded. *Finally - Elena is here,* I'd thought.

But as I turned the corner, a shiny black object led the way out of the elevator before deafening cracks of gunfire assaulted the air. Dashing back through the hallway, I slipped into the laundry room and threw myself into this cupboard before I even noticed my phone was still clutched in my hand. Cursing myself for not locking any doors behind me, I tapped out nine-one-one with shaky thumbs and have been waiting here for what seems like hours, waiting for the sirens to sound.

It's so quiet. No more gunfire, no yelling. If only I knew where anyone was, if anyone was even left inside the manor, I might be able to stop the constant flow of tears lining my cheeks. I'm scared. So fucking scared, terror seizing me. Not even the darkness of the cupboard is enough to coax me outside, a rare sense of solace wrapping around me. If I'm in here, I'm safe. An opposite concept to what I've been led to believe my entire life.

The sound of a handle twisting somewhere in the room beyond freezes the blood in my veins and my breathing automatically halts. The more I try to stay still, the more eccentric my trembling becomes until the sound of my teeth chattering prevents me from hearing any further sounds. The door abruptly whips open. Luckily, my hand was already wrapped around my mouth and catches my scream. A disheveled-looking Huxley sighs, his shoulders sagging in relief.

"Oh thank fuck, you're okay." he whispers. Throwing myself into his arms, he grips me tightly and buries his face into my neck. Leaves litter his blond, wavy hair, the ends muddied. Sweat coats his skin, a similar tremble to his movements as mine.

"What happened to you?" I ask as he puts me down. There's a dirt smear across his cheek and his jersey is torn down the side.

"I was already outside when they entered. I've army crawled through the bushes, climbing through the windows one by one until I found you. We need to move. Now." He whispers, linking his fingers with mine.

"Wait," I tug on his arm. "Aren't the police here yet? I called them ages ago." Shaking his head of messy blond hair, I scramble for a plan. We're too far away from the safe room entrances to risk it, but outside we're exposed. Huxley doesn't want to wait, creeping towards the window while listening intently for foreign sounds. Boots on the wood flooring in the hallway cause us to jerk behind a tall unit, his hand now covering my mouth.

We remain rooted to the spot. Doors are opened and rooms are searched in turn, each one loudly deemed 'clear' before moving onto the next. The room adjacent to this one is opened. We're next. There's no use trying to cover our movements now as we dart for the window. We're several feet from the ground but the fall doesn't concern me. The door flying open does.

"Stop!" a voice yells. Huxley slams his palm against the small of my back, shoving me onto the window ledge with his body weight. Bullets fly into the wall beside us. The pounding of boots echo with the hammering of my heart. I'm straddling the frame, half inside and half out when the warmth at my back disappears.

"Go!" Huxley shouts, throwing himself into the assailant running towards us. He knocks the man off kilter, giving him an opening to swing a fist into his masked face. Again and again, he manages to rain punches down on the man's head and body. A slither of hope flares to life, even if Huxley's face has taken on a terrifying edge. The harsh lines I usually marvel at are contorted by rage, his arm bulged with violence instead of vanity. Tears fill my eyes and I scream for him to come with me, stretching my hand out with strained fingers. We have our opening, now we have to take it. I climb over the windowsill; thankful I chose to wear sweatpants today and brace myself for the fall.

"Huxley, please!" I shout over my shoulder. Nodding, he readies himself to run as I drop myself over the edge and onto the hard ground. My ankles are unable to support the landing so I fall, rolling through the shrubs, thorns catching my hair, face and arms. Huxley's blond hair appears over the edge of the window before he's dragged backwards. Hearing grunts and shouts from above, I have to withdraw my instinct to cry out. He's fighting for me, giving myself away wouldn't help either of us.

I'll get help. I will help. Rolling onto my hands and knees, I crawl through the greenery towards the front of the manor. My phone is clunking against my thigh in my pocket, I can capture some footage until Huxley joins me. Anything concrete to find out what is happening to us. Yeah, that's what I'll do.

Heading in the direction of the windows surrounding the front lobby, a gunshot pierces the air and I freeze. My mind stutters to a standstill, the sound ringing on repeat through my ears. It's as if it's happening again and again, although I only flinched once. When it clears, I peer back up to the open window. The struggling has stopped, and the air has gone deathly quiet, the world also holding its breath.

The wail of several police sirens cuts through me. They're here, but they're taking too long. I wait longer, willing Huxley's face to appear and to let me know he's okay. But it doesn't. Instead, the rush of boots race out of the rear doors, the distant crunch of gravel fading away.

They're escaping and I'm doing nothing to stop it. Somewhere, a tiny voice in my mind forces me to scramble from the bush and run down the driveaway.

"That way!" I scream. "They're escaping out the back!" A black and white striped car skids to a halt in front of me, police appearing in all directions. Hands grab for me, words I can't hear sounding around the roar of blood in my ears. I'm placed into the back seat of a police car, the door slamming me inside. Officers in front of the car and multiple more police vehicles all rush towards the house, guns at the ready and the reality of what has happened hits me like a freight train.

Huxley didn't appear. He would have followed me. Nothing would have held him back. Hiding my face in my hands, I cry so loudly my body shakes with each sob. Huxley came for me, saved me. I need him to be okay. I pray the gunshot I heard is either embedded in the burglar or the wall. If anything happens to him, I can't...I won't...there won't be any coming back from this. I've split my heart and given out pieces so freely. I know better, but I did it anyway, and now I need to suffer when they do. I need to die when they do. The door to my left opening makes me flinch, but the sight of Wyatt sliding in is what really shocks me.

"Come here," he says, his voice so soft that my tears double. Holding his arms out, I hesitate briefly wondering if this is a trap but fall into his body anyway. It's the hauntedness of his green eyes, the scruff of his dark hair, the defeat in his posture. It can be a trap, I don't care any more.

Relaxing back against the leather seat, Wyatt strokes my hair as I cry into his chest. I clutch his t-shirt in my fist, using his deeply intense cologne to soothe me. To ground me. Another siren sounds and I glance up to see an ambulance passing, pulling right up to the front door. Not even Wyatt can hold me back now. Bursting out of the seat, I run to join the group of officers hovering around on the graveled driveaway.

"Holy fuck," Axel runs out of the house and lifts me into his arms. "You're okay. I've got you." Over his shoulder, I see Garrett walk out, his usual cheekiness a distant memory by the taut expression on his face. He doesn't meet my eye, passing by and joining Wyatt on the edge of the display. Placing me down, I keep my arms wrapped tightly around his middle as Axel pulls me out of the way. A stretcher is rushed out of the house, Huxley's blond hair hanging over the edge. Dax is walking by his side, holding Huxley's hand tightly with his white t-shirt covered in blood. *No.*

"Huxley!" I cry out, trying to run forward but Axel keeps me held tightly under his arm. I see the cage he was creating now, pre-empting this. I struggle and fight, needing to see. Huxley's eyes are closed, his mouth slightly parted and his skin an ashy shade of white. The sheet is tightly bound to his body by two orange straps, failing to stop the blood leaking through the gauze stuffed into his wound. Two paramedics lift the stretcher into the ambulance, as an EMT and Dax jump in the back. The other slams the back doors closed and jogs around to the driver's seat, turning the sirens on as he speeds out of the driveaway.

"Let me go, Axel! Get off me," I beg and scream but his grip is unyielding. "This is all my fault. You'd all have been better off never coming here." Hands grip my cheeks, forcing me to stop writhing and face the emerald eyes staring at me.

"If we weren't here, that would have been you," Wyatt saves sternly. "We have to remain calm until we know the facts." I mimic his nodding, copying his deep breaths. He is the voice of reason here and now, his lack of open emotion finally serving a purpose. "We'll take the Bentley and meet them at the hospital. He's going to be okay."

"I'm afraid we're going to need to take some statements," an officer interjects, a notepad open in his hand. Wyatt's scowl is venomous as he releases me and spins on his heel.

"Then you can take them from the hospital," he growls with authority. My bottom lip quivers as Wyatt jogs around to fetch the car and the officer backs away, leaving us to our own thoughts. Noticing Garrett's distant stare, I reach out to grip his hand and tug him towards us. Slipping his hands into my hair, Garrett holds me into his chest while Axel's arms wind around my waist from behind. Garrett places his head onto Axel's shoulder above me, trapping me. We sigh collectively.

"He's going to be okay," Axel rubs his hands over my waist.

"He better be," I whimper, pressing further into their warmth. Garrett grunts overhead, his tone low and barely recognizable.

"Oh, he will be, Peach. Because if Hux even thinks of dying on us, I'll fucking kill him myself."

AXEL

CHAPTER FORTY SEVEN

The next few days pass in a blur. Huxley's surgery took an agonizing amount of time, but went well. The bullet entered beneath his collar bone, missing the subclavian artery. It's a miracle his joint damage wasn't severe and his recovery should be smooth - if he abides by the surgeon's instructions.

As it is, Avery is tucked into his side, propped up in the hospital bed and turning the newspaper pages for him. Both she and Wyatt recently came back from being shouted at down the phone. In Avery's case, it was her lack of updating Meg which she caught shit for. Wyatt got an ear-full from Nixon.

"The police want to take another statement from you," Dax enters the room, six coffees mounted in a cardboard holder. His gaze seeks out Avery, and she groans.

"I've already told them everything." She sinks further into the baggy hoodie she's wearing - I think it's Garrett's. It's true, we've all heard her statement twice before and there's nothing left to say. The phone call Avery made from her closet to nine-one-one was actually intercepted, and it's possible she was speaking to an accomplice of the intruders. Luckily, a jogger passing by the manor heard the gunfire and called the real authorities.

As it stands, that voice on the end of the phone is the only tangible lead the cops have. Huxley's guards were drugged, the surveillance was wiped from an unknown source. This knowledge is the first time we've realized we're not dealing with some simple fan or harmless stalker. This is the big leagues, and we're all but small fish in their pond.

The groaning continues as Dax aids Avery in standing from the bed, puts a coffee in her hands and guides her towards the door. It's better to let the police ask their questions and leave, even if they don't give any advice for what we're supposed to do now. As Dax closes the door, I can see his expression means business.

"Any ideas?" he asks. We all know what he means. We've been passing hallway whispers, scrambling for ways to keep Avery safe. It's clear, to whoever is watching her, the very problem is us. But leaving her alone isn't an option. The attack on the manor was just the beginning. Those men were looking for her. They had instructions to take her.

"Aside from locking her in a basement?" Garrett pitches in from his chair in the corner. Dax remains standing by Hux's bed, the pair of them hitting Garrett with a death glare. "What?! I'll be down there too, caring for her most basic needs, and you guys can deliver us the finest food money can buy. Add in a few chains and whips - sounds like heaven to me." Wyatt hasn't stopped pacing for days, whereas I hover on the edge of a counter, my arms folded.

"This isn't a fucking joke, Garrett," I seethe. His brows hit his hairline but he doesn't say anything further.

"Is it worth having a tail on her, someone discreet who can watch from a distance?" Huxley tries to offer a useful solution. "Maybe from the outside, they might be able to see something we would miss."

"We are far too close to make good judgment calls," Dax admits. The dressing on Huxley's shoulder and chest shows as much. He prioritized her escape over his own, protecting her the way any one of us would have. Seems stupid really, when no commitment has been made, but it feels right. Natural. I'd put Avery's safety over mine without a second thought.

"We have to return to school," Wyatt states coldly. "Regardless of all the pulling of heartstrings happening in this room right now, she is just one girl. Not worth throwing your futures away over."

"What gives you the right-" Hux starts, but Wyatt's sharp tongue is ready.

"I have every right. None of you would be here if it wasn't for me. I've fought for all of you to have bright futures. Now look at yourselves. Throwing it away. You could have *died*, Huxely. What am I supposed to do then? When the gunshot happened in my family's home, because of my family's issues?"

Guilt. The crux of Wyatt's bad moods and terrible decision making. He keeps us all at arm's length, but is the first to buy our way out of trouble. I clear my throat, preparing to rip off the band aid. To alleviate Wyatt of the role he's put himself in. Although incredibly thankful, we never asked for him to be our leader. Especially when that means he'll never actually be one of us, always distanced, always up on a pedestal while we cower underneath. The only relationships Wyatt understands are transactional.

"It's not your job to look after us any more, Wyatt." My voice rings clear through the hospital room.

"Not my job..." Wyatt stalls his pacing and looks up. His eyes are wide, meeting each one of us in turn. I sense everyone holding their breath, side glances being passed around. Out of everyone, I was probably deemed the least likely to voice their thoughts. I'm just the coward, right? The soft, clingy burden they keep around. The one who had his chance at finding Avery before the gunmen and failed. Yeah, Wyatt's not the only one grappling with his guilt.

Wyatt storms out in a flurry, making a point of avoiding me. My eyes lower, sadness twinging the corners of my mouth. Garrett's foot shifts, outstretching to nudge my shoe. I retract it.

We're all running dangerously low on the clothing we'd shoved in our backpacks, expecting to be returning to Waversea within two days. The cops escorted Wyatt back to the manor just once, allowing him to collect the rest of our belongings. He packed Avery's too, a random selection of leggings and toiletries, and a box of their mom's stuff - diary included.

Meeting Gare's questioning gaze, I sigh. "You know I'm right. This dynamic hasn't been working for us since long before Avery turned up. He can't keep ordering us around. We want a brother, not a sergeant." The others turn into themselves, deep in thought or perhaps unwilling to admit the truth. The door reopens, a head of blonde hair appearing

"Woah," Avery stops, sensing the atmosphere before she's even stepped inside. "Who died?" A young and older woman shuffling by in the hallway gasp and sob, rushing to move on by. "Shit, I'm so sorry!" Avery calls after them. Sighing, she tosses her coffee cup into the trash can, the weight of it suggesting she didn't drink any. I'm yet to touch mine either.

"I need some air. Will you walk with me?" I ask Avery, straightening. Her eyes fly to Huxley. Oh, right. "Do you mind, Hux?" I ask for her, although I'm already moving towards the exit. He gestures with his hand for us to go ahead, just as another presence appears at my back.

"It's okay, Garrett. I've got this one." I don't look back, taking Avery's hand and leading her away. I can imagine Garrett's reaction. A swift gasp, the look of hurt bleeding through his dark brown eyes. It's my day for upsetting everyone, it seems.

"What's going on?" Avery blinks up at me, falling into step at my side. I know she's referring to me and Garrett. There's nothing to say, too much tension to wade through and some things, he just can't joke his way through.

My fingers curl around hers, the tightness in my chest eases as we put some distance between us and the others. We've been cooped up for too many days, initially in the waiting room and then in Huxley's private suite. The nurses urged us to leave, to find a room in the small hotel over the road, but we declined. No one was leaving until Huxley was out of surgery. Now, we won't leave until he's discharged.

Placating Avery with a smile, I lead her out into the courtyard. A chill is blowing in, tinted leaves falling from overhanging branches. I use the cold as my excuse to keep walking, guiding Avery over a busy main road to that small hotel. She says nothing as I eagerly grab the first room available, needing to pay for the entire night up front. It may have been a little obvious if I asked for an hourly rate. On the ground floor, I press a keycard into the door and crowd Avery inside, letting base need steer me. Avery doesn't object, her large blue eyes blinking up at me.

"Are you sure about this?"

I lower, grabbing Avery by the back of her thighs and lift her onto the desk. The room is basic; a double bed, wardrobe, ironing board. A small bathroom is reflected in the mirror beyond Avery's head. I dip my mouth to her neck, pressing kisses to her collarbone, her throat, her jaw.

"Without sounding like a total douche, I need this. I'm not like the others. I need to touch and be touched. I need your comfort, I need you to remind me of what it feels like to be taken care of." Avery allows my exploration of her exposed skin, not an inch of her face and neck going unkissed. Her hands lightly settle on my waist over my t-shirt.

"I meant, are you sure about doing this without Garrett?" I still, my fingers tangled in her hair.

Does she know this will be the first time I'll have been alone with a woman since leaving my childhood home? Does she know the exact nature of the horrors those women did to me, and what I've dreamt of doing back to them ever since. Garrett is my keeper, making sure I don't slip into a memory mid-fucking and let my rage bleed out. But I'm safe with Avery, and more importantly, Avery is safe with me.

I slip the hoodie over her head, finding a thin cotton vest underneath. Tracing the line of her strap, I dare a glance at her expression. Glazed eyes assess me above a faint smatter of freckles on her button nose and her golden hair tickles my chest.

"I need to learn to live without Garrett. He says as much himself."

"Axel, no-"

"Don't," I look away. "We all know it's only a matter of time before he leaves me with nothing but empty memories and false notions. It's who he is."

Leaning her forehead against mine, Avery parts her legs and hooks her arms around my neck so we are fully pressed against each other. We stay like that, happy to support one another without judgment for the longest time. This is my method of survival. Gentle touches and soft caresses remind me of how it feels to be loved. To be alive. Without them, I wouldn't see much point in sticking around.

"Axel, we're all shaken up after Huxley, but I really think-"

"Don't think. Just touch me." I'm thrown back into that selfish mode of starved contact. Gripping Avery's nape in one hand and palming her breast in the other, I grind my crotch against hers, driving a groan from her. "Please touch me."

Obeying immediately, Avery throws herself into my kiss. Her hands are everywhere, tracking my abs, scratching at my back. Our lips only part to hastily undress, shoes being kicked in all directions and clothing littering the aged carpet. I drop to my knees, dragging her sweatpants and panties off together. Avery's nails scraping my head as I stop to appreciate her. Fuck, she's beautiful.

From head to toe, from perked nipples to her glistening pussy, she's perfect. I don't need Avery to tug me closer, my mouth closing over her clit in the next instant. I push her thighs wide open for me, the surface of the desk equal to my kneeling height. My tongue is in her, thrusting, licking, laving. She tastes so sweet, my cock strains at full attention. I can't deny myself this time, unable to withhold from standing and sliding straight into her. Avery gasps and moans, a sound that will be imprinted in my mind forever. It's the sound of pure pleasure, and for once, it's all for me.

Lifting her from the desk, I fuck her without restraint. There's no need to pretend we aren't both chasing the same high, the same grip of reality which has been slipping. My breaths slip out in heavy pants between heated kisses, her teeth traveling down to bite my neck. I groan, every nerve ending in my body buzzing and alive. She marks me everywhere she can reach, not holding back. This is what I wanted, an outlet for us both. Avery pretends she isn't shaken by the ordeal at her home, the mystery that's unfurling around her. Now she knows, I'll be here to help her forget.

My balls slap against her ass as I pound harder, faster. There's no telling who breaks first, our matching groans ringing out as we cum together. I push us through, until every drop has been drawn out of me and is seeping down Avery's thighs. I'm still rock hard inside of her, my long legs crossing the room in four steps.

Without withdrawing from her tight cunt, I step into the shower and switch on the faucet. A lukewarm spray washes away the sweat coating our skin. I kiss Avery feverishly, pushing my tongue into her mouth, tangling with hers. Pushing her against the tiled wall, she gasps into me, her back arched. I move slower this time, long and languid thrusts, following the rise and fall of her body with each one. Her arms fall away, giving me full, unregulated control over her body. Reaching for the provided shower gel, I lift her hand and squeeze a huge dollop into her palm.

"Avery sweetheart. Please touch me." I place her hand on my chest. She is so compliant, lathering me, washing me. I lean into her every touch, my body rolling and drawing the sweetest sounds from my parted lips. Once she deems me clean and the water eradicates all of her hard work, Avery looks up at me from beneath hooded eyes, her chest flushed.

"Axel baby. Please make me forget." And I do just that.

HUXLEY

Stepping into the frat house at Waversea is surreal. It feels like a lifetime since we were all last here, not merely two weeks. Having been through surgery, multiple x-rays and a constant drip of the best morphine money can buy, my arm is now held to my chest in a tight sling to support my collarbone. Wyatt ushers in behind me with our bags, micromanaging every move I make. I don't have the energy to chastise him for it. Already, just from walking from the car to the front door, I'm exhausted.

My feet begin to drag as I shuffle towards the staircase and Garrett slides out of the kitchen to help me. I wrap my right arm around his shoulders to lean against him. I gave up resisting when Avery straddled me in the hospital bed and spoon fed me jello. As if reading my mind, Garrett groans.

"Lay off the desserts for a while, big guy. Without your good looks, you've got nothing to fall back on." I bark a laugh, which sends a sharp slice of pain through my shoulder.

"Fuck off, I'll always be beautiful." I say, despite the grease in my hair and the whole hospital ick lingering on me. I just wanted to get out of that damn place as quickly as possible. Easing me to the top of the stairs, Garrett forces me to walk the last twenty feet to where he's opening my bedroom door. An angel is lying upon my bed. Her blonde hair pools around her as she sleeps peacefully, the rhythmic rise and fall of her chest making everything I've been through worth it. I'd jump into the firing line for everyone in this house, including Avery.

"She fell asleep waiting for you," Garrett flashes me a smile as he turns to leave, then pauses. "I'm so glad you're home," his breath whooshes out of him. The smile shifts for something much more vulnerable to take its place. I offer out my right arm and tuck Garrett into my side.

"Me too, brother. Me too." After giving me a tight squeeze and actually making a 'squee' sound, Garrett leaves me. I stand in the doorway, unable to bring myself inside. Avery insisted on coming back to Waversea early to get my room ready – and it looks fucking perfect. Eventually, I shuffle in. Wyatt appears with my bag in his hand, throwing it across the floor and closing the door behind me. Avery's eyes flutter open and her bright smile eases any pain I might have felt.

"You're back." She rises to greet me, kneeling on the mattress. I twist to sit on the bed with a huff, each movement feeling taxing on my usually strong body. Tender hands slowly push their way around my stomach from behind as she rests her head on my good shoulder.

"I know I've said it a hundred times, but I'm still so thankful for you saving me. If you hadn't been there..." she whispers into my ear, ducking her head to place a kiss onto my neck. My right fist clenches. As long as I live and breathe, no one will be taking Avery away from me. Unclenching my fingers, I turn to rest my cheek on her head. Anger has no place in here right now; I'll reserve it all for later.

"If this is leading to a 'thank you blowjob', can I redeem at another time?" Her laughter lifts my heart as she lowers me onto my back, but she doesn't outright say no. Removing my shoes, she flicks on the TV and snuggles up to me. Sleep begins to pull me back under but I'm eager to stay in Avery's company. Her curves are pressed against me in an oversized nightshirt, her bare leg hooked over mine in the flannel pajamas I've been wearing for two days.

"Hey sweetheart, would you be able to run me a bath when I wake up?" I breathe heavily as the darkness takes me away before I can hear the response. The next thing I know, Avery is gently shaking my arms as I wake from the most peaceful sleep, thanks to the effects of the painkillers I was given before leaving the hospital.

"Your bath is ready," she smiles sweetly. The cast of golden hair hanging around her is like a halo, lifting me from one dream into the next. I should tamper down the swell of affection growing within, but I'm done hiding. I came too close to leaving words unsaid and emotions unexplored.

Reaching up to cup Avery's cheek, she shifts and grabs my offered hand, helping me out of bed. Despite feeling much more rested, I allow Avery to lead me into the bathroom I share with Dax, and watch her unbutton my long-sleeved pajama top. Smoothing her hands beneath the red checked material, her lips brush my neck as she tiptoes up to push the top over my shoulders with extreme care. The dressing taped to my chest is huge in comparison to the size of the bullet hole, but that'll work in my favor for the sympathy vote.

"Enjoy your soak," she breathes into my ear before strolling towards my bedroom with swaying hips.

"Aren't you going to help me take my trousers off?" I ask, readjusting my stiffening erection. At least that still works. Avery smiles over her shoulder at me, battering her blue eyes as she opens the door to reveal a topless Dax on the other side. He winks and blows me a kiss before sidestepping Avery to advance on me. "Actually, I think I'll manage," I say in a light tone. Before Avery started slipping into my bed at night, I typically slept and moved around the house naked. Which is why Dax isn't fazed as I shake my pants down, he then helps me into the tub, careful not to get my dressing wet as I relax in the warm water.

"How are you feeling?" Dax asks from his position perched on the sink's counter.

"I'm alright man," I lie, "just trying to focus on getting my strength back. Keep moving forward, right? Besides, this is gonna be a killer scar one day." He chuckles along with me but doesn't say anything else, allowing me to rest my head back. We all have our roles to play, a finely balanced dynamic to maintain, and brooding is Wyatt's forte. But the truth is, I thought I was fine before I re-entered this house. Now I'm not so sure. My mind wanders into nothingness, where no thought or pain can reach. A vast open space that I could easily lose myself in if Dax didn't break the silence.

"Mafia or vampires?" he asks. Him and his damn collection of raunchy paperbacks. Avery reappears with a jug to wash my hair, answering for me.

"Don't hold back the good stuff, Daxy. Be a good boy and dig out the monster smut." Dax does as he's told, while Avery attends to sitting me upright, massaging my scalp with frothy shampoo before rinsing it all out.

"Maybe I'll get shot more often," I joke.

"I'll wash your hair for you whenever you like, if you promise to never take a bullet for me again. We were so worried about you." I snort at Avery's response, knowing full well I would take that bullet for her a thousand times over if it meant she's safe. Once healed and strong enough, I'll be heading the investigation as to why her home was broken into in the first place. From what I've understood, nothing was taken. Those men were there for her.

Dax returns with a book in hand, the cover questionable. Avery finishes my hair and pats her hands dry, sitting on the floor by the tub. I lean my good arm over for her to hug while Dax crosses his legs on the countertop and opens the book.

"Ohh!" Avery straightens excitedly. "I love this one! The minotaur and the milkmaid." I look up at the ceiling blankly.

"You guys are weird," I remark. Either way, Dax and Avery take it in turn to read a chapter each until the water turns cold. I find myself oddly fascinated by the time the milkmaid has got to the actual 'milking' but Wyatt calls through that it's time for dinner. Dax carries over a fluffy towel from the heated towel rack and uses his upper body strength to lift me from the tub. Wiping the soapy water from my chest first, he then wraps the towel around my waist.

Back in my room, Wyatt is placing a stack of pizza boxes onto the dresser with Garrett carrying plates and Axel balancing a tower of smaller containers. The two bedside tables have been moved to the foot of the bed and are covered in bottles of soda, plastic cups and dip pots. Axel moves onto the bed after flicking The Fresh Prince of Bel Air onto the mounted TV so I can lounge in the center. One may think the scene is spontaneous, but it's an exact recreation of how we spent one summer when Dax broke his leg. He couldn't play ball, so none of us did. Instead, we all suffered the consequences of Garrett's terrible diet and needing to get back into shape afterwards.

Despite how Wyatt has been since we arrived here, he has always been the most thoughtful one out of us all. He relishes making others happy even though he will shrug off any praise if we try to give it to him. Opening the box lids, the smells of baked grease flood the room as Dax helps me step into some boxers. Smells like heaven to a man stuck on jello for two days.

After fixing the sling back around my neck and left arm, Dax then helps me to nudge across the bed. Garrett hands me a plate piled high while I'm squished into the Kingside bed by four masses of muscle-two at the headboard and two down by my feet. I glance around, unable to shake the sense that something is missing when I realize it's not something, but someone.

"Where's Avery?" I ask. Wyatt doesn't take his focus off the TV, but his frame tenses and I roll my eyes. I thought we were over this shit.

"I suggested maybe we keep this as a boys night, and she agreed. It's been ages since we all hung out together." He answers tentatively. Probably because he knew it's a surefire way to irritate me. None of the others attempt to argue or agree with him, just continuing to eat with their eyes focused straight ahead. And that seriously pisses me off.

"Okay, everyone out." I say loudly, which does grab their attention, judging by the wide-eyed gaping expressions I receive. "Everyone can fuck right off." I shove my plate into Axel's hands and try to shove Garrett off the bed with my feet, but I only end up hurting myself. Pain slices through my tensed shoulder, causing me to groan and clench my teeth.

"Hey, hey. Take it easy," Dax says, placing a hand on the back of my neck but I shake him off, despite the agony it continues to cause me.

"I may be the one who was shot, but Avery has been stalked by these fuckers for months. They sent a message for us to stay away, and we didn't. As a result, she was hunted down by a gunman in the house she felt safest in. And instead of washing her hands of us then and there, she's been at the hospital comforting me. I don't need a boys night like the old days. That's not how it is any more Wyatt. You need to get with the fucking program or get the fuck out."

Hanging their heads, they all begin to edge out of the room which is actually the opposite to what I had expected. I'd expected Wyatt to hang up his vendetta for tonight, for me, and to fetch Avery with a murmured apology. Despite hugging his empty plate to his chest, Garrett stares longingly at the pizza, but I give him my angriest stare until he leaves too.

Now I'm alone. Swallowed by the darkness within, visualizing that void which I could easily lose myself in. I've never shouted at my brothers before, I don't even know where it came from. But I suppose I'm not myself right now; I'm in pain, I'm fucking furious for no particular reason and all I want is Avery cuddling me again. Yet I don't call for her. She shouldn't see me like this. I've been so mellow in the hospital but now I'm back here, I feel apprehensive. What if Avery is in trouble right now? I couldn't do shit.

A soft knock sounds against my bedroom door just as it opens, and I don't need to look to see who it is. I smell her honey and vanilla shampoo before she kneels beside the bed, her big beautiful eyes looking up at me with worry. "Axel said you might need some female company." Not just any female, this one specifically but I don't tell her that. I may be ready to confess the thoughts I've been having, but whether Avery is ready to hear them is another issue.

"I don't know what came over me," I sigh, leaning into her touch. "I kinda lost my shit." I hang my head, annoyed at myself. She rounds the bed and strokes her fingers up and down my chest gently. I wanted all of us here. It feels right when we are all together but I'm too stubborn to say it out loud. I'm not going to beg Wyatt to put himself in a position I know he'd hate, even if it is for me.

"Trauma isn't something we can control. At times, we may think it's buried so deeply, it almost doesn't exist. But when you least expect it, that damaged part of you will come to the surface and force you to face it." A tear leaks from my eye so I look away from her, desperate for her not to think I'm weak. Her soft hand moves across my cheek and pulls me back to face her. "You never have to hide your pain from me."

"I don't...I would hate myself if..." I fail to find the words. Avery seems to find the exact ones I need to hear without hesitation.

"You can't scare me away, Hux." I close my eyes, focusing on breathing. On not cracking into a thousand pieces with her watching. The faintest touch of lips press against mine. Salt invades the seam of my mouth, my own tears mixing with the lifeline Avery offers me. I reach out with my good arm, my hand encompassing the width of her nape. I hold her steady, keeping her with me, encouraging her to keep kissing me. Avery drowns in my tears as I drown in her comfort.

Peeling back, Avery beams at me with the brightest smile. One I don't particularly feel deserving of after the show I made to my brothers.

"Stop being so proud. I literally owe you my life. Now, can we eat? I'm starving." Her stomach growls on cue. I find myself copying her smile, nodding and sitting upright.

Avery hands me back my plate of food before bending forward to grab herself one. Her perfectly rounded ass, covered in pink frilly panties, peeks out from beneath the nightshirt, my mouth drying up at the sight. I'd do something stupid that I'm definitely not in any position to be doing, if it weren't for the shadow pacing back and forth beneath my doorframe.

"Come in Garrett, the food's going cold." I shout, the action pulling on my throat uncomfortably.

The door bursts open with a loud bang and Gare rushes in with his empty plate like a lion pouncing on its prey. Between his grunts and lip-smacking around a slice of pizza he's barely lifted from the box, he slurps a fizzy drink. I'm morbidly disturbed to say the least, but Avery finds it amusing. Her giggles distract him, like a deer in the headlights as he whips his eyes towards her.

"Shh," I whisper. "If you spook him, he might eat us." A wrong choice of wording, as Garrett's stare grows even more intense. Avery makes a point of shimmying under the cover, barring her body from his view and fully enjoying his pout.

My chest eases, the chokehold of anguish finally loosening its grip and a full smile stretches across my face. I feel semi-normal again. Semi-me again. Avery coos and strokes a spot of the cover in slow circles. Garrett, taking full advantage of her attention, cocks his head back and forth before rounding the bed and curling up between her legs, pizza box in hand. She strokes her fingers through his hair as we eat and watch TV. Despite half of the guys missing, this feels better because if Avery is by my side, I don't need to worry about her being in trouble. And call me selfish, I just want to have her around.

"Little Swan?" I ask after a few episodes, as my eyelids are starting to grow heavy. Avery hums in response. "Read me the rest of the damn minotaur book."

AVERY

Daybreak blends into sunset beyond the closed curtains. Days and nights become irrelevant. There is only Huxley and his needs. Wash his wound, change his dressings, plump his cushions. We've watched so many seasons of multiple shows, they've all blended into each other. I can't keep up with the characters, and I can forget the plot lines. But Huxley is distracted. That's all that matters.

In the moments he drifts to sleep and I'm too restless, I turn to my mom's diary. I've read it front to back, back to front and twice more for good measure. It wasn't until I really looked, I realized why there's a sudden change in her mood. A tiny crease along the spine's edge, so close I missed it on first inspection. There are pages missing.

It was a guy she met by accident, an offered umbrella in the pouring rain. A meal at a diner when her car had broken down. Rich people don't carry wallets, shouldn't drive between shoots alone. But that was my mom, stubbornly independent. She wrote how she would manufacture pockets of time to herself, the car windows down as she belted songs and became lost from a demanding world.

He'd been so kind to her - this man who didn't recognise her face. Who didn't ask for a photo or autograph. She described how he looked at her, as if the world started and ended in her eyes. How Nixon hadn't looked at her in years. He opened the door, offering his hand to aid her over a muddy puddle. She left with his coat, his phone number and a notion that the man who called the recovery van somehow saw something in her that everyone else missed.

She called him that night. They spoke for hours. Their affair didn't start for months, in my mom's opinion. I would question whether weekly luncheons and dinners in the back of dim restaurants would constitute the start of an affair. Darkened movie theater rendezvous' turned to hotel rooms. The rush, the excitement. It was all so out of character for the woman I knew, but she was young. Everywhere my mom went, eyes were on her. Photos were taken, gossip was whispered. This was her escape. *He* was her escape.

I skim the upcoming descriptions of lustful nights. Mom wasn't shy, she detailed every sordid, incriminating detail. So why did she feel the need to remove those pages? A familiar prickle filters up the back of my spine. Maybe she didn't. Maybe someone else did.

A shadow appears at the edge of Huxley's door, a soft 'psst' causing me to lift my head. Dax beckons me. I tuck the diary beneath the pillow and slip out without disturbing Huxley.

"What's up?" I whisper once in the hallway. Pale light streams in through the window at the end of the hallway, no longer blocked by the trees' foliage. Fall has stripped the branches of their leaves. Standing in sweatpants, sneakers and a hoodie, Dax is joined by Axel and Garrett.

"We're going for a morning run," he runs a hand over his short, blond afro. "And thought you might like to join us. Get some fresh air." My eyes slide back to the door. I tug on the long sleeve of my pajama top.

"He'll be fine, Little Swan," Axel takes my hand. "Wyatt is lurking nearby. If Huxley needs anything, Wyatt can take the brunt of his bad mood." I chew on my bottom lip, not fully convinced. It's true, Huxley's moods have been awful in the times I've stepped out and he's woken alone. Beginning to retract my hand, Axel holds it firmer. "Avery, sweetheart, come jog with us.

"Huxley needs me. It's my fault he was injured." I breathe harshly. Axel's hazel eyes are understanding yet firm.

"You didn't have your finger on the trigger, nor did you jump in front of a loaded gun. And you're not moping around with a healed wound, making sure everyone keeps tiptoeing around." Dax steps forward, his tanned features etched with concern.

"You need some space from him." I close my eyes briefly, nodding. They're right. I know they're right.

"Not to mention, you need exercise," Garrett leans against the opposite wall and picks at his nails. "All that takeout in bed is going to be a nightmare for your dance partner to lift in the showcase."

"Yeah, thanks Garrett. I get it." Tugging my hand from Axel's, I walk away and enter my bedroom. A wash and quick change later, I emerge in leggings and a sweater, my hair bundled into a high ponytail. The boys are waiting at the bottom of the stairs, where I steal the chocolate pastry from Garrett's hand and take an aggressive bite in his face. He grins and smacks my ass on the way out.

The boys let me set the pace, although they choose the route. I would suspect they've taken this same jog many times before, given the synchronized way they herd me from one road to the next. The cool morning air fills my lungs, a crisp burn I instantly welcome.

We're nearing the edge of campus, but my focus is on the unique presences surrounding me. Each of the guys have their long, athletic legs. Their arms pumping, their stamina well trained. Garrett's messy hair is damp from a pre-run shower, Axel wearing a hint of cologne. Dax tracks his steps on his smart watch, his lean frame flanking me protectively. A smile warms my cheeks. They were right; I really did need this. Not just the exercise, but the break from the frat house. From Huxley.

My mind is blank. Quiet even. There is only the thump of sneakers on tarmac. The heavy breaths clouding in front of our faces. Exertion revives my limbs. A long road, a peaceful backdrop. It's this false sense of serenity which delays my reaction to a flash of light in the corner of my eye. Then another, and another. Bodies bundle through alleyways, between houses and amongst the shrubs. A swarm of cameras and microphones are angled towards my face.

"There she is! Miss Hughes! Over here!"

They come from all angles, a van pulling up in front to block the road. A flurry of lights blind me. The noise cracks like a whip through the serenity, alerting anyone in the vicinity to our presence. The demands, the shouting.

I cover my ears but the questions continue to leak through.

Hands grip my waist. At first, I jerk out but the arms band around me tighter, pulling me through the horde of bodies. I'm bundled into Axel's and Dax's side, whilst Garrett steps away to give the press something to report. I hear a whole load of cursing, followed by a crash and a further round of shouting. He's laughing when he catches up to us. Our jog back to the house isn't peaceful. It's a race, us against those who take chase. Tires skid against the tarmac. Within seconds, the van is rolling alongside us, filming and whistling for my attention. Dax strips out of his hoodie mid-stride and throws it over my head.

Wyatt appears in the doorway of the frat house, his brows furrowed. We rush inside, nudging him out of the way. I collapse in the lobby, hand on my chest as the door is slammed closed. But that doesn't stop the vultures. Cameras flash, shouted questions continue and that's when I realize - Wyatt is still outside. His outline is visible through the frosted glass, his commanding demeanor quieting the raucous. I crawl forward, despite the hands which grab for me. The Shadowed Souls mean well, but I won't hide away while Wyatt slates me to the press. Those are not headlines I'll allow. Pushing up onto my knees, I peer at the bodies flooding the front lawn.

"Mr Hughes, is your sister safe under your protection?" a woman calls, bravely taking a step from the rest. Wyatt reaches out and snatches the microphone from her hand. Here it comes. The part where Wyatt tells the world how pathetic and weak I am.

"I believe Avery *was* safe under my protection, until you parasites just offered her to the kidnappers on a silver platter. Why don't you do us all a favor and fuck off? There's no story for you here." There's a moment of silence before the shouting kicks off again, cameras flashing as Wyatt throws the microphone into the crowd. He turns to the door and I scramble back, catching his attention through the glass. His pause seems to last an eternity, then the ghost of a smirk touches his mouth and he looks back over his shoulder.

"Oh, and she's not my fucking sister."

I don't wait around any more. I'm shaking with anger. A ruined run. A public disowning. Which one am I more upset about? But none of it matters. Wyatt is right - if the men who broke into the manor didn't know where I was, they sure will now. I climb the stairs, leaving the rest of the curious glances behind.

Entering Huxley's room, I shed my clothes, eager to dive back beneath the sheets. Why did I think leaving was a good idea? Tearing at my socks, I pause, noticing the bedside light is on. He's propped up, his blond hair disheveled. Topless, broad, the sheet pooled at his waist. In his large hands is my mother's diary, his thumb nudged between the open pages.

"What are you doing?" I ask, slowing to a standstill. "That's...it's not yours."

"When are you going to tell Wyatt that Nixon might not be his father?" Huxley asks, his brown gaze steady. I swallow hard, then I'm rushing forward. For a man who's supposed to still be injured, he's swift, holding the diary out of reach. I dive over his legs, straddling him.

"Huxley! Give it to me!" I push his head aside. His arm around my hips is an iron band, rooting me in his lap. I'm careful to avoid his shoulder, soon succumbing to the hug he draws me into.

"You have to tell him," Huxley says against my hair. Slowly, he pushes the diary into my hand. I hug it between us, clinging onto my mom's words. Such simple words, belying actions which she couldn't have foreseen would cause so much pain, anguish and *drama*.

Do I wish I had been adopted by any other couple? Definitely not, but that doesn't change anything now. The only mom I ever had is gone. The only family member I have left is across the country, ignoring my calls, refusing to consult with the police. I sigh.

"You're wrong, Hux. I don't owe Wyatt anything."

DAX

CHAPTER FIFTY

Rolling my shoulders, I close the laptop and sag back in my chair. I've been on a video call all morning with the entire college Board, having convinced them to meet for a virtual hearing. There was no chance of leaving the house without the reporters camping outside jumping on me to comment. I have nothing to say, in particular, nothing about my 'intimate relations' with Avery.

During his time in hospital, Huxley missed an important coursework deadline, which means half of his overall mark for this year is sitting at a big fat zero. After an hour of persuasion, they finally decided to give him until the end of today to get it submitted.

Collecting Hux's laptop, I climb the central staircase to his room and knock softly. Peeking around the door, he's sitting alone in the dark and watching TV. For a moment, I look over the blank expression on Hux's usually cheery face as he stares forward. His eyes are lined with heavy shadows, a frown pulling at the corners of his mouth. His hair is hanging limply onto a white shirt that has a sauce stain down the front. Huxley would never normally be seen with a speck of dirt on him, preferring to go topless rather than look grubby.

"Hey Hux?" I ask, snapping him out of whatever daze he was just in. He attempts a smile that doesn't come across but I return it anyway. Moving into the room, I walk over to open his curtains. "It's lunchtime, do you want anything to eat?" He shakes his head, looking like a lost puppy as he gazes at the full bowl of soggy cereal on the bedside table. Oh thank fuck, I'd briefly thought that smell was him.

Typing out a message to Garrett, asking him to come and collect the bowl, I quickly change my mind in fear he might try to eat it so I copy the message and send it over to Axel instead. Sitting next to Hux, I open his laptop and place it on my crossed legs. "I have good news. In light of-" I glance to his left shoulder where the dressing is poking out the neckline of his t-shirt, "well, you have until four o'clock today to submit your fall coursework. So I've come to help you." I smile but he doesn't return it. The ghost of the Huxley I know just stares back blankly.

Axel strides in without knocking, replacing the bowl with a bottle of water and a banana. "You have to eat Hux, or I'll get Avery to force feed you," he says before leaving. A hint of a real smile flickers across Hux's face, half hidden by the overgrown stubble that now qualifies as the start of a beard.

"Sorry, Dax. I'm not in the mood. I'll just make up the credit next year." I can't hide my shock. Huxley is the best of all of us. Top of his classes, the quickest on the basketball court - not that I'll admit it out loud. He's our golden boy.

"Sorry dude, I can't let you do that. Even if we only send what you've done up to now, it'll be better than submitting nothing at all." I type his password in, since we all know each other's for emergencies, and load up the document. I don't have the first clue about law, but I read through a few pages trying to understand what he's decided to base his most recent paper on.

"Did Avery sleep in your bed last night?" Hux asks unashamedly. "She didn't come back all of yesterday or last night."

"She was revising in the study. Garrett found her passed out on the desk and carried her back to her own room." At Huxley's panicked look, I rush to add, "Don't worry. He dragged his mattress through the halls and slept right outside her door. No one is getting in without one of us knowing." This is one of the instances where I'm glad Garrett is prone to overreacting.

There's a streaming link online with a twenty-four hour rolling video of the front door. On the plus side, the press are doing the police's surveillance for them. On the down side, Avery is now a prisoner inside these walls. Not just those of the frat house, but those of Huxley's room. He's staring longingly at the door, thinking of her. Pining for her. It's not healthy for either of them.

"Hux...She can't be stuck in here every minute of every day. Especially when you are choosing not to leave yourself."

"I know that." He grunts and scowls. Relaxing back against the pillows, his fingers drum and gaze becomes unfocused again. I return to the eighty-seven page essay, highlighting sections which could be worded better and color coding references. At times, I find myself squinting as I reread the same sentence twenty times over, trying to make sense of the legal mumbo jumbo.

"For the love of fuck, stop reading. It looks like the vessel in your head is about to explode." I grimace, rubbing the new addition to my forehead. "Tilt the screen my way. I'll annotate, you type." He says with a roll of his eyes, shifting to make space for me against his headboard.

We spend the next two hours pushing through his essay until Hux eventually drifts off to sleep. I sit beside him, his head flopping over onto my shoulder while I scan through the document again, searching for spelling and grammatical errors. Once I'm satisfied it's as clean as I will get it, I email the essay over to his tutor with a sigh of relief.

In his inbox, I can't help but notice an email from Stephanie Vaughn, Huxley's mother. The subject reads 'Let's Have Lunch' as if she hasn't disregarded him for years. Our pasts are nothing alike. Huxley spent his childhood trying to please the parents who were stealing from him. I was raised with nothing material, but all of the love and respect for the strongest woman I'll ever know. Now she's gone, and it's that feeling of not having second chances which makes me wonder if I should encourage him to reach out while he still can.

Closing the laptop, I readjust Huxley further down the bed, figuring it will strain his injury more if he wakes up with a stiff neck. My arm gets trapped beneath his head, which I consider leaving but I should let him rest properly. As I withdraw my arm, he flinches violently and raises his fists to defend his face, causing a scream of pain to escape his lips as his shoulder is jolted.

"Hux, it's okay! It's just me, just Dax," I say as he comes to. Blinking in confusion, a look of anger falls over his face as he recognises me.

"Get out," he says, shifting onto his right side. I linger, unsure if he means it until he shouts, "Leave me alone!" Confused, and slightly irritated, I place his laptop onto the dresser and exit the room. I get he's struggling with a few issues right now, but surely Hux can see I am trying to be there for him, as I always am.

Just outside the door, I almost crash into Wyatt. He's loitering around, hands in his pockets, unsure what to do with himself.

"He's getting worse, isn't he?" I nod. Wyatt sighs, jerking his chin. "Come with me. I need a witness."

"What for? Where are we going?" But Wyatt doesn't answer. Instead, we descend the stairs and pass through the kitchen.

I know they were harmless, but Huxley's words have really affected me. I was the first to join Wyatt. Or rather, he thought up the Shadowed Souls one night when I was on the verge of becoming a child of the state. In Wyatt's head, a gang name gave him the right to take over, funding my education and housing there after. Then came Huxley, the charming kid who used popularity to his advantage. But when it came to it, he would return to his room and sit alone, slipping into a void much like the one starting to consume him again now.

It was my suggestion to take on Axel after that, saving him from being expelled after he beat a boy shitless for commenting on the hotness of his Mom. And Axel chose Garrett, the guy no one wanted to share a dorm with since he kept eating the entire contents of the fridge overnight. There were many arguments over the legal claim of naming tupperware, whereas in Wyatt's house, everything was fair game. The five of us need each other in our darkest moments, which is why Huxley's outburst probably hurt him as much as it hurt me.

Exiting through the back door, Wyatt stops on the back porch. Curled up on the wooden swing, Avery is covered in a mound of blankets, a book in hand and travel mug stuffed into the crook of her arm. No, not a book - her mom's diary. I briefly look around, wondering why she was out here alone but then I spot Axel and Garrett working on their motorbikes with the garage door wide open. It's not the best vantage point, but close enough should the reporters jump the fence.

"Can I help you?" Avery tilts a brow. The air between those two hasn't been quiet right since the manor, before the attack and everything went to shit. Wyatt crosses his arms, taking a defensive stance.

"Yes, actually. I need you to convince Huxley to take a shower, leave his room and get on with his life." Our presence has attracted the attention of the others, who look at me questionably and I shrug back. Not Avery though, she's growing used to this back and forth, remaining impassive.

"Why me?"

Wyatt thinks over his words. "I believe it can only be you. So I'm asking nicely."

"Strange," Avery hums, her interest returning to her book. A gentle wind blows the chair, a light creak accompanying the shift of her braided hair. "I thought niceties went hand in hand with manners." I take a step back to hide my smirk. I haven't been asked here as a witness, but as a referee. Unfortunately, I'm not in the mood to break the pair of them up today. I'm a one-melodrama-at-a-time kind of guy.

Sighing deeply, Wyatt's arms fall to his sides. Here it comes.

"Please."

My brows shoot to my hairline. Lifting her blue gaze, Avery closes the diary and carefully places it in her lap.

"Sorry, what was that? I couldn't hear you over the grinding of your teeth." Oh she's good. She's learnt so well. Avery doesn't even falter, as if she's been waiting months to deliver back the shit Wyatt's been dealing out to her. I reckon if he were to drag her into a whiskey-infused cupboard now, she'd barely react. Simply wait to be released and then attack him like a lioness, all blonde mane and sharp claws.

"Please can you convince Huxley to leave his room. Perhaps he could join us for dinner tonight. All of us," Wyatt states as an afterthought.

"Are you cooking?" Avery tilts her head. Wyatt clenches his fists, his patience well and truly spent.

"Don't push it."

"I'll cook," I interject, deciding I should have some input here.

"Deal." Avery pushes her blankets aside, slipping her bootie slippers onto the wooden patio. Her flannel pajamas are yellow and striped. Keeping the diary close to her chest, she glides past Wyatt to lean into my side, her mouth beside my jaw. "At least I know you won't poison my food."

Avery disappears inside the house, and Wyatt takes her spot on the porch swing. His limbs are slack, as if being polite took all of her energy.

"You did a good job," I smirk, patting Wyatt's thigh. He takes a swing at me and misses.

"Don't patronize me." My laughter is canceled out by a round of screaming and protests from the top floor. I briefly look up, wondering if I would have been better served as a referee up there, and then quickly decide against it. Avery is a big girl, she can handle herself.

That evening, we all sit around the dining table. I made spaghetti and meatballs, while Garrett was on garlic bread duty and Axel laid the table. Wyatt sits at the far end, nursing his wine glass like a lifeline. Avery decided last minute we should dress up, after she manhandled and shaved Huxley in the shower. Given by the way he keeps tugging at the crotch of his pants, either the razor went on a little journey or he's gained a serious case of blue balls. His hair is still damp, pushed back from his ashy face. But he's smiling, and that means more to us than Avery will ever realize.

GARRETT

CHAPTER FIFTY ONE

Lifting my fist, I rap my knuckles on the door. Avery is quick to open it, blurry eyed and face marked from sleep. I lean forward, using my thumb to wipe the drool from the corner of her mouth.

"Good morning, Peach." From behind my back, I produce a large bouquet of sunflowers. Dax's favorite, I might add. My failsafe incase Avery decides my charm is somehow an offense to her feminism. Luckily for her, but unluckily for Dax, she smiles and accepts them graciously.

"Why do I feel like there's a catch?" she murmurs, stepping back into her room. I take my cue to enter, pushing the door shut with my back.

"I'm offended. Can't a handsome guy give a pretty girl flowers?"

"You're assuming you are handsome," Avery chuckles. Wow, arrow to the heart.

"I won't assume you're a morning person again either. And to answer your original question - I'm here to take you out on a date."

"A date," Avery tilts her head, her hair falling aside and eyes half-lidded in disbelief. I nod enthusiastically. "Outside?"

"Yep. And I'm going to help you get ready." Avery drops onto her unmade bed, smelling her flowers and not making any move to get me out of her wardrobe. Some of the outfits in here are either new, or what Wyatt picked up when he was packing her bags from Hughes Manor. I'm drawn to a pair of metallic leggings, ombre purple to blue to green. I can't find a top I like, so I shed mine, a thin navy sweater which will swamp her. Perfect. Avery places her flowers down just as I'm hunting through her underwear drawer, forgetting the reason I was in here in the first place. Standing, she scuffs her feet over to the bathroom door when I gasp and rush forward to stop her.

"Wait," I grab her wrist, then push the door open with my foot. "I need to help you with that too." Avery jerks then, struggling and failing to get out of my hold.

"With the toilet?! What the fuck Garrett, get off of me!" There's a skirmish with the door which I win, locking myself inside. Digging into my back pocket, I pull out a long rectangular box. "Seriously, can you go? I need to pee." Avery puts her hands on her hips. She's so cute when she's mad.

"Exactly. Did you know the HCG levels in your urine are most concentrated in the morning?"

"What?! Ew, why do you know that?"

"Because a naughty little Peach and an even naughtier big Axel decided to go at it bareback the other week, and I made it my business to know. Just squat and do your thing, I'll hold the stick." I say, unboxing it. I wonder where I am on the scale for offending feminism now.

The noise that comes out of Avery is alarming, and I honestly didn't know a human could do such a thing. It's a mix between a wild banshee and a screaming goat, as she snatches the pregnancy test from my hand and spins me to face the wall. For good measure, she shoves my face against the plasterboard and I'd be lying if her brute force didn't make me a teensy bit hard.

I'm a good boy, continuing to kiss the wall as Avery pees and slams the test down on the counter. She leaves to change while I linger around on nervous feet. Three minutes is a long time when you're counting down the seconds.

"Did you do it right?" I ask impatiently, waiting for the result to appear. Avery groans, the distinct sound of her head slamming into something solid.

"This is the worst date I've ever been on."

"Oh, Peach!" I rush from the room. It was the desk she hit her head on, her legging-clad ass high in the air. "You silly goose! This isn't the date. This is just pre-empting what kind of date we have."

Gathering her upright, I smooth the wild hair back from her face. "It's okay. I promise. Whatever happens, I'm going to make sure it's okay."

Avery shifts her head out of my grasp, frowning at me. "Of all the people in this house, you were in my top two for not being calm about such an opportunity."

Okay, it's true. I internally freaked the fuck out when Axel finally decided to talk to me to make an off-handed comment about their hotel quickie. A release they desperately needed, which is fine. But to be so careless as to not rubber up, well fuck. You know when I'm the voice of reason, there's a problem.

Nothing a little weed and a whole lot of research can't fix. Now, I'm wholly fascinated by the concept of a miniature Axel growing inside of Avery. Imagine how beautiful she'll glow. Imagine all the desserts we could eat together while I sing to her bump, earning my title as Funcle Garrett. It's a blissful image that I spent hours dreaming about while high, but not now. Not while we're in college, and also at risk of murderous stalkers and violent kidnappings.

Holding Avery to me, I kiss the top of her head. "Whatever happens," I promise again. Avery shudders against me and I belatedly realize she's crying. Ahh fuck, I'm the worst at comforting crying women. I usually jump out of the window and wait for them to disappear.

"How could I have been so stupid, Garrett?" Avery's voice breaks. Like Axel, I don't think she spent much time thinking about her actions that day. My hands soothe her back through my sweater, leaving me standing in a white vest and jeans. She molds herself against me, seeking my warmth.

"Well, let's at least find out what we're crying over," I sniffle back a tear myself. I hate seeing those I love in pain. Wait...

"Are you okay?" Avery asks as my footsteps come to an abrupt halt. "What's wrong?" I feel like I've just been hit with a sledgehammer to the chest, but I manage the smallest shake of my head.

"Sorry Peach, I think I had a mini-stroke there." I breathe shallowly. She doesn't look convinced but Avery and I walk arm-in-arm to the bathroom, our bodies rigid and strides wooden. I squeeze my eyes shut, unable to look first. Unfortunately, Avery's head is pressed into my chest too. Cracking one lid the smallest amount, I spy the one pink line boldly sitting upon the strip.

"Oh, thank fuck," I rush out. Avery peeks now too, gasping in delight and throwing her arms around my neck. We squeal and jump together, the weight of stress automatically lifting. "Phew. That was a close call, and let it be a lesson to you, madam." I bop her on the nose. "Now, back to our date."

Avery is elated after that. She fixes her hair and make-up, an easy smile playing about her lips. She doesn't even ask where we're going as I don a leather jacket, grab a stack of pre-packaged pastries in one hand, and hers in the other. I stuff my face before slipping on my bike helmet, buckling hers and cutting through into the garage.

The reporters are half asleep, too delayed to catch my bike speeding out onto the road. Avery's arms are firm around my waist, a real laugh torn from her. We make our great escape off campus, the bike dancing beneath us. What a great day. Maybe I should start every morning with a prenatal scare.

Entering the city, it doesn't take long to approach the tall building made of glass. Avery's squeeze on me tightens, her body straightening as I pull up in a parking lot.

"Hey, I know this place," she shoves the helmet off her head and squints at me. "What the hell are we doing at a gynecologist's office?" I smile, taking her helmet and tucking it into the seat storage box with mine. She's so cute when she's confused.

"You have an appointment at ten," I sling my arm over her shoulders and walk her to the front doors. "Time to get you an IUD fitted."

"And you didn't think to discuss this with me before?" she slaps my chest. There's the feminist offense I've been expecting all morning! But honestly - no, I didn't think to discuss it with her. I made a list of pros and cons, and mass castrations seemed a little dramatic, even for me. This way, we're all protected. The receptionist gives Avery a funny look, but she's too busy scolding me. "And this is your idea of a date?! What was the alternative if the test came back positive?"

"I was going to drive to the nearest airfield and jump out of a plane without a parachute. Wyatt would have probably joined me." A look passes through Avery's face, unsure if I'm joking or not. A nurse passes by, welcoming me by name. I nod, kissing Avery on the temple. "That's my cue."

"Garrett!" Avery yells, her voice booming around the lobby. Everyone is staring now, those reading magazines in the waiting area, those sitting behind the desk. "Where are you going now?!" I tut at myself. Words, Garrett, use your words.

"It's common courtesy to have a full sweep of checks between sexual partners, and I like to do a sperm count for good measure. Always nice to see the little guys flourish, and honestly," I stop to let a couple pass for their appointment. I hold the door open for them and everything. "They have the strangest porn movies here, like old style manga but weirder."

Saluting, I bid Avery goodbye for the next hour, hearing her stomp and grumble around. She's so prickly sometimes, like a little honey badger who may or may not attack me in my sleep for no apparent reason. Shrugging, I whistle a tune down the hallway, an upbeat skip to my strides. All I know is, if Avery and I were alone in the woods - I'd choose the bear.

AVERY

Dragging my feet from the study to the living area, I slump onto the sofa. A defeated groan rumbles through me. Wyatt is lounging in an armchair, an arm over his eyes. Garrett and Axel drop down beside me a moment later, both huffing loudly.

Midterms are kicking all of our asses. Despite being trapped inside, we've been too distracted to study, and I barely keep myself awake through Mrs. Patrick's online lectures. Taking English Lit for extra credit was supposed to mean I didn't have to focus on it so much, but with reporters lingering in the windows and across the front lawn, I'm struggling to focus.

Today, Dax and I both sat a multiple choice and an essay style exam on opposite ends of the desk, ignoring the reporters chatting outside. The vans are a permanent fixture on the other side of the road, camera crews taking shifts for the slightest appearance we make.

At the very least, I'm sticking to my schedule. I have ballet practice in an hour, in a dining room that the guys have cleared out for me. The flooring isn't right, the curtains remain drawn. I can't watch myself in floor-to-ceiling mirrors or check my own technique. It's just not the same, it's not right and this is what I feared about the showcase. That I would come to dread dancing, the one thing that's kept me going all these years.

Fingers touch my shoulder, the firmness deepening into a one-handed massage. I lean my head back against Dax's arm.

"Hey, where do you go? One minute you finished your exam early and then you vanished." A kiss touches my temple.

"You muttered, *I could murder a cheeseburger right now.*" Dax reaches out of sight and hands me a paper bag from the cafeteria. Garrett shoots upright, like a dog catching onto the scent of grease.

"Suck-up," Axel rolls his eyes. Dax produces a second bag and drops it in Garrett's lap.

"Only because I knew you'd steal Avery's if you didn't have your own," Dax gives Garrett a stern stare. Garrett isn't paying attention. The smell hits me as I open the bag and I melt into the sofa. Dax's other hand sinks into my shoulder, massaging the kinks while I stuff my face. Suddenly, life doesn't seem as bad. I try not to let my mind drift about how comfortable I am. Ironic, since there's a man upstairs struggling through his recovery because he chose to protect me.

"Has anyone checked on Huxley today?" I sigh into Dax's touch. He rubs small circles either side of my nape, pushes his thumbs down my spine.

"I was just up there," Wyatt mumbles, leaving the arm over his eyes. "He ate some of his lunch but I found him just staring out of the window." The mood around us sours. I sit up, shaking off Dax's skilled fingers and offering the rest of my burger to Axel. He takes it.

"I'll go talk to him."

"Hey, do you know what we should do?" Garrett's arm whips out to push me back down when I try to stand.

"I'm not screwing you in his bed and forcing him to watch," I drawl, my head tilting and eyes hooded.

"Oh, you minx. Now that's exactly what I want to do. But I was going to say, we should have a party! On Friday, when this hellish midterm week is over."

"Because our last party went so well," I purse my lips. The murder mystery party was an utter shambles, and we didn't even get to finish it. As far as I know, Wyatt hasn't apologized for trying to beat up Garrett, nor has Garrett incessantly made fun of choking Wyatt unconscious like I would have expected.

"Trust me, I'll make it fun." Garrett pleads with wide, brown eyes.

He's perfected the puppy-dog look, but still, I can't trust someone whose idea of romance is to have a heavy-handed man insert a device into my uterus. Planning capabilities aside, I sigh and relent anyway. No one can say Garrett doesn't consider everyone's best interests when it matters.

"Fine. But nothing big, I don't have the energy to mingle with loads of people."

"Just us," Garrett holds up a three-finger salute. I don't know what it is but apparently it means I'm supposed to trust him.

"And tricking me into a gangbang is a copout as a form of entertainment," I add, just to iron out the fineprint.

"I'm out," Wyatt huffs, stands and leaves. I forget he's there half the time, now he's not pushing me around or calling me names. It's more of a mutual decision to ignore each other. Garrett's eyes are sparkling with mischief, his burger still sitting in the box on his lap. Wow, he must be serious for a change.

"You're the best form of entertainment, but I will put my thinking cap on. Now go help Huxley *blow* off some steam." He lets me up this time and I make sure to smack his shoulder. Meg would pull me aside and warn me to keep him in line, that he gets out of hand too easily. Then I'd explain back that Garrett's spontaneity makes life interesting. I never know what he's going to say, what he's thinking. He's a loose cannon, sure, but one that explodes joy and vibrance.

Climbing the stairs, Axel calls after me that I have fifty minutes until ballet practice. He should know, having taken on the role as my time keeper and dance coach. He doesn't know anything about ballet, but he does understand joints and ligaments. He keeps close watch on my stance, how I hold my arms or when my weight leans too much on my stronger leg. Then, he helps me to stretch out afterward.

Wyatt's bedroom door slams shut just as I reach Huxley's. I withhold my frustrated sigh. At some point, I have to question what his friends even see in him and if it's always going to be this way. Maybe he thinks the same about me, but that would mean he'd actually have to think about me.

Entering Hux's bedroom, I find him just as Wyatt said. Propped up against the headboard, staring out of the window, a plate of uneaten food on his bedside table. I don't bother speaking, shedding my sweater.

I climb over his body in my vest and yoga pants, wrapping my arms around his neck. In an instant, I'm enclosed in his heat, his hands smoothing across my back. His hold is strong, desperate. He inhales my neck as if breathing life into himself.

"I've missed you," Huxley says against my skin. His words are soft, his lips chasing. Drifting my hands into his damp hair, I gently ease his head back.

"You've showered," I smile. He exudes my honey shampoo and vanilla body wash. A shine slowly burns to life in Huxley's chocolate eyes.

"And I brushed my teeth too," he flashes a small smile. The kind that makes my heart flutter. To celebrate his small milestone, my head inclines. His mouth meets me halfway, a gentle press, a seeking comfort. Those large hands smooth over my back, drawing me ever closer.

A sigh escapes me. Deepening the kiss, Huxley's mouth moves against mine, carefully building a rhythm. He doesn't press for more, doesn't take us beyond simply enjoying each other's presence. I drown in him, in us. A silent conversation of affection and tenderness takes place between our lips and without thinking, my hand shifts to gentle rest over his healed bullet wound.

But it's more than that. Beyond the sweet kiss, there's a tremor in his fingers, a tremble in his chin. He's withholding an onslaught of emotion that has been buried for too long. I understand it well. I've lived through darkness. I've survived trauma. He can too. Breaking away, I drop my forehead against his.

"There's been so many times I've searched for comfort like this." My chest rises and falls heavily. Huxley's stubble brushes my cheek.

"Don't leave again. Stay here with me." And there is the crux of the problem. Pressing my lips together, I sit back, solidifying the space between us. Huxley's face, previously so filled with hope, falls. "Ahh, I fucked it." My smile is slatted as I cup his cheek.

"You need to try to get out of here, Hux. We can still do this," I gesture between us, "on the other side of that door." He nods knowingly. If it came down to an ultimatum, Huxley wouldn't really push for me to abandon my life. He wouldn't want me to hide from my classes. He wouldn't let the bullet he took be in vain.

A deep inhale helps Huxley to steel himself. His eyes close, blond lashes fluttering over his cheeks. He's searching, hunting for that piece of his soul that helps him to shine. I don't expect him to find it so easily, but there is a hint of a smirk when he looks at me again.

"Hey," I bop him on the nose. "Are you ready to venture downstairs with me?"

"It depends on who sent you to ask," Huxley's brow lifts. I don't know what that means, who Huxley seems to have issues with currently, so I deflect.

"I know you've been cooped up for a while, Hux," I lean forward, resting my forearms on his shoulders. He's easily distracted by my cleavage. "But do you really think I've started taking orders?" He chuckles lightly, playing with my hair.

"I think you're easily bribed." I laugh then. "Maybe I could be bribed too." I bite my bottom lip, which he promptly pulls free with his thumb. His fingers are soft against my cheek, his knuckles stroking a path down my neck. Heat floods my system and it takes everything in me not to roll my hips to see if he is equally affected.

"Is that so? Maybe we can stroll up and down the hallway hand in hand while you tell me what it is you want." I tilt my head back and forth. Huxley shifts, laying us both down on the mattress.

"Nice try, Little Swan," his smile turns sad. "I'll come out soon. Not today, but soon." Huxley nuzzles into me further. Well, this has gone to shit. Nevertheless, my leg becomes locked between his thick thighs. I'm drawn into the protective hold he keeps around me, snuggled in his warmth.

"When you're ready," I agree, unable to withhold my yawn. My eyes have fluttered closed, despite the brightness all around. The midday sun streams through the window, viscerally reminding me that we're all trapped here, whether by the paparazzi or by our own demons. "You've got about thirty minutes before Axel comes looking for me." My voice becomes heavy, the weight of stress being interchanged for the weight of Huxley's bicep.

"That's all I need." Huxley presses a kiss to my forehead and I'm a goner.

AVERY

Friday night. I nod slightly at myself in the bathroom mirror, my blue eyes wide and body coated in droplets from a recent shower.

I've barely seen the guys all day. Granted I've been locked away in my own room. I didn't have half as many midterms as the others and Axel had an online lecture this afternoon so I took the chance to curl up in bed and read. Whenever Garrett's planning is involved, I have no doubt I'll need my energy. Physical, mental and social energy.

Beyond the bathroom, I hear my door open and click shut. Hugging the towel around myself, I peek out. There's no one there, but a lone, nondescript box is on the floor just inside the room. I'm smiling before I've even picked it up and deposited it on the bed. The note on top reads:

'Put it on and drink this. We're already drunk.'

"So romantic," I snort, lifting the lid. Wow, Garrett really pushed the boat out. A set of white lace underwear and a bottle of pink gin lies in the tissue paper. That's all. I try not to overthink, trusting that there's a plan. Or the plan is a drunken orgy, as I predicted. The set is simple and fits perfectly, a soft lace thong and a bra without any underwire. I slip a robe over the top, leaving my feet bare.

Chugging the gin, I spare another look in the bathroom mirror. My face is recently washed, fresh and slightly flushed. A smattering of freckles is visible over my nose. Chewing on my lip, I decide to leave myself free of make-up to match Garrett's simplistic vibe. I twist my blonde hair up into a claw clip, the ends slightly damp and beginning to curl. That's that.

Leaving the room behind, gin bottle in hand, I follow the low sound of music. The only light on is coming from beneath Wyatt's bedroom door. I tiptoe past, eager to leave him to his stewing. The party is hard to locate at first, taking me on a tour through the house. There's no one about, but evidence of empty beer bottles lining the kitchen island. They really did start early, and I have some catching up to do.

I realize the music is coming from the garage. Slipping out onto the back porch, I inch towards the back garage entrance, not trusting the paparazzi not to climb the fence for a photo opportunity. I'm sure seeing me creeping around in my robe would make a front cover somewhere.

Pushing open the door, darkness and music drags me inside. Some type of plastic crinkles beneath my feet, the cars and bikes nowhere to be seen. I can sense those moving about inside, shadows waiting to pounce. A thrill of excitement runs through me. The door is closed and light suddenly flicks on, but not the usual one. UV bulbs flicker, soon revealing four beautifully crafted bodies in white boxers. Our underwear illuminates, as do the smiles closing in. Huxley, with his shaggy blond hair and mischievous grin, catches my attention first.

"Hey," I beam. I fall into his arms, forgetting the rest of our company for a moment. A wealth of emotion hits me, and a weight I didn't realize I'd been carrying suddenly lifts. Huxley is out of his room and joining in again. He kisses my head.

"I won't stay long, but I wanted to try for you." I beam up at him. From behind, my robe is untied and peeled down my arms. My fingers linger on Huxley's hips, the circular pink scar just below his collarbone dull in the current lighting. If I didn't search for it, I could almost convince myself it wasn't there and I didn't owe this man my life. As it stands, I'm well aware of those facts and I can't help seeking out his comfort. My lips press over his heart, leaving a tender kiss there before I'm turned in a slow circle.

"We need to finish getting you ready," Axel says, his voice barely audible over the music. A spotify mix of old school pop leaks from bluetooth speakers, anything with a baseline really. Axel holds up a bottle of neon pink paint, shaking it suggestively. A grin splits across my face as the pieces start to fall into place. He nudges Dax, who's absently bobbing his head to the beat. AKA, drunk out of the other side of his face. It must have been a rough week for him.

Dax, ever the gentleman, reaches out a hand to steady me as Huxley steps back and I lose my leaning post. "Careful," he teases, his blue eyes twinkling. There are hands and chiseled abs everywhere, surrounding me. Garrett wraps an arm around my waist, pulling me towards a bench covered in neon paints. Every color imaginable and a handful of paintbrushes. My eyes flicker to the floor and walls, now noticing the plastic sheets covering every available space.

"Ready to get messy?" he asks, his breath warm against my ear.

"Always," I reply, taking a long swig of gin. Someone plucks the bottle from my grip and replaces it with a bottle of green paint. Dax, with his striking blond hair, is already squeezing out some neon orange paint into his palm. He doesn't hesitate, playfully smearing a streak of paint across Axel's chest. Axel visibly shudders and then laughs, a deep, infectious sound that makes my heart skip a beat.

It's a beautiful sight. The boys are easy, grinning and bumping shoulders. They form a circle around me, each armed with different colors of paint. Garrett, never one to miss an opportunity for theatrics, dips his fingers into the yellow paint and trails them down my arm, leaving a vivid, glowing trail in their wake.

"You look even more beautiful in neon," he murmurs, his dark eyes intense.

"Flattery will get you everywhere," I quip back. Coating my entire hand in green, I slap my palm against his abs. There's a momentary tensing and then it's gone, Garrett's relaxed demeanor returning. I focus on him first, creating a secondary armor to the ink he wears, covering the body he is uncomfortable with. Axel helps, coating Garrett in multicolored handprints alongside mine. In red, I draw a huge heart over his real one. He laughs, the sound blending with the music.

And so it goes. Garrett smears blue paint across Huxley's tattooed back, and Huxley retaliates with a swipe of orange down Dax's arm. The brushes come out, but no one is working on a masterpiece. Smears become splashes, streaks of paint flying across bodies and glowing brightly under the blacklights. Dax gets the brunt of the attack as we gang up, flicking paint all over his tanned skin. I'm swept up in the fun of it, so that I don't sense the shift of attention until they're all facing me once more. A simple smile sits on each one of their faces.

The brushes are on me then. Soft strokes of bristles, tickling my sides, my thighs, my feet. No patch of skin is left untouched. Heat rises to my cheeks, both from the excitement and the attention of their hungry eyes. Garrett pulls me into a playful dance, spinning me around before dipping me low, making me giggle.

"Garrett! You're smudging me!" I cry out, sliding against his torso. He pauses, looking up thoughtfully.

"That's a new one. Usually, it's *'Garrett, you're destroying me.'*"

Without any venom, I slap his cheek with a blue hand, leaving my mark. He responds by shoving his tongue down my throat. Rookie move on my part - assaulting Garrett will only make him cum quicker. Warm hands slide over my back and waist, multiple bodies caging me in. Garrett's mouth consumes my thoughts, my heart swelling and thighs clenching. Every nerve ending is alive, sparking with the electricity in the garage. Breaking away from Garrett but remaining in his hold, I lean my head back onto someone else's shoulder. My head is spinning and I'm far too eager to dive into this headfirst. Whatever *this* is.

"I believe you owe me," Huxley's chest rumbles at my back. His fingers glide along my jaw, tilting my head up to his face.

"Because you took a bullet for me," I nod in understanding. Huxley flinches, his chocolate eyes suddenly pained.

"What?! No! I'm not some asshole who would hold my injury over you for sex."

"I am," Garrett shrugs, kissing a path along my neck. Huxley ignores him. The lightheartedness returns to his features, a playful smirk on his lips.

"You owe me from Silk and Satin. I was promised some kinky fun and I'm ready to cash in." I bite the inside of my cheek. Technically, it was Garrett who was pimping me out that night but I keep it to myself. I've been walking around Huxley on eggshells, not wanting to rush his recovery. But fuck, I want him. I want all of them. Garrett isn't the only selfish one here. Turning in his hold, I push up onto my tiptoes to bring me closer to Huxley's jaw.

"Cash me in," I breathe, using the paint to push my fingers over his pecs. With some gentle assistance, I ease Huxley back to the paint table. Garrett follows, his hands not leaving me for a second. Dax and Axel have stepped back to sip their drinks and watch. Axel's fingers are toying with Dax's, seeking affection, craving comfort. Dax lets it happen.

Taking the initiative, I clear off the paints with a swipe of my arm. They crash to the floor in a messy heap. At the jerk of my chin, Huxley sits, his long legs bent at a right angle and feet still firmly on the floor.

"Garrett," I state clearly. His head raises from the crook of my neck, a dazed hum leaving him. Is he drunk on alcohol or drunk on me? "Switch with Dax. Axel needs your attention." His pause is minimal, the curve of his smile against my ear.

"Oh, I like this side of you, Peach." Kissing my hair, he does as directed. Strolling over to Axel and clapping Dax on the nape, Garrett gives him a light shove in my direction. I grin, holding out my hand. Dax bumbles over, his smile easy, his fingers loose on the neck of a beer bottle. I take it and swig the rest down, tugging him close with my other hand. It's time to put Dax's easygoing attitude to the test. Will he quickly sober up, or will he surprise me like he continues to do?

"Lie on the floor, I'm going to sit on your face." Dax's blue eyes darken, his tongue darting out to lick his lips. He does just that, laying himself across the paint-smeared plastic, his head between Huxley's feet. I have all of their attention, and the accompaniment of Billie Ellish to my strip tease. I pop my bra first, tugging the straps free. Cool air hits my nipples and adrenaline floods my core. Every set of eyes is heated, watching from a distance. No one makes a move to rush me or beckon me closer. Teasing my thumbs in the lace of my thong, I throw a flirtatious look at Garrett.

"I thought I told you to give Axel your attention." Instead of standing still, palming himself through his boxers, Garrett jerks into action. Freeing Axel's cock, he squeezes the base, drawing a moan from Axel which almost undoes me then and there. Raw pleasure contorts his features, as if he's been starving for Garrett's touch. Something I've been wondering since the hospital, since Axel started enforcing the distance between them. They need each other and I'm only too happy to be the one orchestrating their pleasure for once.

My thong slides down my legs and I turn my attention to Huxley. Patient, remarkable Huxley. My fingers trail over the circular scar at his collarbone once more, hiding but still puckered beneath my touch. He's quick to take my hand, running it over his chest and abs. The paint is a mess of colors now, smeared in every crevice. Gripping his waistband, Huxley shifts so the painted cotton lowers and his cock springs free. He's painfully hard, weeping already.

"I've been waiting so long for this," he murmurs. I smile coyly.

"I know." Lowering myself down onto my knees, Dax widens my thighs and positions me over his face. His tongue drags over my cunt at the same time as I lick Huxley's plump, purple head. We all groan in unison. I'm careful not to use my hands, not wanting to cover Hux's shaft in luminescent paint as my mouth glides over the silky, smooth surface. His thighs, though, are fair game.

My fingers dig into the firm muscles, feeling the tension and eagerness beneath my palms. He bucks slightly as I swirl my tongue around the head of his cock, tasting the salty bead of precum gathered there. He's large, as I knew he would be. The gin has helped to relax me enough to take him deep and hold him there until he squirms. There is nothing more empowering than making a fully grown man squirm and whimper.

In the background, Axel is doing an equal amount of just that. His hips buck into Garrett's grip, fucking his hand. His tongue is in Garrett's mouth, a mess of paint smeared over their faces and into Garrett's hair. I could watch them for hours if Huxley's hand didn't grab the back of my head and urge my focus back onto him. I bob up and down, not withholding the building need Dax is creating within me.

Dax's tongue is working wonders, flicking and swirling over my clit expertly, sending waves of pleasure rippling through my core. His fingers are everywhere, parting my pussy to grant him full access, stroking a path over my ass and back again. He eats me out like it's his first meal and I reckon I could let him go for hours. My tender, attentive Dax with a secret devilish tongue. I don't want it to end.

My moans vibrate against Huxley's cock, and he groans too, a deep, guttural sound which spurs me on. I take him deeper, my lips sliding over his shaft, my tongue pressed flat against the underside. Dax's hands grip my hips, pulling me down harder against his mouth. The dual sensations are overwhelming, a delicious blend of pleasure that makes my legs tremble.

I steady myself by gripping Huxley's thighs even tighter, my nails leaving crescent moons in his skin. The intensity of his need is palpable, the throbbing heat against my lips too good to deny. Huxley's breath hitches, and I know he's close. I hollow my cheeks, increasing the suction, and he moans louder, his grip in my hair tightening.

Without realizing, my hips are rocking back and forth, taking my pleasure further. Dax's tongue delves deeper, tension coiling in my belly - a tight, insistent knot of desire that's about to unravel. My movements become more urgent, more desperate, and Huxley's hips thrust up, his cock sliding deeper into my mouth.

Sucking hard on my clit, Dax pushes me over the edge. An orgasm crashes through me, a tidal wave of sensation that has me crying out around Huxley's cock. The vibrations send him spiraling toward his own climax, his hips jerking as he comes, filling my mouth with the hot, salty rush of his release. I swallow him down hungrily. Leaning upwards on my knees, Dax slides free and bands an arm around my waist.

"My turn," he says into my ear, lifting me to stand. I release Huxley with a pop. Pausing for long enough for Huxely to kiss me deep and slow, he smiles.

"I'm done for tonight, Little Swan. Come spoon me later." I nod, my heart swelling. I'm just so glad he came and joined in. It feels right when we're all together. Slipping away, Huxley leaves an empty spot on the table.

"On your back sweetheart," Dax orders, his voice thick with lust. I bite my bottom lip. I could get used to Dom Dax. Sprawling across the table, briefly wondering why garage benches have become my niche, Dax lifts my legs. One at a time, he strokes his fingers from my feet, to calves and then thighs, leaving my legs pressed against his chest. Each shift of movement is caught by the UV lights, our bodies glowing brightly. Lining himself up with my entrance, my head rolls back.

"Wait!" Garrett shouts, skidding across the painted plastic like an ice rink. He slams a foil packet against Dax's chest. "Until I see a full bill of clean health, you're suiting up."

"Are you serious? I've never had anything in my life."

"STD's are no joke, my friend. I made Axel have one before he took Avery to the ball." My brows raise. Dax relents, nodding his thanks. No doubt Dax believes he is feeling the effects of his beer, but I know better. Garrett has always secretly kept my safety at the forefront of his mind. He may be reckless in all other aspects of life, but not with me. Not about this.

Sliding the condom over his cock, I lie there, appreciating Dax's size and the deeply-ingrained V lining his abdomen. Dax is a sculpted work of art, the sinew of muscles tensing when he shifts. His blue eyes raise to mine and I'm lost, ready for this man to do whatever he wants to me.

He enters me slowly, teasingly, his cock stretching me in the most delicious way. The cool sensation of the condom is a stark contrast to the heat building between us. I gasp, my back arching off the table, my legs trembling against his chest. Dax's grip on my thighs tightens, and I can feel his control slipping as he pushes deeper, filling me completely. Once fully seated, Dax withdraws and slams in with harsh, swift thrusts. I gasp, tensing in all the right places.

Garrett moves to my side, his hand coming to rest on my forehead, smoothing back the strands of hair that cling to my skin. I'm certain he's making more of a mess than he's fixing, but I can't complain. His touch is gentle, a grounding presence amidst the overwhelming pleasure. He leans down, his lips brushing against my ear.

"How does he feel?" he whispers, his voice a soothing counterpoint to Dax's rough, primal movements.

"Perfect," I manage to breathe out, my fingers curling around the edges of the table, holding on for dear life. Every movement sends electric sparks shooting through my body, each thrust hitting that perfect spot that makes my vision blur. Axel appears at my other side, his boxers firmly in place. He smiles stupidly like a man sated while a lone finger circles my nipple.

Dax's pace quickens, the sounds of our bodies coming together filling the air, mingling with our gasps and moans. The UV lights cast an otherworldly glow across our skin, highlighting the slick sheen of sweat and the streaks of paint decorating us. It's surreal, a vivid explosion of color and sensation. I'll have many drunk dreams about this later.

Axel's hands slide over my body, squeezing my breasts, tweaking my nipples just enough to send another wave of pleasure coursing through me. Both his and Garrett's touches are light, teasing, and completely opposite to Dax's unrelenting drive. I turn my head, capturing Garrett's lips in a desperate kiss, needing to feel him, to connect with him amidst the whirlwind. Fingers graze my clit and I hear the sharp slap of Dax nudging whoever it is away.

"Avery is only coming for me tonight." I drop my head back against the table, savoring that frantic growl. I didn't know I needed to hear it, but now, all I want is for Dax to talk to me that way. Dark, dirty and desperate.

Dax's rhythm becomes erratic, his breath coming in ragged gasps. I can feel him throbbing inside me, so close to the edge. His hands slide from my thighs to my hips, pulling me even closer, deeper, his thrusts growing more frantic. The sensation is almost too much, pushing me higher. My orgasm reaches its peak at the same time his does. I cry out, my body convulsing as Dax groans, his own release a powerful, shuddering explosion.

We collapse together, Dax's body heavy and comforting over mine. Garrett's arms wrap around us both, holding us close, his breath warm and steady against my skin. Axel continues his gentle, lazy strokes along my sides. The world slowly comes back into focus, the glowing aftermath of our passion a soft, comforting haze.

"Garrett," I murmur, feeling the weight of exhaustion and satisfaction settle over me. He hums his acknowledgement. "This was a really good fucking idea."

"I hope you didn't doubt me for a second." I can't suppress my giggle, and even Dax huffs a laugh. We all doubted him, but he definitely came through. Garrett's lips press against my forehead, a tender kiss I lean into.

"You're a work of art, Peach. Painting you was at the top of my to-do list. The rest was inevitable."

HUXLEY

CHAPTER FIFTY FOUR

Whenever I think it can't get any worse, my finger slips on the laptop mousepad and it gets so much fucking worse. It started with curiosity. Within an hour, I was consumed.

Avery did come to me last night, freshly showered and unconscious within seconds. I cradled her body, inhaling her hair, but I couldn't sleep.

I'm in recovery, confined to my room and the one time I leave - I let Avery suck me off. Guilt racks my mind. I don't want her to feel indebted to me. I'd have taken a bullet for anyone in that house, and despite Garrett's offering, I wouldn't have expected any sexual favors in return. It should be the same with Avery.

And add to that the fact that I'm currently useless physically, possibly mentally, there was nothing else to do but hold her all night, wide awake and fully aware of my downfalls. If I'm not the bodyguard of the group, who am I and what use am I to anyone?

So here I am. Out of my room, as far as the dining table and trying to help in the only way I can. Investigation. Clicking on the next website, my stomach rolls. It's a necessary evil - to know who may have ill intent towards Avery, I need to understand her. To know about her life before and after her adoption.

I close my eyes, needing a moment to focus on breathing before my lungs seize up. I need to know every fact. Every sickening detail. Which is the only reason I find myself clicking onto the next article.

First Look Exclusive: See the childhood home of adopted Hope Hughes.

That's what the media called her at first, before they knew her real name. I've read through many articles which described Wyatt as a spoiled, problem child, and referred to Avery as the Hughes' new 'hope' at their perfect family becoming complete. Did Wyatt know at that time? Did he know the entire world was labeling him, turning on him. Their relationship never stood a chance to be based on anything other than hatred.

Scrolling down, image after image sprawls beneath the headline, a small house with boarded windows and multiple locks on the door. Mess litters the floor in each room, most of which consists of beer cans and dirty clothing. Furniture has been shoved aside, a sign of a struggle. Is that where the police apprehended him? Then there's where Avery was kept. Not a room, but a closet, with soiled sheets and scratches in the wooden walls. My stomach rolls.

If only I'd known. I watched Wyatt scare her, force her to relive past traumas. And everytime, Avery would bounce back with twice the vigor as before. I didn't want to consider the anguish she felt. None of us did. We wanted to live in a world where Wyatt's anger was fleeting, where his hatred was biased and unjust, and no one would really dare to hurt the precious woman who crawls into my bed whimpering at night. She's too precious, too innocent, but fuck me, she's so strong. How she is functioning on a daily basis is a mystery.

But I did know. I read her transcripts. And I still let it happen.

Figures shift around the dining room, people walking past my chair. I pay them no mind, until a shadow leans over my shoulder.

"Whatcha doing?" Garrett cocks his head. "Is this some new docuseries I should know about?" I huff and shake my head. Sensing me tense, he lowers into the seat at my right. He's read the captions. I keep going. Next image, next page. I scour the words, absorbing Avery's pain as if it lives within the black and white text. Next paragraph, next write-up.

"Woah," Dax comments. I didn't realize he had joined us, or that

Axel is in the chair on my other side. "He was released." I've latched onto the same headline as him. Frederick Walters, Avery's father and abuser, was released from prison months ago.

"Oh, hey!" Avery passes by. I quickly slam the laptop shut. "You left your room again!" She pushes through the crowd of bodies, her attention solely on me. Kissing my head, she wraps her arms around my neck. "I knew you could do it."

Tears prick in my eyes. She's praising me for walking down a flight of stairs, but we've never truly appreciated that she's walked through hell. That she walked away from one fuck-up and into the home of another. I've never felt angry with Wyatt before, no matter what he's done. I know in his mind, he feels justified. *It's just a little hazing, what's the harm? A little smell of whiskey. A few harsh words.* Now I see clearer, and I no longer permit him to taunt her. I stand with Avery.

Twisting, I clench my teeth to hold back a grunt and pull her into my lap.

"Little Swan," I breathe against her neck. She smells sweet, vanilla and honey seeping into my senses. Her hair is in a high bun, a jacket and leggings covering her leotard. Make-up free, her questioning eyes seek out mine. Big and blue. She's the personification of beauty and strength. I can't keep this information from her, or the guilt I'm battling against.

"Your father...did you know he wasn't in prison any more?" Her eyes harden. Her arms start to fall away from my neck but I don't let them. I need to do this. "He was released months ago. Just before your mom's accident." I hadn't intended to imply a link in those two statements, but now it's out there, everyone's minds are ticking over.

"The letters from Mr. XO," Axel taps his finger on the table in thought. "You've been receiving them since you were adopted, right? He knows your birthday, your likes and dislikes. It makes sense that he could have been writing to you from prison."

"Stop," Avery states coldly. It's too late to put the lid back on this can of worms.

"Now he's free, and he's escalating. He's seen you with us. It's classic obsessive behavior." Dax adds, his hand curling around her nape protectively. We're caging her in, stopping her from bolting, so she removes herself in another way. Staring straight ahead, I'm not sure Avery is even listening to us any more.

Axel also adds a comforting touch to her thigh, his hazel eyes haunted. "Maybe we should consider that Nixon is on the run. This Walters guy was released, Cathy was killed and you were sent here for safety. Maybe your dad is going after those who he thinks took you away from him."

"Don't call him that," Avery grinds out harshly. We're quickly losing her. But there isn't another time. There might not be any time.

"Do you think Wyatt's on his target list now? What if we all are?" Dax asks, his eyes dropping to my shoulder. I shudder and hug her harder.

"Avery, we need to take you somewhere safe-"

"Stop it! All of you!" Avery shoves her way out of our hold, swiftly moving out of reach. Fury tightens her features as she rounds on me. "You have physio this afternoon, and I have to attend an actual dance practice. Leave the past where it belongs." Garrett stands, tentatively slipping an arm around her lower back. She lets him, her gaze curious but stern.

"Peach, there could be answers here. We can't ignore them." She looks away, straining her neck to the side. I know what she's thinking - when Garrett is the voice of reason, you know it's serious. I turn in my chair, holding out an offered hand. She doesn't take it, but I set aside the hurt that flashes through me. It doesn't matter, I wanted answers and now I'm ready to offer solutions.

"You know I have resources. I can have him dealt with. No one would ever trace it back to you."

Avery scoffs. "I would be first in line for questioning." She analyzes my face, deciding if I'm deadly serious. Realizing I am, her posture stiffens even more. "Don't you dare do anything stupid. We can't get involved in this. There's too much we don't know."

Pushing out of Garrett's hold, he lets her leave. We all watch her storm towards the front door. I almost call after her, wary of the reporters lingering outside about to see her leave unguarded, when I notice Wyatt standing off to the side. His brow is raised, jaw oddly slack as he grabs his jacket and heads after her. The door is closed after them with a definitive slam. As a whole, we exhale.

"Well, what a shit show that was," Garrett rubs the back of his neck.

One by one, the guys disperse and I remain, arms laid on either side of the closed laptop.

Avery is in denial. I understand that. She's scared. I recognize that. But I don't have the option to sit by and wait for the next gunman to make his move. Next time, I might not be so lucky and despite Avery's objections, we're already very much involved.

AVERY

I'm such a hypocrite. I've been forcing Huxley to rush through his demons and leave his room, and at the first sight of my own trauma, guess where I am? Propped against my headboard, my lap covered in Mr. XO's letters. The box of my mom's things, which is usually tucked beneath the bed, sits on the floor, the lid at an angle. I thought I'd find comfort in handling her perfume bottle, hairbrush, a photo frame with the pair of us in...but no. I didn't. Instead, I turned where I probably shouldn't - the letters.

I've re-read them all, and I'm more certain than ever that the boys are wrong. I know my birth father, and he doesn't speak like this. In my entire childhood, there was never so much as a compliment. I was a brat, the waste of space who ruined his life. Everything was wrong and everything was my fault. These letters are precious, understanding. I'd forgotten all about the one crumpled against my chest right now, and I peel it back to read for the fourth time today.

Avery.
Your presence brings so much joy to those lucky enough to be around you. I have written songs I hope to share with you in person someday. I imagine us spending time together, talking about our dreams and passions. I know that if you got to know me, you would feel the same way.
Yours, XO.

It's not the most poetic letter I've received, but there's a hidden hope within. A promise of meeting in the future, whoever this person may be. They care about me, and in turn, they've become my secret guilty pleasure. How many nights have I dreamt of a prince charming turning up on the doorstep, prepared to whisk me away from my tower? Too many to let Fredrick Walters sully those memories.

A light knock sounds on my door. I shove the letters into a hasty pile, put them in the box with my mom's stuff and shove it back under the bed. The door pops open a few inches and I'm stunned to see Wyatt standing there.

"Can I come in?"

"Depends what you want to talk about," I pout. I'm being irrational. The information shared downstairs yesterday afternoon wasn't anything new. But I hadn't wanted the guys to know that version of me, especially Wyatt. He has enough ammunition, and despite his opposing perception, I know I'm so much more than my misgivings.

Wyatt steps into the room, remaining close to the exit. He shifts, unsure of where to put his hands. First in his pockets, then out, then pushing through his hair and back down to his jean-clad thighs. I raise a brow, as if I'm not moping around in pink silk pajamas beneath the covers.

"I just wanted to let you know I'm going to be having some people look into the crash, now that new information has come to light." My stomach plummets. Of course the coincidence of my father's release and Cathy's death is too big to ignore, no matter how much I want to bury my head in the sand. If he really is responsible, and the Hughes' are being targeted by association with me, I don't think I'll be able to live with that knowledge. Her blood will be on my hands.

The silence stretches out, and Wyatt seems to feel inclined to fill it. "There might be...questions for you to answer, and I hope you'll cooperate." He's smoothing his hair back again, avoiding my eye contact.

"It's fine, Wyatt. I get it." I chew on my inner cheek, my mind racing while I have Wyatt's attention. "Have you spoken to Nixon at all?" There's a tick in his jaw and he rolls his neck. Apparently that wasn't the right question to ask.

"He's ignoring my calls."

"Me too," I wince. Exhaling sharply, Wyatt nods and leaves. I sit for a whole three minutes more before deciding the spiral of my thoughts isn't something I can allow to continue.

I need a distraction, and I find it at the kitchen island, a fork in hand and an entire cake on the board in front of him. Fucking animal. Pushing the cake aside, I push myself up onto the countertop, shimmying over so my legs hang either side of Garrett's arms.

"Distract me." His smile is wicked, the strain of yesterday nowhere to be found in his hazel eyes.

"Anytime, Peach."

Huxley's thigh traps me in place as his body radiates an unnatural level of heat. The sunlight is shining beneath black-out curtains to announce the start of a new crisp and winter-filled day, despite the fact I've not had much sleep. My body is exhausted from the back-to-back ballet rehearsals I've been putting in, but with the showcase looming, my mind won't rest. Behind my closed eyes, I either repeat the choreography or slip into a mini dream of falling off stage and breaking an ankle.

Using all of my strength to shift the dead weight of his thigh, I shift up to sit on the bed, looking down at his strong jaw line. A sly smile pulls at his lips. Evidently, this asshole has been awake for a while and has kept me trapped on purpose. Shoving at his chest, he gasps dramatically and holds a hand over his faded bullet scar. What a faker.

"I thought you said you weren't going to hold your injury over me," I tut. Huxley's eyes open to reveal a brief glint of mischief in their brown depths.

"That was for sex. Snuggling is fair game."

"Well aren't you lucky you get both." I comb my fingers through his hair before stroking the stubble lining his jaw. It takes his appearance from surfer boy to blond demi-god and I'm into it. His gaze flicks to my lips, a longing in his eyes I'm eager to fill. Leaning over his broad frame, I hold Huxley's face in my hand and place my lips on his. He instantly responds with a quick kiss that leaves me chasing for more.

"Luckiest man in the world," he grins. A groan sounds from behind me.

"Get a room," Dax mutters into the covers. He is rather cranky in the mornings. My mouth opens to respond when Garrett strolls past the bed, his toothbrush in hand.

"This is their room," he points between Huxley and I. Technically, it's just Huxley's but after the neon party, it quickly became apparent none of us wanted to sleep alone. Hence, the two single beds now pushed against Huxley's four-poster. There's enough mattress space for each of the four men and I'm left hunting for a gap to squeeze into. It's heaven.

Axel exits the bathroom, freshly showered with a towel fastened around his hips. "What do you feel like doing today?" he asks no one in particular. I groan and fall back into the pillow.

"Anything but think about tomorrow night. I need a mental break from Miss Nightingale riding my ass."

"Now there's a mental image I needed," Garrett laughs to himself, disappearing into the recently-vacated bathroom with his toothbrush. I can't muster much of a smile. My legs have begun to tingle, nerves creeping from the tips of my toes to the heavy ball in my chest.

The showcase. The damn showcase that seemed months away and is now almost here. It's not the dance per se; I know the steps, I've got the timing down. It's the audience. It's putting myself in the spotlight, faced with a room of strangers. The only people I'm not worried about watching me bare my soul on stage are those in this room. They'll be my focus, as they have been in each rehearsal. Despite the reporters giving up and leaving weeks ago, I've had a personal entourage to every class, lunch and library study session. The real fun is left for behind closed doors.

Beneath the covers, fingers appear on my feet. Sliding upwards, they skate over my calves and thighs, skimming past the area I tilt for him to touch. A heavy mass crawls up the mattress next, and his shaven head settles onto my stomach. I smile then, absentmindedly stroking Axel's scalp and neck. His weight is a calming presence, stilling the jitters inside. Huxley settles back into my side, Dax's jaw finds the curve of my shoulder. My guys. We all connect on a level of broken that just makes sense for us to try to fix each other. But who said we need fixing? Maybe we can just *be*.

Although, nothing that is happening in this bed right now is acceptable to Garrett.

"Get out of bed, you lazy fuckers!" he yells, whipping the covers aside. Shoving Axel aside, Garrett has the subtlety of a rhinoceros in grabbing my ankles and roughly yanking me down the bed. Dax and Huxley are up within seconds, diving on Garrett.

"Dude," Huxley gets him in a headlock. "Those legs are precious!"

"What use would a fractured ankle be right now?!" Dax grabs Garrett's knees and squeezes them until he buckles. Axel joins and I sit up to watch a tickling match ensue on the floor.

"Bunch of children," I roll my eyes and attempt to leave. I'm not sure who snatches my waist and tugs me down, but all hands fall to my ribs. I'm screaming, writhing in laughter and kicking out. They don't relent until I'm begging for a pause.

"There's no pauses in life sweetheart," Axel grins over me. His groin is firmly pressed between my legs. Heat consumes me. He leans down to place a kiss on my lips, just as fleeting as Huxley's. These men are going to be the death of me. My lids linger closed a moment too long and when I open them, four sets of eyes are fixed on my flushed cheeks.

"I will never tire of watching my brothers fawn over my girl," Garrett smirks. My brow raises.

"That's very presumptuous of you," I laugh, shifting aside. My hand slips into Garrett's jacket pocket while he's frowning at my face.

"What is?"

"Assuming I'm your girl." Pushing upright, I walk back towards the bathroom. "I mean, I'm not even your phone background." Removing my hand from behind my back, I shake Garrett's phone at him. In fact, his background is a bunny in a spacesuit costume. Cute, weird and completely in character. Stupidly, Garrett doesn't have a passcode lock. "Hmmm, I wonder how many porn subscriptions you have."

"Give it back!" he screams, scrambling to his feet. I shriek, diving into the bathroom and locking the door closed behind me. I'm quick to lock the opposite door too, securing myself inside. My grin couldn't be wider. Let Garrett sweat for a while. I chuckle, tossing his phone onto the counter.

After taking a heated shower and brushing my teeth, I pull on a pair of turquoise leggings and off-the-shoulder sweater. *One more day*, I think to myself. One more day and I can slob out for the entire Christmas break, eating far too much and watching festive movies. That's as far as my forward planning has gone, considering I don't know what else to do or where I would go.

Typically, I would be freaking out, feeling like I don't have a home. A base to revert back to. But I don't. There's an odd sense of freedom festering inside. It doesn't matter where I end up; the Shadowed Souls will be there for me. Even Wyatt, who hasn't so much as scowled at me in weeks. He's not talking to me either, but on occasion, we can be in the same room without the tension forcing one of us out.

Exiting the room, I'd almost forgotten about Garrett until he pushes away from the wall, scaring the shit out of me.

"And here is the little minx in question," he announces, angling my own phone's screen to reflect a video of myself. I hold a hand up to cover my face. "Don't be shy, Peach. Your first IG Live is a big deal." My footsteps stall and I shoot Garrett an incredulous look.

"Are you insane?!" I hiss under my breath. Garrett's grin grows.

"Amongst other things," he shrugs. "Come say hi to your adoring fans." Holding my phone at a height I can't reach, I jab my elbow into his ribs, all the while keeping my face hidden from view. A few choice words pass my lips and when he continues to record, I make a small jump for my phone. He evades me easily. "Oh, you want this back? Come get it."

"Garrett, I swear to—" I start, but he's already off, ducking into the hallway.

Darting after him, I fly down the stairs at a dangerous speed. So much for protecting my ankles. I hear laughter and Huxley's voice booming, "She's coming for you, man!" The boys are lounging on the couch, but they spring into action as Garrett bolts past them.

"Bear with me, folks! The cameraman is under duress!" Garrett shouts to his audience. Axel tries to grab him, but Garrett slips out of reach, heading towards the kitchen.

"He's heading to the back!" Dax shouts, and we all pivot, changing course like some sort of chaotic, synchronized dance. Garrett's manic laugh echoes as he slides across the kitchen tiles, narrowly avoiding a collision with the counter and filming all the while. I'm right behind him, arm outstretched, my heart pounding. There's no time to enjoy the thrill of the chase. Not when he's being a fucking idiot, broadcasting me across the internet. Anyone could be watching.

"Garrett! You turn that off right now!" I shout. He's stopped on the far side of the island, shifting everytime I do in the opposite direction. I glare just as he turns the screen back on me, so I do what anyone would in the same situation. I drop to my knees out of sight. Crawling around the stools, another body meets me there. A body I never would have expected to be on all fours, his green eyes glinting with mischief.

"Follow me, I've got an idea." Wyatt whispers and scuttles away. I'm half-stunned, mildly distracted by Wyatt's jersey slipping out the back door and the kerfuffle happening between Garrett and the others.

Axel and Huxley are cornering Garrett by the refrigerator, some more tickling taking place - most of which is instigated by Axel. Warmth spreads through my chest and I linger for a while longer, enjoying the view. Axel and Garrett are like magnets, drawn together by an irresistible force. They don't even realize how much they need each other, and I'm happy to keep subtly reminding them.

But right now - I'm firmly on the Garrett butt-kicking train. Leaving them to their distractions, I duck out undetected. Cool air hits instantly, my toes feeling the winter the most through my cotton socks. I shudder. It could be a trap, or just a horrible mistake to blindly follow Wyatt, but I can't see that far ahead. Not as the play fighting inside is becoming rough and the shadows are nearing the glass plane.

"Here." Wyatt unravels the coiled hose pipe fixed to the side of the house, and my own menacing smile grows. Pushing a finger against his lips, he turns the faucet as I pull a long length of the pipe free. Words are kept to a minimum, but we're standing in close proximity, intently waiting for our target. The door handle rattles and Wyatt places an arm over my front, urging me a step back from view. Hidden around the corner, my fingers tremble on the hose until I hear the men spill out the door.

Without a particular target in mind, since beggars can't be choosers, I step around the corner and twist the nozzle so a fast jet of water sprays over the lot of them. I only consider then that the water is ice cold. The screams are as hilarious as they are horrific. Wyatt is whooping in a way I've never heard, abundantly pleased with himself.

Hollering fills the backyard, until I start to scream as they all advance on me. It's a good job the press aren't nearby. They'd have a field day. Huxley reaches me first, grabbing the hose to yank it from my hands with ease. Twisting it around, he shoves the jet down my jumper before I can stop him. Holy fuck, it's beyond freezing. Throwing my fists into his chest, he doesn't budge until Wyatt switches off the faucet.

Garrett is sputtering, shaking water from his hair, but he's still laughing, holding my phone above his head like a trophy. I seize my chance, dropping the hose and lunging forward to grab my cell. I'm successful, but earn myself a soaking wet hug from behind.

"Did you catch all of that?" Garrett leans over me to speak into my phone's receiver. I minimize the image of myself, only to be flashed with Meg's face.

"What the hell?" I stutter. Meg's leaning on her fist, an amused and dopey smile on her face.

"Yeah, I caught every second," she laughs. "You're right, she is a real bitch when she's on the offense. She'd be perfect on my lacrosse team."

"It wasn't a livestream?" I ask dully, my mind a step behind. I blame the cold seeping into my back.

"Of course not. I'm not a fucking idiot," Garrett plants a sloppy kiss on my temple. Huxley and Axel are groaning, shuddering and soaked through. Their t-shirts are stuck to each muscled outline. Dax, being the hero with the gift of foresight, steps out in his boots with a bundle of towels in his arms.

Garrett peels himself from me to wrap a towel around my shoulders, uncaring of the water dripping from his messy, dark hair. Given his easy smile, no one would be able to guess that the blue shade creeping into his lips was from potential hypothermia. "Just wanted to make your day a little more interesting, Peach."

"You definitely succeeded," I say, catching my breath and looking around at the state of us all. The guys are a mess, I'm no better, and Wyatt is watching on with an emotion that isn't hatred. What is happening in the world?

Garrett doesn't release my shoulders, walking me back to the porch swing. I sit with a thud, and suddenly my legs are being forced apart by Garrett's. Gripping the sides of my face, he pushes his tongue into my mouth before I even realize what he's doing. The warmth of his mouth against mine ignites an immediate fire that mixes with the adrenaline already coursing through my veins.

Duelling his tongue with mine, he mouth-fucks me so hard, my toes are curling. Running a hand across the hard expanse of his chest, he grinds against me deliciously, before snatching the phone I forgot was in my grip and stepping away.

"So, Meg, as I was saying before we were so rudely interrupted," Garrett rolls his eyes in my direction. "I'll make sure to film Avery's dance for you tomorrow. We wouldn't want you to miss it."

I sit stunned, panting from arousal and shock as Axel appears to offer me a hand up. Never mind the cold, all of my limbs are numb now for very different reasons. Garrett is pacing, curling a wet tendril of his hair as he talks to my best friend. Huxley and Dax head in, leaving me standing opposite Wyatt. He hasn't moved an inch, leaning against the house, arms folded. He's taking in the scene from afar, as per usual.

"Let's get you warm and dry," Axel tries to urge me inside. I pause, digging deep for some resolve. Things have been fine with Wyatt, an unspoken agreement to ignore each other, but these past ten minutes have proved there could be more. That it doesn't have to be this way.

"Will you be there too?" I find my voice. Wyatt raises a brow and I shift under his gaze. Axel's arm around my back is all that keeps me in place. "The showcase tomorrow. Will you...come?" I suck my bottom lip into my mouth. Axel is still but doesn't comment, and luckily Garrett is lost in his own conversation down the wooden steps.

"Do you want me to?" Wyatt asks tentatively. His features don't betray if he likes that idea or not, but I nod anyway.

"It'd be nice if everyone was there." *Nice*, ugh - Mrs. Patrick would have a fit at my choice of adjective. Wyatt straightens, pushing his hands into his pockets. He's actually considering it. I was certain he'd laugh cruelly and walk away. Instead, he steps forward and stops right in front of me.

"Okay then."

"Okay then," I parrot back, nodding several times. Axel's arm tightens around my waist, successfully tugging me into the house this time. I'm going to need another shower and a head start of binging food and festive movies.

"I'm proud of you," Axel mutters beside my ear. Guiding me up the stairs, he diverts us to the bathroom he keeps private for himself. "Let me show you how much." I grin from ear to ear. Well, there's an offer I can't deny.

AVERY

CHAPTER FIFTY SIX

I stand backstage, heart pounding, the heavy curtain separating me from the expectant audience. My body shudders beneath the leotard, a proud tutu sticking out from my hips. Months of rehearsals have led to this moment. My muscles are tense, feet poised in my first stance, every detail of the routine running through my mind. The murmur of the crowd fades as I focus on my breathing, the floor cool beneath my ballet slippers.

The scent of the stage—wood, sweat, and a hint of old velvet—grounds me. I hear the faint rustling of the audience settling into their seats, the occasional cough or whisper. It's a full house and the pressure is palpable. My fingers twitch involuntarily, a last release of nervous energy. I flex them, feeling the delicate fabric of my tutu brush against my legs, a reminder of the countless hours spent perfecting every move.

From the wings, Miss Nightingale watches me closely. A small incline of her head seems to speak volumes. She thinks this is where I belong, what I should be doing with all of my time. In reality, I don't know where I belong. I just like to dance.

The curtain begins to rise. I take a deep breath, steadying myself. As the lights flood the stage, I scan the front row and there they are. Garrett, Axel, Dax, and evidently - Wyatt. I tried to convince Huxley to come but he's not ready to face the outside world yet. Inside is fine, he roams freely now and is eating properly, but he still couldn't bring himself to leave. Not even for me. I understand. I'm desperately trying to understand. I suppose the recording Garrett is taking for Meg will have to be enough.

Holding my pose, the silence before the music starting is deafening. Theo is on the ground level, his fingers on the piano keys. An orchestra accompanies him, the music students making their own debut for agents in the audience. I suppress a shiver, looking for a focus. I find it in Axel. His hazel eyes are fixed on mine, and at his neck, a sharp collar and tie. I withhold a gasp, the backs of my eyes pricking. He wore a shirt for me.

The music starts, and I launch into the first movement without a second thought. My body responds, every practiced step flowing with minimal effort. This routine is second nature to me now. The smile spread across my face is a real one, each leap and pirouette a small burst of joy.

The spotlight tracks my every move, but it's the Shadowed Souls smiling up at me that sees my spirit soar. I let myself fully embrace the music. The melody is hauntingly beautiful, and I pour my heart into every step, every gesture. My movements become more fluid, more expressive, telling a story that words could never capture. I am no longer just dancing; I am living the music. I don't even blink as Nikko enters, my counterpart. He joins the outstretched line of my body like a shadow. His fingers trail my arms, his hands on my waist and then I'm lifted.

During one practice, where it was glaringly obvious I was uncomfortable in Nikko's presence, with his hands all over me, Miss Nightingale had taken me aside. *'He's a prop,'* she'd said bluntly. *'You're the prima ballerina. Everybody in the show is a prop at your disposal.'* I didn't have such a hard time dancing with him after that.

Now, we're completely in sync. My extended leg is lined by his, the flourish of my arms mimicked in unison. We feel each movement, ingrained through repetition and muscle memory, giving the piece the precision it demands. Reacting to the crescendos and decrescendos of the orchestra, we effortlessly glide from one piece into the next. Months of practice, and we sail through the first half of the intricate choreography.

My muscles burn, but it's a good burn, the kind that tells me I'm alive and pushing my limits. The music swells, and I execute a series of grand jetés, my feet barely touching the ground. The audience fades into the background, and it's just me, the music, and the feeling of weightlessness. My heart races. My breaths come quick and shallow, my pulse a drumbeat in my ears. I focus on a spot in the audience to maintain my balance, and there he is again, Axel. His eyes shine with pride, his smile widening with every flawless move I make.

As we enter the final section of the dance's first half, Nikko lifts and then dips me low, my legs poised into perfect points. The climax of the piece approaches, a series of fouetté turns. I spin, faster and faster, my leg whipping around with each turn. The world blurs around me, but I am centered, focused. Suddenly, I fall still, chest heaving and arms suspended in front of my tutu.

For a moment, there is silence. The audience seems to hold its breath. Then, the applause erupts, a tidal wave of sound washing over me. I lower my arms, and absorb the energy of the crowd. The applause grows louder, a distant roar through the blood rushing in my ears. I bow deeply, gratitude and relief mingling in a heady rush.

As I straighten, I look out into the sea of faces, but it's Garrett's face that stands out now. His expression is full of admiration. So open, so in awe. I melt as the curtain falls and I step into the wings. I'm met with the hugs and congratulations of my fellow dancers. Miss Nightingale gives me a proud nod, her eyes shining with approval. I smile. I did it. I danced in front of a crowd, and an excited hum beats through me that I'm about to do it again.

"Twenty minutes, dancers," a stage-hand calls out. "Find a place to stretch, make sure you hydrate!" I accept a bottle of water from an assistant, turning to the rear of the stage. As Prima Ballerina, I'm the only one with access to the wardrobe dressing room, whereas the other dancers are settling onto the wooden floor, their legs spread wide. I've barely made a step when a hand harshly grabs my upper arm, dragging me along. I try to yank myself free, only forcing him to hold on tighter.

"Wyatt?" I gasp, jerking against his body. "What the hell are you doing?!" I look around for backup, but we're swallowed by the people bustling around. Elbowing the door open, Wyatt shoves me in the dressing room. He pauses to shut and lock the door, and then he's coming at me. I struggle to stay on my feet, stumbling backwards until my back hits a wall. He doesn't stop advancing.

"What's your problem?!" I scream, shoving at him when he gets in my space. His green eyes are laced with rage, his face hard. I thought we were getting on okay. How freaking naïve that was. Pressing himself along the length of my body, his forehead presses against mine, roughly pinning me between the wall and the bun in my hair. I still, not even breathing as he steals the oxygen from my vicinity.

"Did you think prancing about with strangers was the way to get my attention?" Ignoring the obvious irony there, my lips part, dumbfounded. There's that phrase again. *Prancing about*, as if dancing is some stupid notion to waste time and occupy my simple mind. I want to scream. Shove at him again to no avail, ready to tell him that Nikko isn't a stranger - he's been my dance partner for months. But that's not what tumbles out of my mouth.

"I've been *prancing* around your best friends' bedrooms and you haven't seemed to care." His hands are on my ribs, his fingers digging in through my leotard. He pushes me flush against the wall, the expensive cologne he always wears slamming into my senses. Lowering his head, his lips brush my ear.

"I care," Wyatt growls, dropping his head and sinking his teeth into my neck. I gasp, a jolt of my body putting me flush against him, my head tilts of its own accord to permit him further access. His thigh shifts, pressing hard between my legs. I'm frozen in place, not daring to move as his mouth releases me and shifts. A gentle bite touches the place where my neck meets my shoulder.

"Wyatt," I say, far too breathily. "What's happening here?"

"Shhh," Wyatt's lips push against my skin, his mouth roaming upwards to nip at my jaw. My body betrays me. With each small bite, my hips tilt further forward, shamelessly rubbing myself against his thigh. I'm going to kill Garrett for planting this fantasy in my head. The amount of nights I've fallen asleep picturing it.

My head tilts, my high bun like a cushion. My eyelids lower, my senses taking over. His mouth is hot and seeking, his chest firm. Angling his thigh away, Wyatt's hand palms my pussy through my leggings. The heel of his thumb is directly over my clit, the sweetest torture.

Did he picture me just like this when Garrett made me put on that slutty ballerina's costume at the club? Did he slink off to the bathroom and jerk off over it? Questions I shouldn't ask. Answers I shouldn't want.

His thumb shifts and finds the right spot, pushing into me and drawing tiny little circles. The pressure is intense as I tiptoe to put some space between us. Everywhere I go, he follows. His tongue flicks over my throat, into the dip of my clavicle. I'm blazing from the inside, an inferno building within the leotard I long to shed. But I won't make that move. I won't encourage him. Any second, Wyatt will remember who I am, what I mean to him, and jerk back in disgust. I dare not wonder why I'm not doing just that.

"Kiss me," Wyatt whispers. My head is angled upwards and away from him, even as I shake my head. No, I'm not giving him that. We're not lovers. We're enemies, at the precipice of our misdirected anger. There's nothing else to be said, nowhere else to go, but straight over the blurred line we've been dancing along for months.

Grabbing my chin, Wyatt drags my head down. I struggle against him, shoving at his shoulders but he doesn't budge. He drags my leotard aside and pushes one long finger inside of me. On my gasp, his tongue enters my mouth. I thrash against him, but it only serves to increase his pace. The hand on my ribs lowers to my waist, pinning me with brute strength.

"Fight me all you want. You need this." Wyatt holds my cheek still with his. My hands are clutching the shirt at his shoulders, but I'm not fighting hard enough. We both know it. I want deniability, while doing nothing to actually deny the desire building within. Wyatt's mouth is at my ear, his hushed words barely audible between my stifled moans. "You've been begging me with your eyes. Every time I've let myself slip, you've been just as curious and eager." A second finger pushes inside of my cunt and I clench. "Just as wet and tight as I imagined."

So he has been thinking about me. His knee nudges mine wider.

"Oh, Avery." I swallow hard then. My name lustfully muttered in his voice is my undoing. "Tell me this is good for you. Tell me I'm being so good for you." My eyes snap open. Wyatt - good for me? After everything he's said and done, he wants a clean slate. He wants me to admit I forgive him, before he turns around and throws this in my face too.

"No," I grind out. Pushing his arm hard, his fingers fall free while I grab his crotch through his slacks. He's painfully hard beneath my palm, gasping at my touch. Using the grip, I shoulder Wyatt aside and twist us both, using my free hand to slam his shoulder into the wall. He lets me, his green eyes hooded and cheeks flushed.

"You don't get to do that to me." Unbuckling his belt with sharp movements, I leave it hanging and unbutton his slacks. Tugging them to his thighs, his cock springs free. A trickle of defiance and a fuckload of foreboding hits me. He's so thick, beautifully veined and circumcised. His head is plump and purple. My thighs clench, wetness seeping through my lycra. He just stands there, unmoving, not even breathing. I set my jaw and look up at him with malice.

"You don't get to be an asshole," I grab his shaft as tightly as I can.

"You don't get to be jealous," I pump him in angry jerks.

"You don't get to finger fuck me." Grabbing his tie, I wrap it around my fist and yank him into me. We've been here before, at the Fall Ball, but this time - I'm in charge. I still my movements, glaring into his dazed green eyes.

"You don't get to be praised." I use the fisted tie to shove him back into the wall whilst dragging my other hand up and down his cock. Not once do I release my tightened grip. I want him to hurt. I want him to remember this pain the next time he thinks to insult me. I want him to see how much hatred I hold inside, what his hot-and-cold routine does to me.

Beneath my hold, Wyatt slumps. He's quivering, the collar at his neck pinched. Small, rushed pants cause his cheeks to hollow, the mess of dark hair on his head soon becoming damp with sweat. His hands are pressed against the wall, letting me use his body in any way I see fit. Is this the punishment he was seeking? My thrusts are slickened by his precum, the friction beginning to burn my hand.

"Get on the sofa," he grinds out, daring to grab my hip. "Bend over the arm and let me show you just how much I don't deserve your praise." I jerk him sharply, snapping my hand free of his shaft and grab his balls. I squeeze tightly enough to draw a quick gasp from his parted lips.

"You've taken enough." My voice is laced with anger. "You don't get any more of me." Wyatt's thighs tense, his balls tight. Releasing his tie, my nails drag over his buttoned shirt, feeling the shift of muscle underneath.

I time it perfectly, dropping to my knees and deepthroating his cock. My jaw clicks, the smoothness surprising. A salty blend mixes with the pleasure of hearing his startled cry. He hardens impossibly more, a choked sound preceding the cum bursting into my throat. I swallow every drop. Then I bite down. All teeth and barely any tongue, I scrape the length of Wyatt's shaft, up and down, on and on. He shudders, gasping in pain and jerking against me. His hands lightly touch my head, a faint plea for me to release him. It's at odds with the way his dick is jumping for more.

Finally, I suck down his swollen length and release him with a pop. Sitting back on my heels, I watch Wyatt assess the damage, handing his reddened dick with careful fingers.

"Bitch." Returning to my full height, I plaster a smirk on my face and tilt my head. His green glare is back in full force, but the tension isn't the same. We're thinking the exact same thing. I hate you so fucking much. When can we do this again?

Thumping sounds on my door, a call for the end of the intermission. All dancers need to be back on stage in five minutes. I stand aside, gesturing to the exit.

"Congratulations, Wyatt. You've had *my* fucking attention." He carefully tucks himself away, not in any rush to leave. Righting his hair and suit, Wyatt steps forward, stopping when his bicep brushes my chest. The air is thick with lust but I hold my ground, until Wyatt turns and grabs my pussy roughly beneath my tutu.

"It's cute you think you've won, when you're the one who's left soaking wet and unsatisfied." There's no use denying it. He can feel my heat. But if there's one thing I've learnt from Wyatt, it's to always have the last word.

"Your men are in the hallway waiting to deal with that." His expression hardens.

"Of all the things, I never thought of you as a slut until-" The words have barely left his mouth as my open palm cracks across his cheek. Wyatt's head whips aside, his chest heaving evenly. I've either pissed him off or turned him on further, and I can't tell which one it is. A shudder rolls through his spine and he strides away, leaving the door wide open.

Just as I expected, there's a pair of suits leaning against the opposite wall of the hallway. I'm not an idiot, I knew there was a reason Wyatt wasn't dragged out of here the second he closed us in together. And that reason is currently shedding his jacket and rolling up his sleeves.

"Four minutes isn't long, Peach, but I do love a challenge." Garrett strides in, making a show of checking his watch. Lifting me into his arms, my legs automatically lock around his back. Axel remains back, closing the door behind him, watching through hooded eyes. Dropping me onto the vanity, I grin at Garrett licking his lips.

"I give you two and half."

AVERY

CHAPTER FIFTY SEVEN

Despite the interval intrusion, I finish my showcase with an overwhelming sense of accomplishment. Wyatt doesn't return for act two, thankfully. Although, his scowl in the forefront of my mind fueled the fire to dance like I never have before. I danced in spite of him, committing to Nikko's lifts and holds with renewed vigor. Dancing is a relief, my escape, but the applause. The compliments. The offers that came streaming in from agents and professional dance schools. My chest fights against the weight of it, my head dizzy and my limbs tired yet buzzing with energy.

Could I do this for the rest of my life? End each night on a stage, bowing low with poised feet until the curtain falls. It's not a possibility I've considered, but I haven't had my own band of muscular cheerleaders to spur me on before. Six-foot tall, brazen cheerleaders who are parading me through campus like the most important person in their world.

Garrett has me up on his shoulder, Axel's hand banded around my ankle while he shoulders my bag. They refuse to let me walk, stating that my ballet-slippered feet are too precious to touch the ground. Dax returned at some point during the show's finale, and now he's trailing us beneath the street lights, pretending he isn't tense. I haven't had the chance to ask where he went, and selfishly, I don't want to. Not tonight. Not while I'm riding this high. I deserve to enjoy it.

"Did you see my girl tonight?" Garrett is boasting to anyone nearby. Phones are raised, capturing photos which they'll no doubt try to sell to the press. I don't let it dampen the smile spread across my face as my butt jostles on Garrett's shoulder. "Did you *see* her?! She's incredible!"

"Are you finally claiming me then, Garrett?" I muse in a voice only meant for him. Peering up with glistening brown eyes, there's an earnest tilt to his smirk.

"Oh, Peach. It was never really a question of *me* claiming *you*, was it?" I stroke my fingers through his messy, dark hair. The flash of vulnerability is gone in a blink and I settle further into his hold, his hands on my thighs and long strides gently jostling.

Garrett will never see himself being worthy of affection, using his brazenness to keep people out, using excuses to push them away. But like Axel, I've realized that it's all words. Time will prove that we won't give up on him so easily. I mean, who else could take me dress shopping for another man, to a sex club with other men, to get an IUD fitted for other partners, and still look at me with those '*please don't discount me*' eyes? He's his own worst enemy.

Passing through the courtyard, Garrett sharply turns left. Away from the frat house's direction. Axel's hand falls away, both him and Dax falling into step at our back. The other students move away, having taken their photos. The lighting isn't paparazzi worthy as Garrett climbs the stone steps to a building I know all too well. The library. He produces a key from his pocket, unlocking the arched door and only once inside, permits me to slide down onto the floor.

"What are we doing here?" I ask while Axel grunts, "How did you get the key from Mrs. Russell?" Garrett declines to answer either of us. It's pitch black inside, but he knows exactly where to go.

"This way." He starts climbing the stairs and the three of us follow. By the third floor, my teeth are clamped together. Do you know what I really don't want to do after a two hour ballet recital - climb a million stairs. My hand on the railing drags me higher until we reach the very top level, somewhere I've yet to explore.

The floor opens up beneath a domed skylight. Stars twinkle through clear glass, casting a soft, celestial light over a tiled floor. A sleek, modern telescope stands nearby, a wooden table littered in star maps. Shelves lined with books curve along the walls, their titles gleaming. Chandeliers hang like constellations, illuminating cozy reading nooks created with beanbags. The air is filled with the scent of aged paper. Plush sofas are too inviting to deny. I drop down into the cushions, my head thrown back and limbs limp.

"How have I never been up here before?" I breathe, in awe of the night's sky. How many times have I walked the campus and been too wrapped up in my own thoughts to look up? How many times have I sat downstairs studying, believing my whole world consists of grades and frat house dynamics? Garrett drops down at my side, while Axel looks through the telescope and Dax paces, filled with nervous anxiety.

"Gare, I really think we should-"

"Not yet," Garrett mumbles. His face is upturned, bathed in the light of a half moon. The sharp lines of his face, jaw and Adam's apple catch amongst his dark hair and eyes. Beautiful. Lifting a hand, he vaguely gestures for Dax to stand still. "You clearly know something, which clearly isn't good and clearly is going to throw us another curveball."

"Stop saying the word clearly." I hear Dax's eye roll. Garrett smirks.

"Give us a moment to be still. To bask in Avery's success and each other's presence. Then it can all be fucked up."

Relenting, Dax walks over and lowers on my other side. His back is too straight to enjoy the stars, his hands fisted in his lap. I reach for him, half turning to drag him back into the cushions, my leg thrown over his thighs. My head slips onto his chest at an angle so that I can still stargaze. After a beat, his arms find their way around me, his mouth resting on my head.

It must be eating him up inside, whatever he knows and doesn't want to say. I stroke his abdomen through his shirt, willing time to stand still. To keep the drama and the secrets and the camera flashes and the unknown threats at bay. Garrett takes the silent invitation to spoon my back, his face in my nape.

"So..." I swallow hard. "I think I'm ready to pitch why I have the necessary trauma to be considered for my own skull tattoo. I need to have suffered and overcome, right?"

Garrett's head lifts instantly. "You want to be a Shadowed Soul?"

Dax tenses beneath me as I nod. "I want to be someone to

somebody. And…I'm scared that if I'm not in your gang, there's a higher chance I lose you all."

"That would never happen," Axel drops onto his knees by my legs. His hands on my thighs are as steady and sure as his hazel eyes. "No matter what." I bite my bottom lip. I hear what he's saying but still, it sometimes feels like it's them and me. Despite how far we've come and how much I trust them, there are always going to be these times when we're disjointed and secrets are not being said.

Dax uses a finger under my chin to tilt my head up and meet his gaze. "I'm afraid Wyatt decides who to bring into our fold. It's not something you apply for. His control, his choice." The finality of those words hits harder than I expected. I can screw these guys, dote on them, fall for them, but I will always be on the outside. Never fully accepted.

Garrett's arms tighten around my waist, his mouth at my ear. "You don't want to be one of us, Little Swan. We're fucked up."

"So am I," I whisper. I'm not going to argue. Curling into Dax's chest, I let my eyelids lower. Nothing has changed, only the sinking feeling in my chest.

Axel lightly lifts my leg from Dax and starts to untie my slipper. "You're too precious," he murmurs. His fingers brush my ankles with such care, gently massaging my feet when he's shed my compression sock. Then I'm being dressed, a pair of sweatpants tugged up my calves. My socks and sneakers eased on. "When we get home, I'll give you an ice bath and massage out all of your kinks."

Home. Shadowed Soul or not, I have a home.

Garrett chuckles against my back darkly. "Then I'll fuck out all of your kinks."

Dax doesn't comment, although his deep exhale causes my head to lift higher. Looking up, I cup his cheek and bring his blue eyes down to mine.

"Whatever it is, it's going to be okay." He doesn't look convinced, his full lips pursed. I decide then, there's no use holding this off any longer. It's only hurting Dax. Torment dances between his brows, so I draw him down for a quick kiss and then push upright. Axel stays kneeling when I stand, both shuffling the sweatpants up and the tutu down. He digs around my bag and stands, easing a hoodie over my head without touching my high bun and make-up.

I could say a thousand things in that moment, beneath the stars. Staring into his hazel eyes. I'm in awe of all of them, but Axel hits differently. His body has been tainted, used. His mind has been warped into thinking he's only good for one thing. I drift into his space, pressing my face against the steel firmness of his chest. His fingers trickle over my wrists, arms and shoulders. His touch dips into the hoodie's neck line to brush over the arrow tattoo on my upper back, which he used to cream and massage. I shiver, but I'm not cold. I'm enveloped in his warmth.

Dax's arm winds around my waist just in time, as I'm almost asleep on my feet. We leave our mini sanctuary, exiting the library and pausing for Garrett to lock up. Drifting down the steps, Dax tries to hurry me across the courtyard but it's useless. My legs are wooden, a yawn pulling at my mouth. The night is pitch black now, the half moon hiding behind cloud cover. There's no one around, an eerie silence, which is why I flinch when a white SUV pulls up on the nearest road. Huxley dips his head through the open passenger window.

"Should you be driving?" I ask, thankful nonetheless. The drive is quick, much quicker than I would have been able to walk. I lean over Axel's lap, my feet tucked against Garrett on the backseat. In the front, nervous energy filters around the cab. Not even the radio is on. We enter the garage and I hear it before I've even entered the house. Wyatt is yelling. Or screaming may be a better choice of word. Something crashes, most likely caused by a rogue fist or kick.

I stop mid-stride, throwing my head back and drawing a grunt from Huxley as I hit his bad shoulder.

"Shit," I spin but he waves me off. Just like Dax, Huxley's brow is low and jaw tense. My temper simmers. "So, is this it? We had to rush back because Wyatt can't face his feelings like a big boy?"

"Come on. We need to talk." Huxley moves past me, holding the door wide for the rest of us. Garrett has a similar stance to mine, shoulders sagged as if to say *I had to do something awful to get that library key, and I didn't even get a starlit blowjob for it.*

I nudge him, finding a small smirk for his eyes only. Huxley and Dax get a scowl to the back of the head for thinking I'd give a shit about Wyatt. His hissy fit at my showcase was uncalled for. Outrageous, in fact. He had the nerve to act jealous, after every emotional rollercoaster he's put me through. And once the dam had broken, he wanted it all. He asked me to kiss him, ordered me to bend over and let him fuck me. He would have taken everything if I'd let him, and then given me shit for it afterwards. He's already called me a slut tonight, but *he* was the one freaking out about a male ballet dancer's hands on my waist. A dancer who is flamboyantly gay, by the way.

I enter the house, my eyes glued to the pounding ceiling. Wyatt is having a full-on bitch fit. What a fucking hypocrite. In any other instance, Wyatt would have ruined my entire night. Locked me up, made sure I didn't continue with the show out of pure spite. I love dance and he hates me, why wouldn't he want to take that away? But what was different about tonight is anyone's guess.

Axel places my bag on the kitchen island and I stifle another yawn. I reckon I could head straight upstairs and fall asleep through the banging and crashing. However, Huxley and Dax are by the dining table, standing beside the chair at the head, already pulled out. On the mahogany wood in front of it lies my mother's diary. My face hardens as soon as I see it while Huxley crosses his arms defensively. So it's not just palming my pussy that Wyatt is furious over.

"How much did you tell him?" I jut out my chin. Huxley mimics the action.

"Everything."

"Why?!" My mouth drops open. Maybe there are facts Wyatt should have known sooner, but *everything*? These are my mom's memories, her secrets to tell or take to her grave. They're not in a gossip column for Huxley to pass around. Keeping my eye contact, he reaches into his back pocket and pulls out a crumpled envelope.

"Because this was posted through the letterbox at exactly seven o'clock. I suspect he thought we would all be at your showcase." Prickles encase my nape, goosebumps line my arms. *He.* A single person.

"Huxley," I state firmly. "You didn't interact with this person, did you?" He half shrugs, unable to hide his wince of pain.

"I didn't get the chance. I chased him south off campus, but I'm not as fit as I usually am. My lack of stamina caught up with me."

"What the fuck, Hux?" Axel gasps, slapping his hands on his thighs. I share the sentiment.

"What the hell were you thinking?! You were shot last time, and we wouldn't have known for hours!" I'm furious, discarding the envelope still held in his hand. Closing the space between us, I raise my hand to hit his tender shoulder and stop myself at the last moment, balling my fingers into a fist. "Don't do that again." His chocolate brown stare is steady, not in the least bit regretful. He'd do it again in an instant. I glower at him, at everyone.

"I'm serious. That goes for all of you. If you start putting my safety above your own and I have to spend all of my time worrying if someone in this room has done something stupid, I'm gone. I will walk away." There's a pause and a mixture of expressions in response, ranging from worry to '*No, you won't.*' I double down, but my voice is smaller. My head lowered. "I don't deal with loss well. Don't force me to protect myself like that."

None of them say anything, the air thick with unspoken words. It's too late. They already do value my safety above theirs. Another crash sounds from upstairs, this one juddering the entire house. A hundred bucks says Wyatt's been drinking straight whiskey since he got back.

"Give me the letter," I hold my hand out, sighing. There's no patience left for pleasantries. Huxley gingerly places it into my hand, while Dax scrapes the chair back further. AKA, *you'll want to sit down for this.*

Exhaling loudly, I take the seat. Four men drop into the chairs closest, Axel and Garrett leaning forward to see the pages I'm unfolding. I recognise them immediately. The yellow tinge to the paper, the faintly printed lines, the handwriting in purple pen and large flourishes. The missing pages from mom's diary. My heart stutters to a halt, my body forgetting how to function.

This is what she, or someone, was trying to keep hidden. The entry is short, written in a rush. An excited flurry. She's been for her first scan. Nixon was by her side, holding her hand when they were delivered the news. *Twins.* She couldn't be happier, Nixon is overjoyed. Imagine two sets of feet running around the manor, double birthday parties, the bestest of friends who will never have to walk a day alone. Her heart is so full of love, she might just burst.

"It's not...I don't get...it doesn't mean," I shake my head, squeezing my eyes shut. "We don't know if this is true. It could be fake, forged." It's one hell of a good forgery if so, even through my tear-filled eyes. The handwriting is identical. "I don't understand what you're showing me." Huxley reaches for the envelope and shakes out the rest of the contents. Two tiny hospital bands with the date and timestamp. Both labeled as *Baby Hughes.*

"Okay. So...Wyatt had a twin. Weird but I mean, there's been no mention of it before. There were no pictures in the manor or hint that there was anyone else. Maybe they didn't survive. Either way...I just... why are you looking at me like that?!" I glare at Garrett. Whatever conclusion he's come to, I instantly dismissed when I saw the bracelets. It's Dax's turn to reach across and flip over the diary page in my hand. A list of baby names, all girls, only one circled. *Avery.*

No. No, no. Not happening.

"This is ridiculous. I don't get what you're implying," I toss down the pages. This is a joke. A stupid joke probably orchestrated by Wyatt to push me away again. He hates that I got close enough to see his armor crack. But then why is he flipping out upstairs?

"I think you know exactly what we're implying," Huxley sighs heavily. "Avery, before you were adopted by the Hughes', had you ever met your mother?"

"She had an affair with Fredick Walters," Dax continues. "We know he's your biological father. And we know he fathered these twins."

Whatever happens next, I'm not present for it. I faintly hear voices telling me to breathe, but it's too late. The room goes dark around me, blocking out everyone and everything. Cold spirals through my core. My chest crushes in on itself, squeezing my heart as it fights to keep beating within the tight enclosure. Fear has me gripped firmly in its claws, its nails piercing my flesh as the darkness bleeds out.

Everything spins, a mixture of blue and brown eyes briefly flashing through the haze before I drown in the darkness again. My body starts to shake as I fight for control. In my mind, the attack lasts for hours. Arms band around me, my body airborne before I'm lowered again. Every cold part of me is clung to by a large warm hand. The Shadowed Souls surround me on the sofa, soothing and stroking. Whispering and worrying. Eventually the trembles ease and I can concentrate on inhaling and exhaling deeply.

There's a huge, final crash from above. I hear it so violently, I momentarily believe it came from within my own chest. Stomping follows, booming around the lower level. The guys shoot upright, calling out, pleading. *Wyatt, don't go. Dude, wait - let's talk about this. Come on Riot, we can sort it out.* I peer over the back of the sofa to see him stuff his arms into his jacket and shoulder a large duffle bag. His back is riddled with tension, his brown hair a mess. My lips part on their own accord.

"Wyatt," I breathe. It's a desperate sound, a world of emotion held in that one word. As Wyatt swings the front door wide open, he stills. His head snaps aside and I'm drowning again. Those haunting green eyes physically spear me. The pain, the anguish, the disgust. His lip is snarling, and I watch the deadness of his hatred take over, killing all other emotions. I've lost him. He hates me, with a proper reason this time. Slamming the door behind him, he's gone and my heart cracks wide open.

I'm light-headed. My head lowers into Axel's lap for the second time tonight. Faces fill my vision, someone stroking my hair. Someone wrapped around my legs.

"W-what does this mean?" I manage to force out. I know what it means, I just don't want to admit it. Admit what Wyatt and I did, what we could have done. No wonder he's destroyed the house, my stomach rolls just thinking about it. Dax is there, staring deeply into my eyes. A lifeboat in the ocean, a piercing blue light to my redemption. His lashes flutter over his cheek for a moment, a deep breath preceding the answer I desperately need to hear.

"Oh, Little Swan. It means you always were a Shadowed Soul after all."

To Be Continued...

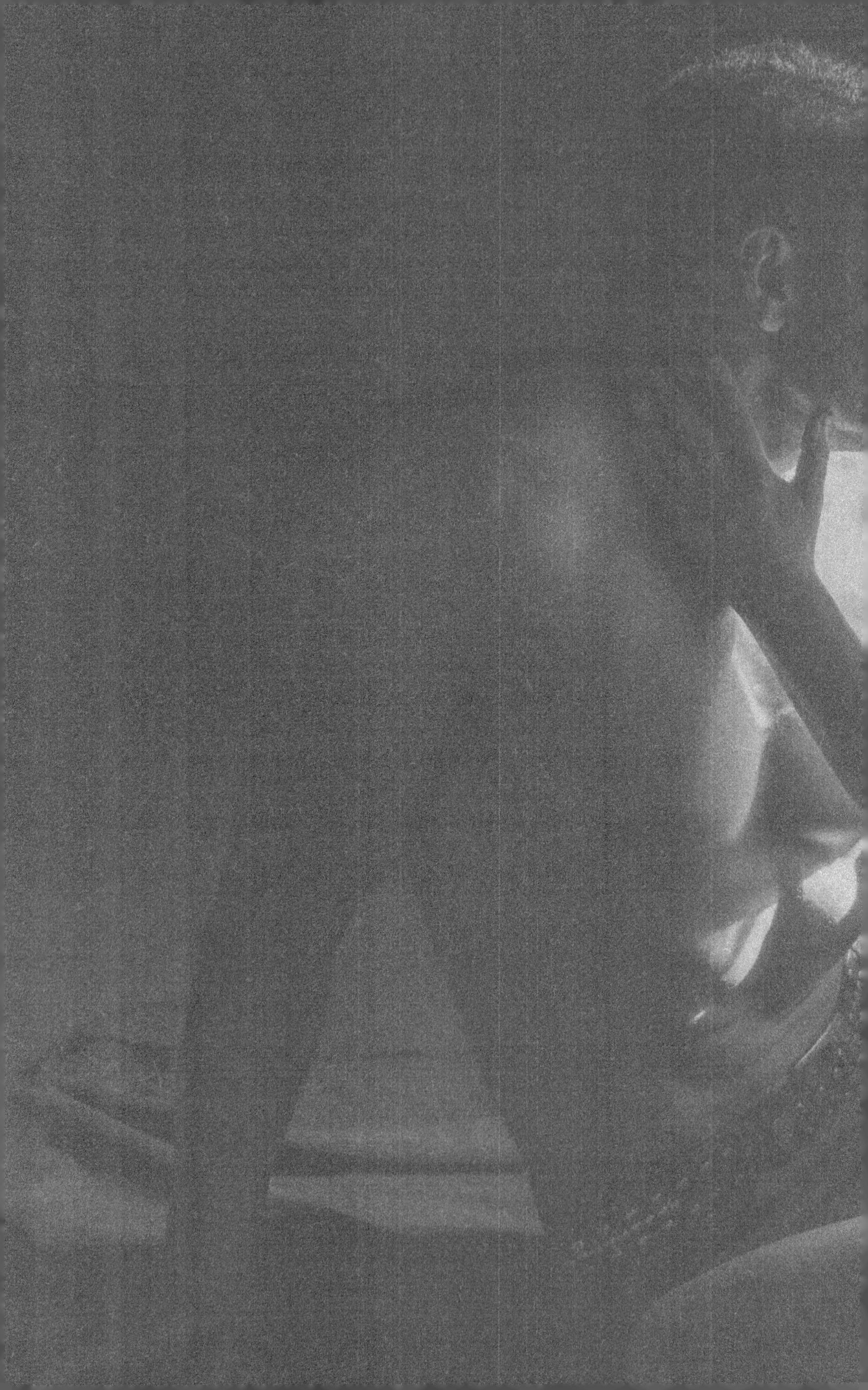

Special Thanks

How are we doing? Are we okay? I promise you, it's all (sort-of) up from here. I mean, it won't be a bed of roses for Wyatt, but everyone is redeemable...I think. **The good news** is, the Shadowed Souls series is completed! So you can binge on through and get your answers right now.

Start the next book in the series right now with:
Bound By Obsession, Shadowed Souls Book Two

I want to take this opportunity to thank you for reading Forged by Shadows. Your support means so much to me. I really hope you've enjoyed it and, if you have, please kindly leave a review on Amazon and Goodreads.

I would like to give a special thanks to:

Melissa from Get Proofreader and Kat Elley PA for the edits.

Victoria and Bianca for being incredible Alphas.

My street team for sharing and getting involved prior to release.

The PA teams who hosted blog tours on my behalf.

Kristina and Ella for being my betas, support system, and mostly importantly, my friends.

And of course, you, the reader!

It's plain and simple; I'm nothing without the readers who support me! Thank you all for devouring my brain-children, and also becoming my friends. I love getting to know you, seeing your gorgeous book shelves and building connections with so many talented and wonderful people.

Notes

Other Works

If you'd like to keep reading from Maddison's backlist, please check out...

Shadowed Souls Series – (set in Waversea)

RH Dark Academy Stepbrother Romance

Forged by Shadows

Bound by Obsession

Haunted by Secrets

Billionaire Brothers RH (set in Waversea) – Standalone

Beautiful Delusions

I Love Candy

Dark Humor RH - Completed Series

Findin' Candy (novella)

Crushin' Candy

Smashin' Candy

Friggin' Candy

All My Pretty Psychos

Paranormal RH with mutants, ghosts and demons - Completed Series

Queen of Crazy

Kings of Madness

Hoax: The Untold Story (novella)

Reign of Chaos

<u>Bound by Fate</u>

<u>Fated Mates RH Shifter – Standalone</u>

Moon Bound

<u>A Deadly Sin</u>

<u>MMA Fighter BSDM RH - Standalone</u>

A Night of Pleasure and Wrath

<u>A Wonderlust Adventure</u>

<u>A Twisted Menage Retellling Duet</u>

Descend into Madness

Embrace the Mayhem

<u>Billionaire Badboys</u>

<u>Con Artist/Billioanire RH Romance – Uncompleted</u>

Wreckin' Amethyst

<u>The War at Waversea</u>

<u>Basketball College MFM Menage - Completed</u>

Perfectly Powerless

Handsomely Heartless

Beautifully Boundless